# CLOAK OF RED

## ARROW TACTICAL SERIES

### BOOK 3

## ISABEL JOLIE

*Choose love.*

*xo,*

*Isabel Jolie*

ISABEL Jolie

Editor: Lori Whitwam

Proofreading: Karen Cimms.

Cover Design: Damonza.com

❈ Created with Vellum

# The End of Grand Strategy

*US Maritime Operations in the Twenty-First Century*

SIMON REICH AND
PETER DOMBROWSKI

Cornell University Press

*Ithaca and London*

First published 2017 by Cornell University Press

Printed in the United States of America

Library of Congress Cataloging-in-Publication Data

Names: Reich, Simon, 1959– author. | Dombrowski, Peter J., 1963– author.
Title: The end of grand strategy : US maritime operations in the twenty-first century / Simon Reich and Peter Dombrowski.
Description: Ithaca : Cornell University Press, 2017. | Includes bibliographical references and index.
Identifiers: LCCN 2017028025 (print) | LCCN 2017032106 (ebook) | ISBN 9781501714634 (epub/mobi) | ISBN 9781501714641 (pdf) | ISBN 9781501714627 (cloth : alk. paper)
Subjects: LCSH: Sea-power—United States—History—21st century. | Military doctrine—United States—History—21st century. | Naval strategy—History—21st century. | United States—History, Naval—21st century.
Classification: LCC VA50 (ebook) | LCC VA50 .R45 2017 (print) | DDC 359/.030973—dc23
LC record available at https://lccn.loc.gov/2017028025

Cornell University Press strives to use environmentally responsible suppliers and materials to the fullest extent possible in the publishing of its books. Such materials include vegetable-based, low-VOC inks and acid-free papers that are recycled, totally chlorine-free, or partly composed of nonwood fibers. For further information, visit our website at cornellpress.cornell.edu.

*For ACDA and AMM, who made this work,*
*and make our lives, so rewarding*

# Contents

# Preface and Acknowledgments

In the opening months of 2017, America is in the process of a dramatic presidential transition. Many commentators are already anticipating drastic foreign policy changes as well as a general sense of administrative incoherence. As evidence, they point to the wide differences between the pronouncements of President Trump and the comments made in their confirmation hearings by many of those he nominated for senior foreign policy positions. Indeed, in *Foreign Policy* in January 2017, Micah Zenko and Rebecca Friedman Lissner pronounced that Trump had no grand strategy, before he was even sworn in as president.

Clearly, the appointment of military officials to senior policymaking positions suggests a tone and approach different from the Obama administration's. As we argue in this book, military personnel generally lack faith in the virtues of any grand strategy. They are pragmatic problem solvers, more comfortable with a response to specific problems than a recourse to abstract principles. That point was tellingly illustrated in James Mattis's congressional confirmation hearing for the post of Defense Secretary. When Mattis was asked about Russia he responded, "I'm all for engagement, but we also have to recognize reality and what Russia is up to. . . . There's a decreasing number of areas where we can engage cooperatively and an increasing number of areas where we're going to have to confront Russia." Circumstances outweighed principle in language, policy, and practice.

In this book, we argue that Zenko and Lissner's comments about the Trump presidency are unwittingly symptomatic of a larger trend: that the link between values and "ways, means and ends" defies the deductive formulations about grand strategies debated by academics and formulated by policymakers. We can look back nostalgically at American grand strategy during the Cold War, but its reputed coherence has been replaced by a new series of challenges in the twenty-first century. Those new challenges are not susceptible to treatment with a one-size-fits-all grand strategy.

Now, we suggest, the stresses and strains of American domestic politics and the exigencies of military operations together conspire to sabotage even the most elegantly articulated and carefully constructed general formulations. Faced with a growing array of hostile actors, a plethora of new threats, and novel forms of conflict, American military officials depend far more on context than on central principles as they decide how to act. Grand strategy may retain a role in defining our central values, but those values are a poor guide to policy in the twenty-first century. President Trump will not be alone in finding that grand strategy has little utility. His immediate predecessors discovered the same—neither President Bush's efforts at na-tion building nor President Obama's pursuit of what we label in this book as Sponsorship were crowned with success.

Strategies, we argue, have to be calibrated according to operational circumstances. They exist in the plural, not in a singular grand strategy. As a result, we show, America employs varying and familiar strategic approaches every day.

Books often have a long pedigree. This one began more than two decades ago. At that time, the authors discussed the possibility of working together as administrators. That particular plot was aborted. But it stimulated a longstanding discussion about administrative failings, principally the gap between strategy, policy, and implementation. Since then, Simon Reich has worked intermittently in both the think tank and academic world. Peter Dombrowski's contribution to public service has been continuous and more substantial, as a regular participant in strategic planning within America's security community. The consequence of that dialogue is this book, one that focuses on strategy limitations from the ground up and defies the vicissitudes of abstract plans.

Swimming against the tide of conventional knowledge inevitably tests the forbearance of those generous enough to patiently and positively respond to our argument. That list includes Robert Art, Hal Brands, Colin Dueck, Christine Fair, and Andrew Ross who all participated with us on a panel at the International Studies Association. Our gratitude also extends to two anonymous reviewers who provided us with a plentiful number of helpful comments. And specifically, we thank Ryan French who provided us with invaluable research and editing support while serving as a research fellow at the Naval War College. Dean Tom Culora and Andrew Winner of the Naval War College also added substantially to the writing of this book. Thierry Balzacq joined the two of us in our continuing debate two years ago. We appreciate our discussions as we continue to learn from his comparative perspective on the concept of grand strategy.

Peter Dombrowski also wishes to express his gratitude to his colleague Peter Swartz (Captain USN retired), who clarified many naval issues great and small. Peter also benefited from the support of the Watson Institute at Brown University while on leave, particularly the assistance of Richard M. Locke, then its director, and Sue Eckert.

Among Peter's intellectual fellow travelers at the Naval War College he thanks Chris Demchak, Mitzy McFate, Michele Poole, Bill Murray, Negeen Pegahi, and Jackie Schneider. Outside the college, Janne Nolan, Judith Reppy, Emily Goldman, Ed Rhodes, Dick Mansbach, John Duffield, and Rodger Payne have all helped him evolve as a scholar. Catherine Kelleher deserves, of course, special mention as she mentored a person congenially averse to mentoring, survived a coauthored volume, and remains a dear friend. Johanna Dombrowski is both a loving daughter and an inspiration for her hard work and tremendous focus.

Simon Reich was the beneficiary of a grant from the Gerda Henkel Foundation and gratefully acknowledges the foundation's support. The grant allowed him to spend the summer of 2015 at a visiting fellow at IRSEM in Paris. There, Marianne Peron-Douse, Céline Marange, and Juliette Genevaz provided invaluable expertise and warm support, and its director, Jean-Baptiste Jeangene Vilmer, proved a welcoming host.

Simon acknowledges the role of those transatlantic family and friends whose enduring support has proven invaluable, in good times and bad: Ruth and Peter Ballard, Carol Bohmer and Ned Lebow, Kate Rothko and Ilya Prizel, Wendy Kates and Martin Schain, Anne and Nicholas Catzaras, Helene Bellanger, Eva Bellanger, Sophie Mahieux, and Stephen Perry. He also wishes to express his gratitude to Richard O'Meara. Truly, a child of the Enlightenment—a soldier, a lawyer, a poet, and a philosopher—Rick is a rugged, Irish personification of the Yiddish term *mensch*.

Like so many before us, we have benefited from the unstinting support of Roger Haydon at Cornell University Press. Roger was instrumental in the framing, writing, and editing of this book. He stewarded it through the review process and weighed in at the end to supervise and participate in the cutting of twenty thousand words—while still managing to maintain his sense of humor. Most important, his unwavering faith in this project buttressed our resilience even when we had our doubts.

And last, but truly by no means least, both Simon and Peter wish to thank their respective spouses, inspirations, critics, and muses—Ariane Chebel d'Appollonia and Ann Marie Martino. This book is dedicated to them with gratitude—for all their love and support.

# The End of Grand Strategy

# Introduction

## Grand Strategies and Everyday Conflicts

In the American intellectual landscape, the literature on grand strategy forms a domain of its own, distinct from diplomatic history or political science, though it may occasionally draw on these. Its sources lie in the country's security elite, which extends across the bureaucracy and the academy to foundations, think tanks and the media . . .

This ambitious environment sets output on foreign policy apart from the scholarship of domestic politics, more tightly confined with the bounds of a professional discipline and peer-review machinery, where it speaks mainly to itself. The requirements of proficiency in the discourse of foreign policy are not the same, because of a twofold difference of office: officeholders on one hand, and an educated public on the other. The body of writing is constitutively advisory—counsels to the Prince.

—Perry Anderson, *American Foreign Policy and Its Thinkers*

The notion of a grand strategy entails the vain search for order and consistency in an ever-more complex world. The very notion is prescriptive. It seeks to impose values and organizing principles on foreign policies; it implies the alternative is muddling through at best, chaos at worst. Truly great powers are the only ones likely to even debate what form their grand strategy should take, because with great power comes hubris—a sense that a country can impose its own blueprint on the global system or at least choose how to engage it. The United States, convinced of its exceptionalism, often attempts to mold the global system to its liking.

Contemporary Europe has no real equivalent, although the European Union continues to debate strategy and issued a global strategy report in 2016.[1] It met with indifference.[2] The Chinese do talk in terms of "peaceful development" and are arguably strategic in their behavior. But they rarely openly debate China's grand strategy.[3] In the United States, by contrast, academics, politicians, the media, and policy pundits engage in ferocious debates about how America should engage the world: what its security priorities should be, what values it should project, what instruments it should use in pursuit of its goals. Strategists argue constantly about the relationship between national ends, ways, and means. The Obama administration, for example, was criticized for having no grand strategy, in part because the President refused to assert an "Obama doctrine."[4] Unlike his predecessors his approach to the Middle East and elsewhere was often characterized as floundering—devoid of a central organizing principle.[5]

Yet the evidence we will present suggests that the very idea of a single, one-size-fits-all grand strategy has little utility in the twenty-first century. Indeed, it is often counterproductive. America faces a novel geostrategic environment with, notably, new threats, actors, and forms of conflict. When these are combined with the more traditional problems inherent in the design and implementation of policy, outcomes are often unanticipated and sometimes perverse—ensuring that American grand strategy is less than the sum of its parts. The very multiplicity of challenges generates a sense of chaos among national security specialists, in sharp contrast to the reputed stability of the one-dimensional, but truly existential, threat posed by the Soviet Union to an earlier generation.

If no unifying doctrine is possible or even desirable in the face of so many diverse and compelling threats, then what is the alternative? Our argument is best summed up by David Milne's suggestion that successful diplomacy requires policymakers to "study dilemmas, contextualize threats, compare their magnitude to the resources available, weigh humanitarian and reputational imperatives, and offer appropriately calibrated responses."[6] The same is true when designing grand strategy. In effect, strategy making in the twenty-first century defies broad rhetorical statements, captivating though they may be. American strategy is now multifaceted and contingent; the United States must address specific problems in a global environment where the utility of military capabilities ebb and flow.

The United States thus employs adaptive responses dependent on circumstances. We avoid simple labels like "smart strategizing," because however seductive, they often mask as much as they reveal. Simplistic solutions are exactly what we critique in this book. Yet even more nuanced strategizing cannot—we readily acknowledge—resolve all of America's foreign policy problems. Indeed, we highlight the fact that the strategies we describe suffer from their own limitations. They are not always functional.

Our primary goal is not prescriptive. Rather, it is to examine the various "calibrated strategies" employed by the United States—efforts to adapt responses to specific geostrategic challenges—and to identify why American policymakers and those military officials charged with implementing policy utilize those strategies on a reasonably regular basis. Simply stated, our goal is to explain *when* these calibrated strategies are used, *why* they are used, and *what happens* as a result.

The classic instrument of grand strategy—the American military—is often asked to perform tasks beyond the traditional application of "kinetic" force. But the military cannot support policies according to any single, highly prescriptive, deductively formulated strategy. Various operational constraints, ranging from inadequate resources to international law and unfavorable geographies, get in the way of simple, prescriptive approaches. Further, Clausewitz's concept of "friction" applies in more than just a shooting war.[7] It applies to the management of the enormous bureaucracies of the American national security state; to the political churn associated with the mass media; and to the gridlock often generated by a powerful legislative branch of government.

In this book, we point to some of the contrarian, unproductive, costly, and occasionally debilitating circumstances that America's military encounters when implementing policies based on singular grand strategic visions drawn up on metaphorical chessboards by academics or Washington policymakers. An anecdote may help illustrate the often-yawning gap, in the words of an old English proverb, "'twixt the cup and the lip" in the attempt to implement grand strategy.

## The Malacca Strait and the Illogic of Grand Strategy

In December 2005, Peter Dombrowski traveled to China to participate in a symposium on Maritime Security in the South China Sea. The agenda included the issue of "chokepoints"—geographically constrained entry and exit points between the high seas. The immediate concern was the Strait of Malacca, a narrow waterway between Indonesia and Malaysia. As the gateway to the South China Sea, it is arguably the single most important maritime passage in the world today.

More than 40 percent of the globe's merchant trade tonnage and a third of oil shipments pass through the strait each year.[8] It is like the Strait of Hormuz or the Panama Canal: American policymakers concerned about piracy, smuggling, and keeping the world's trade flowing, pay particular attention to the security of the strait. American grand strategists likewise consider the Strait of Malacca essential to the "command of the commons" of air, sea, and space; the domains through which goods, information, and people flow.[9] Indeed, the academic literature—dating from Alfred Thayer Mahan's seminal *The Influence of Sea Power* (1890)—emphasizes the importance of controlling the traffic in such chokepoints.[10] For some grand strategists, the United States must demonstrate its "mastery" of the global commons—including chokepoints like Malacca—both to safeguard its access and deny it to enemies if necessary.[11]

Dombrowski asked a Malaysian Navy Captain about policing the strait against terrorists and criminals, and the possibility of keeping open or shutting down shipping lanes when needed. The Captain told him that the sheer volume and nature of maritime commerce made nonsense of the theoretical discussions. He recounted an incident when three visiting Americans stood on the bridge of his vessel and looked at a large radarscope. The screen showed all the vessels in the strait at that time, traffic ranging from small fishing boats and junks to giant container ships and supertankers. There were countless indistinguishable dots on the screen—each one a vessel. It would take an inestimably large force with an incredibly high degree of intelligence to intercept individual ships or boats suspected of carrying contraband. And closing the strait would be an enormously complex operation, fraught with technical, operational, strategic, and economic difficulties and far beyond any navy's resources.[12] His message was clear: there is a major discrepancy between the wish list of theorists and the operational limitations facing navies.

Of course, better technology, better intelligence, and more resources help when it comes to addressing such problems. The United States and its maritime partners have made progress toward "maritime domain awareness"—essentially the sum total of information and intelligence necessary to "police the seas" effectively.[13] But to realize that potential would require a much larger number of costly Coast Guard and Navy vessels to enforce laws.

Operational success in policing the maritime commons often requires a high degree of familiarity with the local environment that American forces lack, as well as a willingness to defer to local authorities. As one analysis observed about the Malacca Strait, "While piracy has certainly been a concern in the waterway in the past, with reported attacks reaching seventy-five in 2000, the number of cases has been falling since 2005, largely as a result of a number of countermeasures introduced by the three littoral states of Malaysia, Singapore, and Indonesia."[14] Tellingly, it was the involvement of local authorities that proved key in the decline in incidents.[15] Still, local initiatives may provide only temporary solutions: in 2014 the number of piracy incidents increased, reminding us that piracy is rarely eradicated but rather ebbs and flows.[16] Strategies must be flexible and fully cognizant of operational limits. The nostrums of grand strategy are often ill-suited to meeting global, regional, and local security challenges—a theme we develop in this book.

Where does this leave grand strategies that rely on controlling the global commons? Certainly, policing or controlling maritime chokepoints is a sine qua non in the lexicon of several prominent grand strategies. There is even a healthy debate over why and how to manage the global commons. Should the United States try to *command* (i.e., dominate) the commons? Or should the United States simply try to *secure* access to the commons and thereby maintain the status quo?[17] These debates show up in major policy documents. The 2010 *National Security Strategy*, for example, suggested that

> across the globe, we must work in concert with allies and partners to optimize the use of shared sea, air, and space domains. These shared areas, which exist outside exclusive national jurisdictions, are the connective tissue around our globe upon which all nations' security and prosperity depend. The United States will continue to help safeguard access, promote security, and ensure the sustainable use of resources in these domains.[18]

But as the Malaysian Captain suggested, there can be a veritable chasm between normative prescriptions about how the United States should engage the world and implementing such prescriptions in a specific place.

Our Malacca vignette offers a telling insight. Scholars and policymakers can devise fundamental principles, coherent rules, or looser guidelines under the rubric of a grand strategy. They can develop reassuring concepts such as *commanding* or *securing* the commons, predicated on America's enviable technological capabilities and seemingly unbridled military budget. But their ingenuity makes little sense for an operator staring at a radar screen full of indistinguishable dots—and trying to figure out which of them may be pirates, smugglers, or terrorists carrying fissile materials. Bureaucratic and organizational impediments—and the occasionally tendentious relationship between civilian and military leaders—complicate the nation's ability to respond to the plethora of threats, differing actors, and various forms of conflict. The cumulative effect obstructs the nation's ability to *implement* any single grand strategy, no matter how sound its overarching principles or how carefully it prioritizes particular threats and allocates resources. This book examines what happens when abstract formulations and operational imperatives collide.

## From What Is Desirable to What Is Feasible

We offer no normative prescription about how the United States should engage the world. Nor do we pillory those who do. Our intent, rather, is twofold.

First, we describe the many ways that the United States engages the world and explain why they differ so markedly. America does not favor one dominant strategy, nor can it. Rather, America employs three concurrent strategies, each of which has two distinct variants. Some are based on strategies advocated by "Primacists" or by liberal internationalists who promote what they regard as a benign form of American Leadership. These are two variants of Hegemony. Others look like those suggested by proponents of "Restraint" or Isolationists—two variants of Retrenchment. A third group involves either a formal or an informal strategy of Sponsorship (though that term is less common in the contemporary strategic lexicon).[19]

So, in effect, we describe six calibrated strategies. In doing so, we demonstrate that the notion of grand strategy is beguiling but illusory. This is not to suggest that the United States cannot implement effective strategies at all. Sometimes strategies achieve their goals, sometimes they do not. Nor do we argue that those strategies lack consistency. Indeed, we will argue just the opposite: that American leaders generally employ military forces according to contingent but predictable strategies.

Yet from policymakers (more abstractly) to senior military officials (more tangibly) and ultimately to frontline personnel (most concretely), strategy is generally "calibrated" in response to context. The demands of operational circumstances take precedence over grand architectural formulations. Explaining which strategy is used and why involves answering a series of questions about the nature of the adversary, the threat posed, and the kind of conflict that may ensue. When these questions combine with the bureaucratic decision-making process, they define what is feasible, not just what is desirable—the latter being the preserve of debates about grand strategy. We illustrate these six standard strategies, advocated by planners, bureaucrats, and occasionally military personnel tasked with their implementation. We accept that they may not cover all the options, nor do they capture the nuance of every response. But collectively they capture America's responses in the vast majority of cases.

Our second goal is to describe the consequences of these six strategies—both when they are successful and when they fail. The lesson here is that American policymakers will have to define their goals realistically, specifically, and transparently, and then tailor their strategies to operational circumstances, if they are to achieve their national security goals. In contrast, the six examples we examine reveal that the benchmarks used by policymakers are often vague or unattainable. Politicians who promise to interdict the global flow of all fissile materials or of illicit drugs or of undocumented migrants into the United States may sound committed and steadfast. But the results are inevitably uneven. Any grand strategy applied without regard for context is rarely even modestly successful. So the potential for failure is deeply embedded in the overarching metaphors we use when debating the desirability of a specific grand strategy. When America pursues a "one-size-fits-all" approach, invariably there will be a disjuncture between expressed goals and their implementation.

We acknowledge that public debates over America's grand strategy can be healthy for a democracy. They can provide transparency, clarify our interests and priorities, and provide for public accountability. Yet there is also a clear downside. America's inability to achieve its major policy goals in the twenty-first century is, in part, tied to an introspective preoccupation with grand debates about which principles should govern its global engagement. The obsession of some high-level officials with controlling outcomes in Iraq, for example, blinded them to the limits of American military power. Mid-level analysts and Beltway pundits bandied about concepts like "shock and awe" and "regime change" as shortcuts to achieving Primacist objectives—often without considering whether they were operationally feasible or would have unintended consequences.[20]

The concept of grand strategy is debated in Washington, academia, and the media in the *singular* rather than the *plural*. The implication is that there is one true path to securing US interests in a complicated world. The debaters also tend to accept a fundamental premise: that the United States has a capacity to control events, and so it can afford to be inelastic in the face of a changing, and increasingly challenging, strategic environment. Other nations must be responsive or deal with the consequences. President Barack Obama implicitly recognized this American shortcoming with his plaintive call for "strategic patience."[21]

When this "dominant principle" approach is employed in decision-making about military operations, it becomes a recipe for failure. Many pundits and policymakers ignore this fact. They often assert that more resources or greater force can achieve their policy goals. One example is the attempt to organize a "surge" in Afghanistan because it was successful in Iraq. There are numerous others. Failures to control America's borders has led to deploying more border guards and redoubling efforts to install expensive, technologically sophisticated deterrents or insurmountable walls.[22] As the 2016 presidential election vividly demonstrated, such failures have seldom led to rethinking immigration policies or altering the federal government's approach to illegal drugs. The interminable cycle of interventions in the Middle East may vary in location, form, and focus, but all are intent on stabilizing a region in the midst of a series of intractable wars. As the invasion of Iraq demonstrated, American efforts at stabilization helped further destabilize the region.

Many in the security elite are unwitting prisoners to one grand strategy or another. Policymakers, exhorted by scholars in books and blogs, too often demand strategies based on a single idea or principle. But if those ideas are not adaptive to context, they create both bureaucratic and political frictions that result in operational failure.

In contrast, when the US military does implement strategies appropriate to context, the results are occasionally more successful—at least when evaluated in terms of declared policy goals. When President Obama, for example, decided to support the battle against Muammar Gaddafi, he employed a strategy of Sponsorship. He relied on American bombing to support local partners rather than fight a professional army in a conventional war. The approach has its detractors but it did result in its evident goal—regime change. Later, in an effort to combat ISIS, he tried a comparable Sponsorship strategy in Syria: the United States embarked on an unsuccessful policy of training locals in order to create a new army.[23] Highly sensitive to criticism if America incurred casualties, this "no boots on the ground" policy also had its detractors among politicians and influential elements of the media.[24] More problematic was the dissent within Obama's own military, many of whom believed that the political imperative ensured that the primary military goal—in the president's words, "to degrade and ultimately destroy ISIS"—would be unattainable.[25] In September 2014, for example, General Martin Dempsey, then Chairman of the Joint Chiefs of Staff, diplomatically told the Senate Armed Services Committee that "my view at this point is that this coalition is the appropriate way forward. I believe that will prove true, but if it fails to be true, and if there are threats to the United States, then I, of course, would go back to the president and make a recommendation that may include the use of US military ground forces."[26] Dempsey's words proved prescient. The Sponsorship strategy that had worked in Libya failed in Syria. But the President stuck with this approach.

Ultimately, the American military does as commanded. The US Navy's ships and surveillance aircraft interdict drug runners off America's shores, for example, although the Navy's leadership would rather that equipment be operating in the Persian Gulf or navigating the South China Sea. Service preferences aside, using expensive ships and aircraft to perform constabulary functions like drug policing is neither efficient nor optimal.

We develop our argument in the next two chapters. Its essence is that America is already inextricably committed to a global role by a series of vested interests and institutional links. Some of them are bureaucratic and organizational, others are legal obligations.[27] Piled onto this is the specific setting in which the military operates. This commitment leaves academics, the press, and politicians to debate what are America's core national interests, often unaware of how little latitude exists to change a strategy in a particular context. Commentators may dispute the extent to which America should engage the rest of the world and deliberate about the form that America's dominant overseas strategy should take. But military officials are guided more by circumstances than by first principles. They respond to the demand for their services in ways that reflect those differing circumstances.

Of course, some scholars and policymakers adopt nuanced positions within the six strategies we discuss. But the grand strategies themselves are not particularly nuanced. Furthermore, we argue, specific and proximate factors inevitably push military commanders to recommend one or another of these strategies even when they conflict with an administration's proclaimed grand strategy. This tension, unsurprisingly, creates debates between and within the civilian and military bureaucracies. These internal debates are distinct from the heated, publicized political arguments that take place both within Congress and between Congress and the executive branch.

The military's role in selecting a strategy varies by issue and sometimes by presidential administration. Yet, in the end, the result is often a return to a familiar option when faced with a familiar confluence of factors, regardless of how functional or wasteful it may be. We keep doing the same things repeatedly with only minor variations, despite their uneven results. More remarkably, however, many of the operations we describe do have surprising elements to them, and we will show this is true even though they are often routine operations that slip below the radar of scholars, policy experts, and media commentators.

What we describe is far more than simple bureaucratic politics. As the threats, actors, and forms of conflict vary, so does the domestic debate. Why do we end up doing things that conflict with our expressed grand strategy or seem unrelated to the president's preferences? As we demonstrate, explaining strategies and their consequences is a very different challenge from prescribing a grand strategy.

## Logic of the Book

The logic of this book is straightforward: little has been written to explain *why* the United States behaves the way it does when it comes to grand strategy.[28] Rather, what we have are three voluminous literatures: one prescribes US grand strategy; a second describes the history of grand strategy, its content and consequence; and a third explains why the United States makes particular policy decisions.

Some authors seek to generalize more than others. Scholars who prescribe grand strategy often proceed from a "top-down" perspective and undervalue the "brass tacks" lessons derived from operational analysis. Historical approaches adopt a moderating position, deriving broad lessons about the nature of grand strategy. In contrast, members of the third group working in the defense establishment on the nuts-and-bolts of policy may take a "bottom-up" approach that eschews generalization. They do not take the particular and broaden it to the context of a grand strategic vision. They "generalize" only to the extent that each individual operational problem is seen as an example of similar operational problems. So, for example, military interventions (say, in Iraq) are seen as a subset of comparable military interventions that require certain types of tools. In effect, scholars and proponents of grand strategy/strategies and students of national security and military operations often talk past each other.

We link these disparate approaches by studying actual naval operations. We chose the US Navy because the maritime domain is central to modern scholarship on grand strategy, global security, and the universalistic approach to remaking the world. Continental military powers, reliant predominantly on armies, simply lack the geographic reach required to be a global power. In contrast, unprecedented maritime force gives the United States access to and command of the world's oceans. Like many great empires, America thus has access to any country, any market, and any global common it wants to influence. Conversely, challenges to good order at sea and American sea power call into question the nation's position as primus inter pares in the community of nations. More modestly, confining ourselves to naval operations is consistent with some of the requisites of social science: by concentrating on maritime cases we hold constant the body of service-specific policies and strategic thought, organizational structures, platforms (ships and planes, for example), equipment, and systems, as well as the physical environment that constrains maritime activities.

In studying maritime operations, we examine the predictable and the effective, the unexpected, and even the tragic in ways that defy the abstract prescriptions of policymakers and scholars. Yet we are not suggesting that these operations are purely haphazard. Indeed, in the following chapters we demonstrate that there is a distinct, discernible logic to maritime operations, albeit a logic that often defies scholarly conventions and policymakers' assumptions. Our goal is to describe and explain, not to prescribe.

Grand strategists, for example, have spent a great deal of energy debating the question of how the United States should respond to the reemergence of China as a global power. Much of the "advice" to be found in the academic literature falls neatly within various schools of thought about international relations. Realists of various hues rely on the assumptions of power transition theory, offshore balancing, or Realpolitik. Liberals look to economic interdependence, regime theory, or the tenets of the so-called democratic peace. But this rich, provocative scholarship provides insufficient guidance for politicians, bureaucrats, and senior officers charged with navigating the issues of the day or institutional inertia. The cacophony of contending perspectives drowns out a deceivingly simple question: what is to be done?

Little of this debate matters to policy analysts who wrestle with the implications of an issue like President Obama's "rebalance" to the Asia-Pacific. Their concerns involve the immediate challenges of fast-breaking developments and crises: what to do about China's construction of artificial islands in the South China Sea? What are the consequences of America's freedom of navigation operations through waters claimed by Beijing? Will it sabotage American and Chinese cooperation in dealing with a bellicose North Korea? And how will it affect China's intention to develop a blue water navy? In essence, policymakers need to pull together varying moving parts in a way that advances US interests.

The goal of many grand strategists is to combat China's regional hegemonic ambitions and to sustain the American-led liberal international order. They debate whether the United States should have a forward offensive capability, adopt an offshore partnership approach, retreat to a defensible perimeter, or even whether America should contemplate a preemptive conflict with China.[29] They are opposed by those who favor a policy of engagement, generally through economic integration, diplomacy, and other aspects of "soft power."[30]

The US Navy, the largest and clearly most capable blue water force in the world, is central to these debates. In some respects, the two other "sea services"—the Marine Corps and Coast Guard—complement the US Navy, even as they reflect unique traditions and bring important capabilities to the maritime domain. One side debates the most effective resolute maritime posture; the other a response in which the instruments of trade and culture predominate, and the Navy's role is to keep the seas free for commerce. *Neither side acknowledges a different fact: that in some contexts the Navy treats China as much as a partner as it does an adversary.*

We describe an unappreciated dimension of the US maritime relationship with China in chapter 4. The US Navy, for example, invites China to participate in joint military exercises in the Pacific even as Chinese forces simultaneously spy on the multilateral exercises the US Navy conducts with its allies and partners—with American forbearance. American military officials, for another example, encounter a conundrum: should they coordinate with China's Navy to interdict vessels that might be smuggling fissile materials or exclude China because their involvement might spur increased investment in a blue water capacity?

Both examples confound the bimodal logic of those who wrestle with the question of whether Beijing should be treated as a challenger or a partner. Clearly, the idea that an adversary should be privy to America's military capacities, even be invited to partner with its Navy, is counterintuitive. So is the notion that we should do anything to encourage the Chinese to develop a blue water force and patrol the seas as another "global sheriff." But in such instances, the mission's goals, the strategy required to achieve those goals, and the US Navy's available resources introduce a contextual logic. As we explore in this book, the US Navy's internal logic and resulting behavior is often at odds with the most cherished assumptions of policymakers and scholars working on grand strategy.

Having examined the evolving nature of threats, the characteristic features of individual prescriptions, and six case studies that each reflect those prescriptions, we conclude by examining the policy implications of our study. Security elites now expend a vast amount of time and energy in attempting to develop overarching policy prescriptions. The evidence suggests that their characterizations don't mesh with the day-to-day demands on the military. What might happen, conversely, if American strategists, policymakers, and officers acknowledge the need for multiple strategies rather than one overriding grand strategy? We discuss the implications of such an approach for the Navy, and military services more generally, in terms of how they meet the demands of calibrated strategies in accordance with their own preferences, based on their service culture, traditions, and experience. But in dabbling in these murky waters, we reject any normative prescription that prioritizes specific values. Understanding how things work is distinct from articulating how they should. Not surprisingly, we suggest that politicians and planners should adopt a smarter strategic approach—one that understands the language of grand strategy is reserved exclusively for what is *desirable* and that of calibrated strategies for what is *feasible*.

# Naval Operations and Grand Strategy in a New Security Environment

> What's the point of you having this superb military you're always talking about if we can't use it?
>
> —Secretary of State Madeline Albright to Chairman of the Joint Chiefs of Staff Colin Powell during the Bosnian crisis, December 8, 1996

> I thought I would have an aneurysm. American GIs were not toy soldiers to be moved around on some sort of global game board.
>
> —General Powell on what he felt when Secretary Albright asked him her question

A massive tsunami struck across the Pacific on December 26, 2004, killing an estimated 280,000 people and displacing another 10 million. China reacted slowly, initially pledging only $2.7 million to hard-hit Indonesia, with whom it had tense relations.[1] The United States, in contrast, immediately pledged $350 million in humanitarian aid in what became known as Operation Unified Assistance, positioning its Pacific naval and air force assets to implement the disaster relief effort.[2] The US Navy (USN) soon dispatched P-3C Orion patrol aircraft and an aircraft carrier to assist with relief operations.[3] The aircraft conducted surveys, assisted search-and-rescue efforts, and cargo planes brought in supplies to shelter the living and dry ice to preserve the dead. This relief effort ultimately involved 12,600 military personnel, 21 ships, 14 cargo planes, and over 90 helicopters.[4]

The US vessels proved crucial for a country lacking electrical power and fresh water supplies.[5] Nuclear-powered aircraft carriers have the capacity to provide a large-scale energy source and the USS *Abraham Lincoln* proved invaluable. In the end, "Abraham Lincoln and its carrier strike group together 'flew 1,800 sorties, delivered 2,700 tons of food, water and medicine and evacuated 3,000 people.'"[6] Even this account underestimates its other contributions, such as providing a centralized communications hub for relief operations, medical treatment for the injured, and even media relations. Eventually the aircraft carrier was replaced by the USNS *Mercy*, a thousand-bed naval hospital ship.[7]

American policymakers recognized the potential strategic significance of being quick and generous in assisting Indonesia. B. Lynn Pascoe, then America's Ambassador to Indonesia, noted that "one thing the Indonesians are never going to forget is who was there first." Paul Wolfowitz, then Deputy Defense Secretary, emphasized the link between US strategy and aid.[8] Indonesia was a potential bulwark against Chinese expansion and a partner in fighting terrorism. And America's tsunami relief initiative proved effective. America's unpopularity among Indonesians dramatically reversed, setting the stage for closer long-term cooperation.[9] In the short term, rapprochement also contributed to Indonesia's new cooperation in patrolling the Strait of Malacca against pirates and its willingness to participate in the Proliferation Security Initiative (discussed in chapter 6). The USN's humanitarian assistance clearly served American strategic interests. But many current conceptions of grand strategy would not have emphasized its significance.

In this chapter, we contrast modern definitions of grand strategy with both the numerous demands placed on the USN by policymakers and the emergent security environment within which it works. Doing so highlights the inadequacy of any single strategic formulation to capture the complexity of challenges the Navy faces and the multiplicity of tasks it now performs. Some argue that the Navy should do less. But between that prescription and its implementation lie a line of vested interests, executive and legislative political institutions, long-standing international commitments, and several layers of a massive military bureaucracy—all before we arrive at the day-to-day complexities of maritime operations.

## Grand Strategy—and What the Armed Forces Do

Definitions and formulations of grand strategy proliferate. They vary in how they define and what they include as part of national security. Barry Posen offers a relatively narrow working definition.

> A grand strategy is a nation-state's theory about how to produce security for itself. Grand strategy focuses on military threats, because these are the most dangerous, and military remedies because these are the most costly. . . . A grand strategy contains explanations for why threats enjoy a certain priority, and why and how the remedies proposed could work. A grand strategy is not a rulebook; it is a set of concepts and arguments that need to be revised regularly.[10]

Definitions of grand strategy that emphasize military threats are in vogue amongst Realist scholars. They have little to say about humanitarian aid, although Posen has acknowledged that the relief effort for the 2004 tsunami proved helpful in the fight against terrorism.[11] Still, this definition of grand strategy leaves little room for aid that could generate spillover benefits.

Eminent military historian B. H. Liddell Hart, widely regarded as the doyen of grand strategy, offers a diametrically opposed definition.

> Grand strategy should both calculate and develop the economic resources and manpower of nations in order to sustain the fighting services. Also the moral resources—for to foster the people's willing spirit is often as important as to possess the more concrete forms of power. Grand strategy, too, should regulate the distribution of power between the several services, and between the services and industry. Moreover, fighting power is but one of the instruments of grand strategy—which should take account of and apply the power of financial pressure, of diplomatic pressure, of commercial pressure, and, not the least of ethical pressure, to weaken the opponent's will.[12]

Liddell Hart stressed that grand strategy is not just about war fighting. It is also about preventing the outbreak of wars in the first place, "winning the peace," and consolidating military victories. His definition—which includes the financial, diplomatic, commercial, and ethical—would have accommodated America's investment in tsunami relief. Assisting the Indonesians was part of a much larger jigsaw puzzle.

Posen's and Liddell Hart's definitions reflect extremes along a continuum between a narrow and expansive definition of grand strategy. Other variants abound, but they often offer little more by way of substance. Stephen Brooks and William Wohlforth suggest that "grand strategy is a set of ideas for deploying a nation's resources to achieve its interests over the long run."[13] John Lewis Gaddis simply defines grand strategy as "the calculated relationship of means to large ends. It's about how one uses whatever one has to get to wherever it is one wants to go."[14] John Ikenberry suggests that "grand strategies are really bundles of security, economic, and political strategies based on assumptions about how best to advance national security and build international order."[15] We could list many other definitions. But these examples illustrate a trend: scholars argue vociferously about the goals and means of a grand strategy but have less to say when defining it.

Still, the contrast between Liddell Hart's formulation decades ago and these more recent definitions demonstrates how much some contemporary scholars have narrowed their lens regarding what constitutes security and strategy. Posen's and Liddell Hart's approaches also differ regarding what constitutes a threat and what are the useful ways and means to respond. Focusing exclusively on direct military threats in the formulation of grand strategy has some benefits: it simplifies the intellectual workload and may do the same for the organizational and policy processes. It also plays to America's clear advantage, given its unrivalled military resources. Finally, it is consistent with both America's traditional "can do" attitude and its increasingly militarized "national security" culture—perennially known as the "American way of war."[16]

There are three obvious problems, however, with this approach. First, it recalls the famous adage that "if you have a hammer, everything looks like a nail."[17] It sees the solution to problems as military rather political, economic, or diplomatic. The tendency was evident in debates during the Obama administration, ranging from how the United States should respond to the Russian annexation of Crimea to US policy regarding Iran's nuclear program.[18]

Second, concentrating on military threats flies in the face of recent public debates over America's international role, which assume that what threatens the United States and its citizens has broadened enormously.[19] This view has been bipartisan. George W. Bush's 2006 *National Security Strategy* and Barack Obama's 2010 version both listed human trafficking as a major concern.[20] By 2015, Obama's NSS had expanded the character of threats to prioritize those posed by an assortment of nonmilitary sources, ranging from illegal drugs and pandemics to climate change.[21]

The third problem is the most relevant to this book: that most of what the military (and specifically the Navy) now does has less to do with war fighting than the twenty-four-hour news cycle implies. True, the amount of time the armed forces spend training and preparing for war is significant. But even that preparation does not dominate their activities. In fact, as Frank Schubert documented, since the Cold War, Military Operations Other than War (MOOTW) have accounted for an increasing percentage of the USN's time and resources.[22] Often to the military's discontent, such operations range from maritime military exercises to enhanced global security (like nonproliferation initiatives) and freedom of navigation initiatives (in the Arctic), to policing missions such as counterpiracy (in African waters) and counternarcotics (in the Gulf of Mexico), all of which we chronicle in the pages that follow.[23] Policymakers drive this expansion of noncombat activities. They want to use their well-financed, well-trained, and readily available military not only to fight wars but also to sustain global stability through policing functions and "win the peace" through humanitarian initiatives. Mission creep has resulted, as both the executive and legislative branches make demands on the military. Tellingly, the term *mission creep* as a term-of-art dates to the years following the Cold War's conclusion.[24]

Another factor contributes to this dynamic: with an end to conscription, fewer policymakers and legislators have served in the armed services.[25] One consequence is an evident gap between the military's and political leaders' understanding of the military's core missions. Central to military culture is a belief that the armed services should focus on improving their capacity to perform essential national security functions. Military officials may welcome more funding, but mission creep is not the way they want to achieve it. Their goal is spending on core functions, not on what they regard as distractions such as policing America's coasts to interdict narcotics. It is a political battle the military's leadership has repeatedly lost.

In sum, "peacetime activities" describes a large portion of naval operations, but such activities are not reflective of the highest priorities of the naval officer corps. Nevertheless, the Navy must integrate these operations into its standard routine in response to policymakers' demands.

*A Cooperative Strategy for 21st Century Seapower: Forward, Engaged, Ready,* the 2015 capstone vision for the Navy, lists five core functions: all domain access, deterrence, sea control, power projection, and maritime security. Many, if not most, naval missions during peacetime come under the rubric of maritime security, including protecting "U.S. sovereignty and maritime resources, support[ing] free and open seaborne commerce, and counter[ing] weapons proliferation, terrorism, transnational crime, piracy, illegal exploitation of the maritime environment, and unlawful seaborne immigration."[26] Yet it is no accident that maritime security is the last of the five listed functions. Dedicating naval vessels, manpower, aviation assets, and an entire range of support systems half a world away from the United States is expensive, in terms both of budgets and of opportunity costs.

Ships patrolling off the Somali coast are not conducting essential missions, as we illustrate in chapter 5. The USN must often neglect combat training when a ship is stationed in the western Indian Ocean for counter-piracy missions. Furthermore, there is a strategic cost: that ship is not readily available to defend Taiwan during what one school of thought calls the "Battle of the First Salvo"—in which a war may be won or lost.[27] Such a scenario would leave the United States with a stark choice: either undertake a costly operation to retake Taiwan or accept a fait accompli. Given the distance from the western Indian Ocean to the western Pacific and Asian littoral, American ships conducting counterpiracy missions are unavailable for deterrence purposes and unlikely to arrive in time to influence a shooting war.[28]

Instead, peacetime naval contributions to national strategy range in practice from "fostering goodwill" to performing more tangible tasks such as disaster management.[29] MOOTW involves routine policing and even includes rescuing people lost at sea and addressing fishing disputes.

Many maritime operations receive little attention. In 2015, for example, the United States supported the Burmese, Thai, and Malaysian navies with maritime surveillance in rescuing thousands of Muslim Rohingya refugees fleeing Myanmar by boat.[30] Most Americans showed little concern about the plight of the Rohingya. But this regional problem attracted the attention of the UN High Commission for Refugees and Muslim states outside Southeast Asia. United States humanitarian intervention supported a diplomatic resolution to the crisis and solidified its position as a broker of regional security. Grand strategists generally ignore these kinds of operations because the regional instability that may result from massive flows of refugees is low on their list of pressing threats. The Navy, however, operates according to a different calculus.

## Three New Trends

There is thus a growing gap. On the one hand, the scope of many popular academic grand strategies is narrowing—what Brooks and Wohlforth characterize as "deep engagement" strategies are often being usurped by "Retrenchment" strategies focusing mainly on security issues.[31] On the other, the list of threats cited by politicians and policymakers is expanding. To further complicate matters, the armed forces' actual activities bear little resemblance to grand strategists' priorities among those threats and (as we shall demonstrate) a simple readjustment is not feasible. The result is a significant challenge to those who prescribe grand strategy.

Of course, not all scholars of grand strategy focus exclusively on security issues. And even those that do may have an expansive conception of security. Notably, they vary as to how they address three critical variables: *the form of threats, the source of these threats, and the nature of conflict that responding to these threats entails.* We now examine how, and to what degree, each of these three elements has evolved. Then we examine how scholars prescribing strategies have responded (or have not responded) to these changes.

## New Threats

It has always been fashionable to focus on the diffusion of advanced military technologies when assessing the proliferation of new threats. General Martin Dempsey, then head of the Joint Chiefs of Staff, for example, wrote in *The National Military Strategy of the United States 2015* report that

> emerging technologies are impacting the calculus of deterrence and conflict management by increasing uncertainty and compressing decision space. For example, attacks on our communications and sensing systems could occur with little to no warning, impacting our ability to assess, coordinate, communicate, and respond. As a result, future conflicts between states may prove to be unpredictable, costly, and difficult to control.

In the maritime realm, perhaps the preeminent example of technological and conceptual diffusion involves the complex, interrelated set of capabilities associated with Anti-Access/Area-Denial (A2/AD) systems. They include short- and intermediate-range missiles, land-based aircraft capable of attacking carrier battle groups, and various undersea warfare weapons. A2/AD capabilities are especially troubling to the Navy because it views its primary mission as ensuring access and projecting power from the sea anywhere deemed necessary. A2/AD systems possessed by China and Russia—and perhaps Iran and North Korea—are judged by most experts to be the single greatest threat to America's dominant maritime position.

The significance of novel technologies can, however, be overstated. There remains an insatiable global demand for conventional weapons systems. The volume of international transfers of major weapons between 2010 and 2014, for example, was 16 percent higher than between 2005 and 2009.[32] But the pace of diffusion of sophisticated military technologies may be more limited than commonly assumed. American policymakers—former president Obama being a good example—emphasize the threat posed by the spread of longstanding WMD technologies or creation of new ones, such as a "dirty bomb in a suitcase."[33] Yet the reality differs. WMD technologies have been relatively slow to diffuse. Few countries have acquired nuclear weapons capability in the last three decades and several have given up their arsenals. The aggregate number of nuclear weapons states has remained stable. Concerns about nuclear proliferation, epitomized by the case of Iran, are largely driven by the single example of North Korea. But few countries have both the will and the capacity to develop a nuclear arsenal that they can accurately deliver.

Furthermore, advanced military technologies are often hard to replicate, with the notable exception of low-end cyberweapons such as distributed denial of service (DDOS) attacks, where attackers make a computer or network unavailable for its intended users by overwhelming it with illegitimate requests, and zero-day exploits, or where attackers take advantage of software or hardware security vulnerabilities previously unknown to the user or vendor. Cyberthreats do consume an increasing proportion of the time, attention, and budget of the military, although independent budgetary assessments are notoriously difficult to calculate.[34] Recent estimates suggest that spending on cybersecurity, broadly defined, has been trending upward—notable given the sequestration in overall military spending associated with the Budget Control Act of 2011. Cyberattacks present both an embarrassing public relations problem—as illustrated by several 2014 and 2015 attacks on the US government and on the Democratic Party in the 2016 electoral campaign—and a potentially serious long-term threat to US military primacy. This is, in large part, because cyberoffensive weaponry is far easier (and cheaper) to develop than defensive systems. But it is falsely portrayed as representative of a possible future dystopia caused by the diffusion of new WMD technologies. Policymakers are more driven by the concern that something might happen "on their watch."[35] This, and public perception, often drives the policy debate and, eventually, military planning.

The issue of high-tech WMD proliferation is often more political and subjective than strategic and objective. Still, the nature of US civilian-military relations demands a response to policymakers' concerns, however misplaced. So, preparedness for what those policymakers fear *might* happen consumes valuable military resources. Other countries may not be able to develop, buy, or use new technologies today, but if left unchecked they *might* in the future. This perception drives US strategy, so America's forces must stand vigilant and make sure it does not happen.[36]

The second and arguably more pressing problem is that conventional arms remain threatening and adversaries have consistently found novel ways to turn ordinary, everyday objects into lethal weapons. Commercial airplanes, not state-of-the-art military aircraft, destroyed the Twin Towers. Crude barrel bombs full of Sarin gas can still kill hundreds if not thousands, and the residual effects of "dumb mines" (that do not automatically deactivate) are a continued scourge, decades after the cessation of conflict. The suicide bomber, C4 strapped to his or her chest, has proved to be an unmanageable global problem. Shocking videos of ISIS members beheading innocent victims using nothing but a knife is perhaps the ultimate symbolic expression of the threat posed by old technologies. What they share is a capacity to maim, kill, and cause terror.

New technologies may diffuse slowly, but however remote the possibility, we disproportionately fear their consequences. The military is therefore asked to address an expanding number of threats, however unrealistic or remote they are from core national security objectives. The Navy faces a long list, from national border patrol to the interdiction of terrorists, drugs, illegal aliens, and arms to patrolling the high seas in an attempt to ensure freedom of navigation, secure chokepoints, thwart the diffusion of WMD technology, and provide disaster relief—while also fighting piracy and human trafficking.

How should we prioritize threats, new and old? The only existential threats to the American homeland come from large nuclear powers and only states have the necessary resources to undermine the statecentric foundations of the liberal international order. Threat perception is often more subjective than objective, even among well-informed policymakers and military officials.[37] Yet policymakers and military commanders devise strategies to combat a dizzying array of threats from states, terrorists, and criminals: realistic low-tech and potential high-tech ones; those that involve offensive and defensive armaments; those that have symbolic targets and those that threaten mass destruction; those that involve the smuggling of people and of drugs; those that can be perpetrated by individuals and those that are digital (and possibly undetectable); and those that involve skirmishes at sea or full-scale warfare.

A new class of novel and nontraditional threats commonly shares three features. First, they are transnational in character, with an expanding geographic scope. Terrorism, for example, has evolved from a domestic to a global problem. Formerly, it was largely contained within national borders—for example, the Irish Republican Army in the United Kingdom, ETA in Spain, or the GIA (Armed Islamic Group) in France. Many governments did not even think about counterterrorism until a wave of plane hijackings by the Palestinian Liberation Organization in the 1970s. Even then, American national security specialists rarely considered it more than a nuisance until September 11, 2001.

Second, each challenge has both domestic and international constituencies seeking to raise the profile of the threat—from climate change and human trafficking to regional conflicts and nuclear war. And in each case, policymakers seek to enlist the extraordinary capabilities of the American military to combat the threat.

Third, some threats do remain directly rooted in human conflict. Others may be at least partly caused by human malfeasance but—like climate change and ensuing natural disasters—are the product of anthropogenic phenomena.[38] These threats have no tangible "enemy" at all. Chinese and Indian emissions of high volumes of hydrocarbons unevenly distribute the costs. Bangladesh, for example, will suffer disproportionately if extreme weather—such as stronger typhoons—becomes more common. New challenges result, such as the creating of "environmental refugees" as well as the prospect of conflict over food, water, and natural resources. In response, advocates insist the US military should apply its unique capabilities to provide humanitarian and disaster relief, or to build levees to protect American cities like New Orleans, even if such missions detract from traditional deterrence and war fighting.

Finally, there are naturogenic threats—those having no human source. These are advertised as new but they are not. Ebola, for example, is terrifying. The Zika virus could change all our best expectations about demographic projections.[39] But the Spanish flu, for which there was no vaccine, killed an estimated 675,000 Americans in 1918–19, and between 30 to 50 million people worldwide.[40] Americans are well aware of these threats, as a Pew public opinion survey conducted in the midst of West Africa's Ebola outbreak made clear.[41] Again, the armed forces were employed, not just to provide security but also to construct facilities and treat patients.

Yet regardless of whether these nontraditional threats are new or have just taken on new form, two things have changed. The first is the speed at which disease and the effects of ecological disaster can diffuse has increased. The transfer to a global population—as SARs, MERS, Ebola, and Zika have all vividly illustrated—is facilitated by the greater volume of people with access to travel by land, sea, and air. A modern pandemic could do far greater damage than the Spanish flu did in 1918–19. The US Centers for

Disease Control and Prevention estimated in 2014, for example, that the number of new Ebola cases in West Africa alone could have doubled every twenty days without stringent quarantine regulations and adequate medical resources.[42] Reinforcing the notion that pandemics have a new scope and scale is the fact that the very term *global health* is relatively new to the American lexicon, largely displacing the more traditional notion of "public" or even "international" health.[43]

The second thing to have changed is that US policymakers have broadened the working definition of *national security* to include more threats. The maritime services—the Navy, Marine Corps, and Coast Guard—have adjusted their top-end strategic documents to reflect this new emphasis. The 2007 vision statement, *A Cooperative Strategy for 21st Century Seapower* (CS21), for example, included humanitarian assistance and disaster relief (HA/DR) among its most important missions.[44] This shift has been reflected in operations, both during crises and on a day-to-day basis—albeit with a significant amount of criticism from within the ranks.[45] In a 2014 interview, for example, President Obama stated:

> There's a reason why the quadrennial defense review—[which] the secretary of defense and the Joints Chiefs of Staff work on—identified *climate change as one of our most significant national security problems* [italics added]. It's not just the actual disasters that might arise; it is the accumulating stresses that are placed on a lot of different countries and the possibility of war, conflict, refugees, displacement that arise from a changing climate.[46]

The Department of Defense is thus preparing to cope with the consequences of climate change,[47] while the armed forces provide manpower, equipment, and technical expertise for disaster relief and humanitarian operations.

Some critics argue that many of the new threats incorporated into major policy documents are marginal to core US national security.[48] Yet, undeniably, more is expected of the American military, adding to the military's planning, training, and operating. Layering new responsibilities on top of old ones has created an unprecedented number of tasks that consume time and resources. Specialized training, equipment, and exercises have been developed, despite concerns that the military's suitability for particular tasks is not always self-evident.

This expansion of functions may partly be explained by the fact that military units are available, adaptable, and willing to undertake complex missions. These considerations often override questions about appropriateness—a propensity demonstrated by then president Obama's dispatching of more than twenty-eight hundred US troops to "combat" the Ebola epidemic. In significant ways that operation was a departure from, if not in conflict with, the military's core mission of safeguarding US national security.[49] But while some civilian medical professionals were willing to volunteer to work with patients, few were willing to volunteer for the complementary logistical tasks performed by the military.

Famously, candidate George W. Bush suggested in 2000 that the US military does not and should not "nation build." He favored reducing America's military involvement in all sorts of noncombat activities, from peacekeeping to humanitarian operations. Eventual National Security Advisor Condoleezza Rice argued that "the president must remember that the military is a special instrument. It is lethal, and it is meant to be. It is not a civilian police force. It is not a political referee. And it is most certainly not designed to build a civilian society."[50] Just as famously, the Bush administration reversed its position after 9/11 with its global counterterrorism campaign and invasions of Iraq and Afghanistan. The US military embarked on a process of nation building, and assumed the greatest variety of political, diplomatic, and economic responsibilities since the Vietnam War. The "military instrument" became a universal solvent.

Afghanistan and Iraq were sometimes characterized as exceptions, or only the province of ground troops. Yet in the same period the Navy also engaged in helping other nations develop the ability to provide for local and regional "Global Maritime Partnerships" and a range of counterterrorism and counterpiracy task forces (described in chapter 5) that had more to do with capacity building than with deterrence or war fighting.[51] Domestic critics often focus on increases in the military budget.[52] They might also focus on increases in the military's roles and missions—and how these increased functions cohere around any single grand strategy.

Our central point is that the responsibilities of the US armed forces have drastically expanded. It is no longer enough to defend the nation against invasion or project power against adversaries; the armed forces are now the nation's first line of defense against threats ranging from cyberattacks to nuclear proliferation, climate change, pandemics, and natural disasters. And like it or not, they are sometimes called on to rebuild societies torn apart by war or support those simply unable to perform security functions like policing the maritime commons.

## New Sources of Threats

The face of conflict has changed. The professionalization of state-sponsored national militaries accelerated in the twentieth century. Both world wars led to a "ratchet effect" in the United States, in which the wartime expansion of militaries never receded to prewar levels. Some scholars suggest that the post-9/11 period has resulted in a new era of state building,[53] resulting perhaps in the development of a "national security state"—a fate the United States reputedly avoided during the Cold War.[54]

Of course, the twentieth century was replete with exceptions. The International Brigade fought in the Spanish civil war in the 1930s; an assortment of irregular and guerilla forces fought in independence movements against colonial rulers across Africa, Asia, and Latin America; and terrorist forces emerged across Europe. Nonetheless, the primary source of threats to national security conventionally came from state actors—a pattern reinforced by the Cold War. After a short period of demobilization following World War II, many states re-created large, technologically advanced militaries designed to fight against mirror-image foes. Conventional, symmetric warfare was the dominant mode of conflict.

In the twenty-first century, however, hostile and violent actors are different. A variety of nonstate actors have been added to state-sponsored militaries with titles such as " paramilitaries," "private defense contractors," "insurgents," "militants," "jihadists," "transnational criminal organizations," and—most recently—"lone wolves." They may vary in their goals. From an American strategic perspective, however, they also vary in another three key respects.

The first is the size of their membership. Although it is hard to calculate with any certainty, ISIS membership was estimated by the CIA to be in the tens of thousands in 2015.[55] At the other extreme are individuals or very small groups who may be dedicated to a large cause but operate independently, such as the Boston Marathon bombers Dzhokar and Tamerlan Tsarnaev or the Orlando assailant Omar Mateen. Between these extremes lies a vast array: the unknown number of Russians who reputedly "volunteered" to serve with the resistance forces in Ukraine in 2014 and 2015; the Ugandan Lord's Resistance Army with an estimated membership of two hundred; and even the "Fort Dix Six" who planned to attack an army base in New Jersey in 2007.

The second variation is the geographic scope of these new actors. Freedom fighters who evolved into criminal gangs, as the Fuerzas Armadas Revolucionarias de Colombia (FARC) did in Colombia or the Shining Path in Peru, remained predominantly nationalists, even if their drug-related activities found customers abroad. But numerous groups have increased their geographic reach. Hezbollah has spread from its primary Lebanese enclave to engage in regional conflicts, most recently in Syria. Mexican drug cartels have expanded their activities south into Central America and north into the United States. And the most expansive have become the most famed. Al Qaeda serves as the model of a transnational terrorist organization that commits acts of varying size and symbolic importance across several continents. ISIS has followed the same pattern. Cyberhackers, often of unknown origin because of attribution problems, may be the ultimate expression of the globalization of violence by a minimal number of actors.[56]

The third variety is to be found in the organizational forms that these actors take. Professional armies are hierarchical and heavily bureaucratized.

At least two alternative (sometimes interrelated) organizational forms have emerged in the last three decades. The first is network structures, in which communication is less transparent or direct, command structures are more attenuated, and lines of authority blurred.[57] Cells heavily populate networks.[58] Again, Al Qaeda provides a notable example. Such networks vary in their degree of formal structure and training, but many of them involve more than simply military forces—as quasi-corporate, public-private structures like Pakistan's A. Q. Khan network illustrates.[59] Many transnational criminal networks (TCOs) still operate on a hierarchical principle. But others link to and intermix with organizations with varied internal structures (hierarchies, networks, franchises, etc.).[60] Threats from organizations with non-state, often nonterritorial and nonhierarchical structures, offer a distinct strategic challenge to the way the United States can respond. Strategies that make sense for deterring states or fighting interstate wars prove generally ineffective when combating networks and other hybrid organizational forms.[61]

Franchises have become widespread. They pledge allegiance to a particular group but operate with a high degree of autonomy, despite seeking material and political support. Both Boko Haram and Egypt's Ansar Bayt al-Maqdis (The Province of Sinai), as examples, pledged allegiance to ISIS in 2015.[62] Yet while the majority of Al Qaeda in the Islamic Maghreb (AQIM) reaffirmed their allegiance to Al Qaeda's core leadership, one AQIM splinter group did not.[63] The fragmentation of command structure across franchises presents a distinct counterintelligence challenge for countries like the United States, which has to infiltrate the franchises themselves rather than identify links between the cells of a network.

Like individual perpetrators, networks and franchises thus present specific problems for the armed forces. Often reliant on agility, invisibility, and dexterity, such groups demand what the military calls "exquisite" intelligence (highly accurate and insightful), along with a familiarity with local geographic, linguistic, and cultural conditions. American forces possess greater counterinsurgency skills as a result of the Afghan and Iraq wars but have yet to master this capacity.

## The Expanding Nature of Conflict

The nature of conflict has expanded and evolved over time. Historically, the civilian population might have been a prize in the spoils of war, enslaved, sexually assaulted, or pillaged. But their involvement in conflict itself was incidental. They were what is commonly termed "collateral damage." Over time, however, civilians moved from being the spoils to the targets of war. German zeppelins, replete with troops throwing hand grenades over the side, terrorized the Belgian and French populations in World War I. The

Holocaust remains the definitive example of a war against an unarmed civilian population.[64] The continuing debate over Armenia, the atrocities of the Balkan wars, and more recently the attacks on unarmed minorities in the greater Middle East have reinforced the use of the term *genocide* in both our common vocabulary and international law.[65]

Just as the targets of warfare have altered, so the nature of potential conflict has expanded, and the geographic focus of the American military has relocated. The form of conflict of greatest interest to American strategists has shifted from the conventional, symmetric war that dominated Cold War thinking to more varied forms . . . and back again.[66] These alternative forms include "asymmetric conflict" and "irregular warfare," tactics that recognize and offset the greater strengths of an adversary. Both are employed by nationalist, ethnic, and now religious insurgencies, involving the kind of guerilla tactics used against American forces in Vietnam and later in Afghanistan and Iraq.

To complicate matters further, these varied actors and approaches sometimes combine, creating another form of conflict. Since the 1990s, national security experts have increasingly used the term *hybrid conflict*, "characterized by a blend of traditional and irregular tactics, decentralized planning and execution, and nonstate actors that use both sophisticated and simple technologies in innovative ways."[67] Peter Mansoor suggests they involve "a combination of conventional military forces and irregulars (guerillas, insurgents, and terrorists), which could include state and non-state actors, aimed at achieving a common political purpose."[68]

Even its advocates recognize that these definitions may lack operational utility.[69] Hybrid conflict has been used to describe everything from the Islamic State's strategy to Russian forces in the Ukraine, cyberhackers in Syria and elsewhere, and China's approach to the South China Sea.[70] But the implications of this new mix are clear. Frank Hoffman summarized the dilemma facing US forces: "This kind of warfare transcends traditional notions of one military confronting another by incorporating conventional and unconventional forces, information warfare such as propaganda, as well as economic measures to undermine an enemy. . . . The critique was, and still is, that America's view of war is overly simplified. . . . We think of things in black-and-white terms."[71]

The categories of warfare are blurring and no longer fit into neat boxes. Robert Gates, former Secretary of Defense, echoed this point when he noted that "one can expect to see more tools and tactics of destruction—from the sophisticated to the simple—being employed simultaneously in hybrid and more complex forms of warfare."[72] Incidents of conventional interstate war may have diminished. But other forms of conflict have increased, and the message is clear: America needs to be prepared to engage in each form of conflict—and sometimes in several of them at once.[73]

Responding to both international developments and public sentiment, American policymakers and the armed services thus prepare for all variants of conflict. The US military has significantly expanded its resources and capacity to engage in cyberconflict over the last decade to combat both sophisticated opponents like China and Russia, and nonstate actors. Clever adversaries also engage in ideological warfare by recruiting and propagandizing online.[74] The contours of conflict have expanded far beyond combat operations.

We have witnessed three key trends in the twenty-first century. Sources of threat have multiplied beyond states to include different organizational forms (networks and franchises populated by terrorists and Jihadists, criminal gangs, corporations) that are often simply grouped under the rubric of "nonstate" actors. Second, conventional warfare has now been joined by several other categories including irregular, asymmetric, and later hybrid warfare. Third, since the Cold War, American policymakers have vastly expanded the definition of what constitutes a national security threat.

Analysts who promote particular variants of grand strategy choose which aspects of these three trends they prefer to prioritize. Policymakers and strategic planners do not have the luxury of priorities, and they have to prepare for all eventualities. The best the military can do is to negotiate among those priorities. In response to the concerns of politicians, it has to plan to counteract the effects of these three new trends. As a result, the US military's missions have expanded to the point that core national security functions like deterrence and war fighting have been usurped by military operations other than war.

# Comparing Grand Strategies—and Their Inherent Limitations

> What, then, should an intelligent strategy be based on? I should say
> first of all on a sound appreciation of existing realities, which will then
> enable us to make predictions which have real planning values—and
> that is easier said than done.
>
> —Bernard Brodie, 1952 lecture
> at the Naval War College, Newport, RI

> A fundamental lesson from history is that strategy is necessarily
> purposeful, but must be designed in a world of ambiguity, complexity,
> and uncertainty.
>
> —Frank Hoffman, "Grand Strategy:
> The Fundamental Considerations," *Orbis*, 2014

The US defense establishment employs an endless cycle of scenario planning, strategizing for the unexpected. The National Intelligence Council, for example, recurrently publishes its *Global Trends* report, projecting far into the future. In the 2030 report's introduction, NIC chairman Christopher Kjom notes, "We distinguish between megatrends, those factors that will likely occur under any scenario, and game-changers, critical variables whose trajectories are far less certain. Finally, as our appreciation of the diversity and complexity of various factors has grown, we have increased our attention to scenarios or alternative worlds we might face."[1]

This scenario building supports preparedness and strategic flexibility, seeking to answer the question "What should we do if . . . ?" Policymakers want a plan and toolbox for every eventuality. Scenario planning has become an industry in the last three decades,[2] both inside and outside of government, yet the United States usually responds to the unexpected in predictable ways.

Our own experience illustrates this point. Two decades ago Simon Reich was among a group invited to meetings with intelligence officials in

Washington, DC. The agenda concerned the likely sources of "instability on the Russian periphery." The timing for scenario building seemed appropriate in the aftermath of the fall of the Berlin Wall. During the first four meetings, the group deliberated about a wide-ranging set of factors that might influence developments in Eastern and Central Europe. The hosts sat on the sidelines, attentive to every word. At the fifth meeting, the group voted on the four most important factors; each participant was then asked to write a paper that configured them and offer a corresponding strategy. The authors presented their findings in the concluding meeting and the group adjourned, never to convene again.

During this process, the hosts enthusiastically encouraged group members to express their views without inhibition. No answer, they insisted, was "right." Indeed, the participants were encouraged to "think outside the box." The participants had initially assumed that the hosts were looking for definitive answers to questions about post–Cold War developments and America's appropriate strategic response. But it gradually became clear that the hosts had different objectives. Was there a factor they had not identified, an eventuality for which they had not planned, or a strategic response not considered? In a period of emergent threats, they needed an assortment of strategies to consider.

Reich never discovered whether this process yielded any tangible product. But today, America's defense establishment is busier than ever, considering scenarios and planning strategies as the world becomes ever more complex. Participating in these events is enjoyable. It allows academics to think about "what if?" questions and hope that they have some faint influence. Yet in the last three decades, neither of us finds evidence that the input of guest academics has much tangible effect on the government's security strategy.

Reality is more formidable than these intriguing discussions would lead us to believe. The forms and sources of threats we identified in chapter 1 do not neatly mesh together with unique forms of conflict. The possible configurations are numerous, and the challenges to the United States are daunting.

Even tabulating all the alternatives would not adequately describe the problem, because both states and nonstate groups can simultaneously adopt multiple, differing tactics. They can, for example, fight conventional, irregular, and hybrid conflicts against the United States simultaneously—as ISIS has done. Transnational criminal networks may fight conventional wars against the Mexican state and irregular wars against the United States—and exacerbate conflicts involving the US military in other areas including the Balkans, Afghanistan, and Colombia.[3] Piracy off the Horn of Africa presents a policing problem on the seas but ultimately may be the result of state failure on Somalia's mainland.[4] The United States often faces a litany of these complex problems. Any conflict may involve a variety of tactics, and scenario building identifies potential problems, not the full range of possible solutions.

The US military—a collection of large bureaucracies rife with such classic pathologies as red tape, duplication, and the ambition to expand—develops strategies and implements them in familiar ways with standard operating procedures. Even the commanding officers of warships are mired in organizational requirements that have little to do with effective leadership or innovative ways to accomplish missions. As one officer reports, onboard "PowerPoint aces" and "check list managers" service requirements "not from a single source, but from volumes of manuals, instructions, notes, and messages" originating from "a host of superior commands at varying degrees of geographical, cultural, and practical distance from the ship."[5] If that is true in the fleet, one of the last bastions of purportedly independent operations, imagine how the same services operate acquisition, personnel, and strategic planning systems. Each response, viewed in isolation, may appear consistent with a specified form of grand strategy. But viewed collectively, it becomes transparent that they are inconsistent with any one of them.

Eliot A. Cohen, former senior State Department official, made a comparable point in his testimony to the Senate Armed Services Committee in the fall of 2015. Commenting on the tendency of bureaucratization to curtail creative military leadership, he argued that

> nothing, but nothing is more important than senior leadership—the creative leaders like Arleigh Burke or Bernard Schriever in the early Cold War. Our problem is that our promotion systems, in part because of the natural tendency of bureaucracies to replicate themselves, and in part because of the wickets (including joint service) all have to pass through, is making it hard to reach deep and promote exceptional talent to the very top.[6]

Cohen made a related point about the dysfunctional nature of routinized bureaucratic review. He noted the example of the military's Quadrennial Defense Review System, "which consumes vast quantities of labor in the Pentagon and much wasted emotional energy as well, [and] seems to be predicated on the notion that the world will cooperate with our four-year review cycle." Moreover, "most public documents, to include the National Security Strategy of the United States, are the vapid products of committees."[7]

These reviews, Cohen noted, are often instantly obsolete because of the rapidly shifting dynamics of global politics. The same could be said of legislative and executive post-hoc reviews of events like 9/11 or Benghazi. They consume vast resources and energy, and provide limited insight or oversight—even when their ambitions extend beyond simple finger pointing. They may publicize problems in the bureaucratic process. But they rarely illuminate or spark significant, lasting change.

In a similar fashion, strategic assessments process the configuration of threats, actors, and potential forms of conflict through the lens of familiar analogs. They are then slotted into traditional boxes in which major strategies reside. It would be an overstatement to suggest that there is never any variance. But America's likely response is shaped by a combination of the rhetoric of policymakers and the standard operating procedures of the military's bureaucracy.

In this chapter, we outline the major strands of contemporary US grand strategy and identify the conditions under which each one is employed by policymakers and, ultimately, the US military. Each of the six main strategies is illustrated in subsequent chapters with maritime cases drawn from the experience of the sea services.

We have two objectives. The first is to note that grand strategists establish priorities, the primary form and source of threat, the character of the opposition, and the dominant form of conflict that the military will encounter. We briefly lay out the variants in the next section. Each of these main types of grand strategy should result in a distinctive profile and repertoire of action. In fact, as we will show, *the United States Navy (USN) often pursues each of these strategies simultaneously.*

Our second goal is to explain why such a variety of strategies are used, and why that variation is inevitable. We argue that, by prioritizing specific threats, all advocates of these competing formulations of grand strategy try to "shoe horn" the world into their prescribed approach. They largely ignore operational requisites, unknown factors, and the messy business of politics—domestic, bureaucratic, and organizational.

Domestic politics involves the push and pull between different constituencies: politicians seeking to address public concerns by offering rhetorical but often vacuous responses; policymakers attempting to impose dominant but ill-suited strategic principles; and military officials who are pragmatic problem solvers well aware of operational limitations. Military officials alone attempt to adapt to the problem they face, the resources at their disposal, and the limitations inherent in existing domestic and international institutions.

These domestic debates vary in scope. Some are narrowly confined to a community of senior officials, strategic experts, lawyers, and military personnel, passing under the radar of media and congressional scrutiny. Others are more expansive, more public, and more belligerent. But in no case is decision making merely nominal, nor is it confined to a debate among policymakers (as much of the grand strategy literature implies). Legislators, commanders close to the action, and pundits weigh in with their opinions.

*America operates six parallel strategies by necessity.* Collectively, they stray too far afield to be amenable to any one guiding principle beyond the obvious: pursuing America's national security interests. In effect, contingent circumstances demand a degree of strategic flexibility that is at odds with any single grand theory. Flexibility entails a calibration of strategy to meet a specific threat under specific circumstances—a calibration that is sacrificed by any unified approach. One size—one grand strategy—does not fit all. But the six strategies we describe define the most prevalent options.[8]

## The Biases of Grand Strategists

All grand strategies make a series of deductive assumptions, notably about the key actors, their relationship, and the appropriate content of a grand strategy. Furthermore, they make choices about the form and source of threats, and how best to respond to them. In doing so they sacrifice flexibility for what proponents characterize as consistency, clarity, and principled policy. Finally, all formulations, by definition, imply cause-and-effect relationships between vision, strategy, policy, and operations. Or as military strategists describe it, between ways, means, and ends.

Our intent is not to misrepresent matters: many proponents of grand strategy do recognize the contingencies that will, from time-to-time, influence capacity to implement any principle.[9] Yet after declaring that contingencies do exist, they proceed largely to ignore them. And, intellectually and organizationally, the key is how each approach builds a dominant strategy.[10] There are three main ways in which these strategies are organized. Each one divides into two different formulations, and that gives us the six distinct strategic options on which we focus.

HEGEMONY

This first form comes in two variants that have commonly vied for supremacy in the American debate. "Primacist" forms are commonly associated with American unilateralism. They are highly assertive, coercive, and often confrontational. Such policies show scant regard for the requisites of international law and thus largely ignore "lawfare"—the use of international legal regulation and instruments (such as the International Criminal Court) to prosecute claims and delegitimate behavior.[11] Primacy is mainly used when dealing unilaterally with territorially defined enemies. Examples include strategic action against countries within the Western Hemisphere during the period of "Gunboat Diplomacy"[12] and more recent unilateral military interventions in Granada and Panama.[13] In the twenty-first century, it has included a neoconservative nation-building variant, in the invasions of Afghanistan and then Iraq.[14] The Obama administration did not embrace this strategy, but it responded to China's newly declared sovereign zone around recently constructed islands in the South China Sea by sending an American destroyer through those waters. Their response was unilateral, used military means, challenged the territorial claim of another state, and—despite American denials—was legally controversial.[15] For Primacists, the United States serves as the world's sheriff or policeman because of its supposedly "indispensable status" in maintaining system stability.[16]

The second variant of Hegemony, what we describe as a Leadership strategy (and others label "cooperative security"), is a traditionally liberal coalition in which the United States assumes a primus inter pares role as a matter of entitlement.[17] Proponents often depict this strategy as benign and respectful of other actors and of national sovereignty. Moreover, they claim that American Hegemony generates public goods that address collective action problems, whether through ad hoc coalition building (such as the first Gulf War), the creation of international institutions (such as the World Bank), or formal alliance structures (such as NATO).[18] Prescribed policies are activist, interventionist, and explicitly promote values such as liberal capitalism and democracy. Having abandoned a broadly Primacist approach in the Middle East, the Obama-inspired, American-led initiative in negotiating the multilateral Iran nuclear agreement of 2015 provides an example of a Leadership strategy. Opponents of the negotiations wanted to coerce or bomb Iran.[19] In contrast, the P5+1 (the five permanent members of the United Nations Security Council plus Germany) negotiations with Iran assumed that other major powers and the United Nations concurred on objectives and processes. The eventual agreement prioritized shared long-term security concerns among the United States' multilateral partners rather than short-term concerns such as Iran's militant regional activities and threats against Israel.[20]

Both Primacist and Leadership grand strategies can be treated as variants of Hegemony because they rely on American global dominance. Yet in addition to unilateralist or multilateralist leanings, they differ in several notable ways. First, the Primacist approach tends toward short-term, resource-intensive, relativist policy in confronting America's adversaries, even if some proponents advocate a long-term process of what critics regard as neoconservative empire building.[21] By contrast, Leadership proponents are inclined to embed American interests in a broader fabric, relying more on global institution building rather than redesign individual countries employing a rule-based system.[22] This approach demonstrates a greater tactical capacity for employing elements of lawfare than its Primacist counterpart.

Ultimately, the multilateralist variant aims to secure greater legitimacy for American policies, both domestically and internationally. It tolerates more free riding by others, because the United States generates an absolute gain. "Burden sharing" is often demanded rhetorically, but the United States invariably assumes a disproportionate share of costs. Washington pays that price because it gets to set the agenda, initiates policy, has clearly preferred outcomes, and is often seen by partners as committed to implementation. The United States may claim that other states want to be led and want the shared benefits of American policies, but often such claims veil coercive American behavior. One example is John Ikenberry's characterization of America's postwar agreement with Western European states as benign and welcomed, when some European historians of the period suggest quite the opposite.[23]

Primacist policies engage other states mainly through the use of military power, whereas the Leadership variant engages with a more diverse set of actors, including international and regional organizations. In 2012, Anne-Marie Slaughter offered a conception of grand strategy for a world composed of networks of both state and nonstate actors. According to Slaughter:

> The most important shift for America is not the rise of China and the realignment of power in the international system, but rather the ubiquity and density of global networks. Existing grand strategies . . . assume a world of states acting essentially as unitary actors with defined military, economic and diplomatic strategies. States certainly continue to exist and to play essential roles in the international system. However, even if they are the principal actors in the international system, they now act side by side with many types of social actors who are able to come together and act independently on the world stage. The resulting system is messy, complex and frustrating.[24]

Slaughter suggests that the task of strategic planners is to prioritize issue areas and to locate the United States as the dominant strategic actor at the center of a hub-and-spoke system.[25]

These two variants of hegemonic strategies lead to different outcomes, exemplified by the 1991 Persian Gulf War and the 2003 invasion of Iraq. George H. W. Bush's administration received the support of the United Nations for the 1991 intervention. His administration worked assiduously to build an able and cohesive coalition to fight the war, with significant burden sharing. George W. Bush's administration, in contrast, ignored the UN's objections in 2003 and prosecuted the Iraq War with limited military assistance from America's usual partners (principally the United Kingdom) and virtually no support from other countries in the region. The Persian Gulf War resulted in the removal of Iraqi forces from Kuwait and the withdrawal of allied combat troops; the Iraq conflict engendered a war from which America has proved unable to extricate itself, even as its partners departed.

SPONSORSHIP

Sponsorship strategies involve the provision of material and moral resources in support of policies largely advocated and initiated by other actors, whether states, global or regional institutions, or nonstate actors. Sponsorship strategies are disproportionately multilateral because of the global nature of the threats they seek to address. When adopting Sponsorship strategies, the United States foregoes the benefits of agenda setting. Such strategies are therefore reactive not proactive from an American perspective. Moreover, the resulting policies generally retain a low profile in the policy discourse, often involving the routine implementation of ongoing, long-standing objectives. Yet the fact that these strategies are neither sensational nor high-profile makes them no less important to national security.

Signature examples include cooperative policing of the global commons, such as antipiracy efforts and campaigns against the smuggling of fissile materials (discussed in chapter 6). They also involve protecting civilians, often in the provision of logistical, intelligence, or tactical support for humanitarian interventions.[26] The United States incurs a political cost because it is not seen to lead, even when playing an invaluable supportive role. Still, it may be rewarded by getting what it wants. Both points were made by Obama about the invasion of Libya when interviewed by Jeffrey Goldberg:

> Of France, he said, "Sarkozy wanted to trumpet the flights he was taking in the air campaign, despite the fact that we had wiped out all the air defenses and essentially set up the entire infrastructure" for the intervention. This sort of bragging was fine, Obama said, because it allowed the U.S. to "purchase France's involvement in a way that made it less expensive for us and less risky for us." In other words, giving France extra credit in exchange for less risk and cost to the United States was a useful trade-off—except that "from the perspective of a lot of the folks in the foreign-policy establishment, well, that was terrible. If we're going to do something, obviously we've got to be up front, and nobody else is sharing in the spotlight."[27]

In practice, Sponsorship strategies divide into two groups. The first are those *formal* strategies that are specifically authorized by international law and protocols, such as America's global fight against human trafficking. These cases involve a high degree of lawfare because the justification for American action is legally codified.[28] Indeed, international law can be used to abrogate sovereignty, as in the case of humanitarian interventions that invoke the UN's Responsibility to Protect doctrine.

The second are those *informal* strategies that respond to the requests of a looser coalition of states or policy entrepreneurs rather than being authorized by intergovernmental organizations. Here the degree of legal justification is more modest, reliant more on norms, and more susceptible to criticism from opponents. But the United States benefits from the fact that it can operate more autonomously in the absence of international law. Nonetheless, the legitimacy of American assistance is still higher than in hegemonic strategies because the United States justifies its actions on the grounds that its participation has been requested.[29]

Proponents of Sponsorship strategies suggest that both variants offer advantages. First, such strategies remain consistent with American interests—they should not be mistaken for altruism. Yet "national interest" here is broadly defined, often supporting universal values such as human rights and protecting vulnerable populations. The conception of interest is long-term, diffuse, and regarded as legitimate by "the international community" precisely because the United States enforces consensual global protocols and agreements advocated by others and responds to requests for assistance.[30]

Second, Sponsorship strategies may enhance American legitimacy because the United States is portrayed as acting as a responsible member of the international community. Some hegemonic approaches make similar claims.[31] Yet their propensity to impose agendas—and to cajole or bribe allies to support them—often diminishes American legitimacy and with it the prospects of garnering support in unrelated policy areas. Sponsorship strategies demonstrate American recognition of an iterative game in which it is attempting to build a residual bank of goodwill that may translate into effective policy issue linkages later.

Third, Sponsorship strategies may reduce financial costs because they entail genuine burden sharing. "Free ridership" is not an option because others are requesting American help. A financial comparison of recent and current conflicts is illuminating. The 2003 invasion of Iraq—a quintessential outcome of a hegemonic strategy—is conservatively estimated to have cost in excess of $800 billion by 2011. By the same date, the war in Afghanistan had reputedly cost $467 billion.[32] Estimates suggest the eventual costs will approach $4 trillion,[33] notwithstanding that (at the time of writing) both wars continue.[34] In contrast, the NATO intervention in Libya, a good example of a Sponsorship strategy, lasted only five months, from the late spring to the autumn of 2011 and cost approximately $1 billion in total.[35]

Daily US costs in the Afghan war (2001–14), the Iraq war (2003–14), and the campaign against ISIS during the Obama presidency (another example of Sponsorship) offer another useful metric. Estimates vary, but the Afghan war had cost well in excess of $100 million a day by 2014. The Iraq war, although shorter, cost more than $190 million a day. The US Congressional Research Service and the Department of Defense both report that by June 2015, the ISIS campaign had cost $9 million a day.[36] Critics may argue that neither Libya in 2011 nor the ongoing war in Syria and Iraq has yielded the desired policy outcomes. Obama admitted as much.[37] But the same was true of the Afghan and the Iraq wars.

Fourth, Sponsorship strategies reduce the likelihood of American casualties because the United States can negotiate limits on its military involvement. Such strategies are consistent with the public's aversion to "boots on the ground." As of May 2016, the American campaign against ISIS had consisted of an aerial offensive supplemented by the use of trainers, in contrast to the hundreds of thousands of ground forces deployed in Iraq and Afghanistan. By comparison, 4,486 US soldiers died in Iraq between 2003 and 2011 using a Primacist strategy, and another 2,372 died in Afghanistan between 2001 and 2015 using a Leadership strategy, for a total of 6,822.[38] In contrast, by May 2016, only three American soldiers had been killed in Iraq in twenty months employing a Sponsorship strategy.[39] At that time the White House deftly defended its approach:

> Secretary Carter earlier today described this death as a combat death. That's accurate. This was an individual who was not in a combat mission, but he was in a dangerous place. And his position came under attack. He was armed, trained, and prepared to defend himself. Unfortunately, he was killed. And he was killed in combat. But that was not part of his mission. His mission was specifically to offer advice and assistance to those Iraqi forces that were fighting for their own country.[40]

The decision of the Obama administration to send "fewer than fifty" special operations troops to Syria in October 2015 to train local Kurdish forces but play no "direct combat role" was consistent with an informal Sponsorship strategy.[41] The first direct American casualty in Syria did not occur until November 24, 2016.[42] Nonetheless, the recruitment of special operations forces and other contributions from key allies to join American forces in advising and assisting Iraqi troops continued.[43]

Finally, Sponsorship strategies allow for easier disengagement, partially because American credibility is not so evidently at stake as in other strategic approaches. Extricating America from Libya was simpler than Iraq because the United States was able to negotiate the terms of its participation from a position of strength. Neither conflict has been satisfactorily resolved. But one has come at a far greater cost in terms of both blood and treasure.

President Obama succinctly characterized a formal Sponsorship strategy in a 2011 interview on Libya.

> So what I said at that point was, we should act as part of an international coalition. But because this is not at the core of our interests, we need to get a UN mandate; we need Europeans and Gulf countries to be actively involved in the coalition; we will apply the military capabilities that are unique to us, but we expect others to carry their weight. And we worked with our defense teams to ensure that we could execute a strategy without putting boots on the ground and without a long-term military commitment in Libya.[44]

Many proponents of the other forms of grand strategy oppose Sponsorship strategies because they believe that the United States should not cede any sovereignty to the UN because the organization does not serve America's national interests.[45] Furthermore, look at what happens to those Sponsorship strategies that attain a higher profile. Some are reinterpreted as examples of American Leadership, even when they are not. America's ongoing global campaign against human trafficking is notable in this regard.[46] The US State Department publishes an annual "Trafficking in Persons" report. It evaluates countries and threatens routine transgressors with sanctions. Additionally, the United States assists countries in constructing and implementing antitrafficking strategies and in building capacity through judicial and criminal reforms. The initiative is justified by global protocols originating from the United Nations' 2000 Palermo Convention on Transnational Organized Crime. They are endorsed by a plethora of NGOs around the globe, legitimating American behavior. In any other context, such action would be characterized as a bullying abrogation of national sovereignty. But in this context, the United States can characterize itself as being a responsible global citizen.[47]

Other opponents criticize Sponsorship strategies either on the grounds that America fails to demonstrate Leadership, or that it is "leading from behind" and is insufficiently aggressive.[48] The Libyan intervention again illustrates such criticism.[49] Such comments resonate with a well-established belief that the United States should lead in agenda setting.[50]

Nonetheless, America's military does routinely implement Sponsorship strategies. American politicians generally fail to recognize this fact, policymakers fail to identify Sponsorship as a strategy unto itself, and the military fails to discuss it—to avoid any political backlash about ceding sovereignty to foreign powers.

RETRENCHMENT

This American grand strategy has been the subject of significant debate among both academics and politicians. Like Hegemony and Sponsorship, Retrenchment comes in two varieties. The first is the Isolationism advocated by several leading Republicans over the last two decades. It was a central component of Donald Trump's presidential campaign in 2016.[51] Isolationists want to withdraw US forces from overseas bases, reduce US alliance commitments, cut foreign and security military assistance programs and humanitarian aid, provide less support for international organizations, and reassert American sovereignty through stricter border control. The last item on that list is primarily intended to deal with illicit flows of people (illegal immigrants and terrorists), of arms (in practice, fissile materials to be used as WMD), and of drugs. Proponents depict these as the most pressing national security issues.[52] Senator Rand Paul, in that spirit, endorsed the view that "there is no good reason for Washington to serve as the world's policeman and many good reasons why it should cease and desist from doing so."[53]

Curiously, some conservatives and right-wing populists share this position with left-leaning liberals and Marxists. The left's variant, of course, differs in its political intent and values, but it also involves a reduction in foreign military commitments. Chalmers Johnson, for example, advocated withdrawal to avoid imperial overstretch and reduce the threat of "blowback."[54] Among politicians, Democratic presidential candidate Bernie Sanders was an avowed opponent of the two wars with Iraq for those reasons.[55] More radically, Noam Chomsky regards American interventionism as an act of military and economic domination over the Global South.[56] The left and right thus arrive at similar conclusions from vastly different perspectives.

One of the few scholars to advocate Isolationism since the end of the Cold War was Eric Nordlinger in *Isolationism Reconfigured*.[57] Nordlinger's contribution, and its applicability to contemporary debates over grand strategy, has suffered from misunderstandings, red herrings, and in some cases, a lack of familiarity with recent historical scholarship on American Isolationism.[58] Isolationism is commonly associated with the interwar period and thus with America Firsters, residual fascism and nativism, and opposition to American entry into World War II. But, as we will show, America does employ Isolationist policies to match its politicians' populist rhetoric from Alaska's Arctic border to southern states bordering on Mexico and facing the Caribbean. These elements resonated when then candidate Donald Trump promised that, if elected, he would construct a wall along the border with Mexico. Trump later pledged to refuse Muslims entry to the United States following an ISIS-inspired terrorist attack in San Bernardino.[59] He then aggressively pursued elements of both in his first months in office. Nonetheless, Isolationism remains in disrepute among scholars and mainstream security experts, despite its appearance in the 2016 presidential campaign and the opening salvos of the Trump administration. Its populist tones resonate with the electorate but key aspects of its implementation will be challenging.

Several scholars have advocated a far less controversial variant known as "Restraint." Restraint is at the forefront of current debates on grand strategy. Proponents of Restraint generally prescribe narrowing America's international goals, limiting global engagement, and using the military sparingly. The origins of recent scholarship on this variant lie in work on selective engagement, offshore balancing, and the "Come Home, America" position.[60] Christopher Layne, for example, advocates offshore balancing, to transition from the twentieth-century grand strategy of preponderance to one "minimizing the risk of U.S. involvement in great power war (possibly nuclear), and enhancing America's relative power position in the international system."[61] Layne concludes that offshore balancing will allow the

United States to reduce its land forces while maintaining "robust nuclear deterrence, air power, and—most important—overwhelming naval power."[62] Eugene Gholz, Daryl Press, and Harvey Sapolsky likewise argue for "a significant reduction in the number of active duty forces and a significant reduction in America's overseas military presence."[63] And Stephen Walt, in the aftermath of 9/11, provided a concrete suggestion in this spirit: that the United States devolve security issues to regional organizations or locally powerful states.[64]

More recently, Barry Posen has combined aspects of selective engagement and Isolationism.[65] His analysis is predicated on the historical example of British nineteenth-century maritime strategy, one entailing a "command of the commons." Today that includes the air, space, and sea, but remains primarily command of the sea. It allows for flexibility and responsiveness in addressing emergent threats. Posen judges the number of serious threats to US interests to be small and believes they can be addressed "with subtlety and moderation."[66]

He offers both a fiscal and a moral defense of his position. The resultant reduction, preponderantly in ground forces, will generate savings for the defense budget. It will reduce the incidence and cost of American intervention and subsequent entanglement, avoiding links to "reckless" allies. Moreover, he contends that it is consistent with democratic values because of its transparency and responsiveness to public opinion. Finally, he argues, Restraint is ethically consistent with a "just war" doctrine, more so than hegemonic options, because preventative war is morally questionable and a recourse to war should be a last course of action.[67]

A "command of the commons" approach is consistent with the American propensity to undertake "freedom of navigation" operations around the globe. It is one that the USN's senior officers enthusiastically support. As Admiral Harry B. Harris, when head of the United States Pacific Command, said on a visit to Beijing soon after the initial US naval incursion into China's self-proclaimed sovereign zone around Subi Reef in the South China Sea, "We've been conducting freedom of navigation operations all over the world for decades, so no one should be surprised by them. . . . The South China Sea is not, and will not be, an exception."[68] With over 100,000 ships traveling through the South China Sea annually, it is exactly the kind of chokepoint that the United States protects as part of a Restraint strategy that defines global commerce and military access as key components of national security.

This description of the three major approaches to US grand strategy is simplified, of course (and we have offered a more systematic tabulation in appendix 1). But ultimately each configures differently, and the policies that are actually implemented differ as well. We recognize that each approach provides benefits and generates costs—although none seem to lead to unmitigated policy successes. So, we do not prescribe any of them. Our goal, rather, is to show that each strategy is used in a particular context. In the next section, we address the question of why a particular strategy is chosen.

## Domestic Politics and the Messy Business of Choosing Strategies

Most scholars understand that American grand strategy is neither a function of the international environment nor the ideational interpretation of that environment. Policymakers are not stupid. They often concur with the notion that operational contingencies may significantly modify strategic responses. Yet they rarely recognize that such modifiers may effectively subvert the very notion of a single grand strategy. And they generally ignore potentially critical intervening factors, especially the influence of the policy organizations charged with implementing strategy.[69]

More than twenty years ago, Richard Rosecrance and Arthur Stein argued that domestic factors had been neglected as determinants of grand strategy.[70] We agree. American strategy is constrained, shaped, and implemented by domestic institutions, bureaucratic-organizational dynamics, domestic politics, and strategic cultures. In sum, military strategies are as subject to domestic influences as other policies. Yet as Robert Putnam noted: "It is fruitless to debate whether domestic politics really determine international relations, or the reverse. The answer to that question is clearly 'Both, sometimes.' The more interesting questions are 'When?' and 'How?'"[71] These are the questions we address in examining what the USN does. Military leaders, under the direction of, and often in collaboration with, civilian leaders, craft strategies that address problems in terms of the character of the threat, the nature of the adversary, and the kind of conflict that they will likely face in the theater of operations. But those strategies are determined within a political context. Military officers can give their civilian counterparts advice but nonetheless remain acutely aware of the imperatives within which they have to operate—for example, not committing to combat operations or only providing trainers to assist local forces.

For the USN, this may mean shadowing ships suspected of carrying contraband but not boarding them—an example we discuss in chapter 6 where we examine the Proliferation Security Initiative (PSI). In such cases, the USN often provides actionable intelligence to allied or partner navies, coast guards, or border patrols who then operate under their own domestic laws to search, seize, and prosecute weapons traffickers. In the PSI case, the USN objected to policymakers about performing this intelligence function. The objections were simply ignored—purportedly in the service of the greater good of reducing proliferation.

Our goal is to explain diverse patterns of behavior, not build theory or prescribe policy. But a focus on military effectiveness and civil-military relations helps bridge the divide between grand theory, where so much appears logically possible, and operational limitations, where so much obviously is not possible. We examine how politics, strategy, and operations interact. Specifically, we want to know how military leaders view the prospects for achieving national objectives, whether through the use or threat of force, or the use of combat units for MOOTW.

## Military Effectiveness and the Domestic Politics of Strategic Planning

Studies of military effectiveness traditionally examine how states achieve victory in warfare.[72] This research concentrates on variables such as regime type, societal characteristics, military culture, state structure, and organizational imperatives to explain why some military forces are successful in fighting wars.[73] Much of it concludes that the US military has been ineffective since the first Gulf War. Neither the Afghan nor Iraq wars can be considered victories. The Taliban government was overthrown and many leaders of al Qaeda, principally Osama bin Laden, have been killed. But both the Taliban and al Qaeda continue to fight, and internal stability remains elusive. Similarly, Saddam Hussein's regime was successfully dismantled. But the country remains an unstable battlefield between ISIS and the Iraqi government, a bastion of terrorism, and Iran has increased its power and influence. Meanwhile, military operations have assassinated terrorist leaders and disrupted cells in countries such as the Philippines, Yemen, and Nigeria. Few, if any, American officials regard the former Global War on Terror as a victory.

Perhaps the reverse is true: the US military is most effective when it serves as a deterrent to war. Put simply, military victory is not a way to measure military effectiveness. In the spirit of Liddell Hart, we suggest that military effectiveness involves peacetime operations as much as wartime ones.

In contrast to the traditional approach, we argue that a study of military effectiveness should examine, first and foremost, how military forces serve America's national interests in war *and* peace, especially in the peacetime operations awkwardly categorized as MOOTW. The unadorned truth is that American military forces serve a wide range of policy ends that only occasionally involve combat. Moreover, military leaders are not always passive recipients of the ways and means of grand strategy. They often participate in the decision-making process, if only to outline operational limitations and preferences. This distinction becomes blurred when military leaders assume positions of authority normally reserved for civilians, as in the Trump administration. Nonetheless, even in more conventional times civilian leaders, seeking to understand what is possible, consult military leaders about strategy, operations, and tactics. The military, in essence, tries to link together the desirable and the possible within a defined operational context.

Finally, bureaucratic limitations apply here. Modern military operations are most often, in military terminology, "joint, combined, and interagency." In short, to complete their assigned missions, each American military service—Navy, Marine Corps, Air Force, Army, and Coast Guard—often have to cooperate: with their fellow services, the militaries of allies and coalition partners, and other US government agencies such as the Central Intelligence Agency, the National Security Agency, and the departments of State, Justice, and Homeland Security.[74]

Elements of research on military effectiveness, broadly defined, have much to offer grand strategy debates that operate at a level of abstraction far removed from operational complexities. Several specific strands offer useful insights into how strategy is developed and implemented.

The first is the focus on civil-military relations found in the classic works of Samuel Huntington and Morris Janowitz. They emphasize both the importance of military autonomy and, in democratic regimes, civilian control over the military.[75] The unresolved tension between the civilian and military leadership helps us understand the limitations of deductive grand strategy approaches. Elected politicians generally assume that military leaders have the professional expertise required to provide overall guidance for national security (and thus the policies adopted) and solutions to particular security challenges.[76] The military leadership is, of course, occasionally ignored. Martin Dempsey (in his capacity as Chair of the Joint Chiefs of Staff) told a congressional committee in 2015 that American forces might be needed to fight alongside "moderate" forces in Syria. He said, "If the commander on the ground approaches either me or the secretary of defense and believes that the introduction of special operations forces to accompany Iraqis or the new Syrian forces, or JTACS, these skilled folks who can call in close-air support, if we believe that's necessary to achieve our objectives, we will make that recommendation."[77] Dempsey's comments reflected a rift between the Obama administration and the military leadership about the appropriate strategy to fight ISIS.[78] So he may well have taken some satisfaction from the fact that, after he retired, the President implemented his recommendations and deployed special operations forces to Syria.[79] As this example demonstrates, the consequences are often dysfunctional when the military's advice is ignored.

A second theme in the military effectiveness literature examines the significance of organizational factors in determining victory in wars, conflicts, and individual battles. High-quality institutional arrangements—for example, those capable of generating innovative technologies and doctrines—lead to positive results both on the battlefield and in fulfilling the state's large political-military objectives.[80]

Assembling suitable data for such studies is often problematic, as is research on the impact of the military on the implementation of any grand strategy. And the problem is exacerbated in low-profile peacetime operations. Tensions between the advice of military professionals and the desires of political leaders rarely reach the national press. That is why the media likes to interview former military officials: they are more likely to stray from official policy. In September 2014, recently retired (and now Defense Secretary) Marine Corps General James Mattis illustrated this tendency when criticizing the Obama White House strategy in Iraq and Syria, in testimony before the House Intelligence Committee. Mattis suggested that "half-hearted or tentative efforts, or airstrikes alone, can backfire on us and actually strengthen our foes' credibility. . . . We may not wish to reassure our enemies in advance that they will not see American boots on the ground."[81] The military's active leadership is generally more diplomatic.

When disagreements between civilian leaders and military leaders are revealed, they are couched in language that obscures rather than illuminates. Consider, for example, common complaints about military "readiness."[82] Military leaders periodically lament that some development is negatively affecting readiness. By this they generally mean that the entire force or some subset (such as the "properly trained" pilots or "properly maintained" aircraft) is unprepared for war. This lack of preparedness is linked to possible defeats during combat or, less commonly, an inability to perform some more modest peacetime mission.

Readiness concerns often serve as a substitute for criticisms about the nature of a particular mission the military is being asked to perform or a controversial priority from political leaders. At the end of the Clinton presidency, for example, the RAND Corporation published a report with a chapter on readiness that specified the dilemma as follows: "The United States could fight and win the major wars, but it had trouble preparing for the big ones while executing a variety of small operations."[83] The subtext was evident: in the aftermath of massive budgetary cutbacks, the authors questioned whether it was possible to conduct peacekeeping and peace enforcement missions without additional resources.

More recently, both senior military officers and politicians (both Democrats and Republicans) have criticized the impact of sequestration on military readiness. In congressional testimony in 2015, the Chief of Naval Operations, Admiral Jonathan Greenert, claimed that "those hits [from sequestration budget cuts], if you will, will take place in our ability to respond, to supplement those forces forward. And [if] those forces forward won't be as modern as they need to be, we'll have dramatic decreases in modernization."[84] Underlying these criticisms are more serious divisions about what the military should and should not do. In a show of solidarity, Christine Wormuth, Deputy Undersecretary of Defense for Strategy, Plans, and Force Development, and Admiral James A. Winnefeld Jr., Vice

Chairman of the Joint Chiefs of Staff, warned that under sequestration, "the United States would likely need to count more on allied and partner contributions in future confrontations and conflicts, assuming they would be willing and able to act in support of shared interests."[85] Some approaches to grand strategy—Sponsorship or Retrenchment—would view the impact of sequestration on US relations with its allies as positive because they want to encourage greater collaboration or circumspection. There is no latitude for free riding. But for some officers and DoD officials, anything adversely affecting the ability of the United States to act unilaterally when necessary (such as in a high-end war with China) is undesirable. Officially the Navy and other services disavow the ability or desire to operate alone;[86] unofficially, many share Robert Kaplan's assessment that

> military multilateralism in the Pacific will nevertheless be constrained by the technical superiority of U.S. forces; it will be difficult to develop bilateral training missions with Asian militaries that are not making the same investments in high-tech equipment that we are. A classic military lesson is that technological superiority does not always confer the advantages one expects. Getting militarily so far ahead of everyone else in the world creates a particular kind of loneliness.[87]

Cordial and productive civil-military relations are important for shaping strategic choices. Yet the preferences of strategists and politicians will often run afoul of the military's judgment—and vice versa. Evidence of conflicts or disarray will, however, appear modest, hidden behind more acceptable debates about "readiness." Evidence of disputes concerning MOOTW cases often lack the deep, vocal, public, documented disagreements between operational experts and politicians that we expect to see during international crises and in wartime.[88] Military officials are generally excluded from these discussions. On occasion, however, the military is more vocal and the fissures more evident, as General Dempsey's controversial comment illustrates. Wherever possible, we chronicle such disputes.

In the chapters that follow we look at a variety of maritime operations. They reflect the diverse strategies represented in the debates among grand strategists. Each chapter examines one variant of each formulation. These operations illustrate issues that are generally regarded as among the most salient to national security: WMD proliferation, "commanding the commons," ensuring critical sea access through chokepoints, fighting piracy and terrorism, addressing the rise of a potential global challenger, and defending the homeland through border control.

In none of these cases, we will show, were grand strategic imperatives determinative. Rather, each strategic choice was a product of a combination of factors. Some factors were external—the type of threat, the actors, the character of any prospective conflict. These dictated the operational imperatives facing officers in the field. These operational limitations were, however, tied to domestic debates between policymakers and the military. In some cases, the military was able to participate in those debates; in others, they were not. In some cases, the contribution of military officials proved significant; in others, nominal. In all cases the operations were consistent with one possible grand strategy—and defied the logic of the others.

# A Maritime Strategy of Primacy in the Persian Gulf

This broader understanding of America's interests, this ideal of world order, has defined our global leadership since 1945. But what Reagan and America's best leaders have also understood is that our ideals do not advance or defend themselves. That takes realism. And it takes power and influence of all kinds—diplomatic, economic, moral, and yes, military. Because when aggressive rulers or violent fanatics threaten our ideals, our interests, our allies, and us—what ultimately makes the difference between war and peace, tragedy and triumph, is not good intentions, or strong words, or a grand coalition. It is the capability, credibility, and global reach of American hard power.

—Senator John McCain when receiving the Peace through Strength award at the Reagan National Defense Forum in Simi Valley, California, November 15, 2014

Primacy has become the default option of American academics and policy-makers who deliberate over grand strategy, largely because of its use during the Cold War.[1] Primacy entails the extended projection of power, and with it comes inherent logistical and technological problems. It is no surprise that the United States maintained more than seven hundred overseas military and intelligence bases during the Cold War. By 2015 this number had declined, for several reasons: force reductions, consolidation, and the fact that fewer countries are willing to host large numbers of US military personnel. The Department of Defense then reported that it was still maintaining 587 sites for the armed services, of which 150 supported naval forces.[2]

This network of bases is crucial to America's ability to operate overseas.[3] But for all their importance in projecting US power and maintaining American commitments, overseas bases carry significant costs. They are vulnerable to attack from air, land, and sea. And host nations may even decide—as did the Philippines in the 1970s—that they no longer want an American presence. The eventual reversal of that decision in 2012 (and threatened rer-eversal by President Duterte in late 2016) only serves to demonstrate the fragility of basing agreements.

Bases are expensive. Some host nations, like Germany and Japan, subsi-dize American bases and even the costs of maintaining American forces. In others, the American taxpayer bears the burden. The United States invests millions of dollars in infrastructure and pumps still more into the local economy to fund support services. Most, if not all, of that investment is lost when its forces leave.[4]

Worse still, bases can be a source of contention with hosts. Politics get in the way, even when dealing with allies. Famously, three weeks before the planned 2003 invasion of Iraq, NATO ally Turkey refused to allow Ameri-can ground troops from the Fourth Infantry Division to invade northern Iraq from its territory, thereby delaying and disrupting the invasion.[5] American strategists and planners fear that the United States will expend vast resources, only to discover that a particular base has limited utility when it is most needed.

Recognizing these problems, American strategists have long sought solu-tions. Characteristically, they have looked for technological solutions— even when such "solutions" are conceptually suspect and not feasible in terms of cost and engineering. Perhaps the most persistent example is the fascination of the US Navy and Marine Corps with the idea of sea bases. "Sea basing, loosely defined, is the capability to sustain, protect and project offensive and defensive military forces at and from the sea without reliance on landward infrastructures."[6] According to the Defense Science Board, sea basing is "a hybrid system of systems consisting of concepts of operations, ships, forces, offensive and defensive weapons, aircraft, communications, and logistics, all of which involve careful planning, coordination, and exer-cising to operate smoothly."[7] In the words of former Chief of Naval Opera-tions Vernon Clark, sea bases present a "sovereign, maneuverable capability to project power."[8] But smaller "lily-pads," or even an enormous "afloat forward staging base, a modified Maersk S-class container ship," remain elusive.[9] New, highly capable platform ships like the recently launched San Antonio-class amphibious transport dock have been developed. Each is a nearly seven-hundred-foot behemoth that carries a crew plus seven hun-dred troops and up to five MV-22 Osprey vertical lift aircraft—at a cost of approximately $1.5 billion. But these platforms are modest compared to some prominent visions.

The impetus to find a technological, sea-based solution to basing acceler-ated during the Iraq war. "The Turks did us a big favor in pushing the sea basing concept," argued one Marine colonel in 2004. "Our most reliable ally became an issue. Sea basing is expensive, but compared to the $26 billion we were prepared to give to Turkey, this is dimes on the dollar," he added.[10]

Even if the more futuristic versions are not feasible, proponents argue, perhaps modified versions are.

The basing debate has had significant implications in perennial hotspots like the Persian Gulf, which ranks among the top places where sea basing might be attractive. The United States first recognized the Middle East's military importance during World War II. Since 1945, the challenges have multiplied. They now include projecting and sustaining regional power throughout the Middle East and North Africa; allowing American and allied forces to transit the region; protecting oil and gas fields as well as their critical infrastructures; and supporting a variety of actors ranging from states like Saudi Arabia to groups such as the Peshmerga in Iraq. With all of its onshore problems, the Middle East appears to be a likely candidate for offshore basing.

Unsurprisingly, a variety of theorists, futurists, and contractors have encouraged the US Navy to consider stationing American forces offshore—either inside the Strait of Hormuz or, better yet, on the open seas. Advocates argue that the ability to operate from "over the horizon" would provide both a continuous, guaranteed presence (at a convenient distance) while sustaining a real military capability. The United States would have less need to accommodate the demands of unstable host governments and far greater freedom for its forces to operate whenever, wherever, and for whatever reason. The idea is especially alluring for Primacist strategies that rely less on collaboration and value American freedom of action.

Unfortunately, the difficulties of large-scale sea basing became quickly apparent. Futuristic visions of sea bases that resemble floating space stations soon gave way to physical and budgetary realities. By 2005, Admiral Mike Mullen, then Chief of Naval Operations, argued that the concept of sea basing itself was open to interpretation. It might instead, according to Mullen, be defined as "a group of ships."[11] In effect, Admiral Mullen was acknowledging that building artificial structures to station American forces where the United States has strategic interests was dauntingly expensive, an engineering nightmare, and (just as important) a tactical and operational mistake. Large, stationary, or even slow-moving sea bases would be highly vulnerable to air and missile barrages, swarming attacks by small boats, and terrorism.[12]

Two things became clear. The military planners' fascination with technological solutions to operational problems often leads to an obsession with massive acquisition programs. It is consistent with a culture that believes that "if we can first imagine the solution, then we can build it," regardless of the costs or feasibility. And a second thing became just as clear: despite an occasional debate about the need for a continued US military presence in the Persian Gulf and the Middle East, that presence will continue to require bases ashore. There is no feasible technological alternative.

## From British Presence to American Primacy in the Persian Gulf

The Persian Gulf is big—about six hundred miles long—and encompasses approximately 97,000 square miles. But Persian Gulf waters are relatively shallow with a maximum depth of 90 meters and an average of 50 meters. At its western end is the Shatt al-Arab river delta, an outlet for the Euphrates and the Tigris which divides Iran and Iraq. At the eastern end is the Strait of Hormuz, the Persian Gulf's narrowest point—about thirty-five miles wide. Iran, Oman, and the United Arab Emirates claim territorial waters in the strait. To complicate matters, the entire gulf is bordered by eight sovereign states: Iran, Iraq, Oman, the United Arab Emirates, Saudi Arabia, Qatar, Bahrain, and Kuwait.

What makes the Persian Gulf significant for international security? It provides access to a set of countries that collectively produce 25 percent of the world's crude oil and hold nearly two-thirds of the world's petroleum reserves. About 40 percent of the world's oil tanker traffic passes through the Strait of Hormuz every year.[13] Furthermore, anyone wanting direct access to Iraq or Iran from the sea must pass through the strait and then the confined, shallow waters of the gulf.

From the eighteenth century until World War II, Great Britain was the dominant power in the Persian Gulf. It guarded its commercial interests and helped protect the commercial waterways linking the region to India and the rim lands of the Indian Ocean, using the Royal Navy, judicious arrangements with local rulers, and the occasional intervention of the British Army or imperial troops from India. The Suez Canal's opening in 1869 enhanced the significance of the gulf in the global economy and as a trade route.

During World War II, the United States co-located its forces with the British and reached its own agreements with local rulers to establish facilities in the region.[14] When World War II concluded, Britain attempted to maintain its traditional role and exclude other powers from the regional security balance. Yet "there was only one exception to the British policy of excluding other external forces. The US Navy was permitted in 1949 to share the Jufayr [sic] base at Bahrain. The American naval force was never more than a token one, even after the Suez crisis of 1956. It was intended, one must assume, to shore up the military credibility of Britain as the chief guardian of Western oil interests in the Gulf."[15] Even with its wide-ranging security responsibilities in the region, Britain's postwar presence was never very large. It maintained a regional headquarters at Aden, along with two army battalions and several Royal Air Force (RAF) bases. The RAF bases each housed two fighter squadrons, along with one-and-a-half transport squadrons, one squadron of support helicopters, and several long-range maritime reconnaissance aircraft. The entire ground force was composed of six thousand British troops. Bahrain was a miniature bastion for the Royal Navy. No more than a handful of Royal Navy ships were in the gulf at any given time, as officials assumed they could send vessels from elsewhere in the event of a crisis.[16]

Yet the debilitating world war had diminished Britain's ability to maintain its empire. By 1968, Britain could no longer afford the political, diplomatic, and military costs of its continued stewardship of the Persian Gulf. In 1971 the Royal Navy withdrew. Nonetheless, with the global economy booming, and with it an increased demand for fossil fuels, the gulf's importance to both the global economy and security architecture grew.[17] The gulf's oil production was rising, and it was projected to continue to rise until the end of the twentieth century.[18] Britain's withdrawal left a power vacuum in an increasingly critical region.[19]

In 1949 the American small naval presence at Juffair consisted of rented office space.[20] It had no permanent presence until the flagship USS *Valcour* was stationed in the gulf in 1961.[21] But the nearest full-service American naval base was nearly three thousand miles away. Even port calls by American vessels were complicated by local requirements.[22]

## Land Basing Becomes a Reality

With the withdrawal of British forces, the United States negotiated with the Bahraini government to take over Britain's former facility. Land basing, albeit on a small scale, became a reality. It did not seem particularly important at the time. But eventually the USN's presence would prove instrumental in molding America's relationships with gulf governments. As Gordon and Trainor note in discussing Bahrain, the USN is "proud that the American naval relationship with the small Gulf state predated the opening of the US embassy."[23]

In 1971, the American presence was no more than a light footprint. By 1979 it was approaching dominance. In the interim, the United States pursued what was termed the Nixon Doctrine—a bargain between the United States and local governments in a region considered to be of critical importance to American national security.[24] In essence, the United States would uphold treaty obligations and provide military and economic assistance to regional partners. In return, those partners would maintain sufficient military capabilities to ensure domestic stability, dominate local forces that might destabilize the region, and in extremis help resist Soviet aggression. For much of the period, the doctrine rested on a "twin pillar policy" in which the United States relied on Saudi Arabia and Iran to provide regional security. Indeed, Iran was initially thought to hold the key. American policy tilted to more of a balance between the two only after the 1973 oil shock demonstrated the importance of Saudi Arabia. The petroleum wealth of Iran and Saudi Arabia also allowed them to make large-scale arms purchases from the United States, which at least in theory, would improve their military capabilities and interoperability with American systems.

The current American approach in the Persian Gulf—Primacy with a focus on keeping the Strait of Hormuz open to international commerce— dates from two events in 1979: the Iranian revolution and the Soviet invasion of Afghanistan. These events prompted the Carter Doctrine in the president's 1980 State of the Union address: "Let our position be absolutely clear: An attempt by any outside force to gain control of the Persian Gulf region will be regarded as an assault on the vital interests of the United States of America, and such an assault will be repelled by any means necessary, including military force."[25]

To give teeth to the new doctrine, the United States established a Rapid Deployment Joint Task Force in 1980. It grew into the unified US Central Command (CENTCOM) in 1983. CENTCOM, headquartered in Tampa, Florida, rather than in the region, is now responsible for 20 countries comprising "4 million square miles and populated by more than 550 million people from 22 ethnic groups, speaking 18 languages."[26].

President Jimmy Carter also issued a secret directive committing the nation to keep the Persian Gulf safe for commercial traffic and ensure the strait could not be closed by either local or extraregional powers. The directive specifically "authorized the Pentagon to use force to prevent Iran from closing the Strait of Hormuz to oil exports."[27] Just days before President Ronald Reagan assumed office, Carter's National Security Advisor Zbigniew Brzezinski issued Presidential Directive/NSC 63, the "Persian Gulf Security Framework," linking the growing American military presence to the free flow of oil and an overarching regional strategy.[28] Indeed, as Bruce Kunihom suggests, "The Reagan administration essentially sought to consolidate the security framework initiated by the Carter administration": continuing to rely on Saudi Arabia while also investing in the smaller gulf states as well as countries that might serve as launch points for direct American intervention.[29] Reagan's corollary to the Carter Doctrine held that United States would not allow Saudi Arabia to become another Iran.[30] It would seek a level of intimacy with the Saudi regime beyond what it had enjoyed with the Pahlavi regime *and* surround the country with friendly states that would amplify US access to the region.

American involvement in the Persian Gulf expanded greatly between 1980 and 1987, with the US Navy committing to protect maritime traffic inside the gulf and through the strait. This commitment was put to the test during the Iran-Iraq War.[30] During the "Tanker War" each side attempted to deny the other financial resources by preventing the export of oil and gas. More than 450 attacks took place against international shipping—until the United States devised a scheme in 1987 to temporarily "flag" commercial vessels and then provide protection using its naval forces.[31] (International lawyers disputed the right of the United States to flag and protect shipping owned and operated by other countries.[32] This secondary issue generated lawsuits and legal wrangling over transit rights through the Strait of Hormuz.)[33]

Resolution of the Tanker War allowed American naval forces to stand down temporarily from their direct policing role. But it also demonstrated how even modest threats and even more modest attacks could disrupt global commerce and provoke a strong response from the United States. Naval planners subsequently debated what to do if Iran or Iraq mounted a sustained effort to disrupt maritime commerce. From a commercial and economic perspective, such action seemed highly unlikely. But given the value of energy exports to all gulf economies, the possibility remained alive, especially given the widespread discussion of regime change against both Saddam Hussein's Iraq and Iran's revolutionary government. Either state might pressure the United States and the global community. Either state might act if the alternative was to lose power or, in the case of Iran, if the United States launched airstrikes against its nuclear facilities.

Concerns about possible disruption to energy flows, however exaggerated, continued to fester, prompting the United States to consolidate its military presence. By 1999 the huge American base, now known as Naval Support Activity Bahrain, assumed a new mission: to support American ships and remote sites throughout the region and into the Indian Ocean. With the Iraq invasion in 2003 and various diplomatic crises between the United States and Iran, planners and strategists worried about a disruption of energy flows.

America's Persian Gulf security policy was often subordinated in this period to the problem of Iraq: first driving Saddam Hussein out of Kuwait, then keeping him contained using sanctions, no-fly zones, and surveillance. Saddam, of course, was defeated and his regime overthrown in 2003 with Operation Iraqi Freedom.[34] Unfortunately, US policy toward Iran suffered from inattention for much of the two-term administration of George W. Bush, despite the "on to Tehran" fantasies of a small group of American strategists.[35] But the Navy remained responsible for keeping the Persian Gulf open to commerce, so operations in the Persian Gulf churned on.

## An Unchanging American Strategy in a Changing Energy Environment

Even as the United States became enmeshed in Iraq—two ground wars and a prolonged period of maintaining a no-fly zone—there was an unwavering focus on keeping the gulf's sea lanes open. This policy has survived despite a steady decline in the importance of the region's energy supplies for the American economy. American naval deployments and planning continued to support a Primacist strategy and do so to this day. Why?

Keeping the Persian Gulf safe became part and parcel first of the Iraqi war effort and later of the recognition that Tehran's nuclear aspirations would have to be dealt with either by high diplomacy or by direct military intervention. One scenario that worried US planners involved Iran taking advantage of the US preoccupation with Iraq to threaten commercial traffic. In another, diplomatic failure and outright war would see Iran retaliate by attacking critical energy infrastructure, destabilizing the Gulf Cooperation Council (GCC) states, using conventional and unconventional means to disrupt sea lanes, or—as many pessimists suspected—through some "hybrid" combination of all these tactics. Preoccupation with Tehran's sabotage plans in the Strait of Hormuz became a Washington pastime.

In organizational terms, America's naval commitment was modest prior to 1995. Overall command of naval forces in the gulf region had rested with the Seventh Fleet, which was based in Honolulu. The Seventh Fleet was responsible for an incredible expanse of ocean, ranging from the West Coast of the United States to the Persian Gulf. During the 1991 Persian Gulf War, operational command over Navy forces supporting CENTCOM was held by the Commander of the Middle Eastern Force. But this arrangement put the Navy at an operational disadvantage to the other military services under CENTCOM's command. Moreover, the Middle East Task Force had insufficient maritime resources to ensure Iraq remained quiescent at sea, watch Iran's maritime activities and deter its nuclear aspirations, not to mention bolster the maritime capabilities of the GCC countries, particularly Saudi Arabia.

The Fifth Fleet and its headquarters within CENTCOM, US Naval Forces Central Command (NAVCENT), was reestablished in 1995. It began with a Carrier Battle Group, including the aircraft carrier the USS *Abraham Lincoln*, and an Amphibious Ready Group as well as several miscellaneous ships—fifteen in total. But the Fifth Fleet has evolved substantially since then.[36] The exact number of ships and warplanes in the region at any given time ebbs and flows with the security situation. The Fifth Fleet's responsibilities have widened to include counterpiracy, counterterrorism, and security missions far outside the gulf itself (we discuss counterpiracy operations off the Horn of Africa in chapter 5).[37]

The growth of the Fifth Fleet—in size, capacities, objectives, responsibilities, and operations—reflects a Primacy strategy in practice. Today it is one of the single most powerful fleets in the US Navy. NAVCENT supervises an enormous area, including the guardianship of "three critical choke points at the Strait of Hormuz, the Suez Canal, and the Strait of Bab al Mandeb at the southern tip of Yemen."[38] Even during peacetime—or perhaps we should say during "routine" operations, given that instability and war seem endemic to the region—the Fifth Fleet controls "20-plus ships, with about 1,000 people ashore and 15,000 afloat."[39]

In addition, hundreds of non-US Navy aircraft (principally part of the Air Force) have airfields in the region and are available to support this naval armada. US Army units, based in the continental United States and Germany, can if needed augment this huge air and sea capacity. Fifth Fleet units have been put to numerous uses. They have contributed to the full range of US military operations across the entire CENTCOM region. Examples include the Afghan and Iraq wars, as well as counterpiracy and counterterror missions associated with the East African littoral. Yet the fleet's primary responsibility remains keeping the gulf open to shipping—to ensure the US "command of the commons" we discussed in the introductory chapter.

The Fifth Fleet is a full-service naval organization capable of blue water operations far out at sea, littoral activities, and power projection against targets ashore. Yet the forces necessary to generate its enormous fighting power come with costs. First, nuclear-powered aircraft carriers and large amphibious ships are not optimized for the types of operation necessary to fight local navies and irregular militias. Indeed, passing through the strait and sailing in the gulf exposes large surface vessels to land-based aircraft and missiles, as well as mines and diesel-electric submarines. Second, the US Navy has downsized over the last decade and struggled to meet the challenge of Chinese naval modernization in the western Pacific. Some strategists believe that far too much of the Navy's fighting force is devoted to the Greater Middle East. But this judgment depends on how one balances US strategic interests in the region versus challenges elsewhere.

The antecedents to the current Primacist strategy of controlling chokepoints clearly date back to the Reagan administration. "By the late 1980s," according to Robert J. Schneller, "the United States had committed itself to the defense of the Arabian Gulf region, created a unified command to carry out the mission, and invested heavily in programs to ensure its success. The entire commitment hinged on the U.S. Navy's ability to control the sea."[40] So the United States had two goals from the 1990s onward. The first was to control the Persian Gulf seaway, to ensure the logistics support necessary for military operations and to deny access to enemies. The second was to ensure access for commercial shipping in times of peace and war, so that oil prices would not spiral.

Policies in support of these goals were enforced. The Fifth Fleet was used to good effect in Persian Gulf War and the Iraq War. It also played a critical supporting role in American and International Security Assistance Force (ISAF) operations in Afghanistan, when American special operations forces first attacked the Taliban regime from aircraft carriers in 2001. Further, the

Fifth Fleet provides ships and ongoing logistical and administrative support to a series of combined maritime task forces that include allied and friendly nation navies and coast guards.

## The Paradox of Contemporary Naval Strategy in the Persian Gulf

Recent events have reinforced this focus on the relationship between the waterways of the gulf and the land that abuts it. With the defeat of Saddam Hussein and the concluded negotiation over Iran's nuclear program in 2015, the proximate national security threats in the Persian Gulf are threefold. The first two concerns are longstanding while the third is situational and, perhaps, temporary. First, a sustained interruption of the flow of gas and oil through the Strait of Hormuz would likely disrupt the global economy. Second, the destruction or disabling of the critical infrastructure associated with energy production and distribution would damage local economies, threaten regime stability, and once again disrupt the global economy (likely for far longer than simply closing the strait).[41] Third, because the United States and its allies rely on access through the strait for troops, logistics, and materiel in its ongoing operations against the Islamic State in Iraq and Syria, maritime insecurity in the Persian Gulf would constrain American operations in fighting Islamic extremists and disrupting terrorist bases.

American political leaders, military officers, and strategists have long assumed that any drastic cut in oil or gas supplies would constitute a substantial threat to the United States and the global economy. Their premise is that even short-term disruptions to supplies will sharply raise global energy prices, slowing global economic growth. America's primary trading partners, China and Europe, remain heavily dependent on the region's fossil fuels. And the oil market has historically proved vulnerable in the face of contractions in supply and volatile when it comes to price movements. Saudi Arabia, the country that could most easily replace lost supplies, would likely be affected by any conflict in the gulf. Further, there is little evidence that other suppliers could address the shortfall.

America, in contrast, has over the last decade increased its energy independence and reduced its demand for gulf petroleum and gas. The reverse is true of its geopolitical competitors; China and the developed economies of northeast Asia are increasingly reliant on imported energy and especially on flows from Iran, Iraq, and the GCC states. As a result, some analysts—attending to national security and geopolitics rather than geoeconomics—question the wisdom of prioritizing the Iran threat.[42] After all, they ask, why spend millions to defend a waterway when the primary beneficiaries are the Chinese? The answer is not obvious.

But strategic adjustment to a changed security (and economic) environment is often slow. The US Navy continues to invest millions of dollars in upgrading its base in Bahrain. It ignores outside calls to seek alternative basing arrangements beyond the gulf—for example, locations on the Indian Ocean close enough to allow for effective operations in and around the Strait of Hormuz. Moreover, as we have noted, the technological panacea of sea basing has proved impractical.

The United States continues to rely on a Primacist strategy in the gulf, one that focuses primarily on state-based threats, although Iran has worked in the past through nonstate proxies (such as Hezbollah) and its own forces, both regular (the Iranian Navy) and irregular (the Iranian Revolutionary Guard Corps). These might all play roles in blocking the Strait of Hormuz. In fact, many observers are skeptical about the ability of Iran and its proxies to close the strait or even threaten the flow of energy through the gulf. As one article concluded, "The notion that Iran could truly blockade the Strait is wrong."[43] Yet, characteristically, the United States prepares for all eventualities, however remote. And so, whether suspicious of the reliability of its own allies, dubious about their capabilities, or seeking to monopolize its control of this critical waterway, it persists in an expensive Primacist strategy from which it gains few immediate and tangible benefits. Like many notions of Hegemony, the strategy of Primacy focuses on short-term gains in power and control. It neglects longer-term considerations about the economic or reputational costs of the strategy.

This leaves a residual question: Does America's military presence serve as a bulwark against Iran's ambitions for regional power? Shahram Chubin doubts the claim, suggesting that

Tehran lacks many components of an advanced military, including power-projection capabilities and strong air-defence, air and armoured forces. It also suffers from a lack of coordination between the IRGC [the Islamic Revolutionary Guard Corps] and the Artesh [the Islamic Republic of Iran Army]. Its military is a shoestring enterprise in comparison to those of its Arab neighbours. It is robust and functional, without being a major challenge.[44]

But the US Navy thinks about this issue very differently. It assumes that the United States can and should have the ability to keep the strait open—whether the form of conflict with Tehran will be conventional, irregular, or some hybrid mix of the two. And, as prudent planners do, the Navy prepares for worst-case scenarios by amplifying the threat, in terms of both the intentions and the capabilities of potential adversaries, while underemphasizing its own strengths.

Navy leaders think about the threat to both shipping and infrastructure. Iran could use its growing number of short- and intermediate-range missiles, tactical aviation, or low-tech terrorist tactics to attack platforms, refineries, and pipelines. Moreover, in extremis, some experts believe. Iran might also supplement direct efforts to destroy infrastructure by using terrorist tactics. Any of these approaches might, in theory, force a favorable settlement. But the chances are remote—and the costs of largely unilateral preparedness are high. Primacy assumes a unilateral approach in addressing a plethora of threats. But what are the possibilities for burden sharing?

## Allied Contributions to Persian Gulf Security

American planners tend to assume that the United States would face any Iranian effort to close the Strait of Hormuz alone. But this judgment rests on controversial interpretations of past events, current practices, and future intentions. In principle, of course, the United States has allies and friends, and other states share America's interest in maintaining the flow of energy through the strait. Potential contributors to gulf security include Iran's neighbors. They also include extraregional powers allied with the United States or willing to join multilateral efforts, those who are similarly interested in the freedom of the seas, and those so dependent on the flow of energy from the region that they too would contribute to naval operations. In the case of the United Kingdom, for example, these three motivations overlap. So, the United States might form a "coalition of the willing" to guard the waters of the gulf. It has done so in the past, including the Gulf War, Operations Southern and Northern Watch (enforcing the no-fly zone and controlling airspace following the Persian Gulf War), the Iraq War, and more recently, related counterterrorism and counterpiracy missions under the aegis of Combined Task Forces 150 and 151.

Other Western navies have worked with the United States in past conflicts with Iran, including the Tanker Wars, when a flotilla of sixty French, British, and Australian vessels gathered in the western Indian Ocean as well as during the Gulf War.[45] But from the Carter Doctrine onward, America's long-term commitment to protect the Persian Gulf has courted controversy. NATO members complained at the time that they had been insufficiently consulted about the doctrine and the subsequent announcement of the Rapid Deployment Force, to which—at least initially—America hoped Europeans would contribute. Other concerns were more substantive. With Warsaw Pact forces still deployed in the heartland of Europe, many NATO leaders worried about the diversion of US forces and resources from what they regarded as the central challenge facing the alliance. Others realized that they lacked the capacity to contribute, or at least to sustain a commitment, to any substantial force operating in the Persian Gulf. They had to prioritize between the threats posed by the Soviet Union and Iran; decide the strategic balance in the locating of military forces; and accurately assess the danger Tehran posed to the flow of energy from the Persian Gulf.[46]

Of course, as the Tanker War, the 1991 Gulf War, and (to some extent) the 2003 Iraq war demonstrate, the Europeans—pointedly the British and the French—did ultimately share the burden. Why they were willing to do so, and how much they contributed to these varied operations, remains an open question.[47] But what is clear is that the Europeans were unwilling to join the United States in making a permanent commitment to Persian Gulf security, as the Carter Doctrine had implied.

The likelihood that European navies will support future efforts to keep the strait open has significantly eroded. NATO members, even France and the United Kingdom, have few ships or aircraft to devote to operations in the gulf.[48] In recent years, for example, the Royal Navy has cut the number of its Type 45 air defense destroyers from fourteen to six, even as it continues plans to replace Trident nuclear submarines. The British do have plans, together with France, to build a sixty-five-thousand-ton Queen Elizabeth-class aircraft carrier. But, by most accounts, even when it is eventually built, it will lack aircraft for its first three years in service. Further, since the Russian war with Georgia in 2008 and the invasion of Crimea in 2014, the British like other European countries are more mindful of maritime threats closer to home—in the Arctic Ocean, the Baltic Sea, the Eastern Mediterranean, and the Black Sea.

This lack of support is a problem. Even the United States has not invested sufficiently in platforms, tactics, training, and procedures, or operational doctrine for certain kinds of missions—those where it has traditionally relied on European forces for what it terms a "surge capacity." A prime example is mine countermeasure operations. For the last two decades, European states (including the Baltic countries) have maintained a formidable force of minesweepers while American capabilities have lagged. Mine warfare is a particularly acute problem in the Persian Gulf. The strait's geography and hydrology, combined with Iran's capabilities and past practices, all place a premium on antimine warfare.[49] The reduced contributions from NATO allies have forced the United States to invest more heavily in an area where burden sharing had made sense.[50]

The US invasion of Iraq proved to be the last straw for those hoping for a major European contribution to American-led efforts. As Robert Hunter comments, "From the moment the initial phase of the Iraq War came to a close in May 2003, the old system of security in the region was shattered, and the United States had no choice, given its own interests, but to take the lead in devising some alternative to put in its place."[51] The origins and prosecution of the war exacerbated burden-sharing tensions among

NATO members, especially regarding "out-of-area" operations. But, more pointedly, the Iraq invasion also sowed distrust in American judgment and led to members questioning the reliability of America's own military capabilities. Reinforcing this trend is Europe's self-imposed focus on austerity, especially in military spending, and worries about the consequences of Brexit. As one analysis summarized the situation, "Power projection and the maintenance of significant forces outside of Europe's immediate neighborhood will be particularly difficult due to reduced force size; limited lift and logistics capability; and a lack of certain key enablers (such as missile defence and unmanned aerial vehicles)."[52] America's Primacist strategy in the Persian Gulf has been reinforced over the last decade by European dissatisfaction over the 2003 invasion and the gulf's increasing military irrelevance when it comes to "hard" security issues.

The local navies of the Gulf States do have some relevant capability. But much of their resources during a conflict would, by necessity, be devoted to protecting their own territory.[53] Since its formation in the aftermath of the Iranian revolution, the GCC has focused largely on political, economic, and social issues rather than external security. It has not institutionalized cooperation nor developed the common doctrine required to serve as an effective military coalition, either among its members or in collaboration with outside partners. Each individual GCC member has invested billions of dollars in hardware, from advanced multirole aircraft and small surface vessels to all the interceptors, radars, and battle management systems necessary for ballistic missile defense. But the collective product of all this expenditure is unimpressive in strategic terms.

Like the George W. Bush administration before it, the Obama administration worked to increase the capacity of the GCC to contribute to their own defense and the region's security. Combined military exercises have been dutifully planned and executed for many years. But few independent analysts are confident that local forces would prove effective, or would be allowed to play a significant role in keeping the strait open. From the point of view of domestic politics, the negatives involved in cooperating with American-led military operations undermine the private willingness of GCC members to fight alongside the US Navy. At best, it is likely that GCC members would concentrate on maintaining domestic stability and protecting their own populations and commercial interests while privately encouraging the United States to maintain its traditional Primacist role.

Other potential collaborators face significant obstacles: political opposition from the United States, especially in the case of China, and technical limitations when it comes to operating far from home in a high-threat environment, such as Japan and India. Over the last five years, the

Chinese People's Liberation Army–Navy (PLAN) has sent small flotillas in support of counterpiracy missions (discussed in chapter 5), and occasionally, Chinese national security experts have speculated about a wider role for the nation. Increasingly, this speculation has entered into American debates; in 2015, for example, one analyst suggested that "the United States may not have to confront a Chinese carrier-strike group in the Persian Gulf just yet, but it still needs to prepare for cohabitation or collision—or both."[54] From the American perspective, the Indo-American security relationship can and should evolve toward greater collaboration and burden sharing in providing security in the Indian Ocean.[55] The Indian Navy has increased its capabilities and strategic horizons—but it has a long way to go before it takes responsibility for a larger share of the security of the Strait of Hormuz.[56]

Iran's maritime forces are sizable enough and capable enough to pose a plausible maritime threat to American forces. Yet any future conflict over the gulf is likely to be asymmetric. Iran lacks the conventional forces to directly challenge the US Navy either in the gulf or on the high seas. It has concentrated on acquiring antiaccess capabilities that use the US Navy's own high-tech, large platform approach to naval warfare against it.[57] Iran deploys relatively low-technology, low-cost naval systems, from small craft to undersea mines and antiship missiles, to make it dangerous for high-tech, incredibly expensive American ships to operate in the gulf. Moreover, it has developed tactics like "swarming" (deploying large numbers of small surface craft to overwhelm the close-in defenses of a modern warship) which, while unlikely to deter an American naval operation, do present operational challenges and the possibility of significant losses.[58]

In the event of war, the conventional wisdom is that Iran would use mines, swarming, submarines, and a variety of missiles to attack both commercial ships and third-party naval forces throughout the region—not just in the gulf.[59] American military forces would be forced on the defensive. In addition to missile exchanges, bombings, and very small-scale naval engagements, much of the US Navy's operations would involve escort duty for convoys, minesweeping, and guarding critical infrastructure.[60] It is highly unlikely that US policymakers would risk deploying ground forces in or around Iran to ensure gulf access.[61] Nor is it clear how helpful such deployments would be.

## The Paradoxical Future of Persian Gulf Security

Some optimistic commentators have projected a thawing of relations between the United States and Iran in the aftermath of the Joint Comprehensive Plan of Action (JCPOA) between Iran, the P5+1, and the

European Union. They have called for the United States to rethink its strategy for the Persian Gulf and in particular the need for a strong military presence in Bahrain. Their logic is clear: the primary driver of the US approach to the region has been the possibility that Iran would destabilize the region. That concern will be remedied through reconciliation. Absent any new threat to core American interests, the United States should pull back because "political and economic developments in the region have reduced the opportunities for effective American intervention to the vanishing point."[62]

The "new normal" in the region for the United States would be a return to its role in the period between 1945 and September 11, 2001. It would entail a "serviceable military presence," without changing its "military footprint." So, it would continue to commit "at least one carrier battle group," and keep "the structure and military bases" it currently has intact. But it would disavow large-scale military intervention and encourage regional partners to assume more responsibility for their own security.[63] This position, of course, begs the question why the United States would maintain such a large military footprint if it did not intend to intervene on land. Part of the answer is that the United States would continue to keep the strait open to naval vessels and commercial traffic, thus maintaining its command of the commons.

Yet, for all the diplomatic breakthroughs that optimists anticipate, this critical change in the US relationship with Iran would presage, at most, a shift from a Primacist to a "Primacy-lite" strategy. The United States would remain the most capable military power in the region and reserve both the right and the capacity to intervene as it has in the past—while hoping that local states achieve greater self-sufficiency. American military forces would remain the net provider of regional security, complete with all the costs and few of the benefits. A change in objective conditions appears to have little impact on the strategy because of the possibility of—in the immortal words of Donald Rumsfeld—a future "known unknown." Iran, apparently, is not really the issue. If it were, then a major shift in relations with Iran would result in a major shift in policy.

So, what explains the continuation of a policy when relations with the enemy appear to be improving? The decline in American dependence on Persian Gulf energy supplies since the 1990s, contrasted with China's growing dependence, has created a perverse incentive for a substantial presence in the gulf. In the event of a war with China, one potential strategy would be to impose a "distant blockade." As James Kurth explains, "A distant blockade allows the adversary the use of his littoral waters, but denies him the use of the waters beyond."[64] From a strategic perspective, such an approach would constitute "horizontal escalation," which would shift "the conflict's focus to areas where the U.S. military has a clear advantage, thus helping create conditions that compel the enemy to seek an end to hostilities. In the case where enemies are dependent on energy resources and raw materials that must be transported by sea, for example, U.S. naval and air forces could establish distant maritime blockades to help achieve these objectives."[65]

Prominent Washington-based defense observers have also posited that, because "Sino-U.S. conventional conflict likely would devolve into a prolonged war," the United States must be prepared to implement a two-stage plan. The first is to withstand China's initial attack and seize the operational initiative. The second is a campaign of attrition—one that would include a distant blockade.[66] Washington defense analysts thus debate the likely efficacy of a blockade, its role in an overarching strategy toward China, and various alternatives. Proponents of "Offshore Control" strategies recommend that the United States can and should "interdict China's energy and raw material imports and industrial exports, while protecting our partners."[67] But they worry that the prevailing focus on AirSea Battle and contesting Chinese actions within the Asian littoral (the Taiwan Strait, the South China Sea, the East China Sea) may be extremely costly to the United States in terms of loss of life and materiel. Others worry that AirSea Battle's focus on deep military strikes on the Chinese mainland would be unnecessarily escalatory. So they too support giving the "American leadership graduated options," including a blockade.[68] Of course, disrupting China's access to energy through the maritime commons and key chokepoints would also be difficult and costly, both for the United States and for the global economy as a whole; indeed, it might not work.[69] But maintaining substantial maritime forces in the Persian Gulf fits neatly into this broader geostrategic view.

Public speculation about war-fighting strategies by American national security specialists has caused Beijing to be "concerned that, in the event of a conflict, India or the United States may attempt to establish some form of a distant blockade of its energy supplies, a large portion of which originates from the Persian Gulf."[70] To date, most proponents of distant blockades have not explicitly linked the Persian Gulf to an anti-China strategy. Rather they have focused on blockading China's near seas and the chokepoints on the eastern edge of the Indian Ocean—such as the Malacca, Lombok, and Sunda straits—even though blockading these chokepoints would put American vessels within the range of Chinese missiles. But it does not take a paranoid Chinese analyst to understand the logic whereby the United States would want to maintain overwhelming Primacy in the Persian Gulf region—safely out of range of China's growing missile capability. Unlike their civilian counterparts, military personnel are increasingly aware of the hazards of sailing too close to the Asian littoral. Bryan Clarke argues that the growth of Chinese surface-to-surface missile stocks "will overcome our ability to defend against it relatively soon."[71]

At the opposite ends of the sea line of communication between China and the Persian Gulf lie the American bases in Bahrain and Singapore. Some commentators outside the US government believe that a distant blockade is a real option in the event of war with China. This position justifies the United States maintaining a strong presence in the Persian Gulf and, indeed, continuing to pursue regional security on the basis of local Primacy. After all, while the ability of the United States to impose a distant blockade would benefit from coalitions with like-minded friends and allies, there is no guarantee that the requisite support from US partners would be available in the case of war. For some grand strategists, prudence dictates the United States should maintain the ability to act unilaterally, not only to keep the Strait of Hormuz open *but also to close it if necessary.* The logic may be compelling, but is virtually impossible to know whether Pentagon planners have developed such contingencies—unless there is a conflict.

Regardless of any strategic calculations about a distant blockade during a future war with China, some well-known hawks remain committed to a Primacist American role in the Middle East. For them, America's trust in Iran's behavior is not a factor. They worry about the general nature of threats and the need to be locally armed and prepared to deal with a variety of local conflicts. As American specialists debate strategic interests and options, the Primacist position will remain alive and well with regard to American security interests in the Persian Gulf.

## Global Concerns, a Regional Strategy

In previous decades, the dominant factor underpinning the size and composition of US forces in the Persian Gulf was to ensure access to energy. Today, there are two major concerns. The first relates to regional instability and global energy markets. The second is the capacity to deny China access to resources by asserting American control of the strait. The major justification for policy has always been the prospect of Iranian sabotage. But, as recent events vividly demonstrate, it does not seem to matter how America's relationship with Iran waxes and wanes; the strategy stays the same. What we see is therefore a Primacist regional policy carried out for global strategic reasons—some to do with the prosperity of the global economy and some to do with geopolitics in Asia, half a world away. America's interest in both of these concerns is unlikely to dissipate soon. It is committed to ensuring global markets remain stable, and China remains dependent for a key natural resource on America's strategic posture in the strait. Neither of these issues is going to disappear in the short to medium term.

European allies are increasingly ill-equipped to assist the United States in patrolling the gulf. The GCC carries political significance as a legitimating force for American action. Other extraregional powers like India and Japan are not ready to assume greater responsibility. But burden sharing would never be more than a supplement to the projection of American regional power. The United States will follow a unilateral Primacist strategy for the indefinite future—even as independent estimates of the overall cost of such a strategy exceed $8 trillion dollars.[72]

CHAPTER 4

# Playing a Follow-the-Leader Strategy on the High Seas

> The Department [of Defense] is also pursuing a robust slate of
> training exercises and engagements with our allies and partners that
> will allow us to explore new areas of practical bilateral and multilat-
> eral maritime security cooperation, build the necessary interoperabil-
> ity to execute multilateral operations, and promote regional trust and
> transparency. We are increasing the size, frequency, and sophistication
> of our regional exercise program, with a particular focus on develop-
> ing new exercises with Southeast Asian partners and expanding our
> multilateral exercise program.
>
> —The Asia-Pacific Maritime Security Strategy: Achieving U.S. National
> Security Objectives in a Changing Environment, August 2015.

Invoking the need for American leadership is a familiar trope of American
presidents, grand strategists, and foreign policy pundits. Liberals define it
as building global institutions and processes, and promoting values such as
the rule of law.[1] But, in practice, leadership often amounts to little more
than exhortations for the United States to "act"—usually militarily and
unilaterally—on the assumption that others are willing to join an American-
inspired initiative.[2] Domestic observers are often disappointed when
American leadership proves insufficient to rally widespread operational
support. Leadership as a grand strategy often tastes great but turns out to
be less filling.

Yet the United States does lead other countries toward its preferred
strategic ends, using all dimensions of power. The military's Leadership
role—military diplomacy—is underappreciated. As former Secretary of
State George Shultz reflected, the "military provided the umbrella
underneath which all our diplomatic cards were played."[3] The United
States may publicly exhort its allies to collaborate under its leadership in
times of war, but evidence suggests that the United States routinely
employs multilateral Leadership through the operations of its military

66

forces during peacetime. Wartime Leadership strategies like the Persian Gulf War are exceptional. War strategies are more often unilateral (Vietnam) or small, loosely based coalitions composed of a few cajoled or bribed allies (Iraq in 2003).

The lower-profile, routinized activities of America's armed forces are amply demonstrated by the US military's consciously developed military-to-military contacts with its formal allies (such as France, Israel, and the United Kingdom) or friendly counterparts (such as Saudi Arabia and Egypt). These linkages have become increasingly sophisticated since 1945, ending America's long-standing tradition of Isolationism and preference for unilateralism. Since then, as we shall illustrate, the United States has developed a complex coterie of institutions and programs, largely under the rubric of theater security cooperation plans.[4] These plans are designed to integrate America's peacetime military activities with broader foreign policy objectives, while also preparing for coalition operations in crises or wars. In addition to diplomatic goals, these activities from a military-to-military perspective enhance communications, interoperability, and the sharing of intelligence.

This multilateralist Leadership strategy is evident throughout the US armed forces, with NATO often used as the preeminent example.[5] But given this book's focus on maritime operations, here we connect the strategy of Leadership to security cooperation plans and, ultimately, multilateral naval exercises. This is one of the principal instruments by which the US Navy creates multilateral linkages, shaping its peacetime environment. The politics of these efforts, however, are often strange.

## Who Is the Enemy?

In 2014, American observers of Asian security affairs offered a barrage of commentary about Chinese spying during China's participation in the Twenty-Sixth Rim of the Pacific (RIMPAC) exercise. RIMPAC is a large, multinational naval exercise conducted off the Hawaiian coast, hosted by the US Pacific Fleet biennially since 1971.[6] Critics were incensed by the appearance of a Type 815 Dongdiao-class auxiliary general intelligence vessel named Beijixing. It was lurking around the port, observing the flotilla of vessels that had been contributed to RIMPAC by the twenty-two participating nations. RIMPAC 2014 was a major event, involving fifty-five vessels, more than two hundred aircraft, and some twenty-five-thousand personnel plus observers from six other countries.[7]

We note four significant points related to China's behavior. The first is at least superficially paradoxical: China was spying on an exercise in which its own People's Liberation Army Navy (PLAN) was a significant participant. China had sent four PLAN vessels for the first time since RIMPAC was established—a supply ship, a missile frigate, a missile destroyer, and a hospital ship.[8] These PLAN vessels were accompanied by multirole helicopters, Changhe Z-8s and Harbin Z-9s, operated by the People's Liberation Army Naval Air Force (PLANAF) as well as a PLAN dive unit. These PLAN units were not marginal to the RIMPAC exercise either. They participated in a "training syllabus [that] included amphibious operations, gunnery, missile, antisubmarine, and air defense exercises, as well as military medicine, humanitarian assistance and disaster response, counterpiracy, mine clearance operations, explosive ordnance disposal, and diving and salvage operations."[9]

Second, this was not the first time the PLAN had sent a spy ship to observe a RIMPAC exercise. China had sent a similar ship to RIMPAC 2012.[10] Presumably, China's earlier surveillance had proved productive and was, quite likely, anticipated by American officials—even as they invited the Chinese to participate. Chinese spying was "business as usual."

Third, prior to 2014, China had been wary about sending ships to participate in RIMPAC. Officers from PLAN worried about what would be revealed if foreign observers had the opportunity to monitor their equipment and activities. But not for the reason one might suspect—the fear of disclosing their latest technology. Rather, in the words of one American retired USN admiral, the PLAN worried about "not only prying (as well as spying) but embarrassment, that its shortcomings and backwardness would be revealed."[11] In contrast, by 2014 the crew of the *Haikou*, a Type 052C (Luyang II-class) destroyer participating in this latest RIMPAC exercise, were eager to show off their vessel's capabilities. "What you have, we have," the *Haikou*'s combat systems officer said.[12]

Finally, even as the PLAN spied, China and the United States had held, and continue to hold, bilateral naval exercises. In November 2015, for example, the USS *Stethem*, a guided missile destroyer, conducted communications exercises with PLAN forces near Shanghai as part of a surface rescue simulation. These drills took place less than a month after the US Navy's 2015 Freedom of Navigation operation in the South China Sea. Despite rising naval and diplomatic tensions, the USS *Stethem*'s commanding officer indicated that his mission was intended to "build mutual trust."[13]

Startlingly, for those who advocate a more confrontational posture toward the Chinese, there is nothing unusual about this behavior. Indeed, bilateral exercises between the USN and the PLAN have become common despite more than a decade of maritime tension.[14] One example involved joint antipiracy training off the Gulf of Aden in December 2014.[15] This combination of hostility on the part of the American national security community and official efforts to promote military-to-military cooperation has confused American allies, notably the Japanese.[16]

At least officially, the USN was not especially concerned over the appearance of the Chinese spy vessel at RIMPAC. Admiral Samuel

Locklear, the officer in charge of the US Pacific Command (PACOM), concluded that "the introduction of the AGI [auxiliary general intelligence vessel] kind of made it look a little odd, but it hasn't stopped the exercise and it hasn't created any difficulties in the exercise. And I guess on the other good side, it gives the Chinese the opportunity to see how their own ships are doing, so which [sic] I understand is pretty good."[17] Analysts outside the government were less sanguine. Rick Fisher, a senior fellow with the International Assessment and Strategy Center, claimed that such spying allowed China's military "to watch how the U.S. Navy interacts with its allies, which could be most useful in the event of actual military incidents or conflict."[18] Politicians were even more forthright. Representative Randy Forbes (R-VA), who chaired the House Armed Services Subcommittee on Seapower and Projection Forces, argued, "Given China's recent disregard for principles like freedom of navigation and the peaceful resolution of territorial disputes, it was already a stretch to reward Beijing with an invite. . . . It is clear their first trip to RIMPAC should be their last."[19]

Yet despite congressional misgivings about China, the US military shows no sign of ending this collaboration with a potential adversary. And the Obama administration ultimately decided to invite the PLAN to RIMPAC 2016—an invitation the Chinese accepted. As PACOM commander Admiral Harry Harris issued warnings about unprecedented PLAN aggression in the South China Sea, an angered Representative Mark Takai (D-HI) threatened to amend the Fiscal Year 2017 National Defense Authorization Act to formally revoke China's RIMPAC invitation.[20] Challenged by Takai, Secretary of Defense Ashton Carter articulated the administration's rationale: "What's the logic for having them [in RIMPAC] in the first place? Our strategy in the Asia-Pacific is not to exclude anyone, but to keep the security architecture going there in which everyone participates." Carter added that "America plays the pivotal role" in that architecture and characterized RIMPAC as "a key to sustaining the American position."[21] Excluding a major regional player such as China would undermine the American-led security framework in the Asia-Pacific.

## Military Exercises as a Component of National Strategy

Exercises are the meat and potatoes of military life during peacetime. The official definition is "a military maneuver or simulated wartime operation involving planning, preparation, and execution that is carried out for the purpose of training and evaluation."[22] Few defense analysts have systematically studied military exercises. But within the ranks of the services, officers acknowledge their importance—for both individual advancement and collective significance in the conduct of military operations.

These exercises are essential for maritime forces. One source suggests the USN participates in approximately "175 unit exercises annually."[23] The majority involve other US military services and/or multinational forces. Operating at sea is a complex minuet of practical activities to maximize both safety and efficiency. These minuets work best if practiced regularly. They also have tactical, operational, and—most important—strategic implications far beyond their "meat and potatoes" reputation. Military exercises help maintain unit readiness, improve joint and combined interoperability, "test" new operational concepts, and—depending on the context—help gather intelligence on both allies and potential adversaries. Generally, bilateral and multilateral military exercises serve American national strategic objectives by enhancing theater security cooperation and/or building the maritime capacity of partner nations.

## Building Security Cooperation, Engagement, and Partner Capacity

During the Cold War, exercises were generally local initiatives, organized and run by forward-deployed American military commanders. They were hosted by one military service, either individually or collaboratively with counterpart services from formal allies and friendly states. Neither the Department of Defense nor the Joint Chiefs of Staff supervised them. This practice began to change with the passage of the Goldwater-Nichols Act in 1986, which created unified geographic chains of command. Goldwater-Nichols also required presidents to periodically issue a strategy document outlining their approach to national security. The combination of regular "National Security Strategy" documents and the newly empowered regional commands presaged a decline in the autonomy of the service branches. The relationship became more hierarchical but simultaneously adaptive: "Theater strategy is derived from U.S. national strategy, and theater strategy determines operations and activities. No two combatant commands follow the same process, format, or procedures for developing theater strategy. Each combatant command has adapted its method to the peculiarities of its region and the personalities of its commanders."[24]

The Clinton administration introduced the idea of theater engagement programs (TEPs) as part of its effort to reform the Armed Services' practices while also consolidating global peace and security. Each geographic command is required to develop TEPs to organize peacetime military contacts and programs with countries in its operational Area of Responsibility. TEPs became a central pillar for the effective conduct of military exercises, themselves a crucial part of a process of building varied forms of multilateral security cooperation.[25] According to the Defense Security Cooperation Agency, security cooperation includes those activities conducted with allies and friendly nations to: build relationships that promote specified U.S. interests, build allied and friendly nation capabilities for self-defense and coalition operations, [and] provide U.S. forces with peacetime and contingency access. Examples include training, combined exercises, operational meetings, contacts and exchanges, security assistance, medical and engineering team engagements, cooperative development, acquisition and technical interchanges, and scientific and technology collaboration.[26]

In 2006, the Chairman of the Joint Chiefs of Staff characterized security cooperation activities broadly as:

1. Military contacts, including senior official visits, port visits, counterpart visits, conferences, staff talks, and personnel and unit exchange programs.
2. Nation assistance, including foreign internal defense, security assistance programs, and planned humanitarian and civic assistance activities.
3. Multinational training.
4. Multinational exercises, including those in support of the Partnership for Peace Program.
5. Multinational education for US personnel and personnel from other nations, both overseas and in the United States.
6. Arms control and treaty monitoring activities.[27]

The Clinton administration viewed TEPs as a means to "achieve resource efficiencies and more direct strategic relevance." Yet this implicit focus on enhanced hierarchy largely failed. According to one observer, the plans have been "developed by Geographic Combatant Commanders with inadequate policy guidance and only limited strategic direction."[28] TEPs remain the province of the geographic commands like PACOM and CENTCOM, which use TEP funds and programs, especially military exercises, to influence allies and partners. TEPs have been less successful in coordinating with national strategies. Such failures do not matter to combatant commanders focused on the security challenges in their own area of responsibility—for instance, the worst-case scenario of a major regional war.

One of our key objectives in this book is to show how specific strategies transcend presidencies. This policy area reinforces that pattern. Drawing on the traditional form of engagement pursued by the Clinton administration, and the George W. Bush administration's demand that partner capabilities be enhanced,[29] the Obama administration emphasized peacetime engagement and increasing the capabilities of American allies, partners, and even potential members of ad hoc "coalitions of the willing." Three documents outlined the Department of Defense's effort to build Partner Capacity during the Obama administration: the *2010 Quadrennial Defense*

*Review*, the *2011 National Military Strategy of the United States of America*, and the *2011 National Strategy for Counterterrorism*.[30] The 2010 QDR emphasized the importance of engaging partner countries: "Sustaining existing alliances and creating new partnerships are central elements of U.S. security strategy. The United States cannot sustain a stable international system alone. In an increasingly interdependent world, challenges to common interests are best addressed in concert with likeminded allies and partners who share responsibility for fostering peace and security."[31]

Promoting regional security through military exercises continues regardless of changes in presidential administrations, the issuance of new national security strategies, or when combatant commanders rotate out (even if the replacement hails from a different military service). The exercises we discuss in this chapter extend back several decades. RIMPAC, for example, was first held in 1971. This broad tendency to integrate theater security over time has been reflected in the continued linkage of capacity building and interoperability with partners. Military exercises serve as a fulcrum for multilateral Leadership strategies, given America's inordinately greater resources and its need for burden sharing. To amplify this point, we examine multilateral maritime exercises in the Indo-Pacific.

## Challenges (and Strategy) in the Indo-Pacific

The Asia-Pacific was regarded as a backwater relative to the European theater during the Cold War. As Admiral William Crowe (USN, retired) observed about his time as the Commander of the US Pacific Command between 1983 and 1985:

> For years, contingency plans for the Pacific called for substantial reinforcements in the event of war with the Soviet Union. But if we ever did find ourselves in a fight with the Soviets, it seemed clear to Long [Admiral Robert L. J. Long, Crowe's predecessor as Commander from 1979 to 1983] (as it did to me) that any early reinforcements of our Pacific Forces would be doubtful. Western Europe would be the centerpiece of a massive conflict, and that theater would claim whatever resources were available. Reminiscent of World War II, Europe's freedom was still America's top priority. The Pacific was still an economy of force theater.[32]

Admiral's Crowe's response was "to take maximum advantage of American air and sea superiority" by relying on America's forward regional presence. After all, the United States has historically had six treaty allies in Asia: Thailand, Japan, South Korea, Australia, New Zealand, and the Philippines. Major American bases are located in Japan and South Korea, in addition to Clark Air Base in the Philippines. The Seventh Fleet's carrier battle groups and amphibious readiness groups were—and remain—the centerpiece of America's regional power.[33] It helped that the Soviet Union's Pacific Fleet was not as formidable as some suggested at the time.[34] The United States relied on allies and mobile naval forces to prepare for a worst-case warfighting scenario. The United States and its allies also had to communicate a credible degree of resolve to their Pacific adversaries. But with the dissolution of the Soviet Union, America's strategic nearsightedness about Asia became even more myopic.

In 2011, President Obama abruptly reversed the pattern of neglect by announcing a "rebalance" of America's strategic focus toward the Asia-Pacific. Multilateral coalition-building became a central pillar of this reallocation, for two reasons. One is the massive combined size of the Pacific and Indian Oceans. American maritime resources are inadequate for waging a multiocean naval war or for policing such an expanse. A second is the region's political complexity. Notably, Asia has a high degree of economic integration but no institutionalized security architecture comparable to NATO in Europe to facilitate coalition command and interoperability.

Underpinning this rebalance to Asia is a widespread American concern that China's rise may undermine the United States' regional role and threaten its allies and partners.[35] Senator Carl Levin (D-MI) and Representative Howard P. "Buck" McKeon (R-CA), for example, inserted a provision—Section 1259—into the National Defense Authorization Act for Fiscal Year 2015 (Public Law 113-291) that requires the Department of Defense to produce an account of its maritime security strategy in the Asia-Pacific region. The ensuing report summarized the department's efforts:

> First, we are strengthening our military capacity to ensure the United States can successfully deter conflict and coercion and respond decisively when needed.
>
> Second, we are working together with our allies and partners from Northeast Asia to the Indian Ocean to build their capacity to address potential challenges in their waters and across the region.
>
> Third, we are leveraging military diplomacy to build greater transparency, reduce the risk of miscalculation or conflict, and promote shared maritime rules of the road.
>
> Finally, we are working to strengthen regional security institutions and encourage the development of an open and effective regional security architecture.[36]

The remainder of this chapter focuses on the second of the DoD's "lines of effort" for the Asia-Pacific rebalance. We examine the use of multilateral exercises to build partners' military capacity to meet the full range of maritime challenges in the region, either unilaterally or in collaboration with the United States. The evidence suggests that exercises will remain a core element of the strategy, even if the Trump administration reverses the regional focus.

## Multilateral Exercises after the Asia-Pacific Rebalance

Many Asia-Pacific exercises predated the Obama administration. But, as a Congressional Research Service report observed, "The [Obama] Administration's 'rebalance' entails not only expanded engagement with the PLA, but also increasing exercises."[37] Both the number of participants and the geographic breadth of exercises have greatly expanded. In many cases, their operational content has changed markedly. For example, while multilateral exercises concentrated on nontraditional, "soft power" military missions such as disaster relief prior to the 2011 rebalance, more recent ones have focused on traditional war fighting such as amphibious landings, antisubmarine warfare, and air defense. Nonetheless, the United States still emphasizes its Leadership role in maritime exercise programs to enhance its regional security.

Appendix 2 provides a list of major multilateral exercises in the Indo-Pacific. From this long list, we select three "mini" cases of particularly important exercises involving US allies and partners—Cobra Gold, RIMPAC, and Malabar. Cobra Gold is one of the oldest series and is hosted by Thailand, one of America's staunchest allies in Asia. RIMPAC draws participants and observers from the largest number of allies and partners. And the Malabar series is important not only because it is hosted by India—the second largest country in the Indo-Pacific and the largest democracy in the world—but because India is America's most valuable regional partner in constraining the spread of Chinese power. Collectively, these three cases illustrate a US Leadership strategy: they are American instigated, collaborative, and involve limited burden sharing.

COBRA GOLD

Hosted annually by Thailand since 1982, Cobra Gold is among the United States' longest-standing military exercises in the Pacific. The number of participants varies but usually involves Thailand, Singapore, Indonesia, South Korea, Malaysia, and Japan. These exercises have focused on interoperability, multinational coordination, and training.

Cobra Gold began in 1982 as a bilateral military exercise between the United States and Thailand, aimed at bolstering the war fighting competencies of the Royal Thai Armed Forces—particularly in conducting and defending against amphibious assaults. As a 1985 article in *Leatherneck*, the US Marine Corps magazine, pointed out, "The training objective of [Cobra Gold] is to enhance the professional capabilities and readiness of U.S. and Thai Armed Forces through participation in joint/combined exercises."[38] The US decision to initiate Cobra Gold is best understood in the strategic context of the Cold War. Communist Vietnam had successfully invaded

Cambodia in 1978 and replaced the Khmer Rouge with a friendly govern-ment. The Soviets invaded Afghanistan the following year. The United States invested resources in the Thai military to bolster its deterrence capacity—not only by strengthening Thai war fighting capabilities, but also by demonstrating a US commitment to the defense of a treaty ally. As the 1988 US National Security Strategy stated, "Thailand . . . our treaty ally, borders Cambodia, which is now occupied by the Vietnamese and the site of an active Cambodian resistance effort struggling to regain self-determination for the Khmer people. In support of Thailand . . . we will continue our close security cooperation to deter any potential aggression."[39]

Cobra Gold's multinational composition actually expanded in the 1990s despite the conclusion of the Cold War, when we might reasonably have expected it to have wound down. Today, Cobra Gold constitutes a bell-wether for US strategic priorities in the Asia-Pacific region.

Amphibious assault and traditional war-fighting competencies have remained important elements of the exercise. But MOOTW, such as human-itarian assistance and disaster relief, appeared on the Cobra Gold agenda in the 1990s. This adaptation came as a result of the redirection of US Cold War defense dollars to other priorities and a diminished threat posed by Vietnam to its neighbors.

The winding down of the Cold War altered US National Security Strate-gies (NSS) in the late 1980s and early 1990s. The 1988 NSS, for example, advocated a highly deterrence-centric US defense policy, to be achieved in large part through the significant forward presence of US forces. As it stated:

> The United States has bilateral or multilateral security commitments with some 43 nations around the globe. . . . In support of those commitments, and to deter adventurism by the Soviets and their client states, we maintain for-ward deployed forces in . . . regions of strategic importance. Our naval forces deployed in the Pacific and Indian Oceans assist in protecting our growing strategic and economic interests, and supporting allies and friends, in Asia and the Pacific.[40]

In contrast, the 1993 NSS discussed paring back these deployments. It noted that

> while reducing our forward-deployed forces, we are redefining our pres-ence abroad with combined exercises, new access and storage agreements, security and humanitarian assistance, port visits, military-to-military con-tacts, and periodic and rotational deployments. Our forward presence forces and operations lend credibility to our alliances and ensure the perception that a collective response awaits any threat to our interests or to those of our allies.[41]

New challenges—by necessity—provoked American operational adaptation. The 1992 iteration of Cobra Gold proved to be a watershed: it was the first time that the exercise emphasized MOOTW over traditional war fighting. Cobra Gold 92 "centered on humanitarian and civic action joint-combined training" as opposed to amphibious assault or coastal defense.[42] Since then, MOOTW has remained a regular feature of Cobra Gold.[43] Moreover, the regional devastation wrought in 2004 by the Indian Ocean tsunami underscored the importance of local militaries well versed in humanitarian assistance and disaster relief.[44]

Consistent with a Leadership strategy, one of the American planners' initial objectives in expanding Cobra Gold was to bolster its political legitimacy with the Thai government and to influence domestic opinion so that, during a crisis, Thailand might permit uninterrupted basing access to forward-deployed US forces. A 2008 Congressional Research Service report underlined this strategy:

> In the past few years, U.S. military planners have emphasized a "places, not bases" concept in Southeast Asia in which U.S. troops can temporarily use facilities for operations and training, without maintaining a lengthy and costly permanent presence. In a State Department press release, a senior Defense Department official pointed to cooperation with Thailand as an example of the military's new approach, citing the annual Cobra Gold exercises. Facilities used by the U.S. military in Thailand fall under the Pentagon's "cooperative security location" (CSL) concept, in which host countries provide access in exchange for upgrades and other aid.

Cobra Gold further evolved in the first decade of the twenty-first century, when new participants joined the exercise: Singapore in 2000, Japan and Indonesia in 2005 and 2006. South Korea followed in 2010, and Malaysia in 2011. Involving additional nations in Cobra Gold offered the United States notable benefits: it demonstrated its commitment to regional security to a wider audience while reinforcing a new security architecture.

Yet just as remarkable have been Cobra Gold's continuities. Notably, the series has been held every year despite numerous outbreaks of Thai political turmoil, including military coups. At most, Cobra Gold has occasionally been "scaled down" in response to such developments. In one recent example, the US government heavily criticized the Thai coup of May 2014, yet the 2015 iteration of Cobra Gold proceeded as normal. This trend indicates the high strategic value that the United States places on the series—all the more so since it has evolved into a multinational exercise that serves as a barometer for the US rebalance to the Asia-Pacific.

The 2015 Cobra Gold, the thirty-fourth in the series, focused as usual on interoperability and strengthening regional relationships. And a portion of its activities were devoted to humanitarian efforts, civil affairs, and medical projects designed to improve the quality of life and local infrastructure for Thailand's population. But significantly, as the US Marine Corps stressed, the "staff exercise and senior leader engagements will sustain and reinforce the foundation and framework for a multinational force to respond rapidly and effectively to regional crises."[45] China, it seems, was once again lurking in the background.

### RIMPAC: THE BIGGEST EXERCISE

The US-hosted RIMPAC exercises are the world's largest series of multinational naval drills.[46] RIMPAC's stated purpose is to enhance interoperability and build relationships with Pacific Rim nations by providing "a unique training opportunity that helps participants foster and sustain the cooperative relationships that are critical to ensuring the safety of sea lanes and security on the world's oceans."[47] Originating in 1971, RIMPAC is held biennially, usually off Hawaii's coastline. It is structured in three parts: "a planning portion, a portion at sea, and a final, massive simulation."[48] The 2016 iteration was the twenty-fifth in the series.

RIMPAC initially involved the United States, Australia, Canada, and New Zealand in a "limited anti-submarine warfare evolution."[49] Its membership was stable in the first decade. It has since expanded significantly, both in the number of international participants and the skills and competencies drilled. In the 1980s and 1990s, Japan, South Korea, and Chile were added at a modest pace; participation has accelerated since then. By 2010, RIMPAC included naval units from fourteen countries. Nonetheless, the greatest expansion of RIMPAC took place following Secretary of State Hillary Clinton's October 2011 announcement of the US "pivot" to the Asia-Pacific.[50] In 2012, twenty-two nations deployed naval platforms for RIMPAC, five times the original number.

In a watershed change in 2014, China was invited to participate. RIMPAC 2014 was an early instance of China "dipping a toe" into the deep waters of multilateral naval cooperation. Its initial foray largely involved medical cooperation in the context of humanitarian and disaster relief operations. Admiral Floyd, in response to a question from a Chinese journalist about China's RIMPAC role, characterized the PLAN's participation as follows:

> China is going to be participating in medical exchanges. That's going on right now. Actually, in fact, I think it started this morning with their—with the hospital ship, *Peace Ark*, working kind of as the basis with our—the U.S. hospital ship, *Mercy*. I was down on *Peace Ark* a couple of days ago. It's a beautiful ship, really great capability. And I believe they brought over—that China has brought over 40 doctors to participate in this. And then there's doctors and medical staff from all the other 22 nations that are participating in the medical exchange going on now.

Now, as part of the medical exchange, they'll talk about humanitarian assistance, disaster relief. That's probably the—that's the most likely areas that we will drop in together and operate in the future, I think, in the real world.

And then once we get out to sea, they will do some gunnery exercises. We'll work some counter-piracy. They also have their explosive ordinance disposal. Their dive teams are here. So there is really a pretty well-rounded list of things that China is participating in over the—gosh, there's over 2,000 different events, I think, and they're in a pretty good chunk of them.[51]

This was also the first time that hospital vessels—China's *Peace Ark* and the USN's *Mercy*—participated in RIMPAC. Chinese and American medical staff "conducted personnel exchanges, military medicine exchanges, and medical evacuation and mass casualty training."[52] This collaboration represents a small but notable step, given both countries' competitive posturing over their timely contribution to humanitarian assistance following the 2004 tsunami rescue efforts.[53]

RIMPAC has taken on more MOOTW operations. Both the 2012 and 2014 exercises involved humanitarian assistance and disaster relief. During RIMPAC 2012, commander of USPACOM, Admiral Samuel J. Locklear, commented that "it's no longer just a maritime exercise. It has grown in scope and become a joint exercise, and we would like to see it continue to grow in that regard."[54] A *Vice* magazine report notes that the inclusion of MOOTW in RIMPAC

ultimately reflects the training priorities of the participating nations. Despite the fact that there's been a lot of fighting around the globe for more than a decade, a lot of . . . conflicts look less like a good, old-fashioned state-to-state slugging match and a lot more like a messier kind of conflict that increasingly forces militaries to look more and more like police. With that transition, the use of force has become an increasingly political activity, demanding the formation of international coalitions [as seen in RIMPAC].[55]

RIMPAC's evolution reflects several other trends. It has recently included aspects of naval war fighting such as antisurface warfare, air defense, and amphibious assault. In a 2014 interview, the Royal Canadian Navy's Rear Admiral Gilles Couturier noted, "While I talk a lot about ships, there are other important elements in RIMPAC, such as submarines and amphibious assault. There is also a significant mine warfare element, which involved about 1,000 folks. This is a very rigorous training event. Mine warfare is also another area where many navies don't get to exercise, so RIMPAC actually gives us the umbrella to get countries together to do that."[56] Another trend has been the multinationalization of command over the exercise, as American planners have sought to expand RIMPAC collaboration and increase burden sharing. According to *Vice*, "The allocation of top roles started changing in 2012, when an Australian was put in charge of the maritime component, and Canada has also taken on a key role as RIMPAC changes to a more global event. This year [in 2014], the seven top leadership positions were held by three Americans, two Australians, with the remaining two held by Japan and Canada."[57]

Yet RIMPAC remains a decidedly American initiative. The United States, through the various subordinate commands of the US Pacific Command, sets the agenda and provides much of the planning. Each RIMPAC takes nearly two years to plan before the first ship or aircraft is deployed. It is American military Leadership and diplomacy that guides these preparations.

Indeed, the turmoil caused by the Chinese spy ship incident described earlier tells us something useful about the US Leadership strategy. Critics suggested at the time that the incident was an attempt to undermine the exercise's utility. Doug Bandow, in a contrasting spirit, argued that "unfortunately, RIMPAC is too small and unimportant to much matter."[58] It is "a nonessential ocean exercise."[59] Many naval officers would reject such a sentiment. Within the Navy, it is an article of faith that exercises are essential to ensure smooth operations at sea. And in deflecting criticism, they ask a series of counterfactual questions. What if the United States simply decided that exercises like RIMPAC were nonessential and declined to invite China, or any other countries for that matter? Would the other participants organize a comparable event? If they did, would it have the same agenda as the current US-led version? Would canceling or divesting exercises like RIMPAC substantively affect the pursuit of American national interests in the Indo-Pacific region? In the absence of (unavailable) evidence to the contrary, the US government's goal is to sustain these exercises and thereby consolidate America's pivotal position.

## MALABAR

The strategic importance of the Malabar exercise lies in US collaboration with India—the greatest potential bulwark against China's rise in the Indian Ocean. This bilateral link is always at the core of the Malabar series, even when it is formally a multilateral event.

An Indo-American rapprochement coincided with the Soviet Union's collapse. The proximate impetus for the Malabar series can be traced to proposals made to New Delhi by Lieutenant General Claude M. Kicklighter, Commander of US Army Pacific, during a 1991 visit. Former Indian Army chief V. P. Malik has suggested that these proposals entailed "service-to-service exchanges and expansion of a defense cooperation framework."[60] The Malabar series of naval exercises, named after the shoreline location of the drills, began the following year. The inaugural event involved only surface combatants.

Sequels were held in 1995 and 1996, each larger in size, scope, and complexity. Submarines and naval aviation assets were added to surface combatants. The series was suspended following India's 1998 Pokhran nuclear tests and subsequent US sanctions. But Malabar was resurrected in 2002, spurred by the George W. Bush administration's determination to forge a strategic partnership with New Delhi in the wake of the 9/11 terror attacks. By 2005 the two nations had signed a ten-year accord known as the "New Framework for the U.S.-India Defense Relationship." It noted that India and the United States would, among other things, "conduct joint and combined exercises and exchanges; collaborate in multinational operations when it is in their common interest; [and] strengthen the capabilities of our militaries to promote security and defeat terrorism."[61]

The exercise continued to expand, reaching a high-water mark in 2007 when two separate iterations were held only five months apart. The second involved three additional nations (Japan, Australia, and Singapore), 20,000 personnel, 28 ships, and 150 aircraft.[62] Alarmed at Malabar's unprecedented scale, China sent a demarche to New Delhi, but the Indian Navy resisted calls by some Indian politicians to cancel the annual event. It eventually responded by scaling back the 2008 Malabar exercise to a bilateral Indo-US exercise. The American reaction to China's demarche and India's response was muted. The Bush administration had recently negotiated the historic India–United States Civil Nuclear Agreement (2005) and regarded the emerging strategic relationship with India as a foreign policy victory.[63] The official American position remained consistent: Malabar "provides a message to other militaries, and our own, that we are capable of operating together and that we work together with our regional partners to ensure stability in the region."[64]

Malabar expanded again after 2008. The 2015 iteration, the eighteenth in the series, marked the second consecutive year that the Japan Maritime Self-Defense Force had been involved. Also, in January 2015, President Obama met with Indian Prime Minister Narendra Modi in New Delhi.[65] The two leaders agreed to expand Malabar, presaging future growth despite Beijing's protests. The following June, US Secretary of Defense Ashton Carter and Indian Minister of Defense Manohar Parrikar signed a ten-year renewal of the 2005 defense framework.[66] Additions to the 2015 framework included agreements to "enhance cooperation in military training and education," "exchange experiences and practices in operating common defense platforms," and "enhance cooperation toward maritime security and to increase each other's capability to secure the free movement of lawful commerce."[67] These activities clearly consolidated an increasingly important bilateral relationship for both countries.

Iskander Rehman concludes that "whereas the MALABAR exercises started with only basic maneuvers and communication drills, they have since expanded in scope and scale."[68] At this point, the public objectives of the Malabar series are extensive: to share best practices and conduct live drills relating to surface and antisubmarine warfare, maritime interdiction operations, underway replenishment, search and rescue, and other core naval competencies. Malabar's location now typically alternates between the Indian Ocean (in the Arabian Sea or Bay of Bengal) and the Pacific Ocean (in waters off the coast of Japan).

Demonstrating the Indian Navy's ability to interoperate—both technologically and in employing relatively similar training, tactics, and techniques—with the cutting-edge capabilities of the USN affords New Delhi advantages in pursuing its own interests. India (and especially its Navy) has long considered the Indian Ocean region to be its own sphere of influence.[69] Yet, even if the Indian Navy's limited budget currently constrains its maritime ambitions, Rehman suggests: "One can assume that, in the future, the Indian navy, absent a major hike in funding, will find itself compelled to focus less on the "visible" components of maritime power, such as maritime multilateralism and soft power projection, and more on the "viable" aspects of developing an effective war-fighting capability in the face of rapidly coalescing threats to India's maritime lifelines."[70] If he is correct, the Malabar exercises will continue to expand in terms of war-fighting missions and technological complexity in the years ahead.

## The Impact of Exercises—and of Budgets

Malabar and the other exercises constitute successes from an American perspective. They provide America's geopolitical rivals with evidence of its leadership, signal its credibility, and demonstrate a capacity to leverage its resources. As a Chinese official newspaper, *The Global Times*, diplomatically observed in a thinly veiled reference to Malabar, "The China-India relationship is on a sound track, and healthy ties are beneficial to both countries . . . India should be vigilant to any intentions of roping it into an anti-China camp."[71] The *Economic Times* reported Chinese Foreign Ministry Spokesman Hong Lei's blunter comment regarding Japan's participation in the 2015 Malabar exercises: "Our position is very clear. It is hoped that the relevant country will not provoke confrontation and heighten tensions in the region."[72]

Then again, the American signal to China and others may be ambivalent. These exercises are meant to convey strength and solidarity in the face of possible Chinese aggression. Yet, given the two countries' extensive economic linkages, American officials often assert that the United States is not seeking to encircle but to engage with the Chinese.[73] The 2015 US maritime

strategy states, for example, that "the U.S. Sea Services, through our continued forward presence and constructive interaction with Chinese maritime
forces, reduce the potential for misunderstanding, discourage aggression,
and preserve our commitment to peace and stability in the region"—even
after acknowledging Chinese provocations (e.g., "China's naval expansion
also presents challenges when it employs force or intimidation against
other sovereign nations to assert territorial claims").[74] Conveying an aggressive message might escalate tensions or engender an adversarial spiral, if
not outright conflict.[75] Such concerns may explain the American decision to
invite China to participate in RIMPAC: providing some degree of reassur-
ance, even if it risks a better vantage point for the Chinese to observe new
technologies and tactics.

Part of the underlying issue concerns budgets—a matter that candidate
Trump promised to address.[76] America's military budget continues to overwhelm that of other nations. It used to be much higher. Chinese military
expenditures accelerated, however, while the Great Recession of 2008 led to
sequestration and Department of Defense budget cuts in 2011 legislation
known as the Budget Control Act. Still, using Stockholm International
Peace Research Institute (SIPRI) data, the Peterson Foundation reported in
2015 it was still larger than the next seven countries combined.[77]

From a budgetary perspective, America's rebalance to the Asia-Pacific
was ill-timed. Nonetheless, "the Department of Defense is on track to position 60 percent of U.S. Air Force and Navy forces in the region by 2020 with
55 percent of the Navy's 289 ships, including 60 percent of its submarine
fleet, already based across Asia."[78] Despite this redeployment, American
military leaders in the Pacific worry about the impact of cutbacks and
accompanying uncertainties on relations with allies. As Admiral Locklear
noted as recently as 2014: "Due to continued budget uncertainty, we were
forced to make difficult short-term choices and scale back or cancel valuable training exercises, negatively impacting both the multinational training needed to strengthen our alliances and build partner capacities as well
as some unilateral training necessary to maintain our high-end warfighting
capabilities."[79]

It is difficult to gauge the practical impact of spending cutbacks in any
given year on individual events like Malabar, RIMPAC, or Cobra Gold, let
alone on an entire class of activities, such as those associated with Theater
Security Cooperation in the Indo-Pacific. The politics involved in efforts to
influence Congress or public opinion when facing the specter of budgetary
changes—whether for new weapons or for day-to-day operations—
encourages skepticism.[80] But one Government Accountability Office report
suggests that the 2011 Budget Control Act has had more impact on recent or
current operations—such as buying fuel, funding travel, and hiring
contractors—than on big ticket items such as procurement or personnel
costs.[81]

It is even more difficult to assess whether the size of America's military budget influences outside perceptions of American power and leadership. But it is unquestionable that America's Leadership strategy entails extensive costs. Rhetoric about America as a model, symbolic action or claims about universal values and global institution building are irrelevant when it comes to concrete military operations. Many modern American overseas military activities—whether entailing MOOTW or kinetic conflict—are likely to involve coalitions. And it remains a truism for the sea services that military exercises are essential for ensuring that coalition operations are successful. In their absence, the USN and its counterparts are likely to encounter steep learning curves, unexpected costs, and expensive mishaps when called on to collaborate. If the Trump administration (and its successors) do continue the Asia pivot, the need (and demand from partners) to expend resources on exercises will remain at least constant and likely grow. Even if the United States and China were to achieve a maritime rapprochement in the near term, the Indo-Pacific is experiencing increasing trans-Pacific trade; an increasing number of capable navies in the region that will want to partner with the United States; and the very real possibility that climate change will lead to more weather extremes such as typhoons that will prompt disaster relief operations and the rescue and care of refugees. The need for increased maritime operations in the area is likely to grow.

American Leadership, through defense cooperation and, more specifically, multilateral maritime exercises, has had limited tangible results in Asia if we compare it to the institutionalized security architecture evident in Europe. No informal structure has yet emerged. As Sheldon Simon concludes, "There has been little movement toward a more networked structure among partners and allies. This means that while virtually all Southeast Asian armed forces exercise and train with their U.S. counterparts, their military relations with each other are almost entirely bilateral."[82]

Yet this reliance on a "hub and spoke" pattern of relations between the metropole and the periphery may be quite intentional. After all, the United States is seeking to "lead" its allies and partners consistent with its own national interests. A benignly articulated "divide and conquer" strategy has a long and distinguished history for great powers. And formal organizations such as NATO carry two risks. First, NATO's Article 5 (an attack on one member is an attack on all members) risks the US being drawn into a conflict by a "reckless driver."[83] Second, institutionalization jeopardizes America's control of the agenda. To create a network of like-minded states that might resist or force modifications to America's approaches to its regional security in Asia is not necessarily a priority for Washington policymakers. But a routine, if informal, multilateral structure that is American-organized may be far more attractive.

We cannot ignore an alternative interpretation: that the creation of a regional network of like-minded states is in process but will simply take more time. America's rebalance to Asia is in its infancy; convincing Asian states to develop new ways to cope with China's military, not to mention changing strategic cultures and long-standing patterns of behavior, is unlikely to proceed quickly or smoothly.

Asia-based military exercises will continue to play an instrumental role for the US-led security network. They serve as a conduit for the United States to develop bilateral and multilateral security arrangements with states across the region by fostering closer military relations for both peace-time and in conflict.

A greater degree of self-consciousness about the nature and form of this undertaking is necessary if we are to assess how multilateral maritime exercises fit into any broader US strategy—particularly America's effort to assert leadership in a region that encompasses more than half the globe. In the words of Vice Admiral Cecil Haney, former commander of the United States Pacific Fleet:

Today the U.S. Navy conducts exercises and training events with over 20 allies, partners and friends in this region, to increase partnership capabilities to address uncertainty in the region. This is something we clearly put a high value on and I look forward to continuing that in the future. But the question is—can we take it up a notch? Can we do more together to ensure the future security in the maritime domain? Are we doing the right things? Are we doing the right things right?[84]

CHAPTER 5

# Pirates, Terrorists, and Formal Sponsorship

At 7:15 a.m. on April 8, 2009, four pirates in a fast-moving skiff used grappling irons and a torrent of firepower to board an unarmed 508-foot US-flagged vessel named the *Maersk Alabama*. The freighter was traversing the Gulf of Aden, between Yemen and Somalia, to deliver food aid to Kenya. Once the pirates boarded, the *Maersk Alabama*'s captain—Richard Phillips—and three other sailors distracted the armed pirates while the rest of the crew disabled the ship before hiding in safe rooms below. With the pirates' skiff sunk during the melee, and the *Maersk Alabama* inoperable, Phillips convinced the pirates to retreat into the ship's lifeboat.

The pirates took Phillips as their prisoner, planning to ransom him for a reported $2–3 million. Things did not develop as they hoped. A US destroyer, the *Bainbridge*, arrived.[1] It pursued the lifeboat while negotiations for the captain's release ensued. After five futile days of discussion, the US authorities concluded that the pirates intended the captain imminent harm. Operating pursuant to authorization provided by President Obama, the US destroyer slowly came alongside the lifeboat.[2]

Aboard were three snipers from Navy SEAL Team 6,[3] one of America's most secretive special operations units. The three snipers, calibrating both the destroyer and the lifeboat's movement, each simultaneously fired one shot, killing all three pirates, and freeing Captain Phillips. A fourth pirate, who had earlier surrendered to US authorities, was brought to the United States to stand trial. Pleading guilty on all counts except that of piracy, he was sentenced to over thirty years in prison.

It is rare that an oceangoing freighter becomes famous once, let alone twice. Most ply the world's waterways, languishing in obscurity. But the *Maersk Alabama* is an exception. It initially captured the world's attention in 2009 when these events took place. Then the freighter enjoyed the spotlight again in 2013 in a film starring Tom Hanks as Captain Phillips.[4] Millions across the globe followed the story of the *Maersk Alabama* twice, once in real time and again in a lightly fictionalized film.[5]

Navy public affairs officials were doubtless elated by the positive publicity. After all, Navy SEALs had rescued an American captain operating a

US-flagged ship, carrying food aid bound for Kenya—albeit the ship was owned by a Danish corporation and crewed by a polyglot group of sailors. And the SEALs completed a daring mission thousands of miles from America's shore. Wins like this are rare, especially when fighting seaborne pirates. Perhaps not since the daring adventures of Lieutenant Stephen Decatur—against pirates sponsored by the Pasha of Tripoli during the First Barbary War in 1804—had the Navy enjoyed such a publicity windfall for its counter-piracy exploits.[6]

Yet the *Maersk Alabama* incident was more representative of contemporary American maritime operations than the casual observer might assume. Rear Admiral Michelle Howard was then commander of Expeditionary Strike Group 2, stationed aboard the USS *Boxer*. That amphibious assault ship was deployed in the Gulf of Aden specifically to conduct antipiracy operations. The assignment proved an important pathway to promotion. Subsequently, Howard became the first African-American woman to achieve the rank of Vice Admiral;[7] then a full four-star Admiral as the Vice Chief of Naval Operations; and finally, in 2016, the commander of some of the Navy's most prominent operational forces—Allied Joint Force Command Naples, US Naval Forces Europe, and US Naval Forces Africa.[8]

Admiral Howard concluded that the *Maersk Alabama* operation was successful because "the Department of Defense is there to protect America's interest, America's property and America's citizens. And in the end there is a deterrence factor. You want the average pirate to look at an American ship and say, 'We'll just let that one go by.'"[9]

From a broader strategic perspective, this public relations coup may deserve a more qualified assessment. Few analysts believe that piracy is a major threat to the United States, its citizens, or even its commercial interests. SEAL Team 6's demonstration of skill and valor masks severe limits on the ability of the US Navy to prevent piracy or to rescue oceangoing vessels attacked by pirates. The costs of unilateral action are enormous—this case involved the use of a multi-million-dollar warship and the expertise of a highly trained force for several days to rescue one American at sea. In part the success of the *Maersk Alabama* was so enjoyable because it was so rare. In practice, the United States needs international cooperation to address the threat of piracy, and that cooperation is achievable only through a global initiative legitimated by the United Nations.

## Piracy as a Historical and Contemporary Threat

The threat of piracy has a long lineage, and so does America's unilateral response. The US Navy has its origins in combating threats to American merchant shipping in the Mediterranean.[10] In the republic's early years, American merchantmen had been protected by the Royal Navy and other states, like Portugal, intent on suppressing piracy to encourage trade. But the seizure of two American ships by Algerian corsairs in 1785 demonstrated an increasing vulnerability.[11] Congress, however, was reluctant to appropriate the funds necessary to construct a national navy and was often content to pay tribute to the Barbary states even as pirates continued to seize American vessels and the efficacy of relying on foreign navies to protect American property was proving unworkable.[12]

President George Washington finally signed the Naval Act of 1794. It created a permanent standing US Navy, initially consisting of six frigates. The new Navy proved to be a sound investment: "The demonstrated willingness of the United States to respond militarily helped American diplomats negotiate a more reasonable financial agreement with Algiers in 1796."[13] Over the next century and a half, the US Navy sporadically devoted its resources to suppressing piracy. It does so today by carrying out cruises intended to deter pirates, intervene ashore, and occasionally engage in armed encounters at sea.

As in 1785, the primary threat posed by pirates now is to commercial shipping, which they attack in both international sea lanes and the littoral. Between April 2005 and 2013, for example, 179 ships were hijacked off the Horn of Africa, costing approximately $400 million dollars in ransoms alone.[14] The direct economic costs of piracy are small if measured against the aggregate value of international shipping: between $7 and $12 billion a year.[15] Yet lost ships, missing cargo, and ransomed merchant mariners can prove expensive for individual firms. More expensive is the aggregate impact on global trade, although this is notoriously hard to calculate. Yet piracy forms part of a historic naval mission. Naval analysts from Alfred Thayer Mahan and Julian Corbett to the contemporary authors of *A Cooperative Strategy for 21st Century Seapower* have consistently argued that a primary naval function is to protect the global economy from disruption.[16] As the authors of *A Cooperative Strategy* noted, "We prosper because of this system of exchange among nations, yet recognize it is vulnerable to a range of disruptions that can produce cascading and harmful effects far from their sources. Major power war, regional conflict, terrorism, lawlessness and natural disasters—all have the potential to threaten US national security and world prosperity."[17] Piracy is one form of "lawlessness." Like the British before them, American policymakers view any global campaign against piracy as consistent with the national interest.[18]

Pirates pose a minimal physical threat to navies, coast guards, or even well-armed merchant vessels. They rarely assault military or paramilitary vessels. Yet the operational challenges posed by counterpiracy off the coast of Somalia and in the Gulf of Aden are daunting. The volume of maritime traffic is high and pirate activities are unpredictable. Added are the difficulties of patrolling vast expanses of ocean while intervening in a timely manner.

Furthermore, for the United States, the purpose of counterpiracy is complex. Nongovernmental analysts commonly regard Somali pirates simply as criminals.[19] Their concern is the protection of trade. Government strategists, however, address recurring questions about links between these pirates and terrorist organizations—notably al-Shabaab, which maintains an enclave in Somalia. Expert assessments of the relationship are split. Nonetheless, a catchall proviso is embedded in the mission statement of the American counterpiracy operation—to "create a lawful maritime order by defeating terrorism, deterring piracy, reducing illegal trafficking of people and drugs as well as promoting the maritime environment as a safe place for mariners with legitimate business."[20]

Establishing a positive link between piracy and terrorism would, inevitably, recast both the nature of the threat and the actors involved. In the absence of definitive evidence, both the Bush and the Obama administrations assumed that such a link either does exist or might develop if the problem were ignored. Other nations remain unconvinced; they contribute to counterpiracy missions because piracy constitutes a serious threat to commercial relations. But for a variety of reasons, they are less willing to engage in counterterror missions led by the United States.

The financial costs for America include the procurement of military platforms and the provision of military personnel, law enforcement, and intelligence assets. The United States has created an umbrella coalition called Combined Maritime Forces, composed of three separate Combined Task Forces (CTFs) operating in the western Indian Ocean, to promote maritime security and fight piracy. Politically, concrete evidence of a relationship between piracy and terrorism would help administrations justify the expenditure. In the meantime, however, the USN proceeds on the assumption that antipiracy operations are in doctrinal terms part of a comprehensive response to the broad array of irregular threats to maritime security.[21]

Historically, the standard American response to piracy has been unilateralist. The USN combed the seas for corsairs—hard to locate but, if in the vicinity, easy to spot. This is untrue today. Even proximity provides no guarantee because small pirate skiffs are hard to detect. Groups of meagerly armed bands of Somalis use commercial small boats and low-tech techniques to find targets. They then attack vessels—large and small, commercial and private. Vast expanses of ocean coupled with few clear markers and swift, unpredictable attacks present formidable operational problems. Yet in 2013 only 23 vessels were attacked, down from the 2011 peak of 237 attacks. The value of these attacks had fallen to $3.2 million, well below the estimated ceiling of $12 billion in 2010.[22] So how was that achieved?

## Formal Sponsorship: A Contemporary Strategy for a Historic Problem

A unilateral counterpiracy strategy would fail today because, given its other missions, the USN simply does not have enough resources to combat piracy alone. Accordingly, the United States applies a Sponsorship strategy to the problem. It addresses the threat to the sea lanes by contributing naval and coast guard assets as one member of a multilateral coalition of states that enforces international laws, including the UN Convention on the Law of the Sea (UNCLOS).[23] As a formal sponsor, rather than leader or sole provider of counterpiracy forces, the United States encourages partner navies to contribute even when resources are limited by material circumstances or domestic politics.

As we will show, the USN plays a key—if understated—operational role. It performs invaluable support functions, using the resources of US Naval Forces Central Command and working through the Combined Maritime Forces (CMF). Furthermore, it provides critical infrastructure; supplies intelligence fusion, a common operating picture, and command and control mechanisms; and maintains a variety of institutional arrangements necessary for a very diverse coalition of navies to coordinate operations.

Formal Sponsorship requires conventions, protocols, and laws. In this case UNCLOS provides the binding framework for maritime cooperation.[24] According to the convention, "piracy" consists of illegal acts committed on the high seas for private ends by the crew or passengers of one ship against the crew, passengers, or property on board another.[25] Legal experts generally treat UNCLOS as a codification of customary international law on piracy and consider all states, whether a party or not, as bound by the UNCLOS definition.[26]

Paradoxically, the United States is the most important state yet to formally ratify UNCLOS—despite the fact that the US government was a driving force behind the agreement and generally follows its provisions. This failure is a product of domestic politics. The US Senate has proved allergic to diluting American sovereignty, and UNCLOS is no exception. Attempts at ratification have persistently faltered there. As with other global protocols, such as the Land Mine Treaty or membership of the International Criminal Court, the United States often demands an exemption or amendment. In this case, not long after UNCLOS was promulgated, it became clear that its provisions insufficiently dealt with certain violent acts at sea—epitomized by the *Achille Lauro* incident in 1985 where an American was killed by political terrorists. In 1988, in response, the UN and the International Maritime Organization promulgated the Convention for the Suppression of Unlawful Acts (sometimes referred to as the Rome Convention).[27] It established "a legal basis for prosecuting maritime violence that did not fall within the UNCLOS piracy framework."[28] The United States did ratify that treaty in 1994.

The UN held meetings in Nairobi, Kenya, in November 2008 and then released a report by the Special Representative of the Secretary-General on the issue of piracy off the coast of Somalia.[29] Around that event, the UN Security Council (UNSC) issued resolutions 1816, 1838, 1846, and 1851, under chapter VII of the UN Charter (which authorizes states to take "all necessary measures").[30] The most important was Resolution 1816. It authorized states to "enter the territorial waters of Somalia for the purpose of repressing acts of piracy and armed robbery at sea" and to "use, within the territorial waters of Somalia, in a manner consistent with action permitted on the high seas with respect to piracy under relevant international law, all necessary means to repress acts of piracy and armed robbery." In October, the UNSC adopted Resolution 1838, calling on states with military capabilities in the region to contribute to antipiracy efforts. Subsequent resolutions extended these mandates. They clarified how counterpiracy operations would be undertaken in accordance with international humanitarian and human rights law, offered provisions regarding technical assistance, and specified agreements regarding the prosecution of captured pirates.[31]

Recognizing the complexity of both the local situation and multilateral coordination, Resolution 1851 in January 2009 encouraged the creation of a multinational Contact Group on Piracy off the Coast of Somalia (CGPCS).[32] The Contact Group, which originally consisted of approximately twenty nations, now includes more than eighty countries in addition to numerous intergovernmental organizations, such as the African Union. It is a "voluntary, ad hoc international forum to coordinate international efforts."[33] It was initially composed of five working groups—Naval Cooperation,[34] Legal Issues, Self-Defensive Actions, Public Diplomacy, and the Flow of Illegal Funds. But as the number of pirate attacks decreased, the Contact Group placed greater emphasis on other aspects of the counterpiracy mission. Today, it also comprises working groups such as Capacity Building, the Legal Forum of the CGPCS, Maritime Counter Piracy and Mitigation Operations, and Disrupting Pirate Networks Ashore.[35]

By 2008, the UN had therefore provided a comprehensive legal justification and framework for maritime powers to combat piracy off the Horn of Africa. As part of its formal Sponsorship strategy, the United States played an important role in facilitating Security Council directives and began both to provide counterpiracy forces and materiel and enable other less-capable navies.

## American Involvement

In December 2008, President George W. Bush's National Security Council issued the "Countering Piracy off the Horn of Africa: Partnership and Action Plan" ("Action Plan") in response to a piracy crisis that had grown since 2006.[36] The Action Plan was the culmination of five years of groundwork on building an institutional infrastructure to address a broad set of maritime security issues.

In 2004, the President had issued National Security Presidential Decision Directive 41, designed to coordinate maritime security affairs through the Maritime Security Interagency Policy Committee. The committee included representatives from the departments of Defense, State, Homeland Security, and Transportation, as well as intelligence agencies. Together they developed the 2005 National Strategy for Maritime Security, as well an annex to that document, which subsequently became the 2007 Maritime Security (Piracy) Policy.[37]

The Bush administration's Action Plan argued that "success in securing the maritime domain will not come from the United States acting alone, but through a powerful coalition of nations maintaining a strong, united international front."[38] It implicitly rejected both Primacy and a Leadership strategy. Rather the National Security Council pledged that

> the United States will encourage other nations to assign more forces, such as law enforcement and naval air and surface assets, in order to increase coverage within the MSPA [Maritime Security Patrol Area]; in return, the United States, within legal constraints, will share information and coordinate with non-CMF member navies that are acting to repress piracy. The United States will also encourage the maritime industry to increase its use of the MSPA, in order to enhance its effectiveness.[39]

The United States promised to establish an interagency Counterpiracy Steering Group to coordinate US activities. To industry (largely shippers) and its international partners, the administration pledged to disrupt pirate financing and facilitate strategic communications about the piracy threat and what was being done to address it. In short, the planning document consisted of exhortation, persuasion, and promises.

The Government Accountability Office criticized the Action Plan in 2010 because it had not been revised since its promulgation in 2008. During those intervening two years, pirates had changed tactics. This included operating further out in the Indian Ocean to avoid detection. Moreover, counterpiracy efforts lacked measures of effectiveness.[40] Still, the GAO credited the US Navy and Coast Guard for achieving an "interdiction-capable presence" by providing "assets and leadership to coalition forces patrolling off the Horn of Africa."[41] Perhaps heartened by this silver lining, Bush pressed forward with a Sponsorship strategy that involved three separate coalitions in the fight against piracy off the Horn of Africa: the US-led Combined Maritime Forces, NATO, and the European Union's EUNAVFOR. This arrangement proved effective, as incidents of piracy declined precipitously after 2011.[42] The US role in this combined operation belies many of the assumptions associated with hegemonic strategies.

## The Combined Maritime Forces

The US Naval Forces Central Command (NAVCENT) directs US counterpiracy efforts off the Horn of Africa. It controls the Combined Maritime Forces, headquartered in Djibouti. CMF involves three Combined Task Forces—150,

151, and 152. Combined Task Force 150 (CTF-150) was established after 9/11, and shortly thereafter was reestablished as a multinational coalition to undertake counterterrorism operations at sea as part of Operation Enduring Freedom. Over time, CTF-150's scope grew "to encompass and address commonly perceived threats to member states and their values."[43] Thus CTF-150 conducted whatever counterpiracy operations were stipulated under the broad mandate of maritime security in the entire region between 2001 and 2009.

As part of its mission, CTF-150 designated a Maritime Security Patrol Area in the Gulf of Aden to protect shipping from "destabilizing activities."[44] This 2008 initiative predated both the creation of CTF-151—CENTCOM's specific counterpiracy operation—and subsequent initiatives by NATO and the European Union. CENTCOM's MPSA defined the geographic and policy parameters for future American counterpiracy operations. This included the establishment of a Piracy High Risk Area Initiative where the shipping industry, encouraged by the United States and United Kingdom, has implemented best practices to make commercial vessels less vulnerable to pirate attacks.

By February 2009, the Internationally Recommended Transit Corridor (IRTC) had replaced the MSPA.[45] The IRTC, depicted in figure 5.1, is "a corridor between Somalia and Yemen within international waters, consisting of two lanes, each of five nautical miles (nm) width, one eastbound and one westbound, with a space of two nm between them. The total length of the transit corridor is 480 nm, and a vessel maintaining 14 knots requires 34.5 hours to pass through it."[46] All three counterpiracy coalitions patrol the IRTC in the Gulf of Aden—the High Risk Area—often escorting commercial vessels registered with the Maritime Security Centre Horn of Africa.

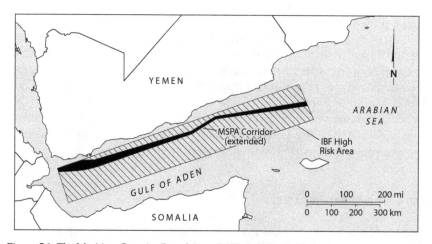

Figure 5.1. The Maritime Security Patrol Area (MSPA) in the Gulf of Aden

Somali pirates established operational bases in Somalian ports. Between 2007 and 2010 they attacked more than 450 ships in shipping lanes abutting the Horn of Africa, taking nearly 2,400 hostages.[47] Combined Task Force-150 operated as a largely US effort with close allies focused primarily on countering "terrorist acts and related illegal activities, which terrorists use to fund or conceal their movements."[48] But in 2009, CTF-151, a second multinational task force, was added under the Combined Maritime Forces.

In 2009, Vice Admiral William Gortney, then commander of the Fifth Fleet, explained that the rationale behind CTF-151's founding was partially institutional: "Some navies in our coalition did not have the authority to conduct counterpiracy missions. The establishment of 151 will allow those nations to operate under the auspices of CTF 150, while allowing other nations to join CTF 151 to support our goal of deterring, disrupting and eventually bringing to justice the maritime criminals involved in piracy events."[49] Numerous UN Security Council resolutions have been invoked by the United States and its partners in CTF-151 to justify the abrogation of the sovereignty of vessels suspected of piracy when boarding them.

Participation in CTF-151 is purely voluntary. It really is a "coalition of the willing." Many members are American allies or partners.[50] No nation is asked to carry out any activity that it is unwilling to conduct. Each country's contribution depends on the timely availability of its naval assets.[51]

The operations of the Combined Maritime Forces, and thus CTF-151, are coordinated from NAVCENT's Naval Support Activity Bahrain. American Coast Guard Law Enforcement Detachments operate aboard American vessels assigned to CTF-151 to support boarding operations and to train personnel on legal issues and evidence procedures.[52] Yet, critically for a Sponsorship strategy, command of CTF-151 rotates among the participating navies.[53] The United States furnishes critical resources and infrastructure but does not lead. It has ceded leadership of the mission to a coalition of countries, operating under the auspices of international law. But it has gained invaluable operational resources required to enhance freedom of the seas.

The size and composition of CTF-151 has varied over time. In 2009, it consisted of approximately twenty ships, drawn from fourteen countries.[54] By 2014, fourteen ships were involved, in addition to maritime surveillance aircraft and requisite shore facilities. But some CTF-151 participants hold joint counterpiracy exercises, drills, and operations to augment capacity. The size of the force is thus not reflective of the total number of resources it can deploy. Two things have remained constant: CTF-151's legitimacy under international law, and the US role in supporting the framework and providing resources.

## Allied and Partner Counterpiracy Contributions

As Vice Admiral Gortney noted, some states that contributed to CTF-151 at its creation did not have the institutional capacity to act unilaterally. Others—the European Union and NATO—were hesitant to participate under the auspices of an American-dominated operation. For domestic political reasons and the need to demonstrate their utility in a changing security environment, both the EU and NATO established their own maritime task forces in the region.

### NATO'S COUNTERPIRACY EFFORT

NATO has undertaken three separate counterpiracy missions since 2008: Operations Allied Provider, Allied Protector, and Ocean Shield. NATO member misgivings about potential American dominance may have led them to establish a separate task force. Yet their counterpiracy missions were and remain intertwined with CTF-151 and, as we will show, an EU operation as well. Thirteen EU members participate in CTF-151, for example, at the same time that the EU is conducting its own operations. All three coalitions share some communications, command and control, and intelligence functions.

NATO's operation has evolved. In October 2008, at the UN's request, NATO deployed three warships to conduct antipiracy duties off Somalia's coast as part of Operation Allied Provider: ITS *Durand de la Penne*, HS *Temistokles*, and HMS *Cumberland*. They were initially assigned to guard World Food Program vessels providing humanitarian aid to Somalia. Thereafter, they patrolled routes considered most susceptible to criminal acts against merchant vessels.[55]

Allied Provider was a temporary operation, largely superseded by an EU mission named Atalanta in December 2008.[56] But in March 2009, NATO returned to the area with Operation Allied Protector. Allied Protector used NATO member state naval vessels to escort shipping ferrying humanitarian assistance.[57] Operation Ocean Shield replaced Operation Allied Protector in August 2009, with a more robust mandate. Ocean Shield had four major objectives: "Deterring and disrupting pirate operations at sea, coordinating international counter-piracy efforts, enhancing the maritime community's capacity to counter piracy effectively, and developing a regional counter-piracy capability."[58] Problematically, the two NATO naval forces that rotated into and out of the Gulf of Aden were not strengthened to meet this mandate.

Four or five ships supplemented by maritime patrol aircraft—all contributed by NATO member states—now routinely deploy off the Horn of Africa. The United States has remained the single largest contributor to Operation Ocean Shield since its inception. But systematically disengaging, it has not contributed a ship since 2013.[59] By 2016, the EU had become a larger contributor to Somali counterpiracy missions, although it too relies heavily on both NATO and the United States to keep its mission operating.

## THE EUROPEAN UNION'S OPERATION

One month after NATO launched Operation Allied Provider, the EU launched Atalanta under the auspices of the European Union Naval Force Somalia (EUNAVFOR). It is a larger and longer-term naval operation than NATO's mission, albeit it with similar purposes.[60] EUNAVFOR is an inter-governmental ad-hoc operation, reliant on voluntary contributions. Operationally headquartered at Northwood, just outside London, it is staffed by officers from the Royal Navy, other contributing EU navies, and representatives from industry.[61] Command rotates among its contributors.

Gradually EUNAVFOR has extended its initial mandate beyond protection for vessels chartered by the World Food Program.[62] Its newer responsibilities include protection for the African Union Mission in Somalia; "the deterrence, prevention and repression of acts of piracy and armed robbery off the Somali coast"; "the protection of vulnerable shipping off the Somali coast"; and even "monitoring of fishing activities off the coast of Somalia."[63]

EUNAVFOR began operations in 2009 with five frigates and two full-time surveillance aircraft. Its complement has increased to a dozen ships assisted by three full-time aircraft and up to eight helicopters. EUNAVFOR's composition inevitably varies, however, with the rotation of national units. The operation's manpower requirement amounts to approximately two thousand personnel.[64] Northwood also hosts the Maritime Security Centre—Horn of Africa. Its purpose is to provide "a secure web-portal with a range of services to merchant vessels including alerts of pirate activity/attacks, risk assessment based on military intelligence, regional and world navigation news and self-protection advisory measures."[65] This intelligence gathering and dissemination center is distinct both from direct operational control on military assets and from EUNAVFOR members and the other maritime task forces operating in the same area. It serves a broader international community involved in international counterpiracy operations, including NATO, the United States, China, Japan, Russia, South Korea, Malaysia, and the Seychelles.[66] Operation Atalanta was initially scheduled to last for one year but was extended several times and has now been funded until the end of 2018.[67]

## CHINA: THE KEY OPERATIONAL "INDEPENDENT"

In addition to these multilateral operations, several states have contributed to counterpiracy campaigns by deploying independent forces. These include the navies of China, India, Russia, and Ukraine. It is relatively easy for countries such as India to contribute, given its cordial relationship with Washington. But that is not true for China and Russia. Both countries will not operate under anything that looks like a US command structure. Their willingness to contribute serves to affirm that the United States is pursuing a Sponsorship strategy, not Leadership. They can participate without risking national embarrassment or domestic opposition. International laws and UN resolutions, coupled with an absence of formal American Leadership, provide them with political cover.

China initially discussed contributing through the NATO and EU counterpiracy missions. It offered, for example, to assist the EU forces in escorting World Food Program shipments to Somalia in 2010.[68] The following year, it engaged in discussions with NATO about counterpiracy operations and subsequently, "China has intersected largely with NATO operations."[69] The size of China's commitment has been noteworthy. Between 2008 and 2012, the PLAN deployed thirteen task forces, amounting to thirty-four ships and ten thousand personnel.[70] Ultimately, from China's perspective, its participation can be characterized as a success. When several attacks were launched in the early months of 2017, after an extended quiet period, it was Chinese forces that captured or repelled the pirate craft.[71]

## The American Sponsorship of Multilateral Counterpiracy Operations

The United States plays a critical operational role, sponsoring the maritime task forces and independent contributors operating in the same location. There are three key elements to its activities.

Perhaps the most important US contribution is organizing communications—specifically its creation and maintenance of a Common Operating Picture (COP) for all participating navies. In military parlance, a COP is a "single identical display of relevant information shared by more than one command."[72] It is critical for "collaborative planning and assists all echelons to achieve situational awareness."[73] The overall operational picture is disseminated via classified military systems (MCCIS, Link11, NSAWAN, and CENTRIXS)[74] and is accessible to most (but not all) countries participating in CMF, NATO, or EUNAVFOR—plus Japan and South Korea as longstanding US allies.[75]

Effective communication presents an ongoing challenge.[76] It can be excruciating for independents supporting multilateral counterpiracy operations. The *People's Daily* captures the dimensions of the problem: "Activities of suspicious ships through network mailbox and radio station every day and shared information resources with 50-odd warships of 20-plus countries and organizations."[77]

Alternatives to the US system have problems. Several partners operate their own communications systems. For Operation Atalanta, the EU established Mercury, an internet-based information exchange between all fleets and "a basic Common Operating Picture displaying merchant shipping transiting the Gulf of Aden." Mercury is a "secure 'real time' chat system for military navies, gathering 120 accounts from almost all the locally involved warships. It is, for example, a key tool for the EU to communicate with the Chinese and Russian fleets."[78] But even in the context of NATO— with decades of operational experience and exercises—there remain numerous complications in using these alternative systems. As one US officer observed, "Within our own services [we] have [an] issue [with] terms and definitions. Then with NATO you have those terms, and then expand to those [navies] you may not necessarily have alliances with, and that does introduce more room for error."[79]

Communications are essential to avoiding mistakes and fatalities. US naval predominance partially stems from its unparalleled technological capacity to link sea services, enduring allies, coalition partners, and countries that are (at best) marginally cooperative and (at worst) possible future adversaries. CENTRIXS is technically superior to other options and is better positioned to overcome this collective action problem. Nevertheless, the United States seeks to improve it. As one officer-turned-analyst suggests, "We must move beyond limited approaches to link a few secure common systems with software applications like CENTRIXS, and get to a fully integrated regional picture from ports to harbors and into the commons."[80]

The second major US contribution is to synchronize (with EUNAVFOR and NATO) much of the organizational framework that underpins regional collaboration. The SHADE (Shared Awareness and Deconfliction) mechanism provides a critical example.[81] SHADE is "not organization but a facilitating venue," open to all navies and associated institutions interested in combating piracy. The United States funds SHADE. But "it is not simply U.S.-led, as U.S. Central Command (CENTCOM) and U.S. Naval Forces Central Command (NAVCENT) do not do any tasking and all involved navies maintain sovereignty and vetoes over their participation."[82]

SHADE is a monthly forum used by naval forces to coordinate counterpiracy operations in the international transit corridor and the high-risk zone of the western Indian Ocean. Members rotate chairing monthly meetings. SHADE initially coordinated CMF, EUNAVFOR, and NATO operations, but it has now grown to include virtually all navies. By 2012 "twenty organizations and twenty-seven countries were participating in SHADE meetings."[83] SHADE played an important role in the dissemination of the Mercury communications systems, encouraging "depoliticized" discussions at the tactical level. Access to CENTRIXS communications remains possible only for NATO members or individual states only by special agreement with the United States. It remains an essential platform for communications between the United States and trusted allies; other partners use Mercury instead. As one senior European Union official characterized it in a confidential interview,

"SHADE is undoubtedly the most important contribution made by the United States to the counterpiracy operation. It is indispensable."[84]

Both communications and facilitating organizational innovations involve predominantly military-to-military relations. America's third major contribution consists of encouraging companies to be active in their own defense. From a governmental perspective, it makes financial sense for shippers to defend their vessels or obstruct armed pirates when attacked. In 2015, for example, Oceans beyond Piracy, a nongovernmental organization, estimated that the world's navies collectively spent approximately $323 million on operations while private firms spent over $618 million providing armed guards.[85] American officials have worked extensively on burden-sharing, to improve awareness and implementation of best self-defense practices in the shipping and insurance industries.[86]

In 2009, the United States and several other governments signed a Commitment to Best Management Practices to Avoid, Deter or Delay Acts of Piracy (the so-called New York Declaration). National signatories to the New York Declaration commit themselves to promoting internationally recognized best management practices for self-protection. Additionally, signatory countries (with the exception of the United Kingdom) commit to ensuring that vessels on their registry have adopted and documented self-protection measures in their Ship Security Plans.[87] Representatives from the Bahamas, Liberia, Marshall Islands, and Panama signed the Declaration during the third plenary of the Contact Group, held at the UN New York headquarters in May 2009.[88] Later, at the fourth plenary, the United States, United Kingdom, Japan, Cyprus, and Singapore joined them.

Yet this description of the US contribution to the counterpiracy initiative does not explain why it chose a Sponsorship strategy. Those reasons are consistent with the logic of American self-interest.

## The Logic and Consequences of US Sponsorship

Sponsorship strategies, whether formal or informal, are commonly employed when all sides share a common agenda. Piracy is clearly a collective action problem. As one European Union official suggested in a confidential interview, "Everyone hates pirates and that was the common denominator."[89] In practice, piracy disrupts international trade without any bias as to its victims' national origins. Maintaining trade flows preoccupies all major trading nations. Smaller countries in the region have an additional concern: the effects of piracy on tourism.[90] But, in a rare example of complementarity, the United States and other forces in this case share a comparable interest in pursuing a policy and—just as important—they share it for largely the same reasons.

All parties had an incentive to join the coalition. None needed to be persuaded, cajoled, bribed, or forced to participate—and the question of free ridership was overcome by a simple principle: contribute what you can. Bigger independent states did not want to be seen as shirking their responsibilities, risking their own vessels or nationals, or (worse yet) viewed as reliant on the United States. Smaller states often wanted to be seen as active, either as a matter of national pride or as a way to demonstrate that they were responsible global citizens. From an American perspective, these are close to ideal circumstances for a Sponsorship strategy.

But why did US planners choose Sponsorship over Leadership in this case? The succinct answer is that it was a logical strategic response to the problem, in terms of the nature of the actors, the threat, and the highly irregular form of conflict entailed. Benefits for the United States were threefold: the reduction in financial cost and the associated capacity for burden sharing; the likely effectiveness of the counterpiracy plan; and the ability to disengage without reputational or strategic loss. All would be accomplished under UN mandates that gave unquestioned legitimacy, even among Somali officials whose sovereignty was transgressed. Those officials characterized the campaign as a means to "build their country's capacity, protect its exclusive economic zone and prosecute criminals."[91]

Asymmetric capabilities often also entail asymmetric costs. Pirates may be ill-equipped, but policing such a huge expanse of ocean still renders this irregular form of conflict a logistical problem. In political terms, the limited regional scope, coupled with a poorly armed enemy, had a distinct advantage—it made the operation appear "winnable" at the outset. Again, this was helpful to the United States.

But the ability to win a "war against piracy" in the abstract is one thing. Doing so at a reasonable price, while using expensive resources that could (arguably) be better employed elsewhere, is quite another. In an era of budgetary stringency, it made better sense to sacrifice the appearance of political leadership in favor of fiscal prudence and the tactical management of military resources. So, the burden has been shared.

Furthermore, the creation of the NATO and EURNAVFOR task forces, coupled with independent states, acted as a force multiplier. Both the Chinese and the Russians have contributed to an extent inconceivable had the Americans led the operation. Yet the Americans contributed the means for communication and organizing that allowed them to coordinate and collaborate with other nations.

The notion of "success" in any American military operation is routinely contested—it is much easier to spot a "failure." But planners chose Sponsorship based on its prospects for dealing with both piracy and, prospectively, terrorism. That choice has proved the right one: the regional campaign against piracy has been a success if judged by the simplest measure, the number of attacks. Since 2010, they have slowly but surely diminished (see table 5.1), although, after a period of stability, four were reported in the first three months of 2017, including one successful hijacking.[92]

**Table 5.1 Piracy off the Somali Coast, 2008–2016**

|  | 2008 | 2009 | 2010 | 2011 | 2012 | 2013 | 2014 | 2015 | 2016 |
|---|---|---|---|---|---|---|---|---|---|
| Suspicious events | 8 | 59 | 99 | 166 | 74 | 20 | 5 | 1 | 1 |
| Total attacks | 24 | 163 | 174 | 176 | 35 | 7 | 2 | 0 | 0 |
| Of which pirated | 14 | 46 | 47 | 25 | 4 | 0 | 0 | 0 | 0 |
| Disruptions | 0 | 14 | 65 | 28 | 16 | 10 | 1 | 0 | 0 |

Source: http://eunavfor.eu/key-facts-and-figures/.

Still, attacks have been rare in recent years.[93] NATO concluded its mission by the end of 2016 and the Americans had effectively done so already. The EU formally extended its mission until the end of 2018 but reassigned assets to the Mediterranean in 2016, to address migrant and arms flows closer to home. Nonetheless, a skeletal force remains and independents are still active, notably Chinese vessels that repelled three of the four more recent attacks.[94]

Analysts argue about what caused this decline. The conventional wisdom holds that the three major maritime task forces deterred regional pirates from attempting to seize commercial vessels. Contrarian analysts argue that "they have actually caused pirates to push out of the Gulf of Aden deep into the Indian Ocean and to adopt more sophisticated technology and weaponry in response."[95] The problem may have been largely displaced rather than resolved, although in a confidential interview a prominent NATO official denied that claim.[96] Still, in terms of the immediate problem, the Obama administration's selection of a Sponsorship strategy seems to have been vindicated. And forces remain present to address any residual problem.

Finally, there is the thorny issue of disengagement. As America's recent wars (and our chapter on the Persian Gulf) vividly illustrate, engagement is easy; disengagement usually comes at a high price. This was not the case with counterpiracy. The American forces involved in the campaign against piracy were skeletal by the summer of 2016.[97] CTF-151 did remain active, although the number of counterpiracy missions for the United States had declined; indeed, it had not contributed a warship to NATO's Operation Ocean Shield since December 2013. Nonetheless, despite the United States' more muted diplomatic and military role, the Contact Group on Piracy in 2016 was composed of more than eighty countries. It had assumed an increasingly significant role in addressing regional maritime threats, even as piracy attacks declined. Indeed, at the spring 2016 meeting of the Contact Group in Mumbai, "members agreed on further regionalizing the work of the group and working towards a sustainable transition strategy as a core objective. Among other points discussed at the meeting were the extensions of the . . . mandate to cover maritime security issues, including illegal fishing and piracy situations in other regions, such as West Africa, or Southeast Asia."[98] As one NATO official suggested, members were reluctant to disband the Contact Group because of its utility.[99] Thus, resolving the immediate problem and the evolution of the Contact Group has left the United States with legitimate options without the constraints associated with many foreign policy initiatives.

Jonathan Stevenson asserts that "most naval commanders do not consider the containment of the piracy problem a central military task, seeing it as a distraction from core counter-terrorism, counter-proliferation, deterrence and war-fighting missions."[100] Stevenson is correct; strategists in general and the USN in particular are certain that there are higher priority missions for their resources. Yet the US Navy adapted to the challenge by establishing a task force (albeit with secondary implications for antiterrorism) when piracy off the Horn of Africa threatened to disrupt a key artery of global commerce.

The US government did not attempt to assume the burden alone, nor did it set the agenda for reluctant partners. Rather, it built on the legal and political foundations established by the UN Security Council to adopt a cooperative approach in which America was a key participant. The USN helped make it possible for NATO and the EU to operate two legs of a tripartite approach. It provided key operational and institutional support that allowed the less-experienced and less-capable navies of its allies and partners to contribute effectively while affording powerful independents a political context in which they could participate. And it did so while avoiding an indefinite presence in the region. Specifically, the United States has molded sustainable institutional arrangements for deconfliction and collaboration to confront piracy that do not require it to play a central political role, while furnishing the technical means for participants with a Common Operating Picture. For states that are not cleared for access to American intelligence, it allows connection at a decreased level of integration

By any reasonable measure, the multinational counterpiracy operation off the Horn of Africa has proved successful. Attacks by Somali pirates within striking distance of the littoral had virtually disappeared by 2015. They reappeared in 2017, but commercial shipping in the region is far safer today than at any time in recent history. The USN has ceased providing ships for counterpiracy operations; but other navies continue to provide smaller numbers of ships. By 2016, debate concentrated on whether to expand the operation, in terms both of geographical scope and of other forms of maritime security.

In the long run, of course, the threat of regional piracy remains unresolved, at the very least until the failed state of Somalia has established effective governance over its own territory. War, poverty, and even famine still tempt prospective pirates. The 2011 testimony of Ray Mabus, then secretary of the Navy, still resonates:

> We are treating the symptoms of piracy, rather than its fundamental cause: Somalia's failure as a state. Despite the international community's commitment, piracy has both continued to increase and move further offshore, a measure of pirate resiliency and the strong economic incentives that underpin it. Nine of ten pirates captured are ultimately freed as there is often insufficient evidence or political will to prosecute them, or to incarcerate them after conviction.

In terms of future strategic options, Mabus noted that "we strongly *endorse* [emphasis added] additional international efforts to address these concerns,"[101] implying continuation of a Sponsorship strategy.

As a practical matter, suppressing piracy was an extremely important first step in guarding the maritime commons. In 2009, Secretary of State Hillary Clinton explained the nation's maritime approach toward Somali piracy by stating that "[you] have to try to put out the fire before rebuilding the house."[102] The international community, with the assistance of the US Navy, appears to have effectively done so. Will it be satisfied with a policy of containment, or will mission creep ensue? The question remains open.

# Navigating the Proliferation Security Initiative and Informal Sponsorship

> Part of his mission as president, Obama explained, is to spur other countries to take action for themselves, rather than wait for the U.S. to lead. The defense of the liberal international order against jihadist terror, Russian adventurism, and Chinese bullying depends in part, he believes, on the willingness of other nations to share the burden with the U.S. This is why the controversy surrounding the assertion—made by an anonymous administration official to *The New Yorker* during the Libya crisis of 2011—that his policy consisted of "leading from behind" perturbed him. "We don't have to always be the ones who are up front," he told me. "Sometimes we're going to get what we want precisely because we are sharing in the agenda. The irony is that it was precisely in order to prevent the Europeans and the Arab states from holding our coats while we did all the fighting that we, by design, insisted" that they lead during the mission to remove Muammar Qaddafi from power in Libya. "It was part of the anti–free rider campaign."
>
> —Barack Obama speaking to Jeffrey Goldberg, April 2015

Sponsorship strategies come in two forms. The distinction is less complex and extensive than that between Primacy and Leadership. Those hegemonic strategies differ fundamentally in terms of values, means, and resources, but they share a fundamental overriding goal: American preeminence. The differences between the two forms of Sponsorship are subtle. In both, the United States defers to other actors, for example when "setting the agenda." Both rely on multilateral coalitions. And both entail a far more equitable degree of burden sharing than is the case with hegemonic strategies.

The two versions of Sponsorship differ in two main respects. The first is the extent to which the policies being implemented have undergone a formal process of codification and juridification. In formal Sponsorship, principles are codified through international law and protocols, often within international organizations. Greater codification reflects a "top-down" strategy in that the protocols and laws agreed by states are implemented locally by authorized actors. Conversely, informal Sponsorship employs a "bottom-up" approach in which the operating principles are based on widely agreed norms, not laws.[1] Formal strategies, as they are based on law, have greater legitimacy. The second difference is their degree of institutionalization. Laws often provide specificity as to where, when, and how they can be applied. Their absence leads to variations in the implementation of informal Sponsorship, depending on context. Lesser degrees of institutionalization imply fewer constraints, and thus greater autonomy, for those implementing the strategy.

This sets up an interesting tension. Formal Sponsorship, as in the American operations described in the previous chapter, benefit from authority derived from law. But that same legal authority also constrains what the actors can do. Informal Sponsorship lacks the same legal authority, and so is fluid and open to interpretation. The norms used to justify informal Sponsorship strategies are often widely accepted. But few are universally embraced.[2] Conversely, they give states more latitude to act.

In tandem, these differences have significant implications. Formal versions are less vulnerable to lawfare because of their juridical character and legal formulation. They may be attacked in international courts but they can be justified by law. Informal Sponsorship strategies are more vulnerable to accusations that those implementing the strategy are acting in a discretionary manner. There is a trade-off between the two Sponsorship strategies: the former has greater legitimacy, the latter a greater degree of discretion.

That distinction is illustrated in the decision to intercept a vessel on the high seas. Doing so breaches national sovereignty—a principal deeply embedded in international law.[3] In the absence of a countervailing law, those carrying out an interdiction rely on evidence of malfeasance by an offending party to justify their actions. Failure to provide evidence undermines the legitimacy critical to any Sponsorship strategy and may also deter future interdictions. This is where our chapter on informal Sponsorship strategy begins.

On May 26, 2011, the USS *McCampbell* intercepted the M/V *Light*, a North Korean–owned and –manned freighter registered under the flag of Belize, in international waters south of Shanghai, China. The United States suspected the M/V *Light* of carrying missile technology, although its manifest acknowledged only industrial chemicals bound for Bangladesh.[4] The M/V *Light* refused the American destroyer's repeated request to board. After consulting with senior officials, the *McCampbell*'s commanding officer chose not to escalate the situation by forcibly boarding the vessel. The *McCampbell* turned over surveillance of the M/V *Light* to planes and satellites. Shortly thereafter the North Korean vessel returned to its home port.[5]

The USS *McCampbell* is an Arleigh Burke–class guided-missile destroyer (DDG 85)—among the most technologically advanced warships in the US Navy. The *McCampbell* had been based in Japan since 2007 as part of the US Seventh Fleet. Designed as a multimission ship capable of performing tasks from straightforward intercept operations to fleet maneuvers during high-intensity operations against technologically sophisticated adversaries, the *McCampbell* was commissioned in 2000, when the Navy estimated its cost to be between $60 and $100 million.[6] The Federation of American Scientists estimates that it costs $20 million per year to operate a single Arleigh Burke.[7] In shadowing the M/V *Light*, the *McCampbell* was operating at the bottom-rung of its capabilities.

Its interception of the M/V *Light* was one of the few publicly acknowledged operations under the Proliferation Security Initiative (PSI). The incident is a classic example of the little-known skirmishes in a high-stakes campaign to prevent so-called rogue states from smuggling fissile materials and WMD components. The PSI itself is an application of a strategy of informal Sponsorship in a key area of national security—the diffusion of nuclear, chemical, and biological materials to adversarial states, terrorist groups, and criminal enterprises.

Many prominent analysts promote the view that the negotiation of multilateral nonproliferation agreements is an area in which America leads.[8] They focus on the principles and proposed measures, reinforcing the idea that the United States benignly "sets the agenda" and in doing so generates collective benefits. But such commentary often ignores the practical implementation of measures designed to thwart the diffusion of fissile materials. In this chapter we examine how American politicians and the US military actually try to address implementation challenges. We find that they employ an informal Sponsorship that departs significantly from conventional characterizations.

## Domestic Politics, PSI, and American Nonproliferation Policies

The United States was the first country to develop and use atomic weapons, and it has spent the decades since attempting to limit their proliferation. American nonproliferation strategies have expanded in depth and complexity, and they currently involve four major initiatives: creating international legal regimes, limiting supplies for those with nuclear ambitions, reducing the demand for weapons of mass destruction, and—most aggressively—military intervention "intended to prevent or destroy nuclear arsenals."[9] Various forms of nonproliferation have been codified into US law with the passage of domestic legislation as well as the ratification of international treaties. Undergirding both American and international efforts is the emergence of international norms regarding nonproliferation.[10]

These, as we will demonstrate, have supported the development of the PSI. Realist scholars and policy analysts sometimes discount these norms, but others suggest that they—and the overarching nonproliferation regime—have been "widely successful" in their own terms.[11] Consistent with a trend toward a global consensus on nonproliferation has been an increasing use of military and law enforcement to support the nonproliferation regime. There are numerous examples of the use of military force against nations thought to possess weapons of mass destruction, such as the 1991 Persian Gulf War and, infamously, the invasion of Iraq in 2003.[12] Yet the ineffective hunt for Scuds missiles in western Iraq during Operation Desert Storm illustrated the extreme difficulty of finding delivery systems that might be used in combination with weapons of mass destruction.[13] Planners thus began searching for better ways to prevent states not party to, or not abiding by, the Nuclear Nonproliferation Treaty (NPT) from acquiring the weapons or the means to produce them.

One primary way to do so entails expanding US activities to curtail the transit of fissile materials. Those operations, justified by UN protocols, are intended to prevent states or nonstate actors from acquiring nuclear fuel and/or building weapons. American intelligence agencies and military services have used their assets to combat proliferation and to destroy weapons, nuclear materials, and various aspects of nuclear programs such as research facilities. A hallmark of these efforts is reliance on collaboration with an increasingly large number of countries, for the pool of potential proliferators has expanded to the point where the United States can help underwrite global initiatives but cannot enforce them unilaterally.

The PSI itself blends civilian-based political, legal, and diplomatic efforts with initiatives that rely on military and intelligence resources. The United States works closely with other countries opposed to the proliferation of WMD-related materials. This chapter focuses on how the US military, largely the maritime services, implements PSI.

From the US perspective, PSI is a marriage of convenience. It links those who advocate strengthening the nonproliferation regime to hawks who advocate military solutions, including preemptive attack.[14] If nothing else, enlisting the intelligence community and military services in nonproliferation efforts—whether to destroy weapons and facilities or to interdict weapons, precursors, or traveling scientists who sell their expertise to the higher bidder—has vastly increased the resources the United States devotes to stopping the spread of WMD.

Nevertheless, the United States does not possess the military reach or legal jurisdiction to pursue a Leadership strategy on nonproliferation. The operational demands are simply overwhelming, and abrogating the sovereignty of foreign countries has too many political consequences in the absence of global consensus. Rather, the "world's sheriff" has followed the lead of other states, while pushing efforts to strengthen global nonproliferation. Certainly, the United States has shouldered the "bulk of logistical, financial, diplomatic, intelligence, and military support for all international non-proliferation efforts, including the NPT."[15] Nonetheless, in concert with like-minded states, the United States has supported an international legal regime to close loopholes and adjust to new technical challenges. It has also pursued a less-publicized strategy with PSI: informal Sponsorship. Despite its evident limitations, PSI has proved to be operationally manageable and politically more palatable to participating states.

## Emergent Threats and Emergent Actors

After a slow start,[16] President Clinton "elevated nonproliferation policy to unprecedented importance" and "declared a national state of emergency."[17] In a September 1993 speech before the UN General Assembly, he argued that "one of our most urgent priorities must be attacking the proliferation of weapons of mass destruction, whether they are nuclear, chemical, or biological; and the ballistic missiles that can rain them down on populations hundreds of miles away. . . . If we do not stem the proliferation of the world's deadliest weapons, no democracy can feel secure."[18] The following year, Clinton issued Presidential Decision Directive PDD/NSC 18 that established the Defense Counter-Proliferation Initiative (DCI).[19] It recognized the shifting away from a Cold War world toward one in which weapons of mass destruction might become available to numerous adversaries. It also gave intelligence agencies and the military services new missions. As Secretary of Defense Les Aspin suggested, the DCI comprised "five elements: One, creation of the new mission by the president; two, changing what we buy to meet the threat; three, planning to fight wars differently; four, changing how we collect intelligence and what intelligence we collect; and finally, five, doing all these things with our allies."[20]

In brief, Clinton had already moved toward interdiction prior to George W. Bush's formal announcement of America's support for the PSI in May 2003.[21] The initiative initially met with resistance from the arms control community outside government and, more important in this context, the Department of Defense and other agencies that supported nonproliferation.[22] Furthermore, critics suggested that the fact Aspin (and not Clinton) made the 1993 announcement reduced US government support for the initiative. One staff member of the House Armed Services Committee suggests that money, the classic weapon of bureaucratic infighting, was the root cause of the lukewarm reception: "The military services reacted skeptically, seeing the DCI as (1) a potential drain on service budgets already strained to the breaking point and (2) as another OSD [Office of the Secretary of Defense] driven "initiative," such as the Strategic Defense Initiative: imposed from above without a great deal of forethought and with little or no involvement of the military."[23] Aspin did not propose a budget increase to buy the hardware needed to implement the DCI. Rather, he proposed that the services themselves provide the required $300–$400 million.[24] It did not help matters when Ashton Carter, then a senior Pentagon official, aggressively used the DCI to assert the policy prerogatives of civilians over the military. With regard to service resistance to spending $400 million on DCI, Carter noted that if the services "do not hear the music, then we will have to do it ourselves."[25] In the end, Admiral William Owen, then Vice Chairman of the Joint Chiefs of Staff, negotiated to reduce DCI funding to roughly $60–$80 million annually for fiscal years 1996–2000 while making counterproliferation a priority of the Joint Chiefs. This ensured a warfighter orientation on the practical meaning of counterproliferation and which systems would be required to fulfill the mission.

An ill-timed incident involving a Chinese vessel suspected of carrying precursor chemicals for the manufacture of Sarin and mustard gas dampened enthusiasm for these interdiction efforts. In the summer of 1993, the US Navy tracked and photographed the *Yinhe* from China to the Persian Gulf. After protracted negotiations, Chinese authorities permitted Saudi officials to inspect the vessel: no chemical precursors were found. This miscue publicly embarrassed the Clinton administration and American intelligence agencies. It also had two lasting consequences: it contributed to China's abiding reluctance to join the PSI, and it encouraged China to build up its naval capabilities (presumably a more powerful navy would dissuade the United States from aggressive treatment of Chinese vessels).[26] Of course, Beijing's reasons for modernizing its navy are far more complex, but it does seem clear that some Chinese officials were embarrassed by their vessel's treatment.

In the aftermath of the 9/11 attacks, the George W. Bush administration focused on threats posed by terrorists and rogue states. Those attacks gave credence to prior warnings that terrorists planned to kill large numbers of Americans using WMD. Eventually, the capture of Al Qaeda research and planning documents confirmed what intelligence warnings had already revealed: Al Qaeda had taken steps to acquire nuclear, biological, and chemical weapons.[27]

As a result, the United States adapted its nonproliferation posture to curtail the access of nonstate actors to fissile materials. The Bush administration moved beyond Clinton's approach by developing more proactive nonproliferation initiatives. President Bush announced the Bush doctrine in a speech in 2002, declaring that the United States would consider preemptive and preventive wars, even regime change, when threatened by terrorists or regimes harboring terrorists.[28] He commented, "We cannot put our faith in the word of tyrants who solemnly sign nonproliferation treaties and then systematically break them. If we wait for threats to fully materialize we will have waited too long." Bush made clear that the term *tyrants* extended beyond states. "The gravest danger to freedom," he suggested, "lies at the perilous crossroads of radicalism and technology. When the spread of chemical and biological and nuclear weapons, along with ballistic missile technology—when that occurs even weak states and small groups could attain a catastrophic power to strike great nations."[29] Beyond the new emphasis on preemption, this declaration also focused US policy on the threatened acquisition of WMD by nonstate actors.

The President's logic justified other proactive military measures. Later that year, with the publication of the *National Strategy to Combat Weapons of Mass Destruction*, the Bush administration served notice that it would use the full range of US government resources, with an emphasis on interdiction: "Effective interdiction is a critical part of the U.S. strategy to combat WMD and their delivery means. We must enhance the capabilities of our military, intelligence, technical, and law enforcement communities to prevent the movement of WMD materials, technology, and expertise to hostile states and terrorist organizations."[30]

Subsequent events encouraged the administration to expand the range of policy instruments for use against proliferators. The first incident related to the initiative, PSI supporters claim, was the interdiction of the German-owned M/V *BBC China*, originating in Dubai and bound for Libya, in October 2003.[31] Based on Anglo-American suspicions, it was diverted to Taranto, Italy, where German and Italian officials found centrifuge parts in the cargo hold.[32] The second, more significant development was the public exposure of the A. Q. Khan proliferation network in 2004.[33] Khan, a leading scientist and one of the founders of the Pakistani nuclear program, confessed to a charge of nuclear trafficking based on evidence provided by several countries including the United States.[34] The Pakistan government shut down Khan's operation and tightened security for its nuclear programs. But the revelation that a high-ranking official of a key American ally had provided equipment, materials, and knowledge to avowed American adversaries (including Libya, Iran, and North Korea) shocked both government officials and the public. The conclusion was simple: if allies were unreliable, a better way to prevent the trafficking of illicit materials was to police the global commons. Based in large part on its experience with Pakistan, the Bush administration stressed preventing "rogue states" from acquiring materials, technology, and equipment that could be used to develop WMD.

## Disavowing US Leadership

The Proliferation Security Initiative (PSI) was formally announced at a high-level political meeting in Krakow, Poland, in May 2003. Its mission was to deter and interdict the flow of nuclear, biological, and chemical weapons and precursor materials destined for, or originating from, both proliferating states (particularly Iran and North Korea) and nonstate actors, prominently terrorist groups.

The United States was one of eleven original members. Within the PSI, the United States has largely relied on other states for leadership, planning, and enforcement.[35] Each participant has publicly endorsed a Statement of Interdiction Principles stating that PSI "seeks to involve in some capacity all states that have a stake in nonproliferation and the ability and willingness to take steps to stop the flow of such items at sea, in the air, or on land," and seeks "cooperation from any state whose vessels, flags, ports, territorial waters, airspace, or land might be used for proliferation purposes by states and nonstate actors of proliferation concern."[36]

The global nature of the problem meant that membership expansion was essential for the PSI to succeed. But to obtain the necessarily broad political appeal, it could not be viewed as a vehicle for narrow American self-interest. Accordingly, the United States adopted the role of the "good international citizen," encouraging membership, compliance, and enforcement.

Yet as Bush made clear in a February 2004 speech, PSI was important for strengthening US nonproliferation efforts:

> First, I propose that the work of the Proliferation Security Initiative be expanded to address more than shipments and transfers. Building on the tools we've developed to fight terrorists, we can take direct action against proliferation networks. We need greater cooperation not just among intelligence and military services, but in law enforcement, as well. PSI participants and other willing nations should use the Interpol and all other means to bring to justice to those who traffic in deadly weapons, to shut down their labs, to seize their materials, to freeze their assets. We must act on every lead. We will find the middlemen, the suppliers and the buyers. Our message to proliferators must be consistent and it must be clear: We will find you, and we're not going to rest until you are stopped.[37]

Other PSI members shared Bush's sentiment, despite concerns over his call for intrusive measures, and PSI's membership grew. Aside from the direct targets of PSI—Iran and North Korea—only five major states resisted international pressure to join. Indonesia, Malaysia, India, Pakistan, and China all refused for a variety of reasons.[38] Malaysia and Indonesia, as archipelagic states with numerous waterways including the Malacca Strait, couched their concerns in terms of controlling territorial seas. Pakistan and India perhaps looked to the day when they might export nuclear weapons, fuel, and manufacturing facilities to other states. China remains resistant, officially over concerns about sovereignty. Nonetheless, by 2015, 133 nations had endorsed the PSI's Statement of Interdiction Principles, with even Malaysia reversing its position.[39]

President Obama explicitly embraced the initiative. In 2009, he advocated that PSI's members continue to "build on our efforts to break up black markets, detect and intercept materials in transit, and use financial tools to disrupt this dangerous trade." Obama further suggested that "because this threat will be lasting, we should come together to turn efforts such as the Proliferation Security Initiative and the Global Initiative to Combat Nuclear Terrorism into durable international institutions."[40] If his push to formalize PSI had succeeded, overcoming the objections of some members, it would have reasserted US Leadership and likely signaled the end of a Sponsorship strategy.

Members balked at Obama's idea. For many countries, greater institutionalization would reduce the scope of PSI's activities, just as formal attempts to bolster the nonproliferation regime had failed in the past—among them a Bush administration push for a UN Security Council Resolution "criminaliz[ing] proliferation on a broad scale." The initiative resulted in "a more narrow resolution that focused on nonstate actors and addressed the terrorist threats."[41]

By 2015, twenty-one countries had served as members of the PSI's Operational Experts Group (OEG)—essentially a "steering committee" for the initiative. But the PSI still has no formal structure—neither a headquarters nor a secretariat. It remains an international "activity, not an institution."[42] Nonetheless, the PSI remains a central component of US nonproliferation strategy.

## Sponsorship and the Strategic Challenge of WMD Proliferation

To understand why the United States adopted a strategy of Sponsorship requires an appreciation of the security challenge posed by proliferation—particularly the black market for weapons, delivery systems, precursor materials, and dual-use technologies. The operational complexity of implementing the PSI is daunting:

> The continued loss, theft, and illegal movement of nuclear and other radioactive materials demonstrate that material is available for terrorists to acquire and use as a weapon. Since 1993, the IAEA has logged some 2,500 cases related to the theft, loss of control, unauthorized possession, or illicit trafficking of nuclear and other radioactive material. The insecurity of nuclear and other radioactive material continues, with some 150 cases of theft, loss of control, or illicit trafficking reported annually. At least 18 cases of confirmed thefts or loss of weapons-usable nuclear material have occurred, the latest in 2011.[43]

This sobering summary may actually understate the problem. First, it focuses only on known losses. It does not account for the target of most PSI scenarios, simulations, and tabletop exercises: the deliberate proliferation of nuclear materials by states with or without the cooperation of private firms, state-owned enterprises, or other types of nonstate actors, including criminals or terrorists.

Second, it does not account for the other targets of PSI interdiction: chemical and biological weapons. Few reliable statistics exist about illegal trafficking in chemical and biological agents and the equipment necessary to weaponize them, but the respective industries suggest the problem is greater than with nuclear capabilities. Nuclear industries are highly regulated and controlled.[44] The same is not always true of the chemical and biological industries (notably, outside advanced industrial countries) and many of the technologies that can be used to manufacture weapons have legitimate commercial applications. Export licenses for "dual-use" technologies must be granted on a case-by-case basis by national customs officials, and the process requires a much higher degree of capacity than many nations can afford. There is a paucity of recent policy-relevant research on the issue,[45] but one effort concluded that "determined proliferators seem able to acquire biological and especially chemical weapons with great effort . . . CBWs [chemical and biological weapons] can be accurately characterized as the 'poor man's atomic weapon.'"[46]

Crucially, a large volume of prohibited materials flows through the international transportation system and finding them is a daunting challenge. The international maritime and air transportation systems are extremely complicated. Large numbers of state and nonstate actors operate with inadequate levels of supervision. Roughly 90 percent of the world's commerce is transported in more than fifty thousand vessels under the flags of at least 150 different nations. Even if we accept the common assumption—which we do not—that weapons and components are most likely to be transported in large container ships and bulk carriers, this still leaves more than twenty thousand ships able to carry contraband.[47]

American administrations have viewed nuclear, chemical, and biological proliferation as a security problem since the 1990s, but more recently other states have redefined proliferation as a threat. The primary distinction between the US perception and that of others is one of scope and scale. The watershed events were the Al Qaeda attacks in Spain, Great Britain, Indonesia, and the United States—and a shared fear that terrorist organizations might acquire the means, and certainly had the will, to use weapons of mass destruction.[48] This concern was magnified by public revelations about the A. Q. Khan network's assistance to Libya, Iran, and North Korea. Neighboring states felt a renewed urgency to address the flow of contraband weapons and materials.[49] The major alternatives were not palatable for other regional powers in Asia (e.g., Japan) and the Middle East (e.g., Saudi Arabia): either acquire their own nuclear weapons as a deterrent or cajole other states to participate in preemptive military action before adversaries developed full WMD capability. In effect, the flow to these "pariah" regimes—more recently termed "outlier states"—had to be stopped.[50] What many states had regarded as a narrow US problem during the Cold War widened to the entire international community.

In practice, PSI consistently targeted North Korea and Iran (at least until 2015) because they have persistently worked with illicit nonstate actors and aspired to build their own domestic military capabilities.[51] Both countries have broken international norms while evading nonproliferation enforcement instruments such as sanctions.[52] Other countries formerly of concern such as Libya or South Africa either dismantled their nuclear programs or negotiated agreements.[53] But the proliferation problem extends far beyond outlier states. The proliferation of weapons, their miniaturization, increased sophistication, and variability in delivery means (including suitcase-sized "dirty bombs" and missiles of all ranges) have made them attractive to various actors—including private-sector firms, criminal enterprises, and smugglers. As recently as 2012 in Mexico City, armed men stole cobalt-60—a "category 1" radiation source, lethal with exposure longer than a few minutes. While local authorities do not believe the material was stolen by terrorists, criminals may have seized it (the opened protective container was found in a field) and sold it to others wanting to make a "dirty bomb."[54]

It is difficult to assess the significance of incidents ranging from insiders selling nuclear materials to possible insurgent attacks on a Pakistani nuclear facility. But their sheer volume is daunting.[55] One systematic effort to document smuggling and security breaches in the Black Sea region lists several hundred events.[56] Even countries historically opposed to trafficking have been caught up in a web of illegal activities when their perceived national security interests are at stake. Yemen, for example, despite its record of "generally positive counter proliferation cooperation," was caught importing ballistic missile technologies from North Korea in 2002 when US and Spanish warships interdicted the North Korean–flagged vessel, *So San*.[57] Even "good" international citizens like Germany have been embroiled in controversy: its firms have exported precursor materials or dual-use technologies to Libya, Iraq, and Pakistan, sometimes skirting the intent of domestic laws and international agreements.[58] Further complicating the operational challenge is that many commercial intermediaries have a symbiotic relationship with proliferators. They have willingly or unwittingly provided intellectual property, subcomponents, fissile materials, precursor chemicals, and (albeit rarely) weapons or direct components.

Terrorists, of course, may also steal fully workable weapons or buy precursor materials and the equipment necessary to manufacture their own. But the conflict between PSI participants and proliferators is generally shrouded in secrecy and rarely sensationalized. It is covert, episodic, and rarely involves the direct use of force.

The response of PSI members to this hybrid challenge has taken two forms. The first has been operational: since 2003 a relatively small community known as the Operational Experts Group (OEG)—composed of lawyers, agency officials, and policymakers who need to justify intergovernmental collaboration, vessel interdiction, and the possible seizure of contraband—and individual sponsors have conducted more than sixty exercises of various types designed to enhance the success of real-world operations (see appendix 3 for a list of PSI multilateral exercises). Participants deploy military (including gendarmerie, coast guards, navy and air force) and law enforcement assets, as well as civilian officials (for example, from Justice Ministries) to conduct practices, mock interdictions, and planning meetings. Participants strive to develop multilateral coordination mechanisms, interministerial cooperative arrangements, and best practices that often result in domestic changes. PSI exercises also help generate trust and familiarity between military services, law enforcement agencies, and legal authorities in countries that rarely if ever work together.

Inspection on the high seas, as in 2002, when the *So San* was boarded six hundred nautical miles off the coast of Yemen, receive a great deal of publicity.[59] Yet in practice, internationally authorized military action is rarely required to force any vessel suspected of transporting illegal materials to enter a port for inspection. And the chance of finding ships on the high seas is low. Hence the need for a second form of response: the use of lawfare, which is better employed against ships docked in port. Indeed, in recent years, many of the publicly acknowledged "successes" of PSI are legal and administrative, not military interdictions. A 2010 assessment, for example, noted that US officials counted as successes "denying export licenses, seizing suspected cargo in ports and, in one incident denying overflight permission."[60] In many cases, vessels suspected of carrying contraband are delayed in port as they are tied up in red tape.

## Opposition to PSI at Home and Abroad

For the United States this is a curious policy area: one where it uses massive, expensive warships to conduct constabulary functions on the high seas, and where the primary "weapons" are domestic and international law. Unlike in several other cases discussed in this volume, the strategic debates are not between civilian and military officials over operational matters or prioritization. Rather, debates on PSI are mainly confined to the OEG (for a list of these meetings see table 6.1).

The USN's lawyers participate in PSI meetings, but civilian strategists do not, leaving military officials frustrated that high-level policymakers do not appreciate the significant costs of playing "traffic cop" on a maritime

**Table 6.1  PSI operational experts group meetings**

| Year | Date | Location | Description |
|---|---|---|---|
| 2003 | Jun 12 | Madrid, Spain | Core Group meeting |
| | Jul 9–10 | Brisbane, Australia | Core Group meeting |
| | Jul 30 | London, UK | Operational Experts Working Group meeting |
| | Sep 3–4 | Paris, France | Core Group meeting |
| | Oct 8–10 | London, UK | Core Group meeting |
| | Dec 16–17 | Washington, DC | Operational Experts Working Group meeting |
| 2004 | Mar 4–5 | Lisbon, Portugal | Core Group meeting |
| | Apr 16–17 | Ottawa, Canada | OEG meeting |
| | Aug 5–6 | Oslo, Norway | OEG meeting |
| | Nov 30–Dec 2 | Sydney, Australia | OEG meeting |
| 2005 | Mar 21–22 | Omaha, Nebraska | OEG meeting |
| | Jul 6–7 | Copenhagen, Denmark | OEG meeting |
| | Nov 24–26 | Hamburg, Germany | Regional (Europe) OEG meeting |
| 2006 | Apr 11–12 | Miami, Florida | OEG meeting |
| | Jul 25–26 | Singapore | OEG meeting |
| | Dec 5–7 | Montreal, Canada | OEG meeting |
| 2007 | Mar 26–28 | Auckland, New Zealand | OEG meeting |
| | Oct 2–4 | Rhodes, Greece | OEG meeting |
| 2008 | Feb 4–6 | London, UK | OEG meeting |
| | Sep 25–26 | Paris, France | OEG meeting |
| 2009 | May 12–14 | Miami, Florida | OEG meeting |
| | Jun 22–24 | Sopot, Poland | Regional (Europe) OEG meeting |
| 2010 | Sep 14–15 | Cairns, Australia | Regional (Asia-Pacific) OEG meeting |
| | Nov 1–2 | Tokyo, Japan | OEG meeting |
| 2011 | Jun 9–10 | Honolulu, Hawaii | Regional (Asia-Pacific) OEG meeting |
| | Nov 8–10 | Berlin, Germany | OEG meeting |
| 2012 | Sep 24–25 | Seoul, South Korea | OEG meeting |
| 2013 | May 28–29 | Warsaw, Poland | OEG meeting |
| 2014 | May 13–15 | Newport, Rhode Island | OEG meeting |
| 2015 | May 26–28 | Ottawa, Canada | OEG meeting |

The information in this table is sourced from the U.S. State Department's PSI "Calendar of Events," http://www.state.gov/t/isn/c27700.htm, as well as the "Activities" page of the German-hosted PSI website: http://www.psi-online.info/Vertretung/psi/en/02-activities/0-activities.html.

highway of thousands of commercial vessels. Much of this frustration stems from the Navy's view that its principal purpose is war fighting, not policing the world's waterways. Discussions among the OEG focus on tactics, techniques, and procedures rather than underlying goals such as how PSI might be improved; whether its activities should be institutionalized rather than the current "web of counter-proliferation partnerships";[61] or how members can enlarge the PSI's ranks to include important holdouts such as India, China, and several Middle Eastern countries.[62]

The US goal, however, remains halting the proliferation of weapons and/ or their precursors. The domestic American debate has remained consistent at both the policy and the strategic level: whether to "enforce international agreements" or act unilaterally in the pursuit of US national interests, even if this means pushing the boundaries of international law and the tolerance of the international community.

Yet, the United States must work with other countries, as a practical matter, to achieve an effective interdiction regime. Alone, it lacks the requisite intelligence and military forces to police the global maritime commons. Moreover, the USN lacks the authority to interdict contraband weapons or components on vessels docked in foreign ports. There is little dissent among US policymakers and military officials over PSI as a cooperative strategy for combating proliferation. Rather, the serious disagreements are about whether the United States should accept the international legal framework enabling such cooperation.

American proponents of PSI have been hampered by fundamental disagreements between a minority of US senators and their very vocal supporters in the House of Representatives and outside Congress and the Senate majority over whether the United States should support those international agreements that legalize interdiction. Both the UN Convention on the Law of the Sea (UNCLOS) and the 1988 Convention on the Suppression of Unlawful Acts against the Safety of Maritime Navigation (SUA) justify PSI activities. UNCLOS is the most important guide to what is permissible in international waters, Exclusive Economic Zones, and territorial waters. Furthermore, "UN Security Council Resolutions 1373, 1540, and 1887 require states to take steps to combat terrorism and prevent the proliferation of nonconventional weapons, including to terrorist and criminal groups."[63] These resolutions, although not specific to PSI, provide a significant legal basis for the PSI's activities and authorize (according to participants) interdiction.[64] For the range of relevant UN Security Council resolutions, see table 6.2.

Many Republican congressional leaders have opposed ratification of UNCLOS since the Reagan administration recommended against it in 1982. They object on the grounds that various UNCLOS provisions would undermine US sovereignty, unduly limiting American freedom of action. Both Republican and Democratic administrations (as well as senior naval

Table 6.2  UN conventions most relevant to PSI

| Year | Name of convention or resolution |
|------|----------------------------------|
| 1944 | Convention on International Civil Aviation (Chicago Convention) |
| 1968 | Nuclear Non-Proliferation Treaty |
| 1972 | Biological and Toxin Weapons Convention |
| 1982 | Convention on the Law of the Sea |
| 1984 | Amendment to the Chicago Convention |
| 1988 | Convention for the Suppression of Unlawful Acts against the Safety of Maritime Navigation (SUA Convention) |
| 1993 | Chemical Weapons Convention |
| 2004 | Security Council resolution 1540 |
| 2005 | Protocol to the SUA Convention |
| 2006 | Security Council Resolution 1695 (North Korea) |
| 2006 | Security Council Resolution 1696 (Iran) |
| 2006 | Security Council Resolution 1718 (North Korea) |
| 2006 | Security Council Resolution 1737 (Iran) |
| 2007 | Security Council Resolution 1747 (Iran) |
| 2008 | Security Council Resolution 1803 (Iran) |
| 2009 | Security Council Resolution 1874 (North Korea) |
| 2010 | Security Council Resolution 1929 (Iran) |
| 2010 | Convention on the Suppression of Unlawful Acts Relating to International Civil Aviation (Beijing Convention) |

officers) have endorsed ratification and, more important, have honored both the letter and spirit of the convention.

Within the international legal community there are also long-standing arguments about the interpretation of UNCLOS, SUA's various protocols, and the large body of customary law that guides the behavior of states in maritime affairs. Debates over the right to board ships suspected of trafficking WMD components are particularly relevant to PSI. Many merchant ships are registered in so-called flag of convenience states, known for their lax regulations and relatively inexpensive fees, among them Liberia, Panama, and the Marshall Islands. According to UNCLOS and customary maritime law, the consent of the vessel's "flag state" is required for a "nonflag state" to board that vessel. Obtaining a flag state's consent often creates a logistical headache in time-sensitive cases. The United States has addressed this issue by negotiating bilateral ship boarding agreements with prominent flag states that either allows it to board ships sailing under their flag or expedites the process of granting permission.[65] These agreements are only a patchwork solution because they are bilateral, not multilateral. They do not set general rules or precedents about what steps other PSI participants are allowed to take in order to halt the flow of contraband.

The UN's International Maritime Organization amended the 1988 SUA Convention in 2005 with a draft protocol to "create a nonflag-state right of visit on the high seas given reasonable suspicion of a ship's involvement in terrorist activities."[66] In Article 3*bis*(1)b, SUA focuses on the transportation of materials that could be used in a terrorist attack.[67] It also protects those lawfully transporting otherwise-prohibited materials. Yet, only thirty-four nations have acceded to the convention since it entered into force in 2010. Even the United States has refused to do so, despite the urging of the US Senate Foreign Relations Committee.[68] Once again, sovereignty and the intrusiveness of the inspection regime seem to be at the heart of reluctance to adopt the 2005 protocol.

The United States nonetheless continues to abide by the international maritime agreements and laws underpinning PSI—even as it has pushed, often unsuccessfully, for greater latitude to act against states and private firms that facilitate illicit flows. These agreements set the legal parameters for interdicting weapons of mass destruction at sea, but they contain lacunae regarding jurisdiction. American diplomats have pushed for modifications that would increase state capabilities vis-à-vis ships operating in international waters. Yet the United States' ability to expand the Law of the Sea remains limited because it is not a "State Party" to UNCLOS. If it becomes a member, "U.S. participation in Convention institutions and meetings of States Parties can help shape the future direction of the law of the sea in ways favorable to U.S. commercial, fishing, environmental, and military interests."[69] Without membership, US officials are severely handicapped.[70] Ultimately—despite overwhelming support for UNCLOS membership historically in the executive branch, the military services, and among business leaders—a small group of Republicans continue to compromise the PSI's implementation.[71]

The operational level has also seen disputes, albeit muted, between US military leaders and senior civilian officials. Tensions have been particularly acute regarding exercises and the military expertise necessary to hold OEG meetings. In the complex American system of funding military operations (including training and exercises), PSI is, in effect, an unfunded mandate.

When American participation in PSI was first debated, policymakers did not allocate new or additional funds for implementation. PSI activities are required by policymakers in the service of political and strategic ends that are several steps removed from those most valued by the military—preparing for combat and serving as a deterrent. To pay for PSI activities, units must siphon funds from preferred activities. Funding PSI therefore requires the sea services to do less of something else. PSI activities were not onerous when budgets were ample in the aftermath of 9/11. With sequestration, however, commanders have begun to view PSI as another unwelcome encumbrance. It costs scarce time and money, with few interdiction successes to bolster morale or prestige and no prospect of a dedicated line of funding. As our account of American-led maritime exercises in the Indo-Pacific shows, Pacific Fleet planners have increasingly focused on drilling war-fighting competencies with allies and partners. PSI prepares US forces and partner nations for what are, in effect, military operations other than war.[72]

How much does the United States spend on PSI relative to other participants? Accurate figures on the cost of PSI to the United States cannot be calculated because they are embedded in numerous parts of the defense budget. Unquestionably, the United States pays more than others. As two experienced international diplomats commented, the burden of enforcement is never equally shared, as "some states do more than others, and all states do only what they wish, not necessarily what needs to be done."[73] Still, with more than 130 participating members, the American burden is less maldistributed than in other security areas, and the benefits that accrue to the United States are significant.

Finally, there is the thorny issue of China, which remains an important nonparticipant. The United States has made unsuccessful efforts to address Chinese concerns about the abrogation of sovereignty. As the Arms Control Association website notes, "U.S. officials have courted China to join the regime, but so far it has kept its distance, citing concerns about the legality of interdictions."[74] But Chinese reluctance to join PSI may partially be a function of its long-standing accusations of American duplicity, that the United States itself exports "weaponry to Pakistan as well as the rogue regimes in North Korea and Iran."[75] Of course, China has a well-documented history of arms sales, technology transfers, and the export of dual-use technologies to those countries.[76]

One perspective suggests that China's reluctance to participate in the PSI is simply part of the PSI's well-documented use of "maritime lawfare,"[77] more recently highlighted by disputes over territorial claims in the East and South China Seas.[78] Contrary to Chinese objections, PSI's application of military assets is circumscribed by a civilian legal framework and undertaken in concert with law enforcement authorities. Moreover, China in effect endorsed Western efforts to halt Iran's nuclear programs in the 2015 Joint Comprehensive Plan of Action. Simultaneously, China may be gradually moving toward an approach to nonproliferation more consistent with international norms and institutions.[79] Still, its formal absence from the PSI remains a glaring omission.

Like many foreign policy initiatives that involve the policing of illicit flows, it is hard to evaluate PSI's success in terms of narrowly defined American national security interests. In the first place, PSI operations—like many nonproliferation policies[80]—occur at the murky intersection of intelligence collection, law enforcement activities, and military operations.[81] They entail a high degree of interagency and intergovernmental cooperation, facilitating slippage and the opportunity for bureaucratic infighting over both strategy and implementation. Internal grumbling over the cost of PSI activities shouldered by the military as well as the allocation of responsibilities among agencies can be found among other PSI participants. Some observers suggest that PSI activities declined in the early years of the Obama administration because of the international economic crisis—and the fact that (like the US military) few countries have a dedicated PSI budget.[82] Further, the PSI may have lost international momentum because of the Obama administration's unsuccessful efforts to formalize it. As one official observed, "PSI is like a shark. It must keep moving or it will die."[83]

Evaluating PSI successes evokes several well-known analytic problems. The first concerns how proliferation "events" are counted when there is no reliable way to estimate events that were never detected. Second, there is no reliable way to calculate how many firms, states, or terrorists abandoned plans to ship materials because they might be caught. Finally, the transshipment of materials may not be the most important problem: experts now believe that the linchpin for most governments or groups seeking chemical, biological, or nuclear weapons is not material goods but intellectual knowledge.[84] Since the Soviet Union's collapse, for example, Western states have been concerned that Soviet-trained weapons experts might make their knowledge available to the highest bidder.[85] PSI operations are ill-equipped to address that problem—especially in an age of electronic communication, where detailed instructions can be transmitted instantaneously.

Only former officials have been willing to speak publicly about PSI. Robert Joseph and Brendan Malley, both officials in the Bush administration, suggested that "dozens of interdictions have taken place slowing nuclear and missile programs in Asia and the Middle East."[86] Yet there simply is "no formal mechanism for measuring its effectiveness (like a database of cases)."[87] Although the US Government Accountability Office has praised interagency cooperation on PSI,[88] it has also repeatedly expressed frustration with PSI's programmatic inadequacies (such as lack of a budget, implementation policies, and procedures) and, significantly, any "measures of effectiveness." Indeed, it concluded in 2012 that "while U.S. agencies have provided years of documentation of a range of activities they have performed or plan to perform under PSI, they have been unable to demonstrate if or how these activities are linked to the PSI objective."[89]

What is demonstrable is that the United States has employed an informal Sponsorship strategy. It has deferred to the leadership of others, respected global protocols, and underwritten the costs of PSI even as several of its own major reform proposals have been rejected. And despite its limitations, this Sponsorship strategy appears to have had positive effects despite the vast geographic expanse that must be policed, the heterogeneity of actors involved, and the multidimensional forms of conflict involved. A Primacist strategy to address the problem of smuggling of WMB across the global commons would face severe limitations—the maritime domain is too expansive for USN to go it alone. The same is true of a Restraint strategy. Finally, is PSI simply a classic case of American Leadership?[90] The evidence suggests otherwise. The United States has attempted to operate within the framework of international law and to respect the domestic laws of participating states.

There remains an abiding political problem. No politician's career could survive the consequences of not doing everything within his or her power to prevent terrorists and hostile regimes from acquiring WMD.[91] Politicians have to be practical: sharing the burden is the only recourse, even if the loss of autonomy associated with PSI is a cost to be endured. Deterring or interdicting contraband is feasible only with the cooperation and collaboration of like-minded states, regional and international institutions (notably the UN and NATO), and private actors such as manufacturing and shipping firms.

The OEG structure extensively delegates authority to group members. They host meetings and exercises. The changing pace and agenda of PSI activities is dictated by what is possible with more than a hundred very diverse participating states, not by US preferences. Congressional members and some American officials occasionally complain (off the record) about the slow pace of PSI's processes. They have also groused about the reluctance of several nonmembers to join. But PSI continues as a living entity that has supplemented—not supplanted—the nonproliferation tools available in the attempt to reinforce global norms and laws.

The benefits of the PSI are tangible despite residual questions over how one benchmarks interdiction. It has made a significant contribution to "the long underappreciated role of American nonproliferation policy, including its efforts to prevent nuclear tests, induce compliance with the NPT, or coerce some of its closest allies into remaining non-nuclear."[92] In several cases, other states have themselves interdicted contraband items.[93] Not surprisingly, the majority of seizures have taken place in port, not on the high seas.[94] Over time, multilateral support for the PSI has widened and deepened. Membership has grown and activities have become increasingly coordinated.

Likewise, American support for PSI has expanded and deepened, despite the misgivings of the military over responsibilities and costs.[95] The United States has been its intellectual and financial sponsor in the key national security area of counterproliferation.[96] Yet geography and global markets dictate a cooperative approach. Even the United States lacks the military capacity or legal authority to police the global trafficking of weapons of mass destruction. PSI is "a more flexible approach to collective action that eschews both ad hoc unilateralism and institutionalized multilateralism."[97]

CHAPTER 7

# Racing for the Arctic
# with a Strategy of Restraint

The effect of changing climate on the Department's operating environment is evident in the maritime commons of the Arctic. The opening of the Arctic waters in the decades ahead that will permit seasonal commerce and transit presents a unique opportunity to work collaboratively in multilateral forums to promote a balanced approach to improving human and environmental security in the region. In that effort, DoD must work with the Coast Guard and the Department of Homeland Security to address gaps in Arctic communications, domain awareness, search and rescue, and environmental observation and forecasting capabilities to support both current and future planning and operations. To support cooperative engagement in the Arctic, DoD strongly supports accession to the United Nations Convention on the Law of the Sea.

—*Quadrennial Defense Review Report*, 2010

We're not even in the same league as Russia right now. We're not playing in this game at all.

—Coast Guard Commandant Paul F. Zukunft, July 2015

On August 2, 2007, Russian divers accelerated a new geopolitical race for mineral and energy resources beneath the Arctic seabed. Using two *Mir* minisubmarines, Russian scientists descended to forty-three hundred meters with the official purpose of collecting water and sediment samples.[1] Their unofficial mission, however, sent a chill across the seven other nations that either border the Arctic Ocean or possess territory within the Arctic Circle—Canada, the United States, Denmark, Norway, Sweden, Iceland, and Finland. A pair of divers planted a titanium flagpole on the Lomonosov Ridge during their hour-long exploration of the sea floor—an event the Russians televised.[2] It was watched by many Russian viewers, their interest piqued by the presence of two

122

Russian parliamentarians, including polar explorer Artur Chilingarov, aboard the submarines.[3] Russia subsequently notified the United Nations that it was claiming the ridge as part of its contiguous continental shelf. This claim has important implications for the future exploitation of the seabed and the passage of surface ships through the Arctic Ocean.[4]

John B. Bellinger III, legal adviser to the US Secretary of State, observed, "We knew they were going to the North Pole, but we didn't know they were going to plant the flag. It was a provocative action, and took us aback."[5] Canada's Minister of Foreign Affairs, Peter Mackay, told reporters, "This isn't the 15th century. You can't go around the world and just plant flags" and claim territory.[6] But neither Canada nor the United States were in a position to plant their own flags on the Arctic seafloor. Canada has few large icebreakers, no deep submersible submarines, and lacks a deep-water port accessible to the Arctic. America's Arctic assets include two older, barely serviceable US Coast Guard icebreakers and no naval surface ships with the double hulls necessary to conduct polar operations. Its infrastructure capable of servicing operations in Alaska—the only American territory adjacent to the Arctic Ocean and above the Arctic Circle—is rudimentary.

Reactions to the event contrasted sharply with those nearly four years earlier. In April 2003, at a site about 150 kilometers from the North Pole, the very same Chilingarov declared, "This is our Arctic, this is the Russian Arctic, and the Russian flag should be here."[7] That declaration was universally ignored.

The flag planting, however, prompted an uncomfortable question: how should the United States respond? This symbol of Russia's Arctic aspirations has its roots in climate change. By 2007 it had become clear that the polar icecap was melting. Seas, icebound for most of the year, were becoming accessible during summer melts. In the long run, experts believe the Arctic will be open to seasonal shipping through both the Northwest Passage, which meanders along the island coastlines of Canada's Nunavut Territory, and year round through the Northern Sea Route (increasing the current very limited volume),[8] which connects the Pacific and Atlantic Oceans along Russia's northern coast. Geologists also believe the Arctic's mineral resources, oil, and natural gas may become accessible if the seas remain open for substantial periods. The temperature recorded in November 2016 was 36 degrees Fahrenheit warmer than the historic average, which suggests these changes will happen sooner than many have anticipated.[9]

Analysts suggest that "the transformation in how humans use the Arctic hinterlands is being driven as much by global economics and natural resource availability as it is by climate change."[10] Optimism about

Arctic resources partially stems from the findings of a 2008 US Geological Survey suggesting that the region's natural gas resources could amount to 30 percent of the world's undiscovered reserves, and oil reserves might constitute 13 percent of the world's remaining supply.[11] Yet the race for Arctic resources can be overemphasized; *The Economist* notes that "according to a Danish estimate, 95% of Arctic mineral resources are within agreed national boundaries."[12] Under the existing international legal regime, there is no "race" because most supplies exist within *terra cognita*.

There are two other important dimensions of the ice melt. The first is its economic implications for global shipping patterns. As James Kraska and Betsy Baker note, "The distance from Shanghai to Hamburg is 5,200 kilometers shorter via the Arctic route than via the Suez Canal."[13] The second, more debatable dimension may be military: a new commons for US maritime forces to patrol. It is a task for which they are ill prepared. In the summer of 2015, during a visit by President Obama to Alaska, Senator John McCain wrote that "as polar ice melts, Russia is rushing to nationalize and control new waterways across the Arctic Ocean that could open not simply to commercial shipping, but also military and intelligence activities. Vast natural resources, including oil and gas, could become available for exploitation, potentially transforming the Arctic into a new theater of geopolitical competition."[14] This is a contentious claim, but American policymakers are beginning to debate it as a possible driver for defense expenditures. McCain's claim that Russia has "hegemonic" ambitions in the Arctic remains open to question.[15] But the concern raises strategic questions about how the United States should respond: embark on a Leadership strategy, or maintain its current strategy of Restraint.

The strategic impact of Arctic climate change stems from its second-order effects on the global resource base, global shipping patterns, and regional geopolitics. The United States, like its regional neighbors, has a variety of interests in the Arctic's opening. Every country involved has a different combination of economic and military tools to exploit these changes.

In our earlier cases we described how strategies have been developed, consolidated, and implemented over time. Here, we describe a strategy that is immature and evolving—a halting transformation from traditional Isolationism to Restraint—in response to a rapidly changing security environment. Some planners accord little strategic importance to the Arctic. But its potential as a trade route, coupled with increasingly crowded sovereignty claims that challenge freedom of navigation, suggest its strategic significance will expand. The US Navy is neither well prepared nor especially enthusiastic about addressing the problem.

## The Origins of America's Arctic Strategy

With more than one thousand miles of Arctic Ocean coastline and fifty thousand citizens residing above the Arctic Circle,[16] the United States has been an Arctic state since Alaska was purchased from Russia in 1867—the so-called Seward's Folly in which the US Secretary of State William H. Seward bought 586,412 square miles for $7.2 million.[17] But the region has rarely constituted a core American security concern or been an essential source of national wealth. Even during the Cold War—when the USS *Nautilus* demonstrated the ability of the nuclear submarine fleet to transit under the ice, hide from Soviet surveillance systems, and transport ballistic missiles capable of targeting wide expanses—the US strategic community largely took the Arctic for granted. It was not an area the United States needed to protect for itself or for use by its allies.

The United States has, nonetheless, maintained a sporadic regional presence. The US Coast Guard arrived in Alaska many decades before the Navy in the form of its institutional predecessor, the Revenue Cutter Service. Its purpose was not related to security, but rather the taxmen stationed a cutter in Alaska to prevent smuggling and collect tariffs.[18] The military first ventured into the Arctic with Admiral Richard E. Byrd's flight to the North Pole in 1926. During World War II, and intermittently during the Cold War, the US Navy conducted operations ranging from scientific expeditions to nuclear-armed submarine deterrence.[19] New military technologies and capabilities—including nuclear submarines, ballistic missiles, and early warning systems—eventually made the Arctic a theater in the US-Soviet rivalry.[20] Furthermore, Alaska hosted listening posts for spying on the Russian Far East, as well as naval and air bases. In the post–Cold War era, Fort Greeley has served as one of two bases for the nation's ground-based ballistic missile defense radars and interceptor missiles.

Aside from missile defense installations, the Arctic receded in significance for US national security: the United States essentially adopted an Isolationist regional strategy. Only in President George W. Bush's second term did the rapid Arctic melt and shifts in the security environment precipitate renewed discussions of the region.[21] The Bush administration's National Security Presidential Directive/NSPD-66 (January 2009) stated that "the United States has broad and fundamental national security interests in the Arctic region and is prepared to operate either independently or in conjunction with other states to safeguard these interests . . . includ[ing] such matters as missile defense and early warning; deployment of sea and air systems for strategic sealift, strategic deterrence, maritime presence, and maritime security operations; and ensuring freedom of navigation and overflight." It further noted that the Arctic as a maritime domain requires the United States "to assert a more active and influential national

Table 7.1 Select Arctic strategy and policy documents

| Document title | Publication date |
|---|---|
| Arctic Policy Directive (NSPD 66/HSPD 25) | January 2009 |
| U.S. Navy Arctic Roadmap | October 2009 |
| National Strategy for Arctic Region | May 2013 |
| United States Coast Guard Arctic Strategy | May 2013 |
| Implementation Plan for National Strategy for Arctic Region | January 2014 |
| U.S. Navy Arctic Roadmap: 2014–2030 | February 2014 |
| Executive Order for Enhancing Coordination of Arctic Efforts | January 2015 |

presence to protect its Arctic interests and to project sea power throughout the region."[22]

In May 2013, the Obama administration issued the first *National Strategy for the Arctic Region*. It focused on protecting the Arctic commons and ensuring freedom of navigation:

> The United States has a national interest in preserving all of the rights, freedoms, and uses of the sea and airspace recognized under international law. We will enable prosperity and safe transit by developing and maintaining sea, under-sea, and air assets and necessary infrastructure. In addition, the United States will support the enhancement of national defense, law enforcement, navigation safety, marine environment response, and search-and-rescue capabilities.[23]

That November, Secretary of Defense Chuck Hagel invoked the 1982 United Nations Convention on the Law of the Sea (UNCLOS) in offering more specific guidance, stressing his department would "help preserve freedom of the seas throughout the region, within existing frameworks of international law."[24] Subsequent US official statements on Arctic policy highlighted the need for regional cooperation (see table 7.1).

Pursuing a legalistic approach to the Arctic presents a dilemma because the United States has not actually ratified UNCLOS—the treaty which defines the rights and responsibilities of nations regarding the world's oceans. So American legitimacy is inevitably undermined when it urges other nations to follow UNCLOS guidelines.[25] More practically, the fact that the United States is not a party prevents it from using the convention's processes for resolving jurisdictional disputes over Economic Exclusion Zones, rights of passage through territorially contested waters, and conflicts between national and international laws.

## Restraint and Commanding the Commons

Barry Posen contends that America's post–World War II Hegemony is largely based on its ability to command the global commons. The commons "in the case of the sea and space, are areas that belong to no one state and that provide access to much of the globe. Airspace does technically belong to the countries below it, but there are few countries that can deny their airspace above 15,000 feet to U.S. warplanes." Posen then clarifies the meaning of "command":

> Command does not mean that other states cannot use the commons in peacetime. Nor does it mean that others cannot acquire military assets that can move through or even exploit them when unhindered by the United States. Command means that the United States gets vastly more military use out of the sea, space, and air than do others; that it can credibly threaten to deny their use to others; and that others would lose a military contest for the commons if they attempted to deny them to the United States.[26]

Such domination, enabled by sixty years of investment in air, sea, and space assets, as well as the worldwide infrastructure to operate these systems, "allows the United States to exploit more fully other sources of power, including its own economic and military might as well as the economic and military might of its allies."[27]

If the Arctic is an emerging global common, then America's future strategic choices need to be clarified. But geography and international legal regimes confound American thinking. Much of the region is encompassed within territorial seas of other states and is accessible only through a few relatively narrow straits. Moreover, likely transit routes through the Northwest Passage and the Northern Sea Route pass through waters controlled by states who use differing interpretations of UNCLOS about how they might be used by commercial and naval vessels. The United States has one of the smallest claims, given the modest length of Alaska's Arctic Ocean coastline. Conversely, as a global power who commands the commons, the United States has a strategic interest in Arctic developments above and beyond its narrow economic and political interests.

The first geographic element is narrow, vulnerable access points, often referred to as "strategic chokepoints." Three routes through the Arctic might become accessible and commercially viable as the polar icecap melts (as illustrated in figure 7.1): the Northwest Passage, the Northern Sea Route, and less likely, a direct route over the pole itself. Access to any of these sea lanes requires passage through chokepoints.

From a Russian perspective, the Northern Sea Route (NSR) consists of "five seas that can provide passage through the Northern Sea Route— Barents, Kara, Laptev, East Siberian and Chukchi—[that] are linked by straits."[28] These straits—the Yugorskiy Shar, the Kara Gates, Matochkin Shar, the Vilkitsky Strait, the Dmitriy Laptev Strait, and the Long Strait—are potential chokepoints for international traffic. The Northwest Passage is the body of Arctic water located between the Davis Strait and Baffin Bay in the east and the Bering Strait in the west.[29] Yet the Northwest Passage is complicated: it is "a series of connected straits that weave through the islands

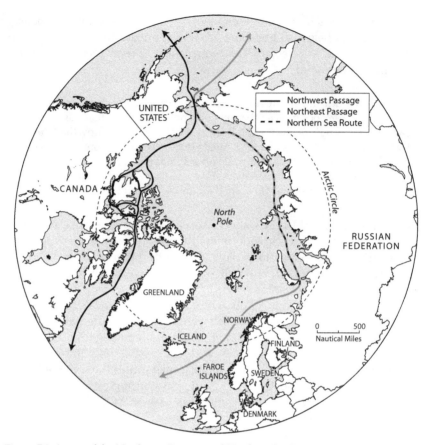

Figure 7.1. A map of the Northwest Passage and Northern Sea Route

that make up the Canadian Arctic Archipelago,"[30] resulting in seven distinct routes.[31] The Department of Defense has acknowledged that "an increase in maritime traffic between Asia and Europe, or Russia, could also raise the prominence of the Bering Strait as a strategic chokepoint and heightened the geostrategic importance of the Arctic region."[32]

Related to this are jurisdictional claims and counterclaims of the Arctic states. Canada, for example, asserts sovereignty over some parts of the Northwest Passage that the United States claims are international waters. Only a small portion of the Arctic Ocean does not fall within the territorial waters or Exclusive Economic Zones (EEZs) of an Arctic state—a predicament for those who characterize the region as a standard global common. That unclaimed portion is the only part of the Arctic Ocean that might credibly be regarded, under traditional interpretations of maritime law, as a common. The region has not yet been ruled part of any nation's jurisdiction. But access to that unclaimed region requires passage through chokepoints claimed by one or more states, although the chokepoints themselves are often governed by maritime law regulating the passage of vessels through straits.

## Threats to the Arctic Commons and the Emerging Commercial Routes?

Some journalists and politicians (like McCain) worry about the threat of Russian military adventurism toward Alaska, Canada, or America's European allies.[33] Yet the principal Arctic threats are not threats but uncertainties about Russian intentions.[34] Since Russia's 2007 stunt, some analysts have argued that Russia might use its preponderant regional military power to control Arctic resources beyond those found within its EEZ. Some have resurrected a Cold War scenario: when the Arctic Ocean becomes navigable, the United States might station Aegis ballistic missile defense destroyers and cruisers there to intercept any Russian missiles attacking the US mainland.[35]

States remain the principal actors in any potential conflict, notably the Arctic Council's eight full members—the Scandinavian countries plus Canada, Finland, Iceland, Russia, and the United States—and the twelve states with observer status, including China. Multinational corporations, environmental NGOs, and groups representing indigenous peoples have lobbied national governments and international bodies, but their ability to operate in the region is severely circumscribed by the harsh climate, geography, small population, and the absence of critical infrastructure. Cruise lines, shipping companies, energy firms, and others that might exploit Arctic resources remain limited without investments in infrastructure, search and rescue capabilities, and robust telecommunications. These factors dictate that, for the foreseeable future, the principal security players will be states.

The Arctic is currently a region of latent conflict. The prospect of a shooting war in the Arctic is minimal. Indeed, there is little precedent for direct security competition aside from undersea and air warning activities on the part of NATO and the Warsaw Pact during the Cold War. Some NATO analysts believe that any future conflict with Russia is likely to be hybrid; NATO has even created a new series of exercises to prepare for complex hybrid threats, including Cold Response in February and March 2016 with fifteen thousand troops from fourteen participating countries.[36] Held in central Norway, the exercise included "an Article 5 scenario, in which the alliance must respond to an attack on a NATO country."[37] As NATO reported, the "exercise included land, maritime and air assets, covering a wide spectrum of scenarios. . . . The main objective was to exercise extreme operations in a joint and combined setting under challenging conditions, focusing on joint action and interoperability."[38]

The limited American military involvement in these exercises indicates a lack of US commitment to a multilateral Leadership strategy, but their character reinforces the view that any conflict would take a hybrid form. NATO officials believe that Russia may work with nonstate actors such as commercial firms (from Russia and perhaps non-Arctic states) to exploit fossil and mineral resources and local populations with political grievances. It may use the full range of coercive and persuasive instruments available, from lawfare to propaganda. Indeed, Russia's hybrid warfare in Ukraine could be a precedent for future action in the Arctic or Baltics.[39]

We disagree with these NATO analysts. If there is to be any actual conflict, however unlikely, it will be symmetric, involving air, surface, and undersea warfare, although these would be minor clashes between ground forces, coast guards, or local law enforcement officials. Our view is buttressed by the fact that the Arctic is an extreme environment, lightly populated, and generally inaccessible to all but the most resource-intensive enterprises. In short, conventional confrontations among national armies, navies, or air forces are the most likely form of conflict *and yet* among the least likely scenarios to occur. Instead, there will be legal and political claims and counterclaims. Indeed, China's policy in the South China Sea may preview Arctic disputes better than Russia's policy in Ukraine. China has pushed the boundaries of international maritime law and received an unfavorable ruling from an international tribunal in The Hague for its activity—from building artificial islands on existing reefs to deploying coast guard vessels and armed fishing boats to assert territorial claims.[40] Given the sustained rapprochement between Moscow and Beijing, Russia may apply lessons from China's recent successes to its Arctic claims. A few analysts argue that both China in the South China Sea and Russia in the Arctic are creating maritime "exclusion areas." Russia's threat to the Arctic and its access points is even more worrisome for maritime transit routes because Russia's interlocking antiship missiles and other A2/AD capabilities may be deployed to reach the Arctic.[41]

Arctic developments depend on unknowable factors, principally the impact of climate change, the pace of the Arctic melt, the evolution of global threats, and how much natural resources are eventually discovered (and where).[42] At a minimum, as commercial activities expand, the need for greater maritime policing will increase the role of states that abut the region. Meanwhile, in at least a tacit recognition of the potential for conflict, both the Arctic Council's members and other international stakeholders are strengthening dispute resolution mechanisms, using both the council and international legal regimes as deliberative forums.

Again, the US Senate's failure to ratify UNCLOS has hampered American efforts. The United States is not eligible to file an official claim regarding an extended continental shelf with the UN Commission on the Limits of the Continental Shelf (an UNCLOS body) because of its lack of legal standing.

In contrast, other states—including Russia, Canada, and Denmark—have filed multiple and often overlapping claims. These filings can be viewed either as legitimate recourse to existing institutional arrangements or cynical attempts to manipulate international agreements. Indisputably, however, the United States suffers from a distinct deficit in lawfare.

Russia remains the wildcard.[43] Its military forces have acted more aggressively since Crimea's annexation in 2014, and its Arctic activities mirror that behavior. Yet some observers conclude that there is no regional arms race: most Russian investments in Arctic-specific capabilities have been designed to address nonmilitary, soft security concerns rather than "hard" security threats.[44] Indeed, "Russia clearly demonstrates that it prefers to use soft power (diplomatic, economic, and cultural methods) rather than hard power (coercive) instruments."[45]

American strategists are inevitably more conscious of Russian military strategy in the Arctic and are more likely to characterize Russian behavior as predatory. Others have reinforced this less-charitable view of Russia's behavior. In December 2014, for example, Russia established a new Arctic Strategic Command based at Severomorsk, the homeport of the Russian Northern Fleet.[46] One analyst concluded that "Moscow is intent on remilitarizing its Arctic territory and is restoring Soviet-era airfields and ports to help protect important hydrocarbon resources and shipping lanes."[47] And in the late winter of 2015, it conducted an Arctic war game "including 38,000 servicemen, more than 50 surface ships and submarines and 110 aircraft," purportedly "to check the readiness of Russia's Northern Fleet and the military's ability to deploy additional forces from central Russia."[48] One senior Russian politician offered a menacing perspective on these developments, even suggesting that Norway's possible hosting of 330 US marines made it a legitimate nuclear target.[49]

Furthermore, Russia has aggressively pushed its case regarding the Arctic seabed, including under the North Pole itself. Since 2001, it has repeatedly submitted evidence to the UN in support of its claim that that it should control oil and gas drilling and seabed mining, as well as fisheries management, over the so-called donut hole—an area of international waters the size of Texas.[50] The UN Committee on the Limits of the Continental Shelf has rejected these representations. Yet Russia continues to submit new evidence buttressing its claims. Denmark and Canada have submitted overlapping claims, but Moscow has petitioned the committee to have its latest claims adjudicated first because it filed an initial claim earlier.

The historical context is relevant. Russia has considered the Arctic a core component of its security sphere for several centuries.[51] Arguably, Moscow's current efforts to strengthen its infrastructure; deploy naval, air, and army assets above the Arctic Circle; and conduct maneuvers and exercises in the High North are intended to restore its position in a region neglected since the collapse of the Soviet Union. As one Russian expert notes, "The Russian Army's withdrawal from the North put the country, which has the world's longest Arctic border stretching for over 17,500 kilometers (one-third of the entire length of Russia's national borders), in danger of losing control of the area."[52] Its strategists argue that the High North has become increasingly central to national security: as Russia drew down Soviet-era forces in the mid-1990s, the "Strategic Northern Bastion" concept was popularized. Russian nuclear forces shifted the country's reliance on a strategic deterrent from land-based to sea-based missiles that are protected by hiding under Arctic ice.[53] Moreover, Russia recently reopened a Soviet-era naval base (established in 1933) on the Island of Kotelny in the New Siberian Islands that it had closed in 1993.[54] A second military installation, in the town of Alakurtti, is thirty-one miles from the Finnish border. By January 2016 that base held approximately eight hundred servicemen from Russia's Northern Fleet but could conceivably accommodate up to three thousand troops.[55]

Another problem for the United States is that its military forces are unprepared to operate in the region's challenging climate. James Kraska suggests that "unlike some navies—Denmark's in particular—the US surface fleet is unaccustomed to operating in extreme cold or navigating ice hazards."[56] Notably, the capacity of USN surface ships and aircraft to operate in the Arctic's extreme conditions is severely limited. Further, the infrastructure necessary to support a higher operational tempo there has been neither planned nor funded.[57] Proponents of American power in the Arctic have attempted to shame Congress and the Navy's leadership by comparing American capabilities with those of Russia: "While countries like Russia see Arctic power as central to their national affairs, the United States pays little more than lip service to our status as an Arctic power. In nowhere else in the world is the U.S. Navy so clearly outclassed in its ability to perform surface operations as in the Arctic."[58] As noted at the start of this chapter, Coast Guard Commandant Paul Zukunft acknowledged in 2015 that "We're not even in the same league" as Russia, although his comment was largely in reference to infrastructure investments.[59]

In May 2009, Admiral Gary Roughead, then Chief of Naval Operations, did establish a Task Force on Climate Change to address urgent concerns about the naval implications of a changing environment.[60] Yet his successor, Admiral Jonathan Greenert, was more cautious: in a 2013 blog post, the Admiral observed, "Initially, these will likely consist of episodic support to Coast Guard operations; over time, periodic deployments of US Navy ships may be needed in the Arctic."[61] And a spokesman for the Navy's Task Force Climate Change succinctly summarized the service's most recent position: "We know there is no immediate threat in the Arctic, and there are [threats] elsewhere."[62]

The reluctance of America's military leadership—especially the US Navy—to invest in military capabilities directly applicable to the Arctic environment is evident in the gaps between official statements, programmatic requests, and actual activities. Formally, the US Navy and Coast Guard have repeatedly pledged to acquire the necessary capabilities—from deep-water ports close to the Arctic Circle to improved command, control, and communications systems. Planned improvements are for the intermediate to long term, meaning beyond 2030. With the ice now receding faster than formerly anticipated, the buildup of Arctic capabilities may not be completed until it is too late to influence the next "Great Game."[63]

The most public point of contention over Arctic assets has arisen over the condition of the US icebreaker fleet. The US Coast Guard and the Navy pointed accusatory fingers at one another in response to questioning by Representative Duncan Hunter (R-CA) at a congressional hearing in 2015. One witness summarized the exchange as follows: "The [Navy] admiral agreed the Arctic is important, but turned to his Coast Guard counterpart, whose service has responsibility for the region. Rear Admiral Kevin Donegan, then acting Deputy Chief of Naval Operations for Operations, Plans and Strategy, "noted that the Navy has its own shipbuilding priorities, including the tens of billions of dollars needed for supercarriers, the next-generation ballistic missile subs, littoral combat ships and amphibs."[64] This disagreement can partially be traced to a long-standing arrangement between the two services:

> The 1965 U.S. Navy–U.S. Treasury Memorandum of Agreement was executed to permit consolidation of the icebreaker fleet under one agency. That rationale was reinforced by a 1982 Roles and Missions Study which stated that polar icebreakers should be centrally managed by one agency and that the Coast Guard was the appropriate one due to the multi-mission nature of polar ice operations. This memorandum of agreement was updated in 2008. The signatories were DOD and DHS and the agreement included an update on responsibilities for coastal security.[65]

In practice, since the mid-1960s, "the Coast Guard operates the nation's icebreakers and uses them, when needed, to support the Navy." And even then, because of Coast Guard priorities and the refitting of one of only two large polar-class icebreakers still in operation, the annual ship resupply to Thule Air Base (on the northwest side of Greenland) has been conducted by Canadian icebreakers.[66] Thule, an American base since World War II, is located roughly 750 miles north of the Arctic Circle and 1,000 miles from the North Pole. Although its strategic importance has varied, today it serves as a critical location for missile warning, space surveillance, and space control sensors. That the American government cannot resupply it without

Canadian assistance is indicative of the military's priorities vis-à-vis the Arctic.

Change is afoot. With high-level strategic guidance in place, lobbying by commercial interests and Alaskan officials, and the creation of a congressional Arctic Caucus in 2015,[67] there is optimism that the Navy and Coast Guard will acquire the resources to defend US interests and enforce international law. But this will depend on strategic debates. As it stands, policymakers and military leaders have accorded higher priority to other regions (e.g., the "Indo-Asia-Pacific") and threats (e.g., NBC proliferation, terrorism, piracy, and narcotics smuggling).

## Framing Arctic "Threats"

We have identified two variants of Retrenchment strategies: Restraint and Isolationism. Restraint focuses on controlling the commons (near and far) for national security purposes. It favors minimal entanglements in alliances and limits the deployment of resources overseas. There should be no engagement with allies who might pull the United States into unwarranted conflicts, nor any "free riders" who can benefit from American efforts to stabilize a region without bearing appropriate costs.

The American strategy in the Arctic is evolving from de facto Isolationism to Restraint. Any major threat to the United States emanating from the Arctic would exclusively be to American homeland security and domestic prosperity. The United States has shied away from engaging allies, partners, national security principles, or international law, primarily because it is an Arctic state with a significant coastline abutting the region. It has largely treated the Arctic as a domestic issue. Indeed, the United States currently bears little security burden in the Arctic. The most recent multilateral discussions conducted by then President Obama with other Arctic states focused on nonsecurity issues such as climate change and economic development.[68]

Yet we believe that US Arctic strategy is being driven toward Restraint by three key factors: emergent security threats (both traditional and novel), new environmental threats, and resource scarcity threats. These factors, combined with a growing Russian hostility and threats to freedom of navigation, presage a gradual shift toward a strategy of Restraint.

## Traditional and Nontraditional Security Concerns in the Arctic

John Herz first coined the term *security dilemma*[69] to describe situations where a destabilizing arms race ensues because states build defensive military capabilities but adversaries are unable to distinguish offensive from defensive moves and so respond with their own military buildup. Kristian Åtlanda describes the Arctic's future in similar terms: "The coastal states' current security and defense policy moves in the Arctic are for the most part intended to reaffirm the status quo, and to make other actors think twice about challenging it. The problem is . . . that the measures sometimes have the unintended and unforeseen effect of making others feel less secure, and compelled to reciprocate."[70]

America's deteriorating relations with Russia during the Obama presidency heightened concerns about Russia's Arctic activities. In 2014, former Secretary of State Hillary Clinton suggested that Canada and the U.S. should form a regional militarized "united front" against Russia.[71] The Canadian response eschewed the offer and focused on diplomatic pressure. Soon after Clinton's speech, Canadian official Leona Aglukkaq announced that "As a result of Russia's illegal occupation of Ukraine and its continued provocative actions in Crimea and elsewhere, Canada did not attend working-group-level meetings [of the Arctic Council] in Moscow this week."[72] This symbolic rebuff carries significant weight in the Arctic Council.

NATO officials neglected the Arctic until Crimea's annexation captured the attention of both politicians and policymakers. In identifying new security challenges for the alliance, neither NATO's 2010 Strategic Concept paper nor its 2012 Chicago summit declaration mentioned the Arctic. As one conference report noted, to date, "the limited interest in the Arctic is partly a result of NATO's strongest member, the USA, being more concerned with the Far East and the fact that the main adversary in the Arctic, Russia, has been willing to abide by international law in the Arctic."[73] Understandably, many American strategists want to avoid conflict on the ice pack, or sea-based clashes given the United States' paltry capabilities and lack of infrastructure.

Yet there is an alternative way to look at the challenges posed by the Arctic's opening. Planners are moving beyond narrow security concerns to recognize that controlling the commons entails a collection of novel economic, environmental, and even human security challenges fundamental to American security and prosperity.[74] So narrow formulations of grand strategy confine their scope to military issues, but policymakers should take account of other security threats.

The first is environmental threats. Analysts who focus on environmental security believe that environmental degradation constitutes a major security risk. Mark Levy dissents from this assumption, arguing that the

> political threat from environmental degradation (involving environmental refugees, resource wars, and so on) is at once both the weakest substantive threat to U.S. security and the strongest intellectual challenge to the field of security studies. That is, the United States has the least to fear from political

conflicts caused by environmental harm (because such conflicts are likely to be limited to regions removed from direct U.S. interests).[75]

We disagree with Levy's assessment. Unlike other environmentally threatened regions, the Arctic is anything but "removed from direct U.S. interests." Few refugees would result from continued degradation in the region, but there would be enormous economic costs in both the short and the long term. The most obvious example concerns oil spills. Scientists still debate the environmental, commercial, and business costs of the disastrous Exxon Valdez oil spill a generation ago. The initial response to the 2010 Deepwater Horizon disaster mobilized approximately forty-eight thousand people and as many as sixty-five hundred vessels. BP spent more than $14 billion, workers devoted more than 70 million personnel hours on response and cleanup activities, and the US Coast Guard took four years to complete its cleanup operations.[76] Plans to drill in the Arctic were shelved as America's shale revolution has provided plentiful supplies of fossil fuel. But the respite in Arctic drilling is more likely a delay than an abandonment, given President Trump's campaign policies and lifting of restrictions in the opening months of his administration.[77] With few ready resources to address a major accident, the effects of a distant spill could be disastrous for America's Alaskan fisheries and coastline.

The second concern is threats in the form of resource competition. Scarcity takes many forms, and the political effects are variable. Michael Klare helped popularize the claim that competition over natural resources leads to war.[78] This view has remained a staple geopolitical assumption, although the empirical evidence is mixed. Klare claims, contrary to other Arctic specialists, that the region is a "new zone of contention," provocatively suggesting that "the risk of tension and conflict in the Arctic is further exacerbated by the determination of key regional policymakers to rely on military power to reinforce their claims to contested territories."[79] Oran Young demurs:

> Much of the resultant literature is marked by persistent expectations that the Arctic will become the scene of escalating jurisdictional conflicts, resource wars, a new great game and even armed clashes during the coming years. Yet these expectations are greatly exaggerated; there is much to be said for the proposition that armed conflict is less likely to occur in the Arctic than in most other parts of the world anytime soon.[80]

Indeed, Royal Dutch Shell's 2015 decision to abandon oil exploration in the Arctic suggests the competition for the region's resources is not as intense as originally projected.[81]

In many respects, Young's view is consistent with the way US planners have defined the Arctic challenge and charted a restrained strategy. Both the Bush and Obama administrations offered subdued responses to Russian saber-rattling in the High North. Both selected the Arctic Council as the appropriate forum to discuss the challenges associated with the Arctic opening but both avoided debate on regional security. When other states proposed adding a defense component to the Arctic Council, for example, the Obama administration resisted. The United States has abided by UNCLOS rules, but—despite the rhetoric—pursued narrow American interests.

Yet the Obama administration began laying the groundwork for a strategic switch from Isolationism to one that prioritizes American economic and military security in the Arctic commons. Its focus was on ensuring rights of access and freedom of navigation. Adopting Restraint as a strategy would have substantial benefits. It embraces the principle of flexibility; limits the commitment of resources (thus prioritizing challenges in other regions); and entails a limited use of existing fora. Most important, the emergent Arctic strategy focuses on control of the commons and ensures that the United States builds on its existing strengths, especially in maritime expertise and assets.

## Freedom of Navigation in the Emerging Arctic Strategy

There is, however, no unanimity about America's preferred national strategy in the Arctic. One major source of disagreement is the division between military leaders and civilian officials. The USN has remained sanguine in the face of demands that it perform military missions in the Arctic in the near to medium term (until 2030).[82] During that timeframe, the US Navy's *Arctic Roadmap* assumes that the "primary risks . . . will likely be meeting search and rescue or disaster response mission demands." But it concedes that "the Navy may also be called upon to ensure freedom of navigation in Arctic Ocean waters."[83] This admission is consistent with the Navy's broader position. Freedom of navigation operations (FONOPs) are an important function of the Navy in ensuring access to both global commons and navigable sea lanes: "United States' policy since 1983 provides that the United States will exercise and assert its navigation and overflight rights and freedoms on a worldwide basis in a manner that is consistent with customary international law. The Navy will guarantee freedom of navigation in Arctic Ocean waters and help ensure the free flow of commerce on the global commons."[84]

The issue of FONOPs in the Arctic may be more pressing than the Navy recognizes. Commercial firms are already lobbying both the Canadians and the Russians for exploration and transit rights in their territories, despite currently brief navigable periods. Both issues relate to freedom of access. More pointedly, these countries embrace interpretations of international waters and areas of national jurisdiction that differ from the United States. FONOPs are a primary tool that the United States uses to communicate its interpretation of free access, using American warships to exercise the right of passage through the global commons.[85]

An unusual chasm exists at the heart of America's Arctic policy, between the ambitious strategy espoused by some planners and the absence of resources to implement that strategy. Both rhetoric and planning show a gradual shift to a Restraint strategy. Yet the behavior of policymakers and the Navy suggests a different story. There is no urgent effort to procure the icebreakers or the surface vessels capable of undertaking FONOPs. American icebreaking capabilities are limited, and no ice-reinforced surface ships are able to make the passage safely. As one maritime expert observes, "The right of transit on the high seas . . . is a practical right, which can be exercised only when a nation uses vessels for commercial and military purposes."[86] Without vessels capable of operating in these contested seas, the US government lacks that "practical right." As the Center for International Maritime Security argues, "The absence of any clear intent to consider permanent presence possibilities, or commit to equipment procurements, evinces the Navy's desire to hedge its commitments to a remote and relatively minor area in the face of important responsibilities elsewhere."[87]

Dissenters want the United States to close the gap between professed strategy and actual behavior. The Coast Guard has received support for its complaints about a lack of suitable ships. State officials, including former Alaska Lieutenant Governor Mead Treadwell, were strongly critical of the unresponsiveness by the departments of Defense and Homeland Security to the rising demand for icebreakers. The United States must "add new polar class icebreakers in the United States Coast Guard's fleet" at least in part because "Congress and the Administration need to recognize that their own mandates and policies—including a significant mandate passed just last year [2010]—have directed that we maintain icebreaking operations."[88] Treadwell appeared to be motivated by Alaska's potential benefit from the Arctic's burgeoning commerce, as well as by traditional pork barrel politics.

The Navy argues that it should focus attention and resources principally on the Indo-Asia-Pacific, a position that generated a surprising response among national security strategists. Over the last decade, many have argued that China should be central to the design of naval strategy, if not indeed the overall US grand strategy.[89] Specialists characterize China as a predatory state that challenges the American-led liberal international order while engaging in neomercantilist practices closely related to its insatiable demand for natural resources.[90] President Trump has echoed that view.[91] This general concern extends to Chinese activity in the Arctic—that they will be the primary beneficiaries from newly opened trade routes and resource-rich lands and seabeds, and will come to dominate the region in the USN's absence. Accordingly, the United States should adopt a muscular assertion of freedom of navigation, nominally as a hedge against unpredictable developments.

The official Chinese response is twofold. First, as a non-Arctic state, China has a right to participate in the global governance deliberations regarding the region. Second, Chinese officials claim their activities are confined to scientific research on climate change and shifting weather patterns, not a search for resources.[92]

Beyond China's formal justifications are underlying concerns. In asserting their rights, China and Russia may transform the Arctic into a venue for collaboration against the United States (a process of "soft" counterbalancing). Just as Sino-Russian coordination in the Shanghai Cooperation Organization may help block US access to Central Asia, so the two may informally cooperate to deny America's access to the Arctic commons. Substantiating this view is evidence regarding Chinese investments in Russian Arctic infrastructure, commercial ventures, and shipping. For example, the French firm Total, Russia's Novatek, and China's National Petroleum Corp. are developing the joint $27 billion Yamal liquefied natural gas (LNG) project in the Kara Sea. Although China is providing only 20 percent of the financing, its investment is critical given Russia's difficulties in accessing Western capital following the sanctions imposed in 2014.[93]

A second concern is the potential role to be played by both the Northwest Passage and the Northern Sea Route in an evolving global supply chain. These Arctic routes will soon be open to commercial shipping for much of the year, and the long-term ramifications are striking. If international shipping can reliably use either or both routes, the distances and transit times between Asian, North American, and European markets will be shortened drastically. This will lower shipping costs. For an export-oriented economy like China's, this will generate tremendous cost advantages. More striking is the geostrategic significance: open Arctic routes would free China from reliance on the Malacca Strait and Suez Canal—chokepoints where the United States and its partners can maintain control of the commons.[94]

## The Future of Arctic Strategy

A chorus of voices—domestic and international, strategic and commercial—have called for greater American engagement in the Arctic region. The early signals from the Trump presidency suggest that resource investment may occur, if profitable. Yet US policymakers and military officials have continued to adopt an abstemious approach. The chief product of nearly a decade of Arctic alarmism is paper: the United States has issued a growing number of relevant policy documents. But the United States—unlike Russia, Norway, and Canada—has taken relatively few concrete steps to implement a strategy despite its Arctic coastline. America has abstained from muscular, unilateral involvement, and it has been loath to employ a moderated, multilateral approach. Instead, the United States has tentatively shifted from Isolationism to Restraint, with only a tepid commitment of resources.

For its part, the US Navy has focused on what it regards as more-pressing hotspots, such as the South China Sea and the European theater, including the Baltic Sea, the Eastern Mediterranean, and the Black Sea.[95] The US Coast Guard has sounded alarm bells over its inadequate fleet and operating budget, but to little avail.[96] Congress has not increased funding or dedicated more resources to icebreakers or infrastructure. Instead, the Navy is pursuing a very deliberate approach. Per the US Navy's *Arctic Roadmap for 2014–2030*:

> Resource constraints and competing near-term mission demands require that naval investments be informed, focused, and deliberate. Proactive planning today allows the Navy to prepare its forces for Arctic Region operations. This Roadmap emphasizes low cost, long-lead activities that position the Navy to meet future demands. In the near to mid-term, the Navy will concentrate on improving operational capabilities, expertise, and capacity, extending reach, and will leverage interagency and international partners to achieve its strategic objectives. The Roadmap recognizes the need to guide investments by prudently balancing regional requirements with national goals.[97]

There are several mutually supportive explanations for America's modest commitment. Timing, for example, matters. An alarming article about the "Arctic Meltdown" appeared in March 2008, just as the Countrywide Mortgage failure forced panicked business leaders and policymakers to recognize that a great recession was starting.[98] Few were willing to publicly call for greater government expenditure to address a security problem that might not emerge for decades. Subsequent sequestration, coupled with other foreign policy challenges, combined to limit Arctic investment. The Department of Defense's thinking was reflected in its 2011 *Report to Congress on Arctic Operations and the Northwest Passage*:

> The near-term fiscal and political environment will make it difficult to support significant new U.S. Government investments. This is an assumption, but also serves as a constraint on action. Agencies will only operate in the Arctic to the level to which they are resourced, meaning that new efforts will likely have to be funded through reallocation of existing resources. The Arctic is currently seen as a peripheral interest by much of the national security community, a situation not likely to change significantly in the next decade or more, absent some external forcing event, such as a major environmental or human disaster or activity in the Arctic viewed as threatening U.S. interests in the region.[99]

This response is puzzling in a broader context: a potential security threat, a possible competition for the region's abundant resources, a more than thousand-mile coastline abutting the region, and an Arctic Council institutional structure that is compatible with multilateral Leadership. Yet these circumstances also led policymakers toward an embryonic Retrenchment strategy in one of the few global commons where America lacks a substantial military presence. The absence of a state-based existential threat to the homeland, a limited but functioning multilateral institutional structure, and a preference for minimizing costs all culminated in an American decision to sustain the status quo.

Among Obama administration officials, only Hillary Clinton was prominent in discussing Arctic strategy—both during her time as President Obama's Secretary of State and subsequently out of government. As one Arctic scholar observed after studying her record, Clinton thinks about the Arctic "in multiple dimensions and as a priority concern."[100] As of the summer of 2016, John McCain was the only leading Republican to have raised the Arctic as an issue worthy of greater attention. At least while campaigning, candidate Trump, notably resistant to the idea of climate change, did not speak publicly about Arctic security.[101] His administration's first draft budget proposal even suggested cutting the Coast Guard's operating budget by over a billion dollars.[102] It is noteworthy however that James Mattis, Trump's Secretary of Defense, asserted soon after his confirmation hearings that it was incumbent on the US military to contemplate the effects of the thawing of Arctic waters and opening of routes on American national security.[103]

By the beginning of 2017, the discourse over Arctic security nonetheless remained nascent. As the region rapidly warms and ice packs melt, demands for action will grow and perhaps resonate with policymakers beyond a small interested community. The salience of the Arctic may also increase if a serious natural disaster occurs, or if other states—even inadvertently—engage the United States in a military confrontation. Alternatively, policymakers may reassess the strategy if global competitors from China, Russia, and Europe take advantage of new shipping routes to gain competitive advantages over American corporations. Under any one or a combination of these circumstances, long-term pressure will build and perhaps force the US Navy to raise the Arctic on its list of priorities. It is likely the Navy will have to broaden its horizons if it hopes to sustain control of the Arctic's commons in the decades to come. To paraphrase a question asked by a long-time Navy analyst during a meeting to prepare a Navy-Coast Guard Arctic strategy, "Can you think of one ocean the Navy does not sail in?"[104]

# Controlling the Southern Maritime Approaches with an Isolationist Strategy

We're going to build a wall, triple the border patrol.
—Donald Trump, campaigning for
the Republican presidential nomination

We are going to be a country of destination.
—US Coast Guard Commandant Adm. Paul Zukunft, 2017

I have met the enemy and he is us.

—Cartoon strip character, Pogo

Since its founding, the United States has sought to control illicit flows, from guns and alcohol to narcotics and people. Smugglers have been ingenious about the routes they choose and the means they use to transport their cargoes. Their cat-and-mouse games with American law enforcement—and, increasingly, the sea services (the USN, USCG, and Marine Corps)—have accelerated over the last few decades, driven both by technology and by market prices. Government authorities have benefited from new surveillance and tracking technologies; smugglers and traffickers have countered with state-of-the-art communications and purpose-built vessels designed to thwart surveillance or avoid capture.

Modern-day Isolationists have defined these illegal flows as the primary national security threat to the United States. They have avoided the term *Isolationism* itself because of its association with Nazi sympathizers and those favoring neutrality in the 1930s. But many of the sentiments foundational to the term have found currency among politicians, notably in the 2016 presidential campaign in which America's problems with drugs, unemployment, and terrorism were all associated with illicit flows.[1] Even the term *America First*, long discredited because of its nativist associations, has come back into vogue.[2] The solutions—build high walls; dramatically increase border controls; pursue assertive unilateral policies;

ban people from the country en masse based on their nationality, ethnicity, or religion—all have their precedents in American history.[3] But as American policymakers strenuously seek to defend America's borders against these illicit flows, their inability to thwart them says more about the magnitude of the task than about their efforts. Whatever the form those flows may take, policymakers can never know how much was not intercepted. They can only estimate their volume or monetary value. Nonetheless, the Navy and Coast Guard (USCG) devote significant resources to implementing the rudiments of an Isolationist strategy every day. Many American politicians either ignore or are blissfully unaware of maritime interdiction efforts. Meanwhile, policymakers feel obliged to respond to public concerns about the noxious effects of illicit flows.

## The Tale of Bigfoot and the Life of a Vessel

In November 2006, a US Coast Guard cutter seized a submersible vessel dubbed "Bigfoot" one hundred miles off the southwest coast of Costa Rica. The cutter's crew reportedly spotted three plastic pipes skimming through the water. Upon investigation, they found a "50-foot wood and fiberglass craft, breathing through the pipes" and motoring "along at about 7 mph, just six feet beneath the surface."[4] With a crew of four, armed with AK-47s, Bigfoot carried three tons of cocaine bound for Mexico, where it would be transported by land into Texas.[5]

Bigfoot's seizure was only one of numerous encounters with submarines and semisubmersibles by the USCG and Navy. In September 2008, the USS *McInerney*, a Navy frigate carrying a Coast Guard law enforcement detachment,[6] spotted Bigfoot II about 350 miles off the Mexico--Guatemala coast. Suspicious about the vessel's contents, they boarded it, only to find four Colombians and 6.4 tons of cocaine with an estimated value of over $100 million.[7] Yet these seizures did not provide a lasting deterrent. By 2016, the USCG and Navy were seizing submarines and semisubmersibles with cargos estimated to be worth twice that amount.[8]

Now decommissioned, the *McInerney* was a guided missile frigate, 467 feet long and at the time of the seizure carrying two helicopters, light armaments, and a crew of 19 officers and 195 enlisted men. The *McInerney* had previously been deployed in environs as diverse as the Mediterranean Sea, the Red Sea, off the coast of Africa, and within the Arctic Circle. It was under the operational control of the US Sixth Fleet—based in Naples, Italy, and responsible for the European area of operations (and parts of Africa) until 2007. In 2008, the *McInerney* was in its thirty-first year of commissioned life and deployed to the mundane task of interdicting makeshift submarines along America's coastline.[9] Today, the rejuvenated vessel enjoys a higher profile. After a $65 million refurbishment that included the installation of antisubmarine warfare systems and new weapons (paid for by the US taxpayer), it serves the Pakistan Navy as the PNS *Alamgir* (F260).[10] Flying Pakistan's flag, it joined Combined Task Force 151 on counterpiracy operations (as discussed in chapter 5).[11]

The USS *McInerney*'s use in counternarcotics operations reveals something important about US strategic flexibility. The USN ships in Joint Interagency Task Force (JIATF)-South, the task force responsible for counterdrug operations, are not assigned to the Fourth Fleet, which is formally responsible for the South Atlantic, Caribbean Sea, and Gulf of Mexico.[12] When ships and other equipment are assigned to SOUTHCOM and the Fourth Fleet, they are provided, or "chopped" (in military parlance), by other Navy commands with wider geographic responsibilities far from the American homeland. The Fourth Fleet's official mission statement reveals the reason: it declares that it "employs maritime forces in cooperative maritime security operations to maintain access, enhance interoperability, and build enduring partnerships that foster regional security in the USSOUTHCOM Area of Responsibility."[13] In less formal language, the United States believes there are few large-scale threats in the region; that interoperability near the American coastline is necessarily with small, low-tech regional navies; and—in the Caribbean and Central America—threats to regional security come from nonstate actors, not powerful states with advanced naval capabilities. The absence of dedicated Fourth Fleet assets demonstrates that its counternarcotics missions are a lower priority for the US Navy than operations in other theaters. Nevertheless, the Navy implements the national counternarcotics strategy.

Operationally speaking, catching smugglers does not require dedicating assets or assigning large numbers of the USN's best ships on a full-time basis. Rather, USN vessels like the *McInerney* play a supporting role to the Coast Guard. JIATF-South, the regional drug interdiction task force led by a Coast Guard rear admiral, uses the resources of the Fourth Fleet or temporarily employs other assets, like the USS *George Washington* Carrier Strike Group or individual ships from other fleets, such as the Norfolk, VA-based Fleet Forces Command or the Third Fleet, headquartered in San Diego, California.[14]

The operational implication is that smaller fleets can flexibly borrow what they need on an ad hoc basis. The budgetary implication is broader: Isolationism, in terms of sealing the nation's maritime approaches, can be achieved relatively cheaply—at least as far as the Navy is concerned—even in the face of novel technologies like semisubmersibles. Finally, the strategic implication is that the United States often uses big, expensive vessels that might be more productively used patrolling the South China Sea rather than the Gulf of Mexico. The strategy potentially leaves the USN short-handed.

## The Bigger Bigfoot Problem

The use of submersibles is not new. Rumors and fragmentary intelligence reports suggest that the Colombian cartels and other transnational criminal networks had been experimenting with underwater systems for two decades before Bigfoot. As Rear Admiral Joseph "Pepe" Castillo, US Coast Guard Eleventh District commander, observed in 2010, "The submarine is both a game-changer and a logical progression in the efforts of the drug runners."[15] Bigfoot I and Bigfoot II were simply indicative of a broader phenomenon:

> The U.S. Coast Guard discovered twenty-three semi-submersibles between 2001 and 2007. From October 2007 to February 2008, that number leaped to twenty-seven. The U.S. government estimates that the drug cartels completed the construction of forty-five submersibles in 2007. By mid-2009, U.S. law enforcement officials estimated that semisubmersibles were supplying at least one third of the U.S. cocaine market.[16]

Indeed, the use of submersibles by drug traffickers—and the response by US law enforcement and the USN—are part of a broader American security conundrum. It involves efforts to protect US citizens from a range of illicit maritime flows, hidden aboard not only submersibles but other types of purpose-built vessels and even commercial and civilian ships.

If narco-submarines can carry five tons of cocaine, Bigfoot clearly has potential for other forms of smuggling within the Western Hemisphere, whether directly into the United States by sea or through Mexico and Canada and then onward by land. Retired Vice Admiral James Stavridis, former commander of US Southern Command, warned in 2015 that "it is important that we collectively consider the potential of these types of vessels to transport more than just narcotics: the movement of cash, weapons, violent extremists, or, at the darkest end of the spectrum, weapons of mass destruction."[17] Authorities believe that maritime traffickers are adapting technologies and operating procedures to counter interdiction efforts. Admiral Charles D. Michel, Deputy Commandant for Operations of the US Coast Guard, for example, testified in 2015 that "today we face a sophisticated adversary that leverages high-tech conveyances such as semi- and fully-submersibles, employs multiple go-fast vessels to move drug shipments, and deploys beacons if forced to jettison bales of contraband to allow later relocation; all are advanced and coordinated means to avoid detection and evade apprehension."[18]

As the increasingly routine use of semisubmersibles demonstrates, protecting America's maritime approaches is more challenging than ever. Well-funded, technologically sophisticated, and globally connected smugglers have a greater capacity to evade the US maritime services and their domestic counterparts, and to transport larger loads effectively.

Thus, at least in the minds of some Isolationists, the world has radically changed since the decades between 1945 and 2001, when American strategists could focus US sea power globally rather than protecting the nation's littorals.[19] The USCG, the primary law enforcement and quasi-military force charged with guarding the nation's coast, has long suffered from a budget and force structure inadequate to carry out its assigned missions. As Admiral Kurt Tidd, the head of Southern Command, told the Senate Armed Services Committee in March 2016, the Coast Guard does not have the ships or aircraft to stop the flow of drugs and migrants from Central America and Mexico.[20] This apparent shortfall has occurred while the federal government's budget for Customs and Border Protection increased by 91 percent, from $6.6 billion to $12.4 billion, between 2003 and 2014. The number of (land-based) border agents over that decade grew from 10,717 in 2003 to 21,391 in 2013, a 99 percent increase, mostly along the southern border.[21] In contrast, there was a combined total of 1,138 (sea-based) interdiction agents for the northern and southern borders by 2013. Huge amounts of money have been spent on land border controls, and the maritime approaches have received a paltry proportion of the overall budget. Air and marine operations, for example, were less than 10 percent of the budget in the FY16 Homeland Security Appropriations Act.[22] Demonstrating a continued inadequate understanding of the maritime dimensions of this problem, the new Trump administration suggested cutting the Coast Guard's budget, in part to pay for a proposed border wall.[23]

The USN contributes expensive vessels, designed for traditional naval missions in the far reaches of the globe, to supplement an underequipped USCG in performing what the Navy considers unglamorous, low-end tasks associated with counternarcotics operations. For the Navy, it is like asking a renowned chef to flip burgers. Furthermore, the Navy argues that operating as a "forward presence" around the globe is efficient and affords the United States a greater ability to influence events abroad. When it comes to acquiring equipment and allocating its resources, the Navy has for decades prioritized ships and aircraft designed for high-intensity combat and long-endurances missions far from the United States. Nevertheless, beginning with the 1980s "War on Drugs," the Navy has diverted ill-suited but expensive ships to help the Coast Guard chase fast boats and low-tech subs and semisubmersibles.[24] How American policy reached this point, and how the maritime services interdict illicit flows, are the focus of this chapter.

## Illicit Flows

Peter Andreas has claimed that America is a "smuggler" nation, built on illegal trade.[25] During the colonial period, new Americans sought to avoid imperial tariffs and taxes with the triangle trade of sugarcane, rum, and slaves. During the Revolutionary War, rebels financed and provisioned their forces through gun running. But these are only two early examples. Indeed, important parts of the American economy subsequently had long-standing business models build on circumventing the law. During Prohibition, for example, smuggling liquor thrived as Americans chose to drink rather than obey the Eighteenth Amendment.

Illicit alcohol helped expand the powers of federal law enforcement agencies,[26] including the US Coast Guard and the Federal Bureau of Investigation.[27] It was during Prohibition, for example, that the "directives of 1923 authorized the [Coast] Guard's use 'all necessary force' to enforce laws at sea, including liquor interdiction."[28] The USN, however, maintained its traditional role, focusing on its overseas missions and guarding against the possibility that other great powers might use their navies to exert influence in the Western Hemisphere.[29]

Smuggling has become more complex in the modern era. Some legitimate businesses, including financial services and transportation firms, have conveniently ignored the activities of what the law enforcement community calls transnational criminal organizations and more specialized drug trafficking organizations (DTOs). Simultaneously, smuggling has also become the province of local gangs and mafias, often in partnership with foreign criminals. The days when a Joe Kennedy Sr. could maintain legal businesses while simultaneously dabbling in smuggled tea or spirits are largely gone. Major smuggling is no longer for part-timers or amateurs.

In response to this "professionalization" of smuggling, the US government has increased its efforts to control borders and provide local, state, and federal agencies with the resources and authority to interdict flows of illegal goods and people. In terms of grand strategy, a renewed emphasis on these issues has forced all military branches to devote resources to these "home games." Their collective mission has been simple: ensure that American borders are defended in support of domestic policy priorities such as immigration, antiterrorism, and drug control.[30] Adaptation has proved more difficult.

Countering the inflow of narcotics has been the heart of American counterdrug policy for more than a century. In 1971, President Nixon declared a "War on Drugs,"[31] leading to the subsequent involvement of the military. By the 1980s, drug trafficking across US borders—or perhaps better stated, the collection and analysis of trafficking data—had expanded, and there were predictable calls for a stronger national response. But the decisive point came a decade later. As Peter Andreas and Angelica Duran Martinez explain, "The end of the Cold War consolidated antidrug policies as the defining element of US security policy in the region [South and Central America as well as the Caribbean]."[32] The military's involvement became routinized.

## Broadening National Security Objectives

A subsequent array of American counternarcotics initiatives—from bilateral ones such as Plan Colombia to regional ones such as the Central America Regional Security Initiative, or CARSI—have utilized the US military in various ways. Some involve engaging local law enforcement officials proactively, whether in capacity building or in military-to-military training. Given America's abiding regional dominance, its defense against drug flows begins in Colombia, Peru, and the smaller countries of Central America. This "active defense" uses the US Army to train local forces, and the Coast Guard and the Navy to interdict drugs and other contraband destined for American shores.

The policy goal is succinctly articulated in the 2015 *Caribbean Border Counternarcotics Strategy*, to "extend the Caribbean Border farther from US shores."[33] Essentially, the American approach is one of layered, external defense: support local efforts to eradicate production and interdict shipments from processing centers. It employs the full range of US law enforcement agencies, the Department of Defense, and the intelligence community to stop traffickers from infiltrating America's land borders and exploiting its maritime approaches. American officials have occasionally been insensitive to the concerns of both producer and transit countries. But in 2006, Anne Patterson, Assistant Secretary of State for International Narcotics and Law Enforcement Affairs, testified that US partner nations have relinquished outdated "sovereignty sensibilities" so that each now "recognizes the links of the drug trade to money laundering, terrorist financing and organized crime, and has been working together to confront the many challenges."[34]

The United States has made efforts to collaborate with these countries, but has devoted most of its resources to unilateral interdiction using assets from the Coast Guard, Navy, and other agencies. Other countries have been forced to relinquish their sovereignty. The United States still regards its borders as the ultimate line of defense for American sovereignty. The Navy and USCG play key roles, attempting to stop the flow of drugs in America's littoral.

Both operate in the eastern Pacific along the coasts of Mexico and California, as well as in the Gulf of Mexico, eastern Caribbean, and the south Atlantic seaboard, all in the name of American national security. Of course, this approach employs a particular and unfamiliar definition of national security, because illicit flows pose no existential threat. It is also a curious definition, given that the sheer volume of drug traffic is driven by huge demand from Americans themselves. In this case, "the enemy," as the comic strip character Pogo famously suggested, "is us."

So, while there is a broad consensus that drugs pose a threat to the health and welfare of Americans, opinions diverge over the importance of drug flows as a national security issue. Isolationists push it toward the top of the list. Liberals characterize it as a threat best addressed multilaterally. Conservatives define it as an issue of domestic law and order. Many Realists simply ignore it as a security issue. Indeed, despite the long-standing challenge of illicit flows, it was not until the Obama administration issued its 2010 *National Security Strategy* that the United States articulated a rationale for military and law enforcement operations to thwart illicit trafficking:

> Transnational criminal threats and illicit trafficking networks continue to expand dramatically in size, scope, and influence—posing significant national security challenges for the United States and our partner countries. These threats cross borders and continents and undermine the stability of nations, subverting government institutions through corruption and harming citizens worldwide. Transnational criminal organizations have accumulated unprecedented wealth and power through trafficking and other illicit activities, penetrating legitimate financial systems and destabilizing commercial markets. They extend their reach by forming alliances with government officials and some state security services. The crime-terror nexus is a serious concern as terrorists use criminal networks for logistical support and funding. Increasingly, these networks are involved in cybercrime, which cost consumers billions of dollars annually, while undermining global confidence in the international financial system.[35]

In 2015, the three sea services echoed the Obama administration's concern in suggesting that

> transnational criminal organizations (TCO) remain a threat to stability in Africa and the Western Hemisphere, especially in Central America and the southern approaches of the U.S. homeland. Their networks facilitate human trafficking and interrelated flows of weapons, narcotics, and money, all of which could be exploited by terrorists to attack *our homeland,* allies, and overseas interests [emphasis added].[36]

In effect, they committed to providing the maritime security necessary to stop these hemispheric flows.[37]

## Redefining Maritime "Threats" and Organizing for Maritime Border Security

Two oceans, one sea, and the presence of two militarily weak and friendly countries on its land borders have protected the United States from invasion. Nonetheless, nontraditional threats to health, prosperity, and rule of law caused by illicit flows have remained a constant problem. With the development of more efficient global transportation networks, the challenge has grown acute. Furthermore, as the US government's ability to detect, surveil, and interdict illicit goods has improved, domestic perceptions of the contraband threat has grown. Nineteenth-century bootleggers, gunrunners, and immigrants could pass through America's porous and ill-defined territorial borders with little fear of detection. Today, the United States has clearly delineated borders and resolutely, if sometimes ineffectually, attempts to govern access to its territory by taxing incoming legal goods, preventing illegal materials from entering, and denying entry to those deemed a national security threat or seeking to work illegally. The US government now has mechanisms to "guesstimate" both the volume of illicit flows and their consequences. Predictably, these new data have generated new concerns.

If the unfettered passage of illicit goods and people was historically considered a "threat," coping with it was predominantly a matter of domestic politics and civilian law enforcement. But since the last several decades of the twentieth century, the executive branch's security agencies and the US military have taken on greater responsibilities for policing land and sea borders. This has led to tensions between the military preference for "away games" and the policymakers' contention that military support is essential for the "home games" of combating the increasingly sophisticated methods employed by TCOs and DTOs.

The antagonists—criminals and smugglers—may be familiar. What is new is their operational scope, scale, and geographic reach, as well as the sophistication of the technologies they employ. Modern TCOs profit from a range of overlapping illegal activities, including "drug trafficking, arms trafficking, human smuggling, human trafficking, counterfeit products, sea piracy, kidnap for ransom, and even the illegal smuggling of commodities such as tobacco and oil."[38] Furthermore, as market demand for contraband has grown, so have the resources at the criminals' disposal. They often operate in failed states where the collapse of government authority has allowed them to flourish. The combination of ungoverned spaces and robust demand for TCO "products" has altered the very nature of the conflict between TCOs and US authorities.[39] An increasing set of "gray area" phenomena parallel in many ways our earlier discussion of hybrid conflicts. These constitute "threats to the stability of nation states by non-state actors and non-governmental processes and organizations" involving "immense regions or urban areas where control has shifted from legitimate governments to new half-political, half-criminal powers."[40] TCOs may not have the trappings of conventional armies, but they have at their disposal resources that many armies lack.

We often think of the consequences of state failure as problems located in countries far from America's borders. But such places exist in the Western Hemisphere. Mexico suffered 164,000 homicides between 2007 and 2014.[41] And its annual figures were actually estimated to significantly increase in 2016.[42] The 2013 report by the United Nations Office of Drugs and Crime lists Honduras, Venezuela, Belize, El Salvador, Guatemala, Jamaica, Saint Kitts and Nevis, and Colombia among the ten countries with the highest homicide rates worldwide.[43] These countries (and others in the hemisphere) host a wide range of criminal organizations. Max Manwaring includes among the list "Transnational Criminal Organizations (TCOs) (cartels and mafia); small private military organizations such as the Zeta enforcer gangs (the Aztecas, Negros, and Polones); mercenary groups (the Central American Maras, Guatemalan Kaibiles, and paramilitary triggermen [*gatilleros*]); and other small paramilitary or vigilante organizations."[44] Aligned along the United States' southern tier are countries that have lost ground to this array of lawless organizations. Government corruption has magnified the problem. Thus, there are few reliable local partners for the United States, despite three decades of efforts at partnership building, including military-to-military cooperation.

The United States has often been reluctant to devote the resources needed to mitigate the consequences of state failure in other regions of the world—an example is the withdrawal of United States and international forces from Somalia after the Black Hawk Down incident in 1993.[45] But it cannot ignore state failures in Central and Latin America. The US military has deemed consequence management—such as enforcing laws to interdict illicit flows—essential to protecting the American homeland. The USCG and Navy have often acted unilaterally in the absence of reliable partners. Formally, regional partners are consulted and often supported with capacity-building measures. But difficult and complicated maritime operations often fall to the American forces. The United States has (at least in principle) therefore chosen to couple the low-cost, low-risk strategy of limited intervention into the domestic politics of Central and Latin American states plagued by insurgencies and criminal enterprises with an Isolationism associated with tight border controls and maritime interdiction programs.[46]

The production, transportation, and distribution of illegal drugs is flexible, innovative, and sensitive to the impact of new law enforcement initiatives.[47] TCOs and DTOs employ "all physical domains: air, sea, and land."[48] But they have a marked preference for shipping large quantities of illicit goods by water. First, the cost is lower. Second, the odds of being caught are drastically reduced because the maritime area involved is much larger than the US-Mexico borderlands. As the US Office of National Drug Control Policy contends, "Illicit drugs coming to the United States from South America pass through a seven million square-mile area called the Transit Zone, roughly twice the size of the continental United States. The Transit Zone includes the Caribbean Sea, the Gulf of Mexico, and the eastern Pacific Ocean."[49] Every Central American country and Mexico adjoin the maritime sections of the transit zone. Further east, several Caribbean islands also serve as occasional transit points, logistical hubs, and safe havens for drugs

151

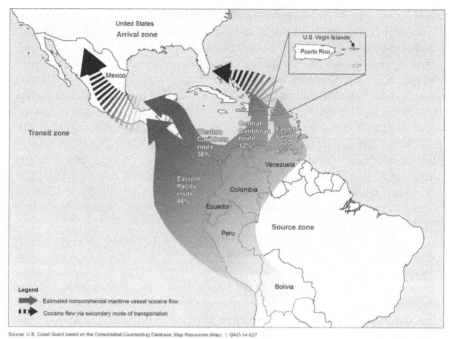

Figure 8.1. Drug flows from noncommercial maritime vessels, fiscal year 2013

bound for America's eastern seaboard. But as figure 8.1 suggests, Mexico is critical, because it has both the longest coastline and a long land border with the United States.

The Coast Guard is historically the lead agency for maritime policing and security operations in the hemisphere, a role largely reaffirmed in the aftermath of the 9/11 attacks. Yet because of the disparity of resources and capabilities, everyone recognizes that the Navy must provide the USCG with air defense, intelligence, and surveillance support.[50] The USN currently serves this function with the goal of targeting suspicious vessels for possible interdiction.[51]

The Coast Guard's authority on drug interdiction stems from Title 14 US Code § 89(a). Title 14 allows it to "make inquiries, examinations, inspections, searches, seizures, and arrests upon the high seas and waters over which the United States has jurisdiction, for the prevention, detection, and suppression of violations of the laws of the United States." That authority can be used by stand-alone Coast Guard units or in conjunction with the US Navy and international partners. Law enforcement detachments accompany naval personnel and occasionally civilian officials in both deep-water and littoral environments.[52] In these operations, the USCG often assumes tactical control of its Navy counterparts.

There are, however, legal limits to the extent to which the USN can support the Coast Guard, other federal civilian agencies such as Customs and Border Control, or even local law enforcement officials. The Posse Comitatus Act (Title 18 US Code § 1385) restricts the use of Department of Defense personnel with respect to law enforcement, specifically prohibiting the "interdiction of a vehicle, vessel, aircraft, or similar activities; and use of military personnel for surveillance or pursuit of individuals, or as undercover agents, informants, investigators, or interrogators" except for "military purpose doctrine" and "indirect assistance." Exceptions include:

(1) Actions that are taken for the primary purpose of furthering a military or foreign affairs function of the United States.

(2) Federal troops acting pursuant to the President's Constitutional and statutory authority to respond to civil disorder.

(3) Actions taken under express statutory authority to assist officials in executing the laws, subject to applicable limitations.

(4) [Counter-drug] operations authorized by statute.[53]

Nonetheless a gap exists between the service with legal authority and the service with the critical capabilities. The Coast Guard has both jurisdiction and the bulk of the ships and aircraft used for patrolling and maritime interceptions. Yet the Navy provides many of the most useful resources—intelligence, surveillance assets, and occasionally, ships. The Coast Guard districts responsible for the waters off the southern coast provide the personnel, cutters, and surveillance aircraft, whereas the Navy contributes ships chopped to the Fourth Fleet and specialized systems including surveillance equipment. To accomplish the counterdrug mission, they work together and with interagency task forces.

## Joint Interagency Task Force-South

In November 1993, President Bill Clinton signed Presidential Decision Directive (PDD) 14. It reaffirmed the drug threat to America and funneled money to help source countries to combat indigenous cocaine production. By 1994, the Department of Defense had created three Joint Interagency Task Forces (JIATFs) and a Domestic Air Interdiction Coordination Center. JIATF-East was headquartered in Key West Florida, JIATF-South in Panama, and JIATF-West in Alameda, California. The Domestic Air Interdiction Coordination Center operated from March Air Force Base in Riverside, California.

These national task forces were to serve as force multipliers and were manned by personnel from various agencies. Their mission was drug interdiction. Together with local, state, and international counternarcotics organizations, they have subsequently been restructured, some have been renamed, and their areas of responsibility have grown, largely due to changing operational demands, new techniques for catching drug runners, shifting national objectives, and shifting patterns of drug production and transit. Questions about jurisdictional boundaries predictably arose after the task forces were created. By 2016, the JIATF-South area of responsibility transcended the seams of SOUTHCOM, NORTHCOM, and PACOM, avoiding issues of command jurisdiction when narcotics are trafficked along combatant command boundaries.

JIATF-South primarily "conduct[s] interagency and international Detection & Monitoring operations, and facilitates the interdiction of illicit trafficking and other narco-terrorist threats in support of national and partner nation security."[54] Key to JIATF-South is the detection and monitoring elements—both necessary for effective interdiction. Thirteen federal agencies and fifteen international partners contribute to what is increasingly a "whole of government" effort,[55] including the departments of Defense and Homeland Security, the Defense Intelligence Agency, Customs and Border Protection, the Drug Enforcement Administration, the National Security Agency, the Federal Bureau of Investigation, and the Central Intelligence Agency.[56] All these organizations in the "interagency process are defined as partners, not subordinate agencies under the command of JIATF-South."[57] The lack of a hierarchy of command to enforce decisions reduces its functional coherence.

JIATF-South's area of operations includes 42 million square miles of ocean and land, ranging from the Gulf of Mexico to Argentina.[58] Its headquarters houses approximately five hundred personnel,[59] including representatives from all five branches of the US armed forces. International partners contribute to headquarter functions at JIATF-South and periodically detach personnel to American surface vessels, submarines, and aircraft.[60] JIATF-South's maritime area of operations doctrine in both national and international waters specifies that the US Coast Guard and Navy are both essential for intercept operations.

JIATF-South has occasionally assumed immigration control functions, in part because of the often-overlapping routes used to smuggle drugs and illegal immigrants across the US border. JIATF-South can expand to incorporate other "threats" because counternarcotic operations prioritize surveillance and monitoring. Intelligence and interdiction may not be designed to include new threats, but they can be expanded quite easily. JIATF-South now tackles drugs, human smuggling, and tax evasion.

TCOs and DTOs comprise most of JIATF-South's adversaries. But these criminal enterprises are often associated with insurgencies.[61] And terrorists are increasingly funded by drug profits.[62] Further, as the 2014 *International Narcotics Control Strategy Report* notes, "No criminal enterprise can function at a high-level for very long without penetrating and corrupting government institutions."[63] And the production, transportation, and distribution of narcotics is assisted by various legitimate businesses operating on the margins of the law—if not beyond them.[64]

The challenges are therefore as varied as the threats, and the form of conflict American personnel face is predominantly asymmetric. TCOs may employ brutal means against civilians and local law enforcement personnel. But even technologically sophisticated traffickers cannot risk using force against US government agencies and military units. There are, however, elements of hybrid conflict because government efforts to combat smuggling often involve nonmilitary institutions, such as the use of banks for money laundering.[65]

In operational terms, JIATF-South's interdiction process begins with intelligence about shipments, ideally from informants. The task force maintains a ceaseless "intelligence watch."[66] Additional intelligence and surveillance assets are used to confirm initial information, and tracking systems (e.g., satellites, aircraft, unmanned systems) are employed to locate a suspect vessel or aircraft.[67] Once confirmation is received, JIATF-South assigns a surface ship to intercept a trafficker. Sending ships to intercept specific vessels is much more efficient than simply patrolling part of the ocean. As one experienced Coast Guard officer observed, "The 'ship in a box' tactic, while effective in detecting strictly military threats to a strike group, is poorly adapted to law enforcement or surveillance operations. As JIATF operations matured through experience, it was determined that active use of intelligence combined with the use of military assets was far more effective in counternarcotics operations than simply assigning ships to patrol certain ocean areas."[68] American naval vessels require that a law enforcement detachment (LEDET)—generally consisting of eight Coast Guard personnel—accompany and direct the interdiction operation, to comply with the Posse Comitatus Act. The tempo of these operations ebbs and flows, but JIATF-South routinely monitors more than a thousand vessels a day. Of these, it directs assets to intercept two or three of the most likely targets.[69]

If a suspicious vessel is spotted sufficiently far out in the Atlantic, the intercept is undertaken by the USN, USCG, or one of the European navies affiliated with JIATF-South.[70] Operations near the coastlines of other countries in the Western Hemisphere are often left to local navies and coast guards, albeit sometimes with the assistance of JIATF-South air assets.[71] When the smuggler's craft is a "go-fast"—a small watercraft "with planing hulls and numerous outboard engines designed to reach high speed without affecting its cargo carrying capacity"—the Coast Guard deploys MH-65D *Dolphin* helicopters aboard patrolling cutters to assist with interdiction.[72]

The US Coast Guard provides most of the assets used by JIATF-South for detection, surveillance, and maritime interdiction.[73] These include major cutters, nineteen maritime patrol aircraft, armed helicopters, and LEDETs Coast Guard personnel.[74] The operation's scale is significant. The Coast

Guard's maritime patrol aircraft—primarily HC-130s and recently some HC-144As—fly approximately 4,700 hours per year.[75] The US Navy and Customs and Border Protection also contribute significant numbers of patrol aircraft.[76] In 2013, the US Navy provided 429 days of vessel deployment. But the financial and resource constraints imposed by sequestration have taken their toll: in 2013 the number of vessels made available to JIATF-South was less than one-half the vessel days in each of the prior four years.[77]

JIATF-South has enjoyed some operational successes despite these limitations: "Over the past 20 years, [JIATF-South] has arrested some 4,600 traffickers, captured nearly 1,100 vessels, and deprived drug cartels of $190 billion in profits."[78] Between 2002 and 2012, JIATF-South seized 1,997 metric tons of cocaine.[79] Yet narcotics are an ever-moving target: these drug busts have simply prompted traffickers to change tactics. Narcotics flows have shifted over time to some less-defended routes in the Pacific and from sea to overland routes.[80] Military cooperation with law enforcement and intelligence agencies has failed to even approximate victory in the "War on Drugs," despite costing billions of dollars.[81] One former JIATF-South director summarized the situation well:

> Our operational successes indicate an increasing level of trafficker sophistication and innovation as they rapidly employ readily available cutting edge technologies, change their tactics, and shift seamlessly between modes of communication and methods of conveyance. Our success is dependent upon our collective capability to be more innovative, more adaptive, and more agile than our adversaries. Currently, we are unable to target 74 percent of high confidence events. Of the 26 percent that we are able to target the principle [sic] impediment to successful detection and monitoring is the lack of the necessary sensors to generate persistent wide area surveillance and precision geolocation.[82]

### The Repeatedly Failed Efforts at Bilateralism and Multilateralism

This Isolationist strategy clearly has its limitations, a product of circumstances rather than preferences. It would suit the United States to share the financial and logistical burden, as in a Leadership strategy. Since the 2008 recession and subsequent budget sequestration, the United States has been forced to rely more on partner nations to carry out intercept operations. According to an official JIATF-South news release on Operation Martillo, an initiative to reduce drug trafficking in the waters off the Isthmus of Panama that commenced in January 2012, "partner nations have supported 67 percent of the law-enforcement interdictions of illicit traffickers."[83] With the availability of US assets questionable, SOUTHCOM has explored numerous ways to maintain operations—including nontraditional surveillance and interception assets for both American and partner forces. The former

head of SOUTHCOM has publicly discussed deploying the RC-12 Project
Liberty aircraft used in Afghanistan to provide intelligence, surveillance,
and reconnaissance in support of counterdrug operations.[84]

But reliance on partners to offset declining resources is unlikely to prove
effective or sustainable. Despite decades of efforts at collaboration, fundamental differences remain between the United States and other countries in
the region. The United States wants to prevent narcotics from reaching its
shores, while its partners have a broader set of goals. Bearing greater costs
for interdiction will inevitably reduce the resources they can use for other
policies and programs. Capacity issues exacerbate this problem. As one
Government Accountability Office report noted, "The inability of transit
zone countries to patrol their shores effectively and conduct other maritime
operations presents a major gap in drug interdiction. In many of the countries we reviewed, [the Department of State] has reported that partner
nations cannot operate U.S. -provided maritime assets for counternarcotics
missions due to a lack of operations and of maintenance resources."[85] These
capacity issues are amplified by political disagreements with and among
the transit zone nations, as well as domestic corruption that undermines
counternarcotics efforts.[86]

American multilateral initiatives run into as many problems as bilateral
ones. There are, of course, global protocols against these various forms of
smuggling, dating back more than a century, a prime example being American support for the 1912 International Opium Convention.[87] Its objective
was to limit the production and use of drugs to medical and scientific purposes.[88] Ultimately US efforts failed, initiating a trend that has persisted for
more than a century.[89] More recent UN conventions include the 1988 Convention against Illicit Traffic in Narcotic Drugs and Psychotropic Sub-
stances, the 2000 Convention against Transnational Organized Crime, and
the 2003 Convention against Corruption.[90] Yet, in contrast to the Sponsorship or Leadership cases we have described, successive US presidential
administrations have been frustrated by a lack of collaboration from other
regional governments in implementing these agreements.

In the Western Hemisphere, the United States has used its formidable
powers to facilitate counternarcotics operations, often blatantly cajoling,
bribing, or coercing smaller countries so that it can adapt global agreements
to its unilateral needs. International law, codified in the UN Convention on
the Law of the Sea, for example, prohibits US law enforcement authorities
from entering foreign territorial sea or air space, or from boarding a for-
eign-flagged vessel, without the foreign state's permission. One American
measure to overcome these legal impediments was the "shiprider" initiative in the 1990s. Agreements between the United States and its smaller
Caribbean neighbors permit American vessels with shipriders—onboard
officials from the relevant country—"to pursue, stop, board, search and
seize American, stateless or third-nation vessels suspected of criminal

activities with the permission of that state."[91] Jamaica and Barbados have complained that such agreements insufficiently respect national sovereignty. Moreover, they alleged that American negotiating tactics were coercive, including threats to limit foreign assistance, intimidation of their citizens by American law enforcement officials, unfavorable positions regarding regional free trade agreements, and even decertification of cooperation with American counternarcotics programs.[92] By the end of the 1990s, however, the United States had signed nearly thirty such bilateral agreements to "streamline the process involved in obtaining permission from a foreign State to enter their territorial sea and air space or to board one of their ships on the high seas."[93]

At times, the United States has acted unilaterally. In 2008, in response to the increasing use of submersibles and semisubmersibles, the US Congress passed the Drug Trafficking Vessel Interdiction Act (DTVIA).[94] Previously, law enforcement personnel had been required to find evidence of drugs to obtain a conviction following a seizure. Criminals therefore built submersibles and semisubmersibles that the crew could scuttle and evacuate, in order to thwart the interception of contraband. With the passage of the DTVIA, Congress criminalized the mere act of operating a vessel on the high seas without a national registration while attempting to evade detection. Some specialists claim "the DTVIA demonstrates an overzealous reach of United States jurisdiction on the high seas."[95]

As the United States has focused on interdicting narcotics traffickers passing through the transit zone, necessity dictated that it enlist the support of the small Caribbean island states. American diplomatic and military-to-military contacts have long sought to overcome island reluctance. But these states are characteristically plagued by inadequate fiscal resources, limited equipment often unsuited for patrolling territorial borders, corrupt officials, and threats posed by traffickers to state security.[96] Even if they want to cooperate, mounting pressure from the United States fuels perennial domestic concerns about maintaining independence. So from an operational perspective, they often prove unreliable.

From a strategic standpoint, the United States may have to devote more American assets and rely less on reluctant partners if American legislators, national security officials, and military officers deem maritime intercept operations sufficiently important. After all, an American Isolationism that seeks to push border controls further from its borders is not in the long-term interest of other states in the region.

The United States has produced an Isolationist strategy by default, not by design—for operational security reasons. Neither bilateral nor multilateral initiatives have proved successful in stemming the flow of drugs and illegal immigrants over the last century. Consequently, American operations have sought to enforce domestic laws unilaterally. As one assessment noted,

"Narcotics trafficking has been declared illegal by several international treaties, but the narcotics trade is not at present considered an international crime over which there is universal jurisdiction."[97] In response to this policy context, American strategy has remained firmly based on littoral border control in the Western Hemisphere.

The United States continues to be the world's largest consumer of illegal drugs. With roughly 5 percent of the world's population, it accounts— according to most estimates—for more than 25 percent of global demand.[98] Demand drives illicit flows, and this Isolationist strategy attempts to protect Americans from themselves. Despite the magnitude of the problem, domestic and civilian law enforcement agencies lack sufficient resources and authority to effectively patrol the borders. The US Navy and Coast Guard will have to continue to provide critical resources in the maritime domain, including aerial surveillance assets, intelligence fusion, and ships and aircraft. This arrangement will persist despite the USN command's reluctance and the enormous expense and inefficiency of deploying Navy platforms for law enforcement missions. As one early report suggested, "The locus of most routine training in the West Atlantic and Caribbean does not fit conveniently with drug interdiction choke and entry points."[99]

Some resources from the Army (active duty and reserves) will support military training and occasional collaborative efforts on the ground with partners in the Andes and Central America. But most of the military's efforts against illicit flows involve maritime surveillance and interdiction. The demand for such support by domestic law enforcement agencies will likely grow, and concerns about terrorist infiltration will make these demands more politically palatable. The suggestion that border control and counternarcotics missions are, at best, diversions from the military's primary missions will gain little traction if politicians evoke the threat of terrorists riding on the backs of drug smugglers.[100]

There is always the prospect of a deviation from the current strategy. But in which direction? The strategic environment is in flux in the aftermath of the 2016 election. Equally fluid are the ways the US national security community interprets that environment and crafts policies to meet changing conditions. Both strategists and politicians have advocated a new understanding of national defense. Some have expanded the notion to include public health, human rights, and economic security, as President Obama did in his 2010 and 2015 *National Security Strategy* documents. Others, notably President Trump, advocate a narrower conception of security that focuses on protecting the American homeland, especially US territories and their maritime approaches. Proponents of this latter conception want the maritime services to insulate the country from the world by operating closer to home rather than deploying across the globe. They emphasize guarding the nation's borders against illegal immigrants, terrorists, and contraband. If necessary, they believe, more military assets can and should be devoted to this task, and Congress should grant the necessary authorities and organizational reforms. Despite the rhetoric of the 2016 presidential campaign, Congress has yet to summon the political will to redirect large numbers of naval vessels and aircraft in such a manner. Hence, the Navy remains free to prioritize its global missions, leaving "home games" predominantly to the Coast Guard.

Among grand strategists, Isolationists have been particularly eager to enlist the military in border control. They believe that the domestic safety of American citizens, and so the impermeability of the country's borders, is the most important national interest.[101] Debates during the 2016 presidential primaries, followed by Republicans winning both the legislative and executive branches, suggest that homeland defense and security will be at the forefront of the political agenda, even if the party itself embraces "America First" while eschewing the term *Isolationism*.[102]

# Conclusion

## Moving beyond the Current Debate

> Every grand strategy involves a set of assumptions about the geopolitical landscape. If those assumptions are accurate and the rest of the logic of the strategy is sound, then the strategy has a good chance of producing success. But if the assumptions are inaccurate, then the strategy will not produce good results, even if the rest of the logic is otherwise sound.
>
> —Peter Feaver, professor and former member of the National Security Council

> As our Armed Forces confront the most diverse and complex array of national security challenges since the end of World War II under extraordinarily constrained fiscal resources, we simply cannot afford to waste our precious defense dollars on unnecessary or poorly performing programs.
>
> —John McCain (R-AZ), chairman of the Senate Armed Services Committee

The term *grand strategy* occupies a revered position in the lexicon of American policy. It assumes that the United States can impose its values and will globally through strategies that link America's ways and means to its ends. So, regardless of its particular form, grand strategy in each of the variants discussed in this book is consistent with a robust and muscular national security culture.[1]

The very notion is presumptuous. It is nonetheless consistent with a Cold War metaphor: the world is a chessboard on which the United States is the dominant player and where it can manipulate others if it pursues a coherent strategy employing all the instruments of national power.[2] It is also consistent with a liberal assumption that others yearn for American-style institutions and free market capitalism. Both assumptions are parsimonious and theoretically elegant.

Within that seemingly broad yet in fact quite limiting rubric, American planners, politicians, and pundits debate alternative grand strategies. They argue about which vision should dominate; to what degree the United States should guide others as a teacher and model; the extent to which it should stride the globe as a colossus; what form its exercise of power should take; or whether it should retreat and simply become an outsized version of an "ordinary" country to avoid the perils of imperial overreach or entrapment.

The very notion of grand strategy is psychologically reassuring. It embraces the view that Americans can determine their future—by virtue of the United States' unprecedented military power and its continued centrality in the functioning of the global economy. Minimally, proponents of Isolationism believe that they can shelter America from global pressures; those of Restraint suggest their preferred grand strategy can (preferably) avert or (effectively) address imminent or embryonic global threats; and maximally, liberals argue that a grand strategy can design the values, processes, and functioning of a global system—what G. John Ikenberry labels milieu or liberal order building.[3]

Inevitably, rival analysts clash on what values a US grand strategy should enshrine; the contours of national security; and the appropriate balance of resources among military power, economic instruments, diplomacy, and "soft power." But they concur in their belief that their recipe, if implemented, will attain the objectives of an appropriate US grand strategy.

When the grand strategies of presidents do not achieve their goals, it is characterized as *their* failure. Their preferred grand strategy was either inappropriate, or their administration's execution was flawed—the latter often a product of a gap between means and ends. Worse still, presidents may have no grand strategy at all and simply be "muddling through." For self-styled grand strategists, this constitutes a lack of "vision"—a vague term often regarded as synonymous with vocal, strident leadership. Ambitious American foreign policy objectives could be achieved, the critics contend, if only the country had presidential leadership with imagination, skill, and sufficient willpower. The former criticism (of a flawed vision) was routinely leveled at George W. Bush, the latter (of no vision) at Barack Obama.[4] Many early critics suggest Donald Trump is simply confused or ignorant, eschewing any grand strategy in favor of "a doctrine of "tactical transactionalism"—a foreign-policy framework that seeks discrete wins (or the initial tweet-able impression of them), treats foreign relations bilaterally rather than multidimensionally, and resists the alignment of means and ends that is necessary for effective grand strategy."[5]

While critics assail recent American presidents for their strategic failings, historians romanticize eras when their predecessors—such as Truman or Nixon—had the vision, command, and acumen to shape global events.

Unfortunately, many of these underlying assumptions are erroneous and the interpretations problematic. Indeed, the historical record is far less generous. Even renowned grand strategist Henry Kissinger suggested at the end of 2016 that "after its early years, America was lucky enough not to be threatened with invasion as it developed, not least because we were surrounded by two great oceans. As a consequence, America has conceived of foreign policy as a series of discrete challenges to be addressed as they arise on their merits rather than as part of an overall design."[6]

Critics thus presume a coherence to global and domestic patterns that is rarely evident. Granted, coherence may have been more apparent during the Cold War, when two superpowers were preoccupied with managing their allies, borders were less porous, identity politics was heavily suppressed, and the enemy was reliably "rational" (itself a contested term)—at least in prioritizing its own survival. But even if it was true then, little of that applies in the post–Cold War context.

Furthermore, proponents of grand strategy generally assume that the US homeland (and its national security policy) remains secure by virtue of two oceans, friendly neighbors, and great resources.[7] This leaves them free to focus on how the United States can shape the behavior of others. In contrast, we have suggested that those forces, in fact, can *shape* American strategies. They often result in reactive, not proactive, American maritime operations.

Rigid organizational structures, bureaucratic imperatives, and operational limitations are often ignored in implementing grand strategies. All three defy the abstract and deductive designs of even the most thoughtful strategic minds. As our diverse case studies have demonstrated, they sabotage even a well-constructed strategy. As a result, it is always easier to identify a grand strategy retrospectively—albeit with a selective reading of history coupled with a high level of abstraction—than to demarcate one in the current era.[8] But even if America's wealth and resources did allow it to implement a coherent grand strategy during the Cold War, despite organizational complications, this is no longer the case. America's resources and institutions are now simply insufficient to the task.

## Navigating a New Environment

We have presented evidence that confounds the prevailing assumptions about the utility of grand strategy as an organizing principle. We provided two types of evidence.

The first is composed of those elements that collectively shape the dynamics of the global system: the mutable character of the actors, the evolving nature of threats, and the consequent forms of conflict in which the United States engages with its adversaries. These elements have shifted the United States away from prophylactic strategies and increasingly toward reactive ones in an increasingly complex security environment.

None of these factors is novel. For two decades, scholars have contended that the global system now resembles the Middle Ages more than the statecentric Westphalian era. The argument, by now well rehearsed, suggests that the global system is fragmenting into one in which many forms of actors have political influence, ranging from popes and moral entrepreneurs to supranational organizations.[9] American national security planners have adapted the military dimensions of grand strategy to this reality. They now worry about terrorist groups with "global reach," transnational criminal organizations, and lone wolves—in addition to great powers and rogue states. These different actors vary in their access to weaponry and choice of tactics. But whatever they may lack in bombs and bullets, they may make up in social power that allows them to influence, coerce, and cajole.

Officially, then, American strategists have adapted their planning, discarding a narrow definition of national security in favor of one that incorporates elements of public, human, and global security. This change has shifted the geographic locus of US action to a variety of failed and fragile states. It is reflected in George W. Bush's repeated adage, in responding to the attacks of 9/11, that it was better to fight—and defeat—terrorists at their source than wait to confront them in the United States.[10] With the exception of traditional Isolationists, modern strategists rarely define homeland security simply in terms of territory. Commanding territory and being secure are no longer correlated. That very belief kept Barack Obama engaged in Central Asia and the Middle East, despite his 2008 campaign promise to end the wars in Afghanistan and Iraq and to withdraw American forces. Unchallenged, the same strategic logic may handcuff future presidents as well.

Over the last two decades, new actors have reduced their focus on territory, expanding their domains of operation and providing them with novel opportunities for conflict. Paradoxically, the growing number of actors has been partially driven by the resurgence of identity politics. A resurgence of ethnicity, race, religion, and populism as the organizing principles of politics has been a response to globalization's cosmopolitan elements—with which traditional American values about capitalism, democracy, and market culture are associated.[11] The Pope and jihadists alike, for example, tout religion as an antidote to the cultural universalism, consumerism, and impiety endemic to Western (read "American") culture. Likewise, nationalism and populism from both the Left and the Right are common responses to the purported economic imperialism endemic in unbridled liberal capitalism, evident in the resurgence of right-wing parties across Europe and the election of Donald Trump.

Dissenters, individually or collectively, often find modernity itself offensive.

Furthermore, traditional military threats are now rivaled by insurgents, terrorist networks, cells, franchises, and even individuals with a capacity to inflict mass casualties. The halcyon days when the pinnacle of military strategy was the ability destroy a nation's armies are long gone. Thus, while media and politicians celebrate the US policy of destroying the ISIS caliphate, including targeting ISIS leadership by drone strikes, the campaign may not solve the overarching problem.[12] ISIS leaders can be replaced, and its fighters can disperse to other nations, living to fight another day in other places and other forms.

Today's characterization of threats is similarly ambiguous, as we can see in the extent to which advocates of differing grand strategies vary their definitions, their preferred approach, and their objectives. These range from narrow conceptions of threats that are militarized and existential (in practice, originating from states and primarily stressing traditional interstate conflicts) to expansive ones that include public health and climate change—what strategic planners and military officials refer to as "nontraditional" security threats. These extend as far as the development of superbugs that could kill, according to one estimate, 317,000 Americans annually by 2050 if unaddressed.[13]

So, it is not surprising that many of the tasks we have described in this book are military operations other than war (MOOTW). If the military is to address these novel threats, then it has to accept new responsibilities. The individual services have not willingly embraced this broader mandate, preferring to respond to narrower definitions of national security. In the American context, the US military undertakes those missions assigned by its civilian leaders. But assuredly, the US military has definite preferences. Furthermore, the political system is sufficiently open that both serving and retired officers have many ways to express their preferences—whether as individuals, representatives of their service branch, or through other organizations.

Finally, new modes of conflict have emerged, among them hybrid warfare and cyberconflict. Conventional forms of warfare for which the military has traditionally trained still exist, of course, although the declining number of deaths from interstate warfare suggests its decreasing importance.[14] More significantly, the increasingly porous character of borders, and the lethal capacities of old technologies coupled with the accessibility of new ones, have made asymmetric warfare more costly and difficult for the United States to address. In the public imagination, the nightmare of nuclear war between superpowers has largely been eclipsed by a dirty bomb set off by terrorists, or a hybrid form of warfare in which our lives are darkened by cyberattacks on the power grid rather than illuminated by the flames of exploding munitions.[15]

## The Strategic Quandary

In tandem, this proliferation of factors—coupled with the popular presumption that threats to the United States can be extinguished rather than managed—has presented American planners with new challenges. Each factor—new threats, new actors, new forms of conflict—can configure in numerous ways and any matrix designed to accommodate all of them would be incredibly complicated. Yet many proponents of hegemonic grand strategies seem to believe that their preferred approach is the appropriate and effective response to all possible eventualities—ideally to prevent their occurrence, but minimally to contain their effects.

Military planners, by contrast, recognize that varied circumstances require a menu of strategic choices. Some threats are unlikely to arise; others are on the very edge of feasibility. But the anxiety created by traditional and social media, and the partisan schisms in the American political system, often dictate that even the most remote or outrageous of possibilities should be treated seriously. Just as important, they have to be *seen* to be treated seriously in a very public way—by presidents, bureaucratic departments, and military leaders. One recent example is the heated debate over China's so-called assassin's mace, alternatively described as a strategy, a technology (for mine warfare, for example),[16] or a set of technologies used by the weak to defeat the strong. The implicit underlying assumption is that some leapfrog technological breakthroughs (equivalent to the American phrase "silver bullet") will threaten US military superiority.[17] Planners are thus preoccupied with the question of what they "don't know that they don't know."

Faced with this inevitable increase in complexity, the standard response is to rely on tried and trusted approaches. Military leaders, for example, develop a veritable library of detailed war plans and various contingencies as they contemplate future conflicts. These plans define their options. When they lack off-the-shelf plans, they will use detailed analyses of historic cases to estimate the military forces necessary to fulfill a particular mission.[18] The opinions of professional military analysts often differ from those of political leaders. General Eric Shinseki, then Army Chief of Staff, encountered strong political resistance from the Bush administration over his assessment of the number of troops required to occupy Iraq after the 2003 invasion. Testifying before the Senate Armed Services Committee, he estimated that "I would say that what's been mobilized to this point—something on the order of several hundred thousand soldiers—are probably, you know, a figure that would be required." In a subsequent Pentagon press conference, Secretary of Defense Donald Rumsfeld demurred. He argued that fewer than 100,000 troops were required, suggesting that "the idea that it would take several hundred thousand US forces I think is far off the mark."[19]

It is generally difficult to alter course when reality collides with this array of strategic options. Indeed, reliably static bureaucratic structures are often essential if the military is to function effectively on a day-to-day basis—from implementing organizational logistics to observing the rules of war. But there are exceptions. When threats lie outside the military's conventional mandate, one organizational axiom is to create joint and interagency task forces—the kind described in our antipiracy and counternarcotics chapters.

The consequences of task forces vary, in terms both of how well they function and of their effectiveness. But they share two common features. First, they are often underfunded, because no single agency or (in the case of multilateral task forces) government has a vested interest in lobbying for funds on their behalf. Second, in practice, they more closely resemble network structures than hierarchies. They may have a formal, authoritative leadership, but given the relative autonomy of different services, agencies, and international partners, nobody is in charge and everything must be negotiated. As a result, they may lack the degree of centralization needed to operate effectively.

This combination has paradoxical effects. One is the use of very expensive manpower and equipment to perform simple operations, such as the use of large naval vessels to interdict drugs or pirates, while significant military threats (in the Indo-Pacific, for example) become harder to manage. This tendency is exacerbated by the USN's preference for "operating forward" while also preparing for large-scale conventional threats. Historically, the USN has kept ships and aircraft stationed around the globe, in countries facing few immediate threats, on the supposition that sea power will be valuable in virtually all contingencies. Naval task forces, especially ones near the US coastline, drain resources, complicating a strategy based on forward presence and forward defense. The inevitable result is the military leadership's call for larger budgets to plug the resource gaps that result from preparing for large-scale wars while simultaneously conducting military operations other than war.

If observers were to accept that no one grand strategy is capable of prescribing responses to the full range of threats to American national security, they would necessarily recognize that the primary purpose of a grand strategy is only rhetorical—a statement of values and principles that lack operational utility. Clearly, such a characterization falls well short of Liddell Hart's formative definition, which we quoted in the second chapter.[20]

Implicitly recognizing at least elements of our argument, proponents of ambitious grand strategies often suggest that their formulation should be malleable, to allow for changing circumstance.[21] But here the metaphor of a house built to withstand an earthquake is appropriate: it can sway if necessary, but it can absorb only so much pressure before collapsing. By definition, the architectural design of any single, abstract strategy is relatively rigid if not indeed static—intellectually, conceptually, analytically, and organizationally. Yet that one grand strategy is expected to work in a context that demands enormous adaptability and that routinely punishes rigidity. A static set of factors—core values linked to ways, means, and ends—inevitably collides with dynamic circumstances and the inflexible organizational structures required if the military is to function effectively on a daily basis. The military's leadership is far more aware than scholars or policymakers of that inherent problem.[22]

## Theoretical and Policy Implications

The adage that one should never let the facts get in the way of a good theory comes to mind when we reflect on debates about grand strategies. We concur with Barry Posen's sentiment that public debates play an essential role in any democracy.[23] We demur, however, when he suggests that "a grand strategy is a nation-state's theory about how to produce security for itself."[24] We believe it is not. A theory explains causal relationships—it does not prescribe. As we have documented, grand strategists make assumptions about how the global system operates, adopt a narrative based on those assumptions, and then prescribe on that basis. They generally do not concern themselves with explanation.

We are not inherently opposed to prescription. But embarking on that course minimally comes after a sequence of understanding, description, and then explanation. We also recognize that social scientists become less adept as they move through that process. So, when it comes to prescription, fortune may favor the brave. But it is not a task to be entered into lightly. We believe that useful policy prescription is based on explaining how things actually work, not on characterizing how they should operate. Explanation must precede prescription and not be skirted.

That is clearly a problem when it comes to the policy design implicit in any grand strategy. Our evidence regarding the US Navy suggests that American policy, in practice, does not replicate any single strategy. It reflects all of them, with different strategic approaches applied, depending on circumstance. In the early weeks of his administration, for example, both academics and analysts repeatedly accused President Trump of either having no grand strategy or the wrong one.[25] But that was a misconception of the situation. In his first three months Trump employed an Isolationist strategy when he attempted to introduce "extreme vetting" for people arriving from select countries, expanded domestic deportations, attempted to secure funds for building a southern wall and retracted his prior suggestion that the Coast Guard's budget should be cut.[26] He employed a Leadership strategy when he walked back prior, more extreme statements in declaring NATO "no longer obsolete," and the United States began engaging in a series of multilateral exercises in Europe.[27] And he employed a Primacist strategy when he claimed to have deployed an American "armada" into regional waters and an THAAD anti-missile system in South Korea in response to the North Korean government's missile tests.[28] None of these decisions may prove durable. Tactical changes may ensue over the life of any administration. But the underlying logic is evident. Even the most rigid, or indeed incoherent, of administrations will offer a plethora of strategies depending on the external factors and the internal organizational parameters.

The conclusion we draw is powerful: theories of grand strategy, as currently constituted, have little value because they do not meaningfully link ways, means, and ends to these various activities. At best, there is a selective linkage between what the US Navy actually does and what various proponents say it should do. And nothing suggests that all the activities we describe can be molded to fit any one formulation.

If correct, what are the policy implications of our work? One option is to persevere with the idea that grand strategies remain useful tools and that the military can be shaped to conform to the requisites of a particular strategy. Posen approximates that kind of approach when he suggests the Air Force, Army, and Marine Corps should be cut (along with overseas bases), consistent with a strategy of Restraint.[29]

A second option is to make the military services more organizationally flexible, strategically "nimble," and tactically adept. This possibility is analytically independent of arguments about the overall number of warships, aircraft, and other types of equipment. At least in theory, aircraft carriers, the symbolic cornerstone of the Navy, could be replaced by smaller craft, a different mix of ships, and greater numbers of stealthy surface vessels and undersea systems. The potential mixes of ships, aircraft, and support systems are virtually infinite if freed from the constraints of service traditions, long-term acquisition policies, and conventional military and grand strategies. Cyberweapons, larger numbers of more capable unmanned vehicles, and other high-tech weapons could displace traditional systems in America's armory. Indeed, former Secretary of Defense Ashton Carter and Deputy Secretary of Defense Robert Work focused on technological investment with the so-called Third Offset Strategy during the second Obama administration. Of course, it will be many years before we know how successful that strategy was and what the unintended consequences of emphasizing high-tech programs were. Precedent suggests that high-tech prescriptions will bring benefits but also incur unexpected costs as adversaries adapt to technological innovations.

Another, related option is to replace large-scale ground forces (armor and associated systems designed to fight opposing armored forces) with smaller-scale rapid reaction forces designed to fight insurgencies and counter terrorism. This option has been tried before, at least by American ground forces.[30] At the height of the Iraq and Afghan wars, as examples, American forces focused on irregular warfare and counterinsurgency operations: popular public figures like Generals David Petraeus and Stanley McChrystal were enormously influential in changing Army doctrine, tactics, and operations.[31] The "regular" army then subsequently counterattacked with renewed emphasis on traditional forms of land warfare. All of this was part of a predictable historic cycle. During the 1970s the revulsion against counterinsurgency operations in Vietnam and the impact on combat effectiveness was replaced by a renewed emphasis on conventional war in Europe.[32] That position was challenged by a resurgence in thinking about small wars and covert intervention during the Reagan administration's adventures in Central America in the 1980s and the Clinton administration's intervention in the Balkans in the 1990s.[33]

Another option is to plan to use the military for MOOTW, instead of doing so on an ancillary basis. It has become commonplace, for example, to declare that America's military is renowned for its war-fighting capacity but not for its peace-building capabilities. If the US military is to be used extensively to combat viruses and irregular violence, there is an argument for designing a strategy where such functions play a central, not a marginal, role.

Most pointedly, however, the logic of our research suggests that American academics, policymakers, strategists, and pundits should abandon the alluring but fruitless search for the holy grail of a single grand strategy. This change will be politically difficult and psychologically painful for those with a vested interest in current debates. But a retreat from a single, one-size-fits-all grand strategy to a plurality of calibrated strategies has several advantages.

First, it will alert policymakers and the public to the limits of American power. It would significantly challenge the hubris that often underlines America's militaristic culture. National pride and patriotism need not be synonymous with arrogance. Lonely but credible voices have been arguing for limits. Andrew Bacevich, a notable voice and retired Army Colonel, has consistently argued in favor of such limits on moral, ethical, economic, and political grounds.[34] He has convincingly demonstrated the perverse impacts and unintended consequences of American efforts to use military force to reshape political orders.[35] Christopher Preble, a former Navy officer, supports that view. Preble argues that the current size of the US military, coupled with America's propensity for interventionism since the early 1990s, is inconsistent with American political traditions and values. Furthermore, Preble suggests, such behavior does not contribute to American national security.[36]

While our analysis both recognizes and documents the limits to American power, we do differ from authors like Bacevich and Preble in one major way. We also attempt to demonstrate how a more nuanced operational approach to strategy—based on the nature of the threat, the actors, and the nature of the conflict—both guides American military engagement and, at least occasionally, will serve broader American interests.

The metric of any individual strategy should not be patriotic flag-waving based on outdated notions of what constitutes military power. Instead, it should be based on the strategy's effectiveness in achieving national ends within the limits of constrained resources and, as Liddell Hart might anticipate, under moral and ethical restraints consistent with American values. As we have shown, declining to commit large numbers of combat forces is not an axiomatic sign of weakness, an abrogation of "indispensable" American leadership, or an unwillingness to bear the burden of America's international commitments and responsibilities.[37] Rather, it may simply be a prudent allocation of resources based on national priorities and military risks.

Second, a debate about calibrated strategies rather than any one optimal grand strategy might engage Americans in a healthy strategic discussion about how the United States is influenced by global forces rather than the current propensity to believe that influence beams outward from America's shores (and this despite a domestic obsession with external threats). The effects of globalization on the US labor market, for example, have provided Americans with a sobering example of how global forces influence both domestic patterns of inequality and electoral politics. Questions concerning Russian involvement in the 2016 presidential electoral process and discussion about terrorism and pandemics suggests a comparable awareness. But a political and policy discussion built on a common understanding of how America needs to respond, flexibly, adeptly, and yet systematically, in a new security environment—rather than simply "using a hammer to bang a nail" or building a wall to keep them out—remains in short supply.

Third, the recognition of the intrinsic need for multiple strategies might also temper policymaker and public expectations of what America's military can reasonably be expected to achieve. The last three decades are replete with examples of unfulfilled, unrealistic, expectations and foreign policy failures: from President Bush's wars in Afghanistan and Iraq to the growth in insurgent militancy across the Middle East; from President Obama's ineffectual containment of Russia's annexation of Crimea to his inability to thwart China's construction of artificial islands in the South China Sea. In part, this frustration has been a product of exuberant ambitions on the part of America's political leadership, coupled with the general public's unfailing belief in the military's adroitness. In part, it is the product of the refusal of political elites to listen to their military leadership. And, we add, in part it is the product of a preference for a "one-size fits all" strategy over an acceptance of the importance of customized strategies for specific and often predictable problems.

Finally, we advocate that the United States embrace a variety of calibrated strategies so that its planners can have maximum latitude. The United States can act preemptively and unilaterally if existentially threatened; lead multilaterally and pay an enlarged proportion of the cost when it requires collaboration with allies to achieve its prized goals; support the initiatives of others—and bear less of a burden—in the pursuit of public goods when it is expedient to do so; protect and patrol key areas of transit through strategic chokepoints when it needs to ensure its own access while denying it to others if necessary; and guard its borders to maintain public security. The military does all of these things already. So, it seems prudent to plan to do so transparently. It makes little sense to relinquish any degree of autonomy in the name of strategic uniformity—to do so is to create a self-imposed straitjacket.

Yet planning to implement all these strategies with greater efficiency and functionality is no small task. It will require a rebalancing of American capabilities, and thus shifts in the defense budget—some within the military services and some across them. It would, for example, make sense to design a Coast Guard with sufficient resources to interdict in the seas to America's south or traverse the frozen waters to its north, even in the depth of winter, without having to rely on the Navy's powerful but expensive fleet. But where would such a redesign leave the Navy?

## Grand Strategy and the Future of the Armed Services

Several versions of US grand strategy seem tailor made for the sea services, especially the US Navy. The Navy prides itself on being flexible and adaptable.[38] Indeed, the breadth of US maritime capabilities is impressive. At the most sophisticated level, naval forces include weapons platforms and systems suitable for the highest ends of war fighting—from nuclear attack submarines to F-35 fighters. But they also include assets useful for the most mundane activities, including domain awareness and routine security missions—from the MQ-4C Triton unmanned aerial vehicle to hospital ships in humanitarian emergencies.[39]

That breadth becomes increasingly evident when one considers the additional capabilities of the US Marine Corps and US Coast Guard. The Marine Corps is a highly lethal ground force that arrives on station in naval vessels and receives (at least part of) its fire support from naval aviation and gunnery. Coast Guard cutters and surveillance platforms play important complementary roles to naval assets. Farther from home waters, Coast Guard law enforcement detachments are deployed on naval vessels to provide legal capabilities in situations short of war.

The US Navy has already recognized that these platforms and capabilities are required to deal with the variety of conflict that will inevitably arise. As Michèle Flournoy and Shawn Brimley have argued:

America's continued advantages in traditional warfighting provide powerful incentives for our adversaries to employ a mix of traditional and irregular approaches that span the range of conflict. The 2007 Maritime Strategy was correct to conclude that modern wars are "increasingly characterized by a hybrid blend of traditional and irregular tactics, decentralized planning and execution, and non-state actors using both simple and sophisticated technologies in innovative ways." Defense Secretary Robert Gates has written that "one can expect a blended high-low mix of adversaries and types of conflict . . . being employed simultaneously in hybrid and more complex forms of warfare."[40]

Equally important, the Navy views itself as a global force, even controversially advertising itself as a "global force for good."[41] Like the combatant commands created by the Goldwater-Nichols reforms in the 1980s, the US Navy divides the world geographically, with each region the responsibility of a numbered fleet. It can deploy ships, aircraft, and personnel to any trouble spot regardless of whether Navy ships are stationed full time in a particular region or sea.

This flexibility is palpable in the USN's military operations. One famous example was the support it provided to Special Operations Forces in carrying out initial strikes against Al Qaeda and the Taliban in the aftermath of 9/11. The USS *Kitty Hawk* deployed to the northern Arabian Sea the following month, commencing Operation Enduring Freedom, where it served as a forward staging base for the 160th Special Operations Aviation Regiment. The *Kitty Hawk's* role extended well beyond its usual mission. In order "to make room for a variety of SOF [special operations] helicopters, *Kitty Hawk* carried only a small presence of eight F/A-18 strike fighters from her normal air-wing complement of more than 50 combat aircraft, primarily to provide an air defense shield for the battle group."[42] For the vessel's crew, this was not a normal mission because they had hardly trained for operations with special operations units.[43] The *Kitty Hawk* served for two months before returning to Japan to perform more familiar functions.[44]

Moreover, naval forces adapt to changing circumstance. They can surge from domestic homeports or overseas bases, and they deploy to other regions as circumstances require. During crises or wars, the Navy concentrates its dispersed forces to achieve combat power. So, when American Primacy is challenged, naval assets can flow into a region within a matter of weeks to reestablish control of the seas and support American land forces. The Persian Gulf War of 1991 is instructive in this regard. When the crisis began, the USN maintained six ships on station, as part of the permanent

Joint Task Force Middle East.[45] By the end of the regional mobilization, the Navy had surged to sixty ships and an amphibious task force (including Marines and their equipment) to support vast numbers of Air Force and Army platforms, personnel, and equipment.[46]

In sum, the Navy can tailor its forces to provide the necessary support for virtually any grand strategy. But the task becomes significantly more challenging if it has to apply any one strategy globally. The US Navy and the other sea services would have a vastly more difficult time if required to support a Primacy strategy that demanded the US military be capable of deterring, fighting, and winning wars unilaterally. To assert Primacy globally would require more warships and other equipment than are currently available. Moreover, it would entail unreasonable demands for future budgets. Yet it is a strategy that many policymakers implicitly demand and often anticipate—whether in Eastern Europe or the South China Sea. Indeed, early reports suggests that the Navy will ask the Trump administration for a much larger fleet—up from the projected 308 to 355 ships—and that his key advisors may be inclined to devote more resources to the task than any presidential administration since Ronald Reagan's.[47]

Whether intentionally or not, naval strategists and planners design America's naval force structure with exactly this sort of flexibility in mind. One of the modern era's premier naval theorists, Wayne Hughes of the US Naval Postgraduate School, for example, has long advocated a "bimodal force" with regard to naval acquisition. He suggests that "a future combination of high- and low-end bimodal forces to deal with major contingencies cannot be perfectly suited. . . . The combination might be imperfect but sufficient."[48]

Tellingly, the Navy buys a myriad of ships, aircraft, and other capabilities on the assumption that it will always need to support both peacetime operations *and* high-end war fighting operations. Not surprisingly, the idea of what is termed a "high-low" mix dates back to Robert McNamara's term as Secretary of Defense between 1961 and 1968, and the notion that "a small number of highly capable ships would perform the limited number of missions that must be carried out in a high-threat environment. For less demanding missions, a larger number of moderately capable and more affordable ships would be procured."[49]

Beyond the three maritime services lies a larger policy question: how well placed are the Army and the Air Force to support our notion of calibrated strategies? One textbook answer is that the official approach of the United States to all phases of conflict (from peacetime to postconflict operations) is one of "jointness," where joint connotes "activities, operations, organizations, etc., in which elements of two or more Military Departments participate."[50] Dating from President Roosevelt's wartime creation of the Joint Chiefs of Staff (JSC), the US armed forces are, by intent, organization, and design, supposed to operate together, in a coordinated fashion that takes advantage of each service's capabilities. Roosevelt's decision, undertaken mainly to enhance military cooperation with Great Britain, was codified by the National Security Act of 1947 and serially modified in the 1950s. Jointness was reinforced and expanded by the Goldwater-Nichols Department of Defense Reorganization Act of 1986, which sought, in part, to redress imbalances between service interests and joint interests.[51] The United States is therefore legally and organizationally committed to a vision that places a premium on interservice collaboration. Given the distinct capabilities the military services bring to all phases of conflict in all war-fighting domains—from land to air, sea, cyber, and space—the US armed forces are theoretically well suited to provide the flexibility and adaptability required by calibrated strategies.

A more nuanced answer disaggregates jointness in two ways. First, for several of the most dangerous future conflict scenarios, in the western Pacific against China or in the European littoral against Russia, the interests and capabilities of the US Navy (and by definition the other sea services) and the US Air Force are both compatible and synergistic. Both services prefer "away games"; both specialize in high-intensity conflict; their missions require surveillance and intelligence collection; and neither requires large "footprints" on the ground. Indeed, the recent concept of Air-Sea Battle was jointly developed by the US Navy and the Air Force as a means to defeat Anti-Access/Area Denial strategies on the part of potential adversaries.[52] In sum, for many maritime missions involving both military operations other than war and actual wars, the maritime services and the Air Force have the capabilities necessary to operate in the emerging global security environment.

Second, the US Army has also been quite flexible in the post–World War II period, despite external criticism, occasional introspective expressions of doubt, and well-known failures. Through a succession of wars ranging from Korea to Iraq, the Army has alternated between conventional conflicts and irregular challenges—and occasionally has had to face both simultaneously.

The Army has often proved agile, as its current deliberations about any future conflict in the western Pacific illustrate. There is a long-standing American strategic axiom: "no land wars in Asia." Yet the Army has eagerly sought roles there—such as deterring China or fighting a potential war on the Korean Peninsula. These efforts underline the paradoxical point that in the post–Goldwater-Nichols era, interservice rivalries reinforce the preferred jointness approach to military operations. The Army's leadership is trying to adapt to the challenge and remain relevant by being flexible. Such a logic suggests it has the adaptive resources for a nuanced approach to grand strategy.

Ultimately, the US military services can and do implement calibrated strategies, and they have done so in recent decades. There is a little reason to doubt that they can continue to do so in the coming decades. It would admittedly be wise to acquire new capabilities, revisit the divisions among them, and transform the institutions to better protect the United States against emerging threats. That, however, is a task for another volume.

## The USN's Understanding of Its Contribution to American Grand Strategy

The Navy has had a prominent role in American grand strategy since the 1890s. Alfred Thayer Mahan, America's most influential naval scholar, not only founded an entire school of naval thought but is sometimes credited as one of the progenitors of the very notion of grand strategy itself.[53] As Edward Rhodes observes, "By nearly all accounts, the dominant American images of naval warfare in the postwar period, as in the half century prior, were strongly influenced by the teachings of Alfred Thayer Mahan."[54] In essence, as Geoffrey Till notes, "There was, in many of Mahan's books, a strong focus on the battle between concentrations of heavy warships as the ultimate decider of naval power."[55] Yet, by the mid-1980s, Philip Crowl, a well-known naval historian, could confidently assert that "traditionalism aside . . . there is scant indication that the U.S. Navy today holds to the Mahanian view of strategy that exalts sea power over all other forms of military action, claims for navies an autonomous domain in the realm of warfare, and equates command of the sea with victory."[56]

These contrasting views about the role of the Navy match the eras in which they were written. In the 1980s, the principal threat to the United States and its interests remained the Soviet Union, whose dominant military focus was central Europe. If war broke out between the United States, the Soviet Union, and their respective allies, experts fully expected the main battle to occur on the European mainland. The US Navy's role would concentrate on ensuring that the transatlantic "bridge" between North America and Europe remained open so that critical troops and supplies could flow freely.[57]

Today, close observers of the Navy cannot so confidently assert that Mahan's "philosophy" is dead and buried. With the rise of China's People's Liberation Army Navy—a foreign fleet capable of challenging the US Navy (within the confines of the western Pacific)—the USN once again thinks and acts in Mahanian terms. Indeed, in his first major policy statement following his appointment as Chief of Naval Operations in 2015, Admiral John Richardson explicitly linked America's twenty-first-century Navy to the views of the nineteenth-century doyen of sea power: "The essence of Mahan's vision still pertains: America's interests lie beyond our own shores. What was true in the late 19th century holds true today—America's success depends on our creativity, our entrepreneurism, and our access and relationships abroad. In an increasingly globalized world, America's success is even more reliant on the U.S. Navy."[58]

But to which Mahan was he referring? The oft-invoked caricature of Mahan as an imperialist, or the more nuanced portrait of Mahan as a grand strategist evident in Jon Sumida's work? It is hard to answer that question definitively from a reading of the Navy's influential 2007 document, *A Cooperative Strategy for 21st Century*, which describes, almost poetically, a global brotherhood of naval cooperation.

Yet delving deeper into the views of Admiral Richardson and his predecessor, Admiral Jonathan Greenert, and carefully examining the official communications and budget submissions of the Navy reveals the prominence of "main force conflict" on the high seas in the minds of the Navy's leadership. *The Design for Maritime Superiority* states that the USN will "maintain a fleet that is trained and ready to operate and fight decisively—from the deep ocean to the littorals, from the sea floor to space, and in the information domain."[59] This comment reinforces Admiral Greenert's famous assertion that "our primary mission is warfighting."[60]

If this Mahanian approach is resilient, and the US Navy—and to a lesser extent, the allied sea services—maintains a clear preference for playing "away games," then US grand strategy *should* be one of Primacy and entail patrolling the global commons. The other strategies discussed in this book—from the Sponsorship of counterpiracy operations to the Isolationism of counterdrug missions—are sideshows to the main event: preparing for and fighting wars at sea. But that aspiration, as we have demonstrated, may be unattainable in the twenty-first century.

# Appendixes

# The Strategies of American Foreign Policy

| Forms of conflict | Hegemony (Primacy) | Hegemony (Leadership) | Sponsorship (formal) | Sponsorship (informal) | Retrenchment (Restraint) | Retrenchment (Isolationism) |
|---|---|---|---|---|---|---|
| Primary US goals | Maintain international order | Enhance capitalism & democracy | Enforce international norms and the rule of law | Enforce international agreements | Strengthen U.S. defense through command of the commons | Strengthen U.S. defense through border control |
| Operating principle | Domination | First among equals | Selective engagement | Selective engagement | Limited disengagement | Significant disengagement |
| Modality | Assertive Interventionism | "Deep engagement" or "liberal hegemony" | Iterative legislated collaboration | Iterative coalitional collaboration | Command and control | Isolation |
| Definition of threats | Narrow—national security but include nation building | Broad—economic, political and security through and nation building and protecting interconnected global system | Broadest—economic, political, human, public, international and national security | Broadest—economic, political, human, public, international and national security | Narrow—sovereignty, territorial integrity, power position and safety against imminent threats | Very narrow—sovereignty, territorial integrity, and threats to domestic order |

(continued)

(continued)

| Forms of conflict | Hegemony (Primacy) | Hegemony (Leadership) | Sponsorship (formal) | Sponsorship (informal) | Retrenchment (Restraint) | Retrenchment (Isolationism) |
|---|---|---|---|---|---|---|
| Key actors | Homogenous (states) | Heterogeneous (states, international organizations) | Heterogeneous (states, international organizations, and nonstate actors) | Heterogeneous (states, international organizations, and nonstate actors) | Largely Homogeneous (states) | Heterogeneous (states, criminals, terrorists and illegal migrants) |
| Relationship to other actors | Unilateral | Multilateral | Sublateral | Sublateral | Unilateral | Unilateral |
| Primary policy instruments | Military Force (coercive) | Military Force (coercive and U.S.-led) | Military Force (MOOTW and rotational command) | Military Force (MOOTW and rotational command) | Military Force (navy, space, air force) | Military Force (navy, air force, USCG, national guards and LEAs) |
| | Diplomacy (nominal) | Diplomacy (moderate) | Diplomacy (high) | Diplomacy (high) | Diplomacy (low) | Diplomacy (low) |
| | Institution building (national) | Institution building (global) | Institution building (global and regional) | Institution maintenance (global and regional) | Institution maintenance (global and regional) | Institution maintenance (global and regional) |
| | Lawfare (low) | Lawfare (moderate) | Lawfare (high) | Lawfare (moderate) | Lawfare (low) | Lawfare (low) |

# Select Multilateral Exercises in the Indo-Pacific

| Exercise Name | Participants | Start year | Sequencing |
|---|---|---|---|
| KEY RESOLVE/FOAL EAGLE | U.S., South Korea | 1961 | Annual |
| RIMPAC | Pacific Rim countries (in 2014, there were 22 participating countries and six observers) | 1971 | Biennial |
| HONG KONG SAREX | U.S., Hong Kong (and China) | 1976 | Biennial |
| COBRA GOLD | U.S., Indonesia, Japan, Malaysia, Singapore, South Korea, Thailand | 1982 | Annual |
| PHIBLEX (amphibious landing exercise) | U.S., Philippines | 1984 | Annual |
| KEEN EDGE | U.S., Japan | 1986 | Biennial |
| KEEN SWORD | U.S., Japan | 1986 | Biennial |
| ANNUALEX | U.S., Japan | 1989 | Annual |
| COMMANDO SLING | U.S., Singapore (and Australia, since 1998) | 1990 | Annual |
| BALIKATAN | U.S., Philippines (and Australia, since 2014) | 1991 | Annual |
| MALABAR | U.S., India (occasionally Japan, Australia, Singapore) | 1992 | Annual |
| Cooperation Afloat Readiness & Training (CARAT) | U.S., Bangladesh, Brunei, Cambodia, Indonesia, Malaysia, Singapore, Philippines, Thailand, and Timor Leste (note that CARAT is a series of bilateral exercises held throughout the year and is not a single, multilateral exercise) | 1995 | Annual |
| SPITTING COBRA | U.S., India | 2004 | Periodic |
| TALISMAN SABER | U.S., Australia | 2005 | Biennial |

*(continued)*

(continued)

| Exercise Name | Participants | Start year | Sequencing |
|---|---|---|---|
| SALVEX | U.S., India | 2005 | Periodic |
| SHATRUJEET | U.S., India | 2005 | Annual |
| HABUNAG | U.S., India | 2006 | Annual |
| PACIFIC PARTNERSHIP | U.S., Australia, Chile, Japan, Malaysia, New Zealand, Singapore | 2006 | Annual |
| VIETNAM NAVAL ENGAGEMENT ACTIVITY | U.S., Vietnam | 2009 | Annual |
| DAWN BLITZ | U.S., Canada, Japan, New Zealand | 2010 | Annual |
| ULCHI FREEDOM GUARDIAN | U.S., South Korea | 1976 (the exercise was South Korea-only from 1968 through 1975) | Annual |
| MULTI-SAIL | U.S. (and Japan, since 2015) | 2002 (est.) | Annual |
| Southeast Asia Cooperation And Training (SEACAT) | U.S., Brunei, Indonesia, Malaysia, the Philippines, Singapore, Thailand | 2002 (under the name Southeast Asia Cooperation Against Terrorism); renamed in 2012 to reflect a broader scope of activities | Annual |

# PSI Multinational Exercises

| Year | Date | Location | Exercise Lead | Exercise Name | PSI-Related Focus |
|------|------|----------|---------------|---------------|-------------------|
| 2003 | Sep 10–13 | Coral Sea | Australia | Exercise PACIFIC PROTECTOR | Maritime interdiction |
| | Oct 8–10 | London, UK | UK | Unnamed command post exercise (CPX) | Air interdiction |
| | Oct 13–17 | Mediterranean Sea | Spain | Exercise SANSO 03 | Maritime interdiction |
| | Nov 25–27 | Mediterranean Sea | France | Exercise BASILIC 03 | Maritime interdiction |
| 2004 | Jan 11–17 | Arabian Sea | United States | Exercise SEA SABER | Maritime interdiction |
| | Feb 19 | Trapani, Italy | Italy | Exercise AIR BRAKE 03 | Air interdiction |
| | Mar 31–Apr 1 | Frankfurt, Germany | Germany | Exercise HAWKEYE | Customs exercise |
| | Apr 19–21 | Wroclaw, Poland | Poland | Exercise SAFE BORDERS | Ground interdiction |
| | Apr 19–22 | Mediterranean Sea, off of Sicily | Italy | Exercise CLEVER SENTINEL | Maritime interdiction |
| | Jun 23–24 | France | France | Exercise APSE 04 | Air interdiction |
| | Sep 27–Oct 1 | Newport, Rhode Island | United States | Unnamed tabletop exercise (TTX) | Unspecified |
| | Oct 25–27 | Tokyo, Japan | Japan | Exercise TEAM SAMURAI 04 | Maritime interdiction |
| | Nov 8–18 | Key West, Florida | United States | Exercise CHOKEPOINT 04 | Maritime interdiction |

*(continued)*

(continued)

| Year | Date | Location | Exercise Lead | Exercise Name | PSI-Related Focus |
|------|------|----------|---------------|---------------|-------------------|
| 2005 | Apr 8–15 | Alfeite, Portugal | Portugal | Exercise NINFA 05 | Maritime and ground interdiction |
| | Jun 1–2 | Ostrava, Czech Republic | Czech Republic and Poland | Exercise BOHEMIAN GUARD 05 | Ground interdiction |
| | Jun 7–8 | Mediterranean Sea and Zaragoza Air Base, Spain | Spain | Exercise BLUE ACTION 05 | Air and ground interdiction |
| | Aug 15–19 | Singapore | Singapore | Exercise DEEP SABRE | Maritime and ground interdiction |
| | Oct 3–7 | Bergen, Norway | Norway | Unnamed TTX | Air interdiction |
| | Nov 14–19 | Indian Ocean | UK | Exercise EXPLORING THEMIS | Maritime interdiction |
| 2006 | Apr 4–5 | Rotterdam, Netherlands | Netherlands | Exercise TOP PORT | Maritime interdiction |
| | Apr 4–6 | Darwin, Australia | Australia | Exercise PACIFIC PROTECTOR 06 | Air interdiction |
| | May 24–26 | Ankara, Turkey | Turkey | Exercise ANATOLIAN SUN | Maritime, air, and ground interdiction |
| | Jun 21–22 | France | France | Exercise HADES 06 | Air interdiction |
| | Sep 13–15 | Gdańsk, Poland | Poland, Denmark, Russia, and Sweden | Exercise AMBER SUNRISE | Maritime and ground interdiction |
| | Oct 10–31 | Persian Gulf | United States | Exercise LEADING EDGE 06 | Maritime and ground interdiction |
| 2007 | Apr 26–27 | Vilnius, Lithuania | Lithuania | Exercise SMART RAVEN | Air interdiction |
| | May 27–29 | Portoroz, Slovenia | Slovenia | Exercise ADRIATIC GATE | Maritime and ground interdiction |
| | Jun 18–22 | Newport, Rhode Island | United States | Unnamed TTX | Maritime and air interdiction |
| | Aug 29–Sep 7 | Miami, Florida and Panama | United States | Exercise PANAMAX 07 | Maritime interdiction |
| | Oct 12–15 | Yokohama, Japan | Japan | Exercise PACIFIC SHIELD 07 | Maritime interdiction |
| | Oct 29–31 | Odessa, Ukraine | Ukraine | Exercise EASTERN SHIELD 07 | Maritime, air, and ground interdiction |

| Year | Date | Location | Exercise Lead | Exercise Name | PSI-Related Focus |
|------|------|----------|---------------|---------------|-------------------|
| 2008 | Mar 10–12 | Djibouti | Djibouti and France | Exercise GUISTIR 08 | Maritime interdiction |
| | Apr 8–22 | Mediterranean Sea | United States | Exercise PHOENIX EXPRESS 08 | Maritime interdiction |
| | May 12–14 | Rijeka, Croatia | Croatia | Exercise ADRIATIC SHIELD 08 | Maritime interdiction |
| | Aug 11–22 | El Salvador, Honduras, and Panama | United States | Exercise PANAMAX 08 | Maritime interdiction |
| | Sep 15–19 | Auckland, New Zealand | New Zealand | Exercise MARU 08 | Maritime interdiction |
| 2009 | Apr 22–May 13 | Mediterranean Sea | United States | Exercise PHOENIX EXPRESS 09 | Maritime interdiction |
| | Apr 26–27 | Tel Aviv, Israel | Israel and United States | Unnamed U.S.-Israeli TTX | Unspecified |
| | Sep 11–22 | Panama | United States | Exercise PANAMAX 09 | Maritime interdiction |
| | Sep 14–15 | Panama | Panama and United States | Unnamed U.S.-Panama TTX | Ship-boarding agreement operationalization |
| | Oct 27–30 | Singapore | Singapore | Exercise DEEP SABRE II | Maritime interdiction |
| 2010 | Jan 24–28 | Abu Dhabi, UAE | UAE and United States | Exercise LEADING EDGE 10 | Maritime interdiction |
| | May 10–Jun 2 | Kenitra, Morocco | United States | Exercise PHOENIX EXPRESS 10 | Maritime interdiction |
| | Aug 20–27 | Panama | United States | Exercise PANAMAX 10 | Maritime interdiction |
| | Sep 16 | Cairns, Australia | Australia | Exercise PACIFIC PROTECTOR 10 | Air interdiction |
| | Oct 14–15 | Busan, ROK | South Korea | Exercise EASTERN ENDEAVOR 10 | Maritime interdiction |
| 2011 | Feb 22–23 | Ulaanbaatar, Mongolia | Mongolia, United States | Unnamed U.S.-Mongolia TTX | Ship-boarding agreement operationalization |
| | Apr 25–29 | Cape Verde and Senegal | United States | Exercise SAHARAN EXPRESS 11 | Maritime interdiction |
| | May 23–Jun 15 | Mediterranean Sea and Souda Bay, Crete | United States | Exercise PHOENIX EXPRESS 11 | Maritime interdiction |
| | Aug 14–26 | Panama | United States | Exercise PANAMAX 11 | Maritime interdiction |
| | Sep 9–10 | Bogota, Colombia | Colombia, United States | Unnamed U.S.-Colombia exercise | Unspecified |

*(continued)*

187

(continued)

| Year | Date | Location | Exercise Lead | Exercise Name | PSI-Related Focus |
|------|------|----------|---------------|---------------|-------------------|
| 2012 | Apr 23–30 | Cape Verde and Senegal | United States | Exercise SAHARAN EXPRESS 12 | Maritime interdiction |
| | May 7–30 | Mediterranean Sea | United States | Exercise PHOENIX EXPRESS 12 | Maritime interdiction |
| | Jul 3–5 | Sapporo, Japan | Japan | Exercise PACIFIC SHIELD 12 | Air interdiction |
| | Aug 6–17 | Panama | United States | Exercise PANAMAX 12 | Maritime interdiction |
| | Sep 26–27 | Busan, ROK | South Korea | Exercise EASTERN ENDEAVOR 12 | Maritime interdiction |
| 2013 | Jan 27– Feb 7 | Abu Dhabi, UAE | UAE | Exercise LEADING EDGE 13 | Maritime, air, and ground interdiction |
| | Aug 6 | Panama | Panama and United States | Unnamed U.S.-Panama TTX | Air interdiction |
| | Aug 12–16 | Panama | United States | Exercise PANAMAX 13 | Unspecified |
| | Nov 20–21 | Zagreb, Croatia | Croatia and United States | Unnamed regional (southeast Europe) TTX | Unspecified |
| 2014 | January | Miami, Florida | United States | Unnamed regional (Western Hemisphere) TTX | Unspecified |
| | May 13–15 | Newport, Rhode Island | United States | Unnamed TTX | Maritime and air interdiction |
| | Aug 4–7 | Honolulu, Hawaii | United States | Exercise FORTUNE GUARD 14 | Maritime interdiction |

Note on Appendix 3: The information in this table is sourced from the U.S. State Department's PSI "Calendar of Events," http://www.state.gov/t/isn/c27700.htm, as well as the "Activities" page of the German-hosted PSI website: http://www.psi-online.info/Vertretung/psi/en/02-activities/0-activities.html.

# Notes

## Introduction: Grand Strategies and Everyday Conflicts

1. See European Union European External Action Service, "Shared Vision, Common Action: A Stronger Europe," June 2016, http://europa.eu/globalstrategy/en.

2. As one EU analyst noted in a confidential interview for this book, the report focuses on security, not defense, and was greeted with indifference, if not hostility, when presented by Federica Mogherini, high representative of the Union for Foreign Affairs and Security Policy, to the European Commission.

3. Wang Jisi, "China's Search for a Grand Strategy: A Rising Great Power Finds Its Way," *Foreign Affairs* 90, no. 2 (March/April 2011): 68–79.

4. See Barack Obama's interview with Thomas L. Friedman in "Iran and the Obama Doctrine," *New York Times*, 5 April 2015, http://www.nytimes.com/2015/04/06/opinion/thomas-friedman-the-obama-doctrine-and-iran-interview.html; Jeffery Goldberg, "The Obama Doctrine," *The Atlantic*, April 2016, http://www.theatlantic.com/magazine/archive/2016/04/the-obama-doctrine/471525/.

5. For a discussion of this claim in the context of the Middle East and Europe, see Jeff Mason, "Obama Faces New Dynamic with Europe at G7 Summit," *Huffington Post*, 6 June 2015, http://www.huffingtonpost.com/2015/06/06/obama-g7-summit_n_7525760.html?utm_hp_ref=tw.

6. David Milne, *Worldmaking: The Art and Science of Diplomacy* (New York: Farrar, Straus and Giroux, 2015), 526.

7. For a modern treatment of friction in conflict, see Alan Beyerchen, "Clausewitz, Nonlinearity, and the Unpredictability of War," *International Security* 17, no. 3 (winter 1992–1993): 59–90.

8. See "FACTBOX—Malacca Strait Is a Strategic 'Chokepoint,'" Reuters, 4 March 2010, http://in.reuters.com/article/2010/03/04/idINIndia-46652220100304; US Energy Information Administration, *World Oil Transit Chokepoints*, 10 November 2014, http://www.eia.gov/countries/regions-topics.cfm?fips=wotc&trk=p3; "China Seeks Great Power Status After Sea Retreat," *Bloomberg Business*, 3 July 2014, http://www.bloomberg.com/news/articles/2014-07-02/china-seeks-great-power-status-after-centuries-of-sea-retreat.

9. Joshua R. Itzkowitz Shifrinson and Sameer Lalwani, "It's a Commons Misunderstanding: The Limited Threat to American Command of the Commons," in *A Dangerous World:*

*Threat Perception and U.S. National Security*, ed. Christopher A. Preble and John Mueller (Washington, DC: Cato Institute, 2014), 223.

10. Alfred Thayer Mahan, *Influence of Sea Power upon History, 1660–1783*, is in its twelfth edition and available for download at http://www.gutenberg.org/files/13529/13529-h/13529-h.htm.

11. Barry R. Posen, *Restraint: A New Foundation for U.S. Grand Strategy* (Ithaca, NY: Cornell University Press, 2014), 136.

12. Sean Mirski, "Stranglehold: The Context, Conduct, and Consequences of an American Naval Blockade of China," *Journal of Strategic Studies* 36, no. 3 (June 2013): 385–421.

13. "Maritime Domain Awareness is the effective understanding of anything associated with the maritime domain that could impact the security, safety, economy or environment of the United States." See Department of the Navy, *Navy Marine Domain Concept*, 29 May 2007, http://www.navy.mil/mda/, 4.

14. Catherine Zara Raymond, "Piracy and Armed Robbery in the Malacca Strait: A Problem Solved?" in *Piracy and Maritime: Crime Historical and Modern Case Studies*, Newport Paper no. 35, ed. Bruce Elleman, Andrew Forbes, and David Rosenberg (Newport, RI: Naval War College Press, 2010), 109.

15. See Ted Kemp, "Crime on the High Seas: The World's Most Pirated Waters," CNBC, 15 September 2014, http://www.cnbc.com/id/101969104.

16. See Executive Director's Report 2014, "Situation Update 2014," ReCaap Information Sharing Center, available through http://www.recaap.org/AboutReCAAPISC.aspx.

17. Itzkowitz Shifrinson and Lalwani, "It's a Commons Misunderstanding," 223–231; Posen, *Restraint*, xiii–xiv.

18. Cf. Robert Gates, *National Security Strategy* (Washington, DC: Department of Defense, May 2010), 49–50.

19. For a discussion of the concept of Sponsorship, see Simon Reich, *Global Norms, American Sponsorship, and the Emerging Patterns of World Politics* (Basingstoke, UK: Palgrave, 2010), 178–205; Simon Reich and Richard Ned Lebow, *Good-Bye Hegemony! Power and Influence in the Global System* (Princeton, NJ: Princeton University Press, 2014); and Peter Dombrowski and Simon Reich, "The Strategy of Sponsorship," *Survival* 57, no. 5 (2015): 121–148.

20. Cf. Jeffrey Michaels, *The Discourse Trap and the U.S. Military: From the War on Terror to the Surge* (New York: Palgrave Macmillan, 2010); Timothy Noah, "Meet Mr. 'Shock and Awe': Harlan Ullman Says They're Doing It Wrong," *Slate*, 1 April 2003, http://www.slate.com/articles/news_and_politics/chatterbox/2003/04/meet_mr_shock_and_awe.html.

21. See *National Security Strategy of the United States 2015* (Washington, DC: The White House, February 2015), iii, https://www.whitehouse.gov/sites/default/files/docs/2015_national_security_strategy.pdf.

22. For figures on the US resource commitment on its southern border, see The White House "Continuing to Strengthen Border Security," https://www.whitehouse.gov/issues/immigration/border-security.

23. Michael D. Shear, Helene Cooper, and Eric Schmitt, "Obama Administration Halts Program to Train Syrians to Combat ISIS," *New York Times*, 9 October 2015, http://www.nytimes.com/2015/10/10/world/middleeast/pentagon-program-islamic-state-syria.html?_r=0.

24. Cf. David Rothkopf, "Other People's Armies: Why Obama's Bet on Letting Our Friends and Enemies Slug It Out in the Middle East Is So Risky," *Foreign Policy*, 19 May 2015, http://foreignpolicy.com/2015/05/19/other-peoples-armies-middle-east-camp-david-obama/.

25. President Obama: "We Will Degrade and Ultimately Destroy ISIL," *The White House Blog*, 10 September 2014, https://www.whitehouse.gov/blog/2014/09/10/president-obama-we-will-degrade-and-ultimately-destroy-isil.

26. Quoted in Mark Landler and Jeremy W. Peters, "U.S. General Open to Ground Forces in Fight against ISIS in Iraq," *New York Times*, 16 September 2014, http://www.nytimes.com/2014/09/17/world/middleeast/isis-airstrikes-united-states-coalition.html?_r=0. For an overview of the issue, see James Fallows, "The Tragedy of the American Military," *The Atlantic*, January/February 2015, 73–80.

27. For an illustration of the extent of this commitment, see "Map: The U.S. is Bound by Treaties to Defend a Quarter of Humanity," *Washington Post*, 30 May 2015, http://www.washing

tonpost.com/blogs/worldviews/wp/2015/05/30/map-the-u-s-is-bound-by-treaties-to-defend-a-quarter-of-humanity/.

28. As exceptions, see Kevin Narizny, *The Political Economy of Grand Strategy* (Ithaca, NY: Cornell University Press, 2007); Robert Jervis, "US Grand Strategy: Mission Impossible," *Naval War College Review* 51, no. 5 (summer 1998): 22–26; Harvey M. Sapolsky, Eugene Gholz, and Caitlin Talmadge, *U.S. Defense Politics: The Origins of Security Policy*, 2nd ed. (London: Routledge, 2014), 13–31; David M. Edelstein and Ronald R. Krebs, "Delusions of Grand Strategy: The Problem with Washington's Planning Obsession," *Foreign Affairs* 94, no. 6 (November/December 2015): 109–116.

29. Cf. Zbigniew Brzezinski and John J. Mearsheimer, "Clash of the Titans," *Foreign Policy*, January/February 2005; Aaron L. Friedberg, "The Future of U.S.-China Relations: Is Conflict Inevitable?" *International Security* 30, no. 2 (fall 2005): 7–45; and Charles Glaser, "Will China's Rise Lead to War? Why Realism Does Not Mean Pessimism," *Foreign Affairs* 90, no. 2 (March/April 2011): 80–91.

30. Joseph S. Nye, Jr., *Soft Power: The Means to Success in World Politics* (New York: Public Affairs, 2005).

## 1. Naval Operations and Grand Strategy in the New Security Environment

1. Dana Dillon and John J. Tkacik Jr., "China's Quest for Asia," *Policy Review*, 1 December 2005, http://www.hoover.org/research/chinas-quest-asia.

2. George W. Bush, "Text: Bush Announces Formers Presidents to Lead Tsunami Aid Effort," *Washington Post*, 3 January 2005, http://www.washingtonpost.com/wp-dyn/articles/A44342-2005Jan3.html.

3. Rhoda Margesson, "Indian Ocean Earthquake and Tsunami: Humanitarian Assistance and Relief Operations," CRS Report for Congress, Updated 10 February 2005, https://www.fas.org/sgp/crs/row/RL32715.pdf, 7; and table 5, 45.

4. In the first month, the United States Agency for International Development (USAID) initiated debris cleanup projects, created temporary shelters, provided water and sanitation, and delivered 21,220 metric tons of food relief. American Presidency Project, "Fact Sheet: Continuing Support for Tsunami Relief," Office of the Press Secretary, 9 February 2005, http://www.presidency.ucsb.edu/ws/index.php?pid=81661. Americans privately donated $200 million. "Tsunami Aid: Who's Giving What," BBC, 27 January 2005, http://news.bbc.co.uk/1/hi/world/asia-pacific/4145259.stm.

5. See Bruce A. Elleman, *Waves of Hope: The U.S. Navy's Response to the Tsunami in Northern Indonesia*, Newport Paper no. 28 (Newport, RI: Naval War College Press, February 2007). Available at https://www.usnwc.edu/Publications/Naval-War-College-Press/-Newport-Papers/Documents/28-pdf.aspx.

6. Margesson, "Indian Ocean Earthquake and Tsunami," 93. Elleman explains the *Mercy*'s mission in the tsunami relief effort in *Waves of Hope*, chapter 7.

7. Margesson, "Indian Ocean Earthquake and Tsunami," 7.

8. Both in Kathleen T. Rhem, "USS *Lincoln* Sailors Greet Deputy Defense Secretary," American Forces Press Service, 15 January 2005, http://www.defense.gov/news/newsarticle.aspx?id=24349.

9. See Terror Free Tomorrow, "One Year Later: Humanitarian Relief Sustains Change in Muslim Public Opinion," undated. Available at http://www.terrorfreetomorrow.org/articlenav.php?id=82.

10. Posen, *Restraint* (Ithaca, NY: Cornell University Press, 2014), 1.

11. Ibid., 86.

12. Basil Henry Liddell Hart, *Strategy*, 2nd rev. ed. (London: Faber & Faber, 1967), 322.

13. Stephen G. Brooks and William C. Wohlforth, *America Abroad: The United States Global Role in the 21st Century* (New York: Oxford University Press, 2016), 75.

14. John Lewis Gaddis, "What Is Grand Strategy?" Prepared as the Karl von Der Heyden Distinguished Lecture, Duke University, 26 February 2009, 7. Available at http://tiss-nc.org/wp-content/uploads/2015/01/KEYNOTE.Gaddis50thAniv2009.pdf.

15. G. John Ikenberry, "American Grand Strategy in the Age of Terror," *Survival: Global Politics and Strategy* 43, no. 4 (winter 2001–2002): 25–26.

16. Thomas Mahnken, *Technology and the American Way of War since 1945* (New York: Columbia University Press, 2010).

17. Notably, this is a comment Gordon Adams pithily used to describe James Mattis, then Donald Trump's nominee as Secretary of Defense. Gordon Adams, "If You Have a Mattis, Everything Looks like a Nail," *Foreign Policy*, 2 December 2016, http://foreignpolicy.com/2016/12/02/if-all-you-have-is-a-mattis-everything-looks-like-a-nail-civil-military-balance-of-power-trump/.

18. On Ukraine, see Kirk Bennett, "The Realist Case for Arming Ukraine," *American Interest*, February 20, 2015. On Iran, see Matthew Kroenig, "Time to Attack Iran: Why a Strike Is the Least Bad Option," *Foreign Affairs* 91, no. 1 (January/February 2012), https://www.foreignaffairs.com/articles/middle-east/2012-01-01/time-attack-iran.

19. Cf. Pew Research Center, "Climate Change Seen as Top Global Threat," 14 July 2015, http://www.pewglobal.org/2015/07/14/climate-change-seen-as-top-global-threat/; Pew Research Center, "As New Dangers Loom, More Think the U.S. Does 'Too Little' to Solve World Problems," 28 August 2014, http://www.people-press.org/2014/08/28/as-new-dangers-loom-more-think-the-u-s-does-too-little-to-solve-world-problems/.

20. *National Security Strategy of the United States*, March 2006, 7; *National Security Strategy*, May 2010, 38.

21. Cf. *National Security Strategy* (2015).

22. Frank N. Schubert, *Other Than War: The American Military Experience and Operations in the Post-Cold War Decade* (Washington DC: Joint History Office and Office of the Chairman of the Joint Chiefs of Staff, 2013).

23. Admiral Jonathan Greenert, the former chief of naval operations (2011–15) has stressed that "our primary mission is warfighting. All our efforts to improve capabilities, develop people, and structure our organizations should be grounded in this fundamental responsibility." Jonathan Greenert, "Sailing Directions," (undated). Available at http://www.Navy.mil/cno/cno_sailing_direction_final-lowres.pdf.

24. Michael Lind, "Beirut to Bosnia," *New Republic*, 18 December 1995, 19. For an examination of the term *mission creep* from a variety of perspectives, see Gordon Adams and Shoon Murray, eds., *Mission Creep: The Militarization of U.S. Foreign Policy?* (Washington, DC: Georgetown University Press, 2014).

25. Fewer than 18 percent of congressional members served in the US military in the 114th Congress. See Rachel Wellford, "By the Numbers: Veterans in Congress," *PBS Newshour*, 11 November 2014, http://www.pbs.org/newshour/rundown/by-the-numbers-veterans-in-congress/.

26. Joseph F. Dunford, Jr., Jonathan W. Greenert, and Paul F. Zukunft, *A Cooperative Strategy for 21st Century Seapower: Forward, Engaged, Ready* (Washington, DC: Department of the Navy, March 2015), 19–26, http://www.Navy.mil/local/maritime/150227-CS21R-Final.pdf. The quote is on 26.

27. Naval analysts have resurrected term to examine how war with China might unfold. See, for example, Robert C. Rubel, "Command of the Sea: An Old Concept Resurfaces in a New Form," *Naval War College Review* 65, no. 4 (autumn 2012): 29.

28. This hypothetical entails worst-case conjecture about potential adversaries. But the US military generally engages in planning for "bolts from the blue." Cf. John Lewis Gaddis, *Surprise, Security, and the American Experience* (Cambridge, MA: Harvard University Press, 2004).

29. Larissa Forster, *Influence without Boots on the Ground: Seaborne Crisis Response*, Naval War College Newport Paper no. 39 (Washington, DC: GPO, 2013), 9; Linton Brooks, "Naval Power and National Security: The Case for the Maritime Strategy," *International Security* 11, no. 2 (1986): 58–88.

30. Associated Press, "U.S. Military Begins Search Flights for Stranded Rohingya," *Military.com*, 28 May 2015, http://www.military.com/daily-news/2015/05/28/us-military-begins-search-flights-for-stranded-rohingya.html.

31. Brooks and Wohlforth, *America Abroad*, 73.

32. Cf. Siemon T. Wezeman and Pieter D. Wezeman, "Trends in International Arms Transfers, 2014," SIPRI Fact Sheet, March 2015, 1.

33. Roberta Rampton, Matt Spetalnick, and David Brunnstrom, "'Madmen' Must Not Be Allowed to Get Nuclear Material: Obama," Reuters, 2 April 2016, http://www.reuters.com/article/us-nuclear-summit-obama-treaty-idUSKCN0WY52M.

34. Government Accountability Office, *Defense Department Cyber Efforts: Definitions, Focal Point, and Methodology Needed for DOD to Develop Full-Spectrum Cyberspace Budget Estimates* GAO-11-695R (Washington, DC: GAO, 29 July 2011).

35. For a simple illustration of this "not on my watch" syndrome, see Matt Apuzzo and Michael S. Schmidt, "F.B.I. Emphasizes Speed as ISIS Exhorts Individuals to Attack," *New York Times*, 28 July 2015, http://www.nytimes.com/2015/07/28/us/fbi-emphasizes-speed-as-isis-exhorts-individuals-to-attack.html.

36. Cf. "Lindsey Graham on the Issues," *New York Times*, 1 June 2015, http://www.nytimes.com/2015/06/02/us/politics/lindsey-graham-republican-presidential-candidate-on-the-issues.html.

37. Cf. David L. Rousseau and Rocio Garcia-Retamero, "Estimating Threats: The Impact and Interaction of Identity and Power," in *American Foreign Policy and the Politics of Fear: Threat Inflation since 9/11*, ed. Jane Cramer and A. Trevor Thrall (New York: Routledge, 2009), especially 76.

38. Marc A. Levy, "Is the Environment a National Security Issue?" *International Security* 20, no. 2 (fall 1995): 35-62.

39. Lauren Garrett, "The Zika Virus Isn't Just an Epidemic. It's Here to Stay," *Foreign Policy*, 28 January 2016, http://foreignpolicy.com/2016/01/28/the-zika-virus-isnt-just-an-epidemic-its-here-to-stay-world-health-organization/.

40. US Department of Health and Human Services, "The Great Pandemic 1918-1919," http://www.flu.gov/pandemic/history/1918/the_pandemic.

41. Pew Research Center, "Ebola Worries Rise, But Most Are 'Fairly' Confident in Government, Hospitals to Deal with Disease," 21 October 2014, http://www.people-press.org/2014/10/21/ebola-worries-rise-but-most-are-fairly-confident-in-government-hospitals-to-deal-with-disease/.

42. Centers for Disease Control and Prevention, "Questions and Answers: Estimating the Future Number of Cases in the Ebola Epidemic—Liberia and Sierra Leone, 2014-2015," (undated), http://www.cdc.gov/vhf/ebola/outbreaks/2014-west-africa/qa-mmwr-estimating-future-cases.html.

43. Theodore M. Brown, Marcos Cueto, and Elizabeth Fee, "The World Health Organization and the Transition from 'International' to 'Global' Public Health," *American Journal of Public Health* 96, no. 1 (January 2006): 62-72.

44. As we later discuss, the 2015 revised triservice vision statement unceremoniously downgraded the priority of HA/DR.

45. One former assistant secretary of the navy excoriated the Navy for it brief effort to recognize operational realities and the preferences of the nation's political leadership. Seth Cropsey, *Mayday: The Decline of American Naval Supremacy* (New York: Overlook Press, 2014).

46. Thomas Friedman, "Obama on Obama on Climate," *New York Times*, 7 June 2014, http://www.nytimes.com/2014/06/08/opinion/sunday/friedman-obama-on-obama-on-climate.html?_r=0.

47. Cf. US Department of Defense, *2014 Quadrennial Defense Review* (Washington, DC: GPO, 2014), http://www.defense.gov/pubs/2014_Quadrennial_Defense_Review.pdf; US Department of State, *United States Climate Action Report 2014* (Washington, DC: GPO, 2014), http://www.state.gov/documents/organization/219038.pdf; *National Defense Strategy* (2012); *National Security Strategy* (2010); and Defense Intelligence Agency, *Threat Assessments* (2013). For a topical example, see Department of Defense, *2014 Climate Change: Adaptation Roadmap* (2014).

48. These consist of buying and deploying the weapons, platforms, and support systems necessary to fight kinetic conflicts; naval, doctrine training, tactics, and procedures; performing exercises on scenarios involving maritime conflicts; and finally, actually participating in conflicts.

49. Ralph Ellis, "U.S. Bringing Home Almost All Troops Sent to Africa in Ebola Crisis," CNN, 27 February 2015, http://www.cnn.com/2015/02/10/us/ebola-u-s-troops-africa/. See also the military's Southern Command use in an R&D and MOOTW support capacity to combat the Zika virus. See Patricia Kime, "Zika Virus: Pentagon Will Relocate At-Risk Family Members," *Military Times*, 1 February 2016, http://www.militarytimes.com/story/military/benefits/health-care/2016/02/01/zika-virus-pentagon-relocate-risk-family-members/79515660/.

50. Condoleezza Rice, "Promoting the National Interest," *Foreign Affairs* 79, no. 1 (January/February 2000): 45–62; quote is on 53.

51. "The original U.S. concept of a 'Thousand Ship Navy' has broadened into 'Global Maritime Partnership' (GMP) that includes not just naval forces but the capabilities of civilian departments, law enforcement and regulatory agencies, industry representatives and nongovernmental organizations, all working together to forge enduring maritime security partnerships" (226). James Kraska and Brian Wilson, "The Global Maritime Partnership and Somali Piracy," *Defense and Security Analysis* 25, no. 3 (2009): 223–234.

52. See Gordon Adams and Cindy Williams, *Buying National Security: How America Plans and Pays for Its Global Role and Safety at Home* (London: Routledge Press, 2009); Gordon Adams and Matthew Leatherman, "A Leaner and Meaner Defense: How to Cut the Pentagon's Budget While Improving Its Performance," *Foreign Affairs* 90, no. 1 (January/February 2011), https://www.foreignaffairs.com/articles/united-states/2010-01-01/leaner-and-meaner-defense; Gordon Adams, "Budget Hope Springs Eternal at the Pentagon," *Foreign Policy*, 11 February 2015, http://foreignpolicy.com/2015/02/11/overseas-contingency-operations-budget-obama-ash-carter-pentagon/.

53. Bartholomew H. Sparrow, "American Political Development, State-Building, and the 'Security State': Reviving a Research Agenda," *Polity* 40 (July 2008): 355–367.

54. Aaron L. Friedberg, *In the Shadow of the Garrison State* (Princeton, NJ: Princeton University Press, 2000). Contra Friedberg, see Linda Weiss, *America Inc.? Innovation and Enterprise in the National Security State* (Ithaca, NY: Cornell University Press, 2014).

55. At the time of writing, all estimates are unreliable, varying significantly in recent years from 3,500 to 50,000. But illustrating this vast discrepancy in figures, see Jim Sciutto, Jamie Crawford, and Chelsea J. Carter, "ISIS Can 'Muster' between 20,000 and 31,500 Fighters, CIA Says," CNN, 12 September 2014, http://www.cnn.com/2014/09/11/world/meast/isis-syria-iraq/; "'Islamic State' Has 50,000 Fighters in Syria," *Al Jazeera*, 19 August 2015, http://www.aljazeera.com/news/middleeast/2014/08/islamic-state-50000-fighters-syria-2014819184258421392.html; Priyanka Boghani, "What an Estimate of 10,000 ISIS Fighters Killed Doesn't Tell Us," *Frontline*, 4 June 2015, http://www.pbs.org/wgbh/pages/frontline/iraq-war-on-terror/rise-of-isis/what-an-estimate-of-10000-isis-fighters-killed-doesnt-tell-us/.

56. Peter Singer and Allan Friedman, *Cybersecurity and Cyberwar: What Everyone Needs to Know* (London: Oxford University Press 2014).

57. Marc Sageman, *Understanding Terror Networks* (Philadelphia, PA: University of Pennsylvania Press, 2004), especially chapter 5.

58. Marc Sageman and Bruce Hoffman, "The Reality of Grass-Roots Terrorism [with Reply]," *Foreign Affairs* 87, no. 4 (July/August 2008): 163–166.

59. David Albright and Corey Hinderstein, "Unraveling the A. Q. Khan and Future Proliferation Networks," *Washington Quarterly* 28, no. 2 (2005): 109–128.

60. For a discussion of the varied organizational forms used by TCOs, see Peter Andreas and Ethan Nadelmann, *Policing the Globe: Criminalization and Crime Control in International Relations* (New York: Oxford University Press, 2006).

61. John Arquilla and David Ronfeld, *The Advent of Netwar* (Santa Monica, CA: RAND Corporation, 1996); and John Arquilla and David Ronfeldt, eds., *Networks and Netwars: The Future of Terror, Crime, and Militancy* (Santa Monica, CA: RAND Corporation, 2001).

62. Sarah Almukhtar, "How Boko Haram Courted and Joined the Islamic State," *New York Times*, 10 June 2015, http://www.nytimes.com/interactive/2015/06/11/world/africa/100000003734334.app.html.

63. Hamdi Alkhshali and Steve Almasy, "ISIS Leader Purportedly Accepts Boko Haram's Pledge of Allegiance," *CNN*, 12 March 2015, http://www.cnn.com/2015/03/12/middleeast/isis-boko-haram/; Abdallah Suleiman Ali, "Global Jihadists Recognize Islamic State," reprinted in *Al-Monitor*, undated, http://www.al-monitor.com/pulse/tr/security/2014/07/syria-iraq-isis-islamic-caliphate-global-recognition.html; Thomas Joscelyn, "AQIM Rejects Islamic State's Caliphate, Reaffirms Allegiance to Zawahiri," *Long War Journal*, 14 June 2014, http://www.longwarjournal.org/archives/2014/07/aqim_rejects_islamic.php; "OSINT Summary: AQIM Splinter Group Pledges Allegiance to Islamic State," *IHS Jane's Intelligence Review*, 15 September 2014, http://www.janes.com/article/43133/osint-summary-aqim-splinter-group-pledges-allegiance-to-islamic-state.

64. Lucy Dawidowicz, *The War against the Jews* (New York: Holt, Rinehart and Winston, 1975).

65. On the Balkans, see Wesley K. Clark, *Waging Modern War: Bosnia, Kosovo, and the Future of Combat* (New York: Public Affairs, 2001). For a brief discussion of the history and laws regarding genocide see United States Holocaust Memorial Museum, "The Genocide Convention in International Law," http://www.ushmm.org/confront-genocide/justice-and-accountability/introduction-to-the-definition-of-genocide.

66. Nonstate, nontraditional threats existed during the Cold War. Yet policymakers subsumed them within the overarching conflict. Indeed, the current irregular forms of warfare and conflict that dominate today's strategic debates such as terrorism and insurgencies had Cold War analogues (e.g., the Palestine Liberation Organization and the People's Movement for the Liberation of Angola, or MPLA).

67. James T. Conway, Gary Roughead, and Thad W. Allen, *A Cooperative Strategy for 21st Century Seapower* (Washington, DC: October 2007), unpaginated document, https://www.ise.gov/sites/default/files/Maritime_Strategy.pdf.

68. Peter R. Mansoor, "Introduction: Hybrid War in History," in *Hybrid Warfare: Fighting Complex Opponents from the Ancient World to the Present*, ed. Williamson Murray and Peter R. Mansoor (Cambridge: Cambridge University Press, 2012), 2.

69. For examples of how the term *hybrid* is employed, see Frank J. Cilluffo and Joseph R. Clark, "Thinking About Strategic Hybrid Threats—In Theory and in Practice," *Prism* 1, no. 4 (2014): 47–63; John J. McCuen, "Hybrid Wars," *Military Review* (March/April 2008): 107–113. For a critique see Russell W. Glenn, "Thoughts on Hybrid Conflict," *Small Wars Journal*, 2 March 2009, http://smallwarsjournal.com/jrnl/art/thoughts-on-hybrid-conflict. Still, "hybrid" has been utilized in official documents. Cf. Conway et al., *A Cooperative Strategy for 21st Century Seapower*.

70. Cf. US Army Operational Command, "Countering Unconventional Warfare: White Paper," 26 September 2014, 3; Scott Jasper and Scott Moreland, "The Islamic State Is a Hybrid Threat: Why Does That Matter?" *Small Wars Journal*, 2 December 2014, available at http://www.smallwarsjournal.com/printpdf/18345; Bill Gertz, "Russia, China, Iran Waging Political Warfare, Report Says," *Washington Free Beacon*, 25 November 2014, http://freebeacon.com/national-security/russia-china-iran-waging-unconventional-warfare-report-says/.

71. Frank Hoffman, quoted in Thomas Gibbons-Neff, "The 'New' Type of War that Finally Has the Pentagon's Attention," *Washington Post*, 3 July 2015, https://www.washingtonpost.com/world/national-security/the-new-type-of-war-that-finally-has-the-pentagons-attention/2015/07/03/b5e3fcda-20be-11e5-84d5-eb37ee8eaa61_story.html. For a full exposition, see also Frank Hoffman, *Conflict in the 21st Century: The Rise of Hybrid Wars* (Potomac Institute for Policy Studies, December 2007), http://www.projectwhitehorse.com/pdfs/HybridWar_0108.pdf.

72. Robert M. Gates, "A Balanced Strategy: Reprogramming the Pentagon for a New Age," *Foreign Affairs* 88, no. 1 (January/February 2009): 28–40.

73. Robert A. Newson, "Why the U.S. Needs a Strategy to Counter 'Hybrid Warfare,'" *Defense One*, 23 October 2015, http://www.defenseone.com/ideas/2014/10/why-us-needs-strategy-counter-hybrid-warfare/97259/.

74. Mark Mazzetti and Michael R. Gordon, "ISIS Is Winning the Social Media War, U.S. Concludes," *New York Times*, 12 June 2015, http://www.nytimes.com/2015/06/13/world/middleeast/isis-is-winning-message-war-us-concludes.html?smprod=nytcore-ipad&smid=nytcore-ipad-share&_r=0.

## 2. Comparing Grand Strategies—and Their Inherent Limitations

1. Christopher Kjom, *Global Trends 2030: Alternative Worlds,* National Intelligence Council, December 2012, preface, available at www.dni.gov/nic/globaltrends.

2. Peter Schwartz, *The Art of the Long View: Planning for the Future in an Uncertain World* (New York: Currency Doubleday, 1996).

3. For a controversial approach, see Mary Kaldor, *New and Old Wars: Organized Violence in a Global Era,* 3rd ed. (Palo Alto, CA: Stanford University Press, 2012); on the Balkans, Peter Andreas, "The Clandestine Political Economy of War and Peace in Bosnia," *International Studies Quarterly* 48, no 1 (March 2004): 29-51.

4. Cf. Idress Ali, 'US Watching Piracy Increase off Somalia, sees ties to Famine,' Reuters, 23 April 2017, http://www.reuters.com/article/us-usa-mattis-africa-idUSKBN17P0C7

5. Nathan D. Luther, "Bureaucracies: The Enemy Within," *Proceedings Magazine* 132, no. 2 (February 2006): 65.

6. Eliot A. Cohen, "Global Challenges, U.S. National Security Strategy, and Defense Organization," Testimony before the Senate Armed Services Committee, 22 October 2015, 4, http://www.armed-services.senate.gov/imo/media/doc/Cohen_10-22-15.pdf.

7. Ibid., 5.

8. We recognize that some authors offer variants within these six options. Robert Art, for example, combines elements of Primacy, Leadership, and Restraint to offer a unique configuration he titles "selective engagement." Cf. Robert Art, "Geopolitics Updated: The Strategy of Selective Engagement," *International Security* 23 no. 3 (winter 1998/99): 79–113. Francis Hoffman also offers an original configuration. Francis Hoffman, "Forward Partnership: A Sustainable American Strategy," *Orbis* 57 no. 1 (winter 2013): 20–40. They may be original, notable, and have utility, but these are variations on the themes we specify in the six approaches discussed.

9. Hew Strachan, "Strategy and Contingency," *International Affairs* 87, no. 6 (November 2011): 1281–1296.

10. Colin Dueck, "Ideas and Alternatives in American Grand Strategy, 2000–2004," *Review of International Studies* 30, no. 4 (October 2004): 522.

11. The definition of lawfare comes from Charles J. Dunlap Jr.: "The employ of regulation as an armament of conflict." Charles J. Dunlap Jr., "Law and Military Interventions: Preserving Humanitarian Values in 21st Century Conflicts," Harvard Carr Center working paper, 29 November 2001. See also Charles J. Dunlap Jr., "Lawfare Today: A Perspective," *Yale Journal of International Affairs* 3, no. 1 (winter 2008): 146–154.

12. James Cable, *Gunboat Diplomacy 1919–1991: Political Applications of Limited Naval Force,* 3rd ed. (Basingstoke, UK: Palgrave Macmillan, 1994).

13. Lawrence Yates, "Military Operations in Latin America, 1961–2001," in *A Companion to American Military History,* ed. James C. Bradford, vol. 2 (Hoboken, NJ: Wiley-Blackwell 2009), 572–583.

14. Francis Fukuyama, *Nation-Building: Beyond Afghanistan and Iraq* (Baltimore, MD: Johns Hopkins University Press, 2005).

15. Jane Perlez, "China Pushes Back against U.S. Influence in the Seas of East Asia," *New York Times,* 28 October 2015, http://www.nytimes.com/2015/10/29/world/asia/china-pushes-back-against-us-influence-in-the-seas-of-east-asia.html.

16. President Obama reiterated American indispensability in "President Obama: What Makes Us America," CBS News, 28 September 2014, http://www.cbsnews.com/news/president-obama-60-minutes/. For the original statement of that position, see Michael Dobbs and John M. Goshko, "Albright's Personal Odyssey Shaped Foreign Policy Beliefs," *Washington Post,* 6 December 1996, A25; Madeleine K. Albright, Interview on NBC-TV *Today Show,* Columbus, Ohio, 19 February 1998. For Obama's repudiation see his "Remarks by the President in Address to the Nation on Syria," 10 September 2013, http://www.whitehouse.gov/the-press-office/2013/09/10/remarks-president-address-nation-syria.

17. See Ashton B. Carter, William J. Perry, and John D. Steinbruner, *A New Concept of Cooperative Security,* Occasional Paper (Washington, DC: Brookings Institution, 1992); Paul B. Stares and John D. Steinbruner, "Cooperative Security and the New Europe," in *The New*

*Germany and the New Europe,* ed. Paul Stares (Washington, DC: Brookings Institution, 1992), 218–248. For an application, see Rodger Payne, "Cooperative Strategy in the Indian Ocean Region," in *The Indian Ocean and U.S. Grand Strategy: Ensuring Access and Promoting Security,* ed. Peter Dombrowski and Andrew Winner (Washington, DC: Georgetown University Press, 2014), 119–138.

18. There is a long list of subscribers to this view. But for a relatively recent recapitulation, see G. John Ikenberry, *The Liberal Leviathan* (Princeton, NJ: Princeton University Press, 2011).

19. Cf. Lindsey Graham, "Sen. Lindsey Graham: Nuclear Deal with Iran 'Has to Include Their Behavior,'" *All Things Considered,* NPR, 15 July 2015, http://www.npr.org/2015/07/15/423263343/sen-lindsey-graham-nuclear-deal-with-iran-has-to-include-their-behavior; Jon Rainwater, "McCain Joins Bolton, Invites Israel to Bomb Iran," *Huffington Post,* 31 May 2015, http://www.huffingtonpost.com/jon-rainwater/mccain-joins-bolton-invit_b_6973978.html.

20. Cf. Ryan Grim, "Iran Tried to Stop Houthi Rebels in Yemen, Obama Says," *Huffington Post,* 6 August 2015, http://www.huffingtonpost.com/entry/iran-tried-to-stop-houthi-rebels-in-yemen_55c3ba1be4b0d9b743db627c; Thomas Erdbrink, "Iran's Supreme Leader Says Israel Won't Exist in 25 Years," *New York Times,* 9 September 2015, http://www.nytimes.com/2015/09/10/world/middleeast/iran-ayatollah-khamenei-israel-will-not-exist.html.

21. Cf. Richard Haass, "What to Do with American Primacy?" *Foreign Affairs* 78, no. 5 (September/October 1999): 37–50; Niall Ferguson, "Welcome to the New Imperialism," *The Guardian,* 31 October 2001, http://www.guardian.co.uk/world/2001/oct/31/afghanistan.terrorism; and Niall Ferguson, *Civilization: The West and the Rest* (London: Allen Lane, 2011).

22. G. John Ikenberry labels this "milieu" order building. See G. John Ikenberry, "Grand Strategy as Liberal Order Building," unpublished paper, 29 May 2007, 2; Stephen G. Brooks, G. John Ikenberry, and William C. Wohlforth, "Don't Come Home, America: The Case against Retrenchment," *International Security* 37, no.3, Winter 2012: 7–51.

23. See G. John Ikenberry, *The Liberal Leviathan,* 10. For critiques of Ikenberry's claims, see Simon Reich and Richard Ned Lebow, *Good-bye Hegemony! Power and Influence in the Global System* (Princeton, NJ: Princeton University Press, 2014), 22; Simon Reich, "Interview with Charles Kindleberger," in *Return of the Theorists: Dialogues with Great Thinkers,* ed. Richard Ned Lebow, Peer Schouten, and Hidemi Suganami (London: Palgrave MacMillan, 2016), 268–273.

24. Anne-Marie Slaughter, "A Grand Strategy of Network Centrality," in *America's Path: Grand Strategy for the Next Administration,* ed. Richard Fontaine and Kristin M. Lord (Washington, DC: Center for a New American Security, May 2012), 43.

25. Ibid., 46.

26. For a historical perspective on this approach, see Stephen Sestanovich, "The Long History of Leading from Behind," *The Atlantic* (Jan/Feb 2016), http://www.theatlantic.com/magazine/archive/2016/01/the-long-history-of-leading-from-behind/419097/.

27. See Barack Obama, quoted in Jeffrey Goldberg, "The Obama Doctrine," *The Atlantic,* April 2015, http://www.theatlantic.com/magazine/archive/2016/04/the-obama-doctrine/471525/.

28. In international disputes, China and a number of other countries have sought to overturn established legal principles as part of a strategy to challenge the United States using so-called American soft power. See Peter Dutton, "Three Disputes and Three Objectives: China and the South China Sea," *Naval War College Review* 64, no. 4 (autumn 2011): 42–67.

29. For a discussion of a variety of relevant cases, see Peter Dombrowski and Simon Reich, "The Strategy of Sponsorship," *Survival: Global Politics and Strategy* 57, no. 5 (October/November 2015): 121–148.

30. Cf. Michael Barnett and Raymond Duvall, "Power in International Politics," *International Organization* 59, no. 1 (2005): 61; Ian Hurd, "Legitimacy and Authority in International Politics," *International Organization* 53, no. 2 (spring 1999): 379–408, especially 402.

31. For a prescient analysis see John Gerard Ruggie, *Winning the Peace: America and World Order in the New Era* (New York: Columbia University Press, 1998). Ruggie anticipated the difficulties of sustaining Realist grand strategies based on the logics of the balance of power (or

offshore balancing) and the resurgence of Isolationism in variants symptomatic of Restraint strategies.

32. David R. Francis, "Iraq War Will Cost More than World War II," *Christian Science Monitor*, 25 October 2011, http://www.csmonitor.com/Business/new-economy/2011/1025/Iraq-war-will-cost-more-than-World-War-II.

33. Watson Institute, Brown University, "Costs of War," http://costsofwar.org/article/economic-cost-summary.

34. Karen DeYoung, "Obama to Leave 9,800 U.S. Troops in Afghanistan," *Washington Post*, 27 May 2014, https://www.washingtonpost.com/world/national-security/obama-to-leave-9800-us-troops-in-afghanistan-senior-official-says/2014/05/27/57f37e72-e5b2-11e3-a86b-362fd5443d19_story.html; Mark Landler, "U.S. Troops to Leave Afghanistan by End of 2016," *New York Times*, 27 May 2015, http://www.nytimes.com/2014/05/28/world/asia/us-to-complete-afghan-pullout-by-end-of-2016-obama-to-say.html; Peter Baker, "Lessons of Iraq Loom Over Obama's Decision to Keep Troops in Afghanistan," *New York Times*, 15 October 2015, http://www.nytimes.com/2015/10/16/world/asia/lessons-of-iraq-loom-over-obamas-decision-to-keep-troops-in-afghanistan.html.

35. See Barack Obama, quoted in Goldberg, "The Obama Doctrine."

36. See "U.S. Spending on Islamic State Fight Totals $2.7bn," BBC, 12 June 2015, http://www.bbc.co.uk/news/world-us-canada-33104829; Geoff Dyer and Chloe Sorvino, "$1tn Cost of Longest U.S. War Hastens Retreat from Military Intervention," *Financial Times*, 14 December 2014, http://www.ft.com/cms/s/2/14be0e0c-8255-11e4-ace7-00144feabdc0.html#slide0.

37. See Goldberg, "The Obama Doctrine."

38. See updated figures for Afghanistan and Iraq at http://icasualties.org/ and at "Faces of the Fallen," *Washington Post*, http://apps.washingtonpost.com/national/fallen/.

39. Krishnadev Calamur, "American Casualties in the Fight against ISIS," *The Atlantic* (4 May 2016), http://www.theatlantic.com/national/archive/2016/05/american-death-toll-isis/481206/.

40. Press Briefing, Press Secretary Josh Earnest, 3 May 2016, https://www.whitehouse.gov/the-press-office/2016/05/03/press-briefing-press-secretary-josh-earnest-532016.

41. Peter Baker, Helene Cooper, and David E. Sanger, "Obama Sends Special Operations Forces to Help Fight ISIS in Syria," *New York Times*, 30 October 2015, http://www.nytimes.com/2015/10/31/world/obama-will-send-forces-to-syria-to-help-fight-the-islamic-state.html.

42. Alissa J. Rubin, Karam Shoumali, and Eric Schmitt, "American Is Killed in First Casualty for U.S. Forces in Syria Combat," *New York Times*, 24 November 2016, http://www.nytimes.com/2016/11/24/world/middleeast/syria-warplanes-turkey.html?smprod=nytcore-ipad&smid=nytcore-ipad-share&_r=0.

43. Terri Moon Cronk, "Carter: Counter-ISIL Defense Ministers Unanimously Support Objectives," *DoD News*, 11 February 2016, http://www.defense.gov/News-Article-View/Article/655155/carter-counter-isil-defense-ministers-unanimously-support-objectives; Chris Church, "U.S. Pushes Other Countries for Special Operators in Islamic State Fight," *Stars and Stripes*, 8 December 2015, http://www.stripes.com/news/us-pushes-other-countries-for-special-operators-in-islamic-state-fight-1.382686.

44. See Barack Obama, quoted in Goldberg, "The Obama Doctrine."

45. For a classic example of one of the most vociferous proponents of this view, see "Profile: John Bolton," BBC, 4 December 2006, http://news.bbc.co.uk/1/hi/4327185.stm.

46. For a summary of such examples, see Barbara Kralis, "U.S. Government Leads Battle against Trafficking," *Renew America*, 3 August 2006, http://www.renewamerica.com/columns/kralis/060803.

47. For a detailed description of America's antitrafficking Sponsorship strategy, see Simon Reich, *Global Norms, American Sponsorship, and the Emerging Patterns of World Politics* (Basingstoke, UK: Palgrave, 2010), 178–205. For a defense of this approach, see Leslie H. Gelb, "In Defense of Leading From Behind: So What If It's a Terrible Slogan? It's Still the Right Strategy," *Foreign Policy*, 29 April 2013, http://www.foreignpolicy.com/articles/2013/04/29/in_defense_of_leading_from_behind?page=0,1; Ryan Lizza, "Leading from Behind," *The New Yorker*, 26 April 2011, http://www.newyorker.com/news/news-desk/leading-from-behind.

48. Cf. David Remnick, "Behind the Curtain," *New Yorker*, 5 September 2011, http://www.newyorker.com/talk/comment/2011/09/05/110905taco_talk_remnick; Zach Carter, "Lindsey Graham Criticizes Obama on Libya Days after Gaddafi's Death," *Huffington Post*, 23 October 2011, http://www.huffingtonpost.com/2011/10/23/lindsay-graham-criticizes_n_1027098.html.

49. Reich and Lebow, *Good-Bye Hegemony!* 131–142.

50. Gordon Adams, "Don't Call It Isolationism: America's Not Retreating—It's Just Going Undercover," *Foreign Policy*, 26 June 2013, http://www.foreignpolicy.com/articles/2013/06/26/dont_call_it_isolationism.

51. Proponents of pruning American international commitments include Patrick J. Buchanan, *A Republic, not an Empire: Reclaiming America's Destiny* (Washington, DC: Regnery, 1999); Ron Paul, *A Foreign Policy of Freedom: Peace, Commerce, and Honest Friendship* (Lake Jackson, TX: Foundation for Rational Economics and Education, 2007). For a support of Isolationism see Rand Paul (with Jack Hunter), *The Tea Party Goes to Washington* (New York: Center Street, 2011), especially 129–168.

52. See Andrew Bacevich, *The Limits of Power: The End of American Exceptionalism* (New York: Holt Paperback, 2009), 3.

53. Former CIA official Philip Giraldi quoted in Rand Paul, *The Tea Party Goes to Washington*, 142.

54. Chalmers Johnson, *Blowback: The Costs and Consequences of American Empire* (New York: Metropolitan Books, 2010); Chalmers Johnson, *Dismantling the Empire: America's Last Best Hope* (New York: Metropolitan Books, 2010).

55. Cf. "Bernie Sanders on Iraq," undated, Feelthebern.org, http://feelthebern.org/bernie-sanders-on-iraq/.

56. Noam Chomsky, *Hegemony or Survival: America's Quest for Global Dominance* (New York: Holt Paperbacks, 2004).

57. Eric Nordlinger, *Isolationism Reconsidered* (Princeton, NJ: Princeton University Press, 1996).

58. See Bear F. Braumoeller, "The Myth of American Isolationism," *Foreign Policy Analysis* 6, no. 4 (October 2010): 349–371; David Dunn, "Isolationism Revisited: Seven Persistent Myths in the Contemporary American Foreign Policy Debate," *Review of International Studies* 31, no. 2 (April 2005): 237–261.

59. Cf. Frank Bruni, "An Overdose of Donald Trump at the G.O.P. Debate," *New York Times*, 16 September 2015, http://www.nytimes.com/2015/09/17/opinion/an-overdose-of-donald-trump-republican-gop-debate.html; Jeremy Diamond, "Donald Trump: Ban All Muslim Travel to U.S.," CNN, 8 December 2015, http://www.cnn.com/2015/12/07/politics/donald-trump-muslim-ban-immigration/.

60. Eugene Gholz, Daryl G. Press, and Harvey M. Sapolsky, "Come Home, America: The Strategy of Restraint in the Face of Temptation," *International Security* 21, no. 4 (spring 1997): 5–48.

61. Christopher Layne, "From Preponderance to Offshore Balancing: America's Future Grand Strategy," *International Security* 22, no. 1 (summer 1997): 87.

62. Ibid., 113.

63. Gholz, Press, and Sapolsky, "Come Home, America."

64. Stephen M. Walt, "Beyond bin Laden: Reshaping U.S. Foreign Policy," *International Security* 26, no. 3 (winter 2001–2): 76.

65. Barry R. Posen, *Restraint* (Ithaca, NY: Cornell University Press, 2014): 44–45; See also Barry R. Posen, "The Case for Doing Nothing in Iraq," *Politico*, 16 June 2014, http://www.politico.com/magazine/story/2014/06/the-case-for-doing-nothing-in-iraq-107913.html. For a fiscal defense of Restraint, see Joseph M. Parent and Paul K. MacDonald, "The Wisdom of Retrenchment: America Must Cut Back to Move Forward," *Foreign Affairs* 90 no. 6, 14 October 2011, http://www.foreignaffairs.com/articles/136510/joseph-m-parent-and-paul-k-macdonald/the-wisdom-of-retrenchment.

66. Posen, *Restraint*, xii.

67. Ibid., 3, 5, 17, 24–27, 69, 141–143; Barry R. Posen, "Pull Back," *Foreign Affairs* 92, no. 1, 1 January 2013, http://www.foreignaffairs.com/articles/138466/barry-r-posen/pull-back; Barry R. Posen, "The Case for Doing Nothing in Iraq."

68. Harry B. Harris, quoted in Jane Perlez, "U.S. Admiral, in Beijing, Defends Patrols in South China Sea," *New York Times*, 3 November 2015, http://www.nytimes.com/2015/11/04/world/asia/south-china-sea-navy-patrols-beijing.html.

69. Rarely is implementation a serious concern in the grand strategy or foreign policy literature. For one counterexample, see Steven Smith and M. Clarke, eds., *Foreign Policy Implementation* (Boston: Allen and Unwin, 1985).

70. Richard N. Rosecrance and Arthur A. Stein, "The Study of Grand Strategy," in *The Domestic Bases of Grand Strategy*, ed. Richard N. Rosecrance and Arthur A. Stein (Ithaca, NY: Cornell University Press, 1993): 11.

71. Robert D. Putnam, "Diplomacy and Domestic Politics: The Logic of Two-Level Games," *International Organization* 42, no. 3 (summer 1988): 427–460.

72. Allan R. Millett, Williamson Murray, and Kenneth H. Watman, "The Effectiveness of Military Organizations," *International Security* 11, no. 1 (summer 1986): 37–71.

73. Michael C. Desch, *Power and Military Effectiveness: The Fallacy of Democratic Triumphalism* (Baltimore, MD: Johns Hopkins University Press, 2008); Stephen Peter Rosen, "Military Effectiveness: Why Society Matters," *International Security* 19, no. 4 (spring 1995): 5–31; and Risa Brooks and Elizabeth Stanley, eds., *Creating Military Power: The Sources of Military Effectiveness* (Palo Alto, CA: Stanford University Press, 2007).

74. See Nora Bensahel, "Alliances and Military Effectiveness: Fighting Alongside Allies and Partners," in Brooks and Stanley, *Creating Military Power.*

75. Samuel Huntington, *Soldier and the State* (Cambridge, MA: Harvard University Press, 1957); and Morris Janowitz, *The Professional Soldier* (New York: The Free Press, 1964). For a public administration perspective of this literature, see Suzanne Christine Nielsen, "Civil-Military Relations Theory and Military Effectiveness," *Public Administration and Management* 10, no. 2 (2005): 61–84.

76. Scholars like Cohen argue that civilian leaders must intervene in military decision making. Eliot A. Cohen, *Supreme Command: Soldiers, Statesmen, and Leadership in Wartime* (New York: Free Press, 2002).

77. Andrew Tilghman, "Dempsey Does Not Rule out U.S. Ground Troops in Syria," *Military Times*, 4 March 2015, http://www.militarytimes.com/story/military/pentagon/2015/03/04/dempsey-us-ground-troops-in-syria-is-an-option/24380755/.

78. Craig Whitlock, "Rift Widens between Obama, U.S. Military over Strategy to Fight Islamic State," *Washington Post*, 18 September 2014, https://www.washingtonpost.com/world/national-security/rift-widens-between-obama-us-military-over-strategy-to-fight-islamic-state/2014/09/18/ebdb422e-3f5c-11e4-b03f-de718edeb92f_story.html.

79. Peter Baker, Helene Cooper, and David E. Sanger, "Obama Sends Special Operations Forces to Help Fight ISIS in Syria," *New York Times*, 30 October 2015, http://www.nytimes.com/2015/10/31/world/obama-will-send-forces-to-syria-to-help-fight-the-islamic-state.html.

80. Barry R. Posen, *The Sources of Military Doctrine: France, Britain, and Germany between the World Wars* (Ithaca, NY: Cornell University Press, 1986); Peter Dombrowski and Eugene Gholz, *Buying Military Transformation: Technological Innovation and the Defense Industry* (New York: Columbia University Press, 2006).

81. Quoted in Whitlock, "Rift Widens between Obama, U.S. Military."

82. See Richard K. Betts, *Military Readiness: Concepts, Choices, Consequences* (Washington, DC: Brookings Institution, 1995).

83. Carl Dahlman and David Thaler, "Ready for War but Not for Peace: The Apparent Paradox of Military Preparedness," in *United States Air and Space Power in the 21st Century*, ed. Zalmay Khalilzad and Jeremy Shapiro (Santa Monica, CA: RAND Corporation, 2002), 438.

84. Megan Eckstein, "CNO Greenert: Navy Could Fix Readiness Shortfall by 2020 if Sequestration Is Avoided," *Proceedings* (10 March 2015), https://news.usni.org/2015/03/10/cno-greenert-navy-could-fix-readiness-shortfall-by-2020-if-sequestration-is-avoided.

85. Quoted in Nick Simeone, "Budget Cuts Threaten Military Readiness, Officials Say," *American Forces Press Service*, 3 April 2014.

86. "We cannot go it alone." Joseph F. Dunford, Jr., Jonathan W. Greenert, and Paul F. Zukunft, *A Cooperative Strategy for 21st Century Seapower: Forward, Engaged, Ready* (February 2015), https://www.uscg.mil/seniorleadership/DOCS/CS21R_Final.pdf.

87. Robert D. Kaplan, "How We Would Fight China," *The Atlantic*, June 2005, http://www.theatlantic.com/magazine/archive/2005/06/how-we-would-fight-china/303959/.

88. Thomas E. Ricks, *The Generals: American Military Command from World War II to Today* (New York: Penguin Books, 2012); and Eliot A. Cohen, *Supreme Command: Soldiers, Statesmen, and Leadership in Wartime* (New York: Free Press, 2002).

## 3. A Maritime Strategy of Primacy in the Persian Gulf

1. Samuel P. Huntington, "Why International Primacy Matters," *International Security* 17, no. 4 (spring 1993).

2. Department of Defense, *Base Structure Report: Fiscal Year 2015 Baseline* (Washington, DC: Office of the Secretary of Defense, 2015), 6 (for total numbers of overseas bases), http://www.acq.osd.mil/ie/download/bsr/CompletedBSR2015-Final.pdf.

3. Yet relatively few academic works have explored the significance of bases. Important exceptions include Richard Harkavy, *Bases Abroad* (London: Oxford University Press, 1989); Alexander Cooley, *Base Politics: Democratic Change and the U.S. Military Overseas* (Ithaca, NY: Cornell University Press, 2008); Kent E. Calder, *Embattled Garrisons: Comparative Base Politics and American Globalism* (Princeton, NJ: Princeton University Press, 2008); Catherine Lutz, *The Bases of Empire: The Global Struggle against U.S. Military Posts* (New York: New York University Press, 2009); and Carnes Lord and Andrew S. Erickson, eds., *Rebalancing U.S. Forces: Basing and Forward Presence in the Asia-Pacific* (Annapolis, MD: Naval Institute Press, 2014).

4. When a military operation is complete or troops withdraw from a country, the United States often leaves behind everything from permanent infrastructure to combat equipment and munitions that cost American taxpayers millions, if not billions, of dollars. See Paul D. Shinkman, "Trashed: U.S. Gear in Afghanistan to be Sold, Scrapped," *U.S. News and World Report*, 4 June 2014, http://www.usnews.com/news/articles/2014/06/04/us-military-equipment-in-afghanistan-to-be-sold-scrapped.

5. Michael R. Gordon and Bernard E. Trainor, *Cobra II: The Inside Story of the Invasion and Occupation of Iraq* (New York: Pantheon, 2006), 115–117.

6. Richard Scott, "Staying Afloat: Sea-basing Plan Still Struggles to Make First Base," *International Defense Review* 44, no. 5 (7 April 2011): 44–48.

7. Office of the Under Secretary of Defense for Acquisition, Technology, and Logistics, *Defense Science Board Task Force on Sea Basing* (Washington, DC: Office of the Secretary of Defense, August 2003), iv.

8. Lawrence P. Farrell, "'Access Challenges in Expeditionary Operations," *National Defense* 88, no. 601 (December 2003): 4.

9. Norman Polmar, "Sea Base Ships for the Future," United States Naval Institute, *Proceedings* 131, no. 3 (March 2005): 104–105.

10. Christian Lowe, "Attack Platform Sea Basing Could Render Reluctant Allies Irrelevant," *Armed Forces Journal* 141, no. 9 (1 April 2004): 36.

11. Christian Lowe, "CNO Raises Questions about Sea Basing Plan: Comments Cast Doubt on the Exact Makeup of Ships and Forces," *Marine Corps Times*, 24 October 2005, 20.

12. One 2005 study—friendly to the concept of sea basing but independent of the Department of Defense—found that any such project would be constrained by "sea state limitations, space limitations on the sea base, and limitations imposed by the need to transfer cargo between the connectors and the sea base in the open ocean in a seaway." Committee on Sea Basing: Ensuring Joint Force Access from the Sea, National Research Council, *Sea Basing: Ensuring Joint Force Access from the Sea* (Washington, DC: National Academy of Science 2005), 3.

13. Rick Gladstone, "Strait of Hormuz Once Again at Center of U.S.-Iran Strife," *New York Times*, 1 May 2015, http://www.nytimes.com/2015/05/02/world/middleeast/strait-of-hormuz-once-again-at-center-of-us-iran-strife.html?_r=0.

14. Geoffrey Gresh, *Gulf Security and the U.S. Military: Regime Survival and the Politics of Basing* (Palo Alto, CA: Stanford University Press 2015), chapters 1–2.

15. J. C. Hurewitz, "The Persian Gulf: British Withdrawal and Western Security," *Annals of the American Academy of Political and Social Science* 401 (May 1972): 111.

16. The British military presence is summarized by Joshua Rovner and Caitlin Talmadge in "Less is More: The Future of the U.S. Military in the Persian Gulf," *Washington Quarterly* 37, no. 3 (fall 2014): 49.

17. For an evocative summary of the role of energy in the global economy, see Daniel Yergin, *The Prize: The Epic Quest for Oil, Money, and Power* (New York: Simon & Schuster, 1991), especially chapter 27, "Hydrocarbon Man," 541–560.

18. Hurewitz, "Persian Gulf," 113–114.

19. In both the Nixon and the Carter administrations, senior national security officials expressed concern about a Soviet threat to the energy-rich region. See David Crist, *The Twilight War: The Secret History of America's Thirty-Year Conflict with Iran* (New York: Penguin Press, 2012), 35.

20. "NSA Bahrain," Military.com Installation Guide, http://www.benefits.military.com/misc/installations/Base_Content.jsp?id=5230.

21. Anthony H. Cordesman, "USCENTCOM Mission and History," Center for Strategic and International Studies (April 1998). Unpaginated manuscript available at https://csis-prod.s3.amazonaws.com/s3fs-public/legacy_files/files/media/csis/pubs/uscentcom3%5B1%5D.pdf.

22. Crist, *Twilight War*, 37.

23. *COBRA II*, 41.

24. Like many presidential national security doctrines, the Nixon Doctrine has garnered the attention of historians and other foreign policy analysts, who have spilled a great deal of ink debunking it in both theory and practice. As Jeffrey Kimball states, "The Nixon Doctrine did not constitute a foreign-policy doctrine in the sense of having been a grand strategy or a master set of principles and guidelines controlling policy decisions. Whether it truly was a doctrine or not, however, Nixon did not practice its principles consistently or even intend to do so when he first announced them. The so-called doctrine, moreover, did not represent a major shift in U.S. foreign policy: previous administrations had applied or attempted to apply the Nixon Doctrine's core principles in selected areas of the world." In "The Nixon Doctrine: A Saga of Misunderstanding," *Presidential Studies Quarterly* 36, no. 1 (March 2006): 59–74. The quote is from 60.

25. Jimmy Carter, The State of the Union Address Delivered before a Joint Session of the Congress, 23 January 1980, http://www.presidency.ucsb.edu/ws/?pid=33079.

26. In territorial terms CENTCOM is smaller today than when it was created, because in 2008, Sudan, Eritrea, Ethiopia, Djibouti, Kenya, and Somalia where transferred to the newly established Africa Command (AFRICOM) area of responsibility. See http://www.centcom.mil/aor.

27. Crist, *Twilight War*, 48.

28. Available online at http://www.jimmycarterlibrary.gov/documents/pddirectives/pd63.pdf.

29. Bruce R. Kuniholm, "The Carter Doctrine, the Reagan Corollary, and Prospects for United States Policy in Southwest Asia," *International Journal* 41, no. 2 (spring 1986): especially 345–346.

30. On the rise of US CENTCOM, see James K. Dobbins, "U.S. Central Command: Where History is Made," in *America's Viceroys: The Military and U.S. Foreign Policy*, ed. Derek S. Reveron (Basingstoke, UK: Palgrave Macmillan 2007), 163–184. The official version of CENTCOM's history, "Growing American Interests," lists key developments, http://www.cusnc.navy.mil/command/2007%20History%20of%20Fifth%20Fleet.pdf.

31. Ronald O'Rourke, "Tanker Wars," *Proceedings Magazine* 114, no. 5 (May 1988): http://www.usni.org/magazines/proceedings/1988-05/tanker-war.

32. George K. Walker, *The Tanker War, 1980–88: Law and Policy* (Newport, RI: U.S. Naval War College, 2000).

33. James Kraska, "Legal Vortex in the Strait of Hormuz," *Virginia Journal of International Law* 54, no. 2 (April 2014): 324–366; and George P. Politakis, "From Action Stations to Action: U.S. Naval Deployment, 'Non-Belligerency' and 'Defensive Reprisals' in the Final Year of the Iran-Iraq War," *Ocean Development & International Law* 25, no. 1 (1994): 31–60.

34. Michael MacDonald, *Overreach: Delusions of Regime Change in Iraq* (Cambridge, MA: Harvard University Press, 2014).

35. David Hastings Dunn captures the giddy spirit of the period surrounding the 2003 invasion with anecdotes involving Richard Perle, President George W. Bush, and General James Garner (US Army, retired). David Hastings Dunn, "Real Men Want to Go to Tehran: Bush, Pre-Emption and the Iranian Nuclear Challenge," *International Affairs* 83, no. 1 (2007): 19.

36. Michael A. Palmer, *On Course to Desert Storm: The United States Navy and the Persian Gulf* (Honolulu, HI: University Press of the Pacific, 2003).

37. Robert John Schneller, *Anchor of Resolve: A History of U.S. Naval Forces Central Command/ Fifth Fleet* (Washington, DC: Naval Historical Center, Dept. of the Navy, 2007).

38. http://www.public.navy.mil/surfor/swmag/vol45/swm_Jan2015_final.pdf.

39. http://www.globalsecurity.org/military/agency/navy/c5f.htm.

40. Robert J. Schneller, Jr., *Anchor of Resolve*, 11. Note the quote's use of the term "Arabian Gulf." Some official US government communications and publications now use the term Arabian Gulf out of respect for the sensitivities of Arab friends and allies in the region. For this book, we will continue to use the historically more common term "Persian Gulf." See "Navy Causes Controversy by Changing 'Persian Gulf' to 'Arabian Gulf,'" *AllGov.Com*, 9 December 2010,http://www.allgov.com/news/us-and-the-world/navy-causes-controversy-by-changing-persian-gulf-to-arabian-gulf?news=841875.

41. Charles Glaser summarized the threat of closure in "How Oil Influences U.S. National Security," *International Security* 38, no. 2 (fall 2013): 127–129.

42. Eugene Gholz and Daryl G. Press, "Protecting 'The Prize': Oil and the U.S. National Interest," *Security Studies* 19 (2010): 453–485.

43. Caitlin Talmadge, "Closing Time: Assessing the Iranian Threat to the Strait of Hormuz," *International Security* 33, no. 1 (summer 2008): 84.

44. Shahram Chubin, "Is Iran a Military Threat?" *Survival* 56, no. 2 (2014): 80.

45. Charles A. Kupchan, *The Persian Gulf and the West: Dilemmas of Security* (London: Allen & Unwin, 1987), 185.

46. Ibid., especially 177–209, "The Out of Area Problem for NATO."

47. Andrew Bennett, Joseph Lepgold, and Danny Unger, "Burden-Sharing in the Persian Gulf War," *International Organization* 48, no. 1 (winter 1994): 39–75.

48. Alexandre Sheldon-Duplaix, "Franco-British Relations at Sea and Over Seas: A Tale of Two Navies," *Naval War College Review* 64, no. 1 (winter 2011): 79–94.

49. Office of Naval Intelligence, *From Guerilla Warfare to Modern Naval Strategy* (Suitland, MD: Office of Naval Intelligence, Fall 2009), 15.

50. Michael Knights, "Political-Military Challenges of Demining the Strait of Hormuz," *Policy Watch, 1987*, 28 September 2012, http://www.washingtoninstitute.org/policy-analysis/view/political-military-challenges-of-demining-the-strait-of-hormuz.

51. Robert E. Hunter, *Building Security in the Persian Gulf* (Santa Monica, CA: RAND Corporation, 2010), 84, http://www.rand.org/content/dam/rand/pubs/monographs/2010/RAND_MG944.pdf.

52. John Gordon, Stuart Johnson, F. Stephen Larrabee, and Peter A. Wilson, "NATO and the Challenge of Austerity," *Survival* 54 (2014): 140.

53. Kenneth M. Pollack, "Security in the Persian Gulf: New Frameworks for the Twenty-First Century," *Middle East Memo*, no. 24 (Washington, DC: Brookings Institution, 2012), http://www.brookings.edu/~/media/research/files/papers/2012/6/middle-east-pollack/middle_east_pollack.pdf.

54. Keith Johnson, "China's Thirst," *Foreign Policy* 211 (March–April 2015): 76–77.

55. Peter Dombrowski and Andrew C. Winner, eds., *The Indian Ocean and U.S. Grand Strategy: Ensuring Access and Promoting Security* (Washington, DC: Georgetown University Press, 2014).

56. David Scott, "India's Aspirations and Strategy for the Indian Ocean—Securing the Waves?" *Journal of Strategic Studies* 36, no. 4 (2013): 484–511.

57. Sam J. Tangredi, *Anti-Access Warfare: Countering A2/AD Strategies* (Annapolis, MD: US Naval Institute Press, 2013), especially chapter 7, 183–202.

58. IISS, "Strait of Hormuz: Iran's Disruptive Military Options," *Strategic Comments* 18, no. 1 (9 February 2012), https://www.iiss.org/en/publications/strategic%20comments/sections/2012-bb59/strait-of-hormuz-iran-s-disruptive-military-options-2-b41b.

59. Dennis Blair and Kenneth Lieberthal, "Smooth Sailing: The World's Shipping Lanes Are Safe," *Foreign Affairs* 86, no. 3 (May–June 2007): 7–13. A summary of the Iranian threat to the Strait of Hormuz can be found on 10.

60. One potential wildcard is the possibility that Israel (or perhaps an aggressive American president) will use an effort to close the strait as a justification to attack Iranian nuclear and weapons production facilities—potentially stimulating a much wider regional conflict.

61. Scholars have long recognized the limited utility of US ground forces in keeping the Persian Gulf open. Robert H. Johnson, "The Persian Gulf in U.S. Strategy: A Skeptical View," *International Security* 14, no. 1 (summer 1989): 122–160.

62. Steven Simon and Jonathan Stevenson, "The End of Pax Americana: Why Washington's Pullback Makes Sense," *Foreign Affairs* 94, no. 6 (November–December 2015): 2.

63. Ibid., 7–8.

64. James Kurth, "Confronting a Powerful China with Western Characteristics," *Orbis* 56, no. 1 (winter 2012): 54.

65. Mark Gunzinger, *Shaping America's Future Military: Toward a New Force Planning Construct* (Washington, DC: Center for Strategic and Budgetary Assessments, 2013), 34, http://www.csbaonline.org/wp-content/uploads/2013/06/CSBA_ForceStructure-Report-web.pdf.

66. For a succinct summary of the CSBA approach, see the briefing by Jan Van Tol, Mark Gunzinger, Andrew Krepinech, and Jim Thomas, "AirSea Battle," 18 May 2010, slide 27, http://www.csbaonline.org/wp-content/uploads/2010/05/2010.05.18-AirSea-Battle-Slides.pdf. More details can be found in Jan Van Tol (with Mark Gunzinger, Andrew Krepinech, and Jim Thomas), *AirSea Battle: A Point-of-Departure Operational Concept* (Washington, DC: Center for Strategic and Budgetary Assessments, 2010). The quote is on 32 and CSBA's conception of a maritime blockade is on 76–78, http://www.dtic.mil/dtic/tr/fulltext/u2/a522258.pdf.

67. T. X. Hammes, "Offshore Control: A Proposed Strategy for an Unlikely Conflict," *Strategic Forum* 278 (June 2012): 1–14.

68. Jeffrey E. Kline and Wayne P. Hughes Jr., "Between Peace and the Air-Sea Battle: A War at Sea Strategy," *Naval War College Review* 65, no. 4 (autumn 2012): 37.

69. Gabriel B. Collins and William S. Murray, "No Oil for the Lamps of China?" *Naval War College Review* 61, no. 2 (spring 2008): 79-95.

70. Iskander Rehman, "From an Ocean of Peace to a Sea of Friends," in *Shaping the Emerging World: India and the Multilateral Order*, ed. Waheguru Pal Singh Sidhu and Pratap Bhanu Mehta (Washington: Brookings Institution Press, 2013), 145.

71. Allyson Versprill, "Analysts: China's Missile Program the Greatest Long-Term Threat to U.S. Security," *National Defense*, 20 August 2015, http://www.nationaldefensemagazine.org/blog/Lists/Posts/Post.aspx?ID=1925. For a detailed analysis, see Mark Gunzinger and Bryan Clark, *Winning the Salvo Competition: Rebalancing America's Air and Missile Defenses* (Washington, DC: Center for Strategic and Budgetary Assessments, 20 May 2016), http://csbaonline.org/publications/2016/05/winning-the-salvo-competition-rebalancing-americas-air-and-missile-defenses/.

72. Roger J. Stern, "United States Cost of Military Force Projection in the Persian Gulf, 1976–2007," *Energy Policy* 38, no. 6 (June 2010): 2816–2825.

## 4. Playing a Follow-the-Leader Strategy on the High Seas

1. Cf., G. John Ikenberry, *Liberal Leviathan: The Origins, Crisis, and Transformation of the American World Order* (Princeton, NJ: Princeton University Press, 2011).

2. President Obama characterized the distinction between leadership in peace and war when he suggested that American leadership in the world "is not just a matter of us bombing somebody." See "Press Conference by the President," 18 December 2015, https://www.whitehouse.gov/the-press-office/2015/12/18/press-conference-president-121815.

3. As quoted in William J. Crowe Jr., "U.S. Pacific Command: A Warrior-Diplomat Speaks," in *America's Viceroys: The Military and U.S. Foreign Policy*, ed. Derek Reveron (New York: Palgrave-Macmillan, 2004), 75.

4. "Theater Security Cooperation Plans" is the latest iteration of the term for the geographic combatant command's annual planning process and a set of documents relating to security cooperation and engagement with countries located within the command's area of responsibility.

5. Christopher Layne, "U.S. Hegemony and the Perpetuation of NATO," *Journal of Strategic Studies* 23, no. 3 (2000): 59–91.

6. For more RIMPAC details, see http://www.public.navy.mil/surfor/Pages/RIMPAC-2016.aspx#.WQd0bFKlm_g.

7. http://www.cpf.navy.mil/rimpac/2014/.

8. William Wan, "Chinese Spy Ship Lurks around U.S.-Led Pacific Naval Drills," *Washington Post*, 21 July 2014, https://www.washingtonpost.com/news/worldviews/wp/2014/07/21/chinese-spy-ship-lurks-around-u-s-led-pacific-naval-drills/.

9. http://www.cpf.navy.mil/news.aspx/030454.

10. William Cole, "Chinese Spy Ship off Hawaii Keeps Track of RIMPAC," *Star Adviser*, 18 July 2014, http://www.staradvertiser.com/news/breaking/20140718_Chinese_spy_ship_off_Hawaii_keeps_track_of_RIMPAC.html?id=267736251.

11. Eric A. McVadon, "China's Maturing Navy," *Naval War College Review* 59, no. 2 (spring 2006): 95, http://www.dtic.mil/dtic/tr/fulltext/u2/a531028.pdf.

12. Michael Fabey, "Why Did China Participate in RIMPAC with One Ship and Spy on It with Another?" *Aviation Week Network*, 15 August 2014, http://aviationweek.com/military-government/why-did-china-participate-rimpac-one-ship-and-spy-it-another.

13. Agence France-Presse, "U.S., Chinese Navies Train Together Despite Tensions," *Defense News*, 16 November 2015, http://www.defensenews.com/story/defense/2015/11/16/us-chinese-navies-train-together-despite-tensions/75881522/.

14. For a general chronology, see Michael McDevitt, "PLA Naval Exercises with International Partners," in *Learning by Doing: The PLA Trains at Home and Abroad*, ed. Travis Tanner, Roy Kamphausen, and David Lai (Carlisle, PA: Strategic Studies Institute of the U.S. Army War College, November 2012), 96–97.

15. Sam LaGrone, "U.S. and China Conduct Anti-Piracy Exercise," *USNI News*, 12 December 2014, http://news.usni.org/2014/12/12/u-s-china-conduct-anti-piracy-exercise.

16. Author discussions with Japan Maritime Self Defense Force officers, 2011–12. The subtext underlying Japan's concerns is, apparently, maximally a fear of betrayal or, minimally, a bilateral deal between the two great powers that will not take into account Japan's interests.

17. Michael Fabey, "U.S. Navy Says China Spy Ship Proves International Waters Recognition," *Aviation Week,* 30 July 2014, http://aviationweek.com/defense/us-navy-says-china-spy-ship-proves-international-waters-recognition.

18. Quoted in Bill Gertz, "Spying Concerns, Regional Belligerence Cloud Chinese Role in Pacific Naval Exercises," *Washington Free Beacon*, 25 June 2014, http://freebeacon.com/national-security/spying-concerns-regional-belligerence-cloud-chinese-role-in-pacific-naval-exercises/.

19. William Wan, "Chinese Spy Ship Lurks around U.S.-Led Pacific Naval Drills," *Washington Post*, 21 July 2014, https://www.washingtonpost.com/news/worldviews/wp/2014/07/21/chinese-spy-ship-lurks-around-u-s-led-pacific-naval-drills/.

20. William Cole, "Rep. Mark Takai Wants to Stop China from Participating in Wargames," *Honolulu Star Advertiser*, 22 March 2016, https://takai.house.gov/media-center/in-the-news/rep-mark-takai-wants-stop-china-participating-wargames.

21. Ibid.

22. See "DOD Dictionary of Military and Associated Terms," March 2017: 85, http://www.dtic.mil/doctrine/new_pubs/dictionary.pdf.

23. Federation of American Scientists, "United States Military Exercises," http://fas.org/man/dod-101/ex/.

24. Clarence J. Bouchat, *An Introduction to Theater Strategy and Regional Security* (Carlisle, PA: US Army War College Strategic Studies Institute, 2007), 13–14.

25. Thomas M. Jordan, Douglas C. Lovelace Jr., and Thomas-Durell Young, *"Shaping" the World through "Engagement": Assessing the Department of Defense's Theater Engagement Planning Process* (Carlisle, PA: Strategic Studies Institute, 2000), especially 4–10.

26. Jennifer D. P. Moroney, Joe Hogler, Lianne Kennedy-Boudali, and Stephanie Pezard, *Integrating the Full Range of Security Cooperation Programs into Air Force Planning: An Analytic Primer* (Santa Monica, CA: RAND Corporation, 2011), 1.

27. Chairman, US Joint Chiefs of Staff, Joint Operation Planning, Joint Publication 5-0 (Washington, DC: CJCS, 26 December 2006), I-3, http://www.bits.de/NRANEU/others/jp-doctrine/jp5_0%2806%29.pdf.

28. Gregory J. Dyekman, "Security Cooperation: A Key to the Challenges of the 21st Century," 7 June 2007, 1–2, http://www.strategicstudiesinstitute.army.mil/pubs/display.cfm?pubID=820.

29. The term *Building Partnership Capacity* was first used in the 2006 Quadrennial Defense Review when, after 9/11 and the invasions of Afghanistan and Iraq, "U.S. and Department of Defense leaders concluded that the traditional set of security assistance and security cooperation tools did not meet the needs of the changed strategic landscape." Kathleen J. McInnis and Nathan J. Lucas, *What Is "Building Partner Capacity"? Issues for Congress* (Washington, DC: Congressional Research Service, 18 December 2015), 1.

30. Government Accountability Office, *Building Partner Capacity: Key Practices to Effectively Manage Department of Defense Efforts to Promote Security Cooperation* GAO-13-335T (Washington, DC: Government Accountability Office, 14 February 2013), http://www.gao.gov/assets/660/652159.pdf.

31. See US Department of Defense, *Quadrennial Defense Review*, February 2010, 57, http://www.comw.org/qdr/fulltext/1002QDR2010.pdf.

32. Crowe, "U.S. Pacific Command: A Warrior-Diplomat Speaks," 75.

33. Edward J. Marolda, *Ready Seapower: A History of the U.S. Seventh Fleet* (Washington DC: Naval History & Heritage Command, 2012), https://archive.org/stream/ReadySeapower/ReadySeapower_djvu.txt.

34. Admiral William J. Crowe, Jr., "U.S. Pacific Command: A Warrior-Diplomat Speaks," 75.

35. Tanguy Struye de Swielande, "The Reassertion of the United States in the Asia Pacific Region," *Parameters* 42, no. 1 (spring 2012): 75–89, especially 76.

36. US Department of Defense, *The Asia-Pacific Maritime Security Strategy: Achieving U.S. National Security Objectives in a Changing Environment* (August 2015), unpaginated introduction.

37. Shirley A. Kan, *U.S.-China Military Contacts: Issues for Congress*, no. RL32496 (Washington, DC: Congressional Research Service, 27 October 2014). Quote from unpaginated summary page following title page, http://fas.org/sgp/crs/natsec/RL32496.pdf.

38. Dan Guiam and Ron Appling, "Cobra Gold '85," *Leatherneck*, October 1985, 25.

39. The White House, *National Security Strategy of the United States*, January 1988, 19, http://nssarchive.us/NSSR/1988.pdf.

40. Ibid.

41. The White House, *National Security Strategy of the United States*, January 1993, 14, http://nssarchive.us/NSSR/1993.pdf.

42. See United States Marine Corp History Division, *Yearly Chronologies of the United States Marine Corps—1992*, http://www.mcu.usmc.mil/historydivision/Pages/Chronologies/1992.aspx.

43. See, for example, Head, Current Operations Branch, "Monthly Operations Summary," 30 April 1993, E-12, http://www.mcu.usmc.mil/historydivision/Status%20of%20Forces/Other/1993/May%201993.pdf.

44. Cf. Kathleen T. Rhem, "USS *Lincoln* Sailors Greet Deputy Defense Secretary," *American Forces Press Service*, 15 January 2005, http://osd.dtic.mil/news/Jan2005/n01152005_2005011509.html.

45. Excerpt from the website of the US Marine Corps Forces, Pacific, "About COBRA GOLD 2015," http://www.marforpac.marines.mil/Exercises/CobraGold/About.aspx.

46. Like Cobra Gold, RIMPAC also has a Facebook page, this one dating from 2012: https://www.facebook.com/RimofthePacific.

47. Commander, US Pacific Fleet, *RIMPAC 2014*, http://www.cpf.navy.mil/rimpac/2014/.

48. Ryan Faith, "What the World's Largest Naval Exercise Reveals about Modern-Day Warfare," *Vice News*, 11 August 2014, https://news.vice.com/article/what-the-worlds-largest-naval-exercise-reveals-about-modern-day-warfare.

49. Memo from R. E. Kirksey, Command Officer, USS *Kitty Hawk* to Chief of Naval Operations, 22 February 1974, http://www.history.navy.mil/content/dam/nhhc/research/archives/command-operation-reports/ship-command-operation-reports/k/kitty-hawk-cv-63-ii/1973.pdf.

50. Hillary Clinton, "America's Pacific Century," *Foreign Policy*, 11 October 2011, http://foreignpolicy.com/2011/10/11/americas-pacific-century/.

51. Foreign Press Center Briefing on Rim of Pacific Maritime Exercise, 1 July 2014 (Washington, DC: Washington Foreign Press Center, US Department of State), http://iipdigital.usembassy.gov/st/english/texttrans/2014/07/20140702303141.html#axzz3wA8yVeS9.

52. John Sorensen, "RIMPAC 2014 Concludes with Enhanced Cooperation among 22 Nations," *Navy.mil*, 2 August 2014, http://www.navy.mil/submit/display.asp?story_id=82545.

53. For critical reviews of China's contribution see Rhoda Margesson, CRS Report for Congress, *Indian Ocean Earthquake and Tsunami: Humanitarian Assistance and Relief Operations*, 10 February 2005, https://www.fas.org/sgp/crs/row/RL32715.pdf; John Chan, "China's Tsunami Aid: Political Interests not Humanitarian Concern," 18 January 2005, https://www.wsws.org/en/articles/2005/01/chin-j18.html; "Tsunami Aid: Who's Giving What?" BBC, 27 January 2005, http://news.bbc.co.uk/2/hi/asia-pacific/4145259.stm. For a positive Chinese view of its contribution see The State Council, "China's Aid to Tsunami Victims Sets Record: Official," 18 January 2006, http://www.gov.cn/misc/2006-01/18/content_162616.htm.

54. Quoted in Donna Miles, "Locklear RIMPAC Exemplifies Pacom's Multilateral Focus," *DoD News*, 12 July 2012, http://archive.defense.gov/news/newsarticle.aspx?id=117089.

55. Faith, "What the World's Largest Naval Exercise Reveals."

56. Ibid.

57. Ibid.

58. Doug Bandow, "Include China in 2016 RIMPAC Exercise: 'Punishing' Beijing by Exclusion Would be Short-Sighted," *China-U.S. Focus*, 3 June 2015. Available at http://www.cato.org/publications/commentary/include-china-2016-rimpac-exercise-punishing-beijing-exclusion-would-be.

59. Ibid.

60. V. P. Malik, "Indo-U.S. Defense and Military Relations: From 'Estrangement' to 'Strategic Partnership'" in *U.S.-Indian Strategic Cooperation into the 21st Century: More than Words*, ed. Sumit Ganguly, Brian Shoup, and Andrew Scobell (New York: Routledge, 2006), 83.

61. "New Framework for the U.S.-India Defense Relationship," 28 June 2005, http://library.rumsfeld.com/doclib/sp/3211/2005-06-28%20New%20Framework%20for%20the%20US-India%20Defense%20Relationship.pdf, 2.

62. Olivia Giger, "Kitty Hawk, Allies Complete Malabar Exercise," *Navy.mil*, 10 September 2007, http://www.navy.mil/submit/display.asp?story_id=31737.

63. On the wider geostrategic context between the United States and India during this period, see for example, the views of two highly placed American officials: R. Nicholas Burns, "America's Strategic Opportunity with India: The New U.S.-India Partnership," *Foreign Affairs* 86, no. 6 (November/December 2007): 131-146; and Evan A. Feigenbaum, "India's Rise,

America's Interest: The Fate of the U.S.-Indian Partnership," *Foreign Affairs* 86, no. 6 (March/ April 2010): 76–91.

64. "Kitty Hawk, Allies Participate in Malabar Photo," U.S. Navy press release, 10 September 2007.

65. "U.S.-India Joint Statement: Shared Effort, Progress for All," The White House, 25 January 2015, https://www.whitehouse.gov/the-press-office/2015/01/25/us-india-joint-statement-shared-effort-progress-all.

66. "Framework for the U.S.-India Defense Relationship," 3 June 2015, http://www.defense.gov/pubs/2015-Defense-Framework.pdf.

67. Ibid., 2–3.

68. Iskander Luke Rehman, "From an Ocean of Peace to a Sea of Friends," in *Shaping the Emerging World: India and the Multilateral Order*, ed. Waheguru Pal Singh Sidhu, Pratap Bhanu Mehta, and Bruce Jones (Washington, DC, Brookings Institution Press, 2013), 147. Rehman's chapter is available at http://carnegieendowment.org/files/IRehman_Chapter_Brookings_Volume_PDF1.pdf.

69. For a comprehensive assessment of this issue, see Peter Dombrowski and Andrew C. Winner, eds., *The Indian Ocean and U.S. Grand Strategy: Ensuring Access and Promoting Security* (Washington, DC: Georgetown University Press, 2014).

70. Rehman, "From an Ocean of Peace to a Sea of Friends," 146.

71. Yu Jincui, "Concurrent India Drills Spark Unnecessary Speculation," *Global Times*, 14 October 2015, http://www.globaltimes.cn/content/947001.shtml.

72. PTI, "China reacts sharply to Japan's inclusion in Malabar exercises," *Economic Times*, 14 December 2015, http://economictimes.indiatimes.com/news/defence/china-reacts-sharply-to-japans-inclusion-in-malabar-exercises/articleshow/50172813.cms.

73. See Denny Roy, "Southeast Asia and China: Balancing or Bandwagoning?" *Contemporary Southeast Asia* 27, no. 2 (2005): 305–322.

74. Joseph F. Dunford Jr., Jonathan W. Greenert, and Paul F. Zukunft, *A Cooperative Strategy for 21st Century Seapower: Forward, Ready, Engaged* (Washington, DC: Department of the Navy, March 2015), 3–4, http://www.Navy.mil/local/maritime/150227-CS21R-Final.pdf.

75. For two helpful articles on Chinese and US bandwagoning strategies, see Charles Glaser, "Will China's Rise Lead to War? Why Realism Does not Mean Pessimism," *Foreign Affairs* 90, no. 2 (March/April 2011): 80–91, http://www.foreignaffairs.com/articles/67479/charles-glaser/will-chinas-rise-lead-to-war; and Randall L. Schweller and Xiaoyu Pu, "After Unipolarity: China's Vision of International Order in an Era of U.S. Decline," *International Security* 36, no. 1 (summer 2011): 41–72.

76. Charles Tiefer, "President Trump Is Likely to Boost U.S. Military Spending by $500 Billion to $1 Trillion," *Forbes Magazine*, 9 November 2016, http://www.forbes.com/sites/charlestiefer/2016/11/09/president-trump-is-likely-to-boost-u-s-military-spending-by-500-billion-to-1-trillion/#18102c234108.

77. Peter G. Peterson Foundation, "The U.S. Spends More on Defense Than the Next Seven Countries Combined," 12 April 2015, http://www.pgpf.org/chart-archive/0053_defense-comparison.

78. Janine Davidson and Lauren Dickey, "Fact: America's Rebalance to Asia Has Some Serious Military Muscle," *National Interest*, 16 April 2015, http://nationalinterest.org/blog/the-buzz/fact-americas-rebalance-asia-has-some-serious-military-12652.

79. PACOM Senate Armed Services Committee Posture Statement by Commander, US Pacific Command, Adm. Samuel J. Locklear, III, 25 March 2014, http://www.pacom.mil/Media/SpeechesTestimony/tabid/6706/Article/565154/pacom-senate-armed-services-committee-posture-statement.aspx.

80. Cf. Gordon Adams, "The Fiscal Slide: Five Reasons the Pentagon Will Avoid the Pain of Sequestration," *Foreign Policy*, 17 October 2012, http://foreignpolicy.com/2012/10/17/the-fiscal-slide/.

81. GAO report to Congressional Committees, "Sequestration: Documenting and Assessing Lessons Learned Would Assist DOD in Planning for Future Budget Uncertainty," (Washington DC: GAO, May 2015), http://www.gao.gov/assets/680/670476.pdf.

82. Sheldon W. Simon, "The US Rebalance and Southeast Asia: A Work in Progress," *Asian Survey* 55, no. 3 (May/June 2015): 572–595, quote from 578.

83. Barry R. Posen, *Restraint: A New Foundation for Grand Strategy* (Ithaca, NY: Cornell University Press, 2014) 44.

84. Cecil Haney, "Naval Diplomacy and Maritime Power Projection," in *Navies and Global Security*, ed. Andrew Forbes (Canberra, Australia: Sea Power Center-Australia, 2014), 49. Available at http://www.navy.gov.au/sites/default/files/documents/SP13.pdf#page=31.

## 5. Pirates, Terrorists, and Formal Sponsorship

1. Coincidentally, the USS *Bainbridge* was named for the captain of the American frigate—the USS *Philadelphia*—that ran aground in Tripoli harbor during America's first campaign against pirates that lasted from 1801 to 1805. William Bainbridge and crew were released after a sea and land campaign orchestrated by William Eaton, one in which Stephen Decatur led an operation to burn the captured USS *Philadelphia*. See http://www.bainbridge.navy.mil/.

2. Account based on summary in Daniel L. Pines, "Maritime Piracy: Changes in U.S. Law Needed to Combat this Critical National Security Concern," 25 March 2012, *Seattle University Law Review*, SSRN, http://ssrn.com/abstract=2028676.

3. SEAL Team 6 is now officially named the Naval Special Warfare Development Group. Mark Mazzetti, Nicholas Kulish, Cristopher Dre, Serge, F. Kovaleski, Sean D. Naylor, and John Ismay, "SEAL Team 6: A Secret History of Quiet Killings and Blurred Lines," *New York Times*, 6 June 2015, http://www.nytimes.com/2015/06/07/world/asia/the-secret-history-of-seal-team-6.html?_r=0.

4. For details, see http://www.imdb.com/title/tt1535109/.

5. Forrest Wickman, "How Accurate Is Captain Phillips?" *Slate*, 11 October 2013. Available at http://www.slate.com/blogs/browbeat/2013/10/11/captain_phillips_true_story_fact_and_fiction_in_tom_hanks_and_paul_greengrass.html. See also Richard Phillips, *A Captain's Duty: Somali Pirates, Navy SEALs, and Dangerous Days at Sea* (New York: Hyperion 2010).

6. For an account of America's first wars against pirates, see Frank Lambert, *The Barbary Wars: American Independence in the Atlantic World* (New York: Hill and Wang 2007).

7. Phil Beaufort, "Navy Promotes First African-American Female Three-Star Officer," *America's Navy*, 24 August 2012, http://www.navy.mil/submit/display.asp?story_id=69192.

8. http://www.navy.mil/navydata/bios/navybio.asp?bioID=394.

9. Beaufort, "Navy Promotes First African-American Female Three-Star Officer."

10. Ian W. Toll, *Six Frigates: The Epic History of the Founding of the U.S. Navy* (New York: W. W. Norton, 2008).

11. "Navy History: Federal/Quasi-War Historical Overview of the Federalist Navy, 1787–1801," Naval History and Heritage Command Website, http://www.history.navy.mil/research/library/bibliographies/reestablishment-of-the-navy-1787-1801/navy-history-federal-quasi-war.html.

12. Rosa Brooks, *How Everything Became War and the Military Became Everything* (New York: Simon and Schuster, 2016), 48.

13. Michael A. Palmer, "The Navy: The Continental Period, 1775–1890," *Empire Patriot* 6, no. 3 (August 2004): 1, http://www.saratogabattle-sar.org/pages/patriot/ESSSAR_patriot_0804.pdf.

14. The primary piracy hotspots today are the Gulf of Guinea, Horn of Africa, and Southeast Asia.

15. See Anna Bowden, "The Economic Cost of Maritime Piracy," working paper, One Earth Foundation, December 2010, 2, https://oneearthfuture.org/sites/oneearthfuture.org/files//documents/publications/The-Economic-Cost-of-Piracy-Full-Report.pdf. On calculating indirect costs, see Jens Vestergaard Madsen, Conor Seyle, Kellie Brandt, Ben Purser, Heather Randall, and Kellie Roy, *The State of Economic Piracy 2013*, www.oceansbeyondpiracy.org.

16. James T. Conway, Gary Roughead, and Thad W. Allen, *A Cooperative Strategy for 21st Century Seapower* (October 2007), unpaginated, https://www.ise.gov/sites/default/files/

Maritime_Strategy.pdf.; and Robert C. Rubel, *Writing to Think: The Intellectual Journey of a Naval Career*, Newport Paper no. 41 (Newport, RI: Naval War College Press, 2014), especially 55–70. Originally published as Corbett Paper No. 11, The Corbett Centre for Maritime Policy Studies, King's College London, October 2012, http://www.kcl.ac.uk/.

17. Conway, Roughead, and Allen, *Cooperative Strategy*, 1.

18. Peter Earle, "Pirates: The Royal Navy and the Suppression of Maritime Raiding 1620–1830," *Military History*, 27 April 2012, http://www.military-history.org/articles/17th-century/pirates-the-royal-navy-and-the-suppression-of-maritime-raiding-1620–1830.htm.

19. Sarah Percy and Anja Shortland, "The Business of Piracy in Somalia," *Journal of Strategic Studies* 36, no. 4 (2013): 541–578.

20. As quoted in Lesley Anne Warner, "Pieces of Eight: An Appraisal of U.S. Counterpiracy Options in the Horn of Africa," *Naval War College Review* 63, no. 2 (spring 2010): 72.

21. Gary Roughead, "The US Navy's Vision for Confronting Irregular Warfare" (Washington, DC: Department of the Navy, January 2010), 3, http://www.navy.mil/navydata/cno/CNO_SIGNED_NAVY_VISION_FOR_CONFRONTING_IRREGULAR_CHALLENGES_JANUARY_2010.pdf.

22. See Jens Vestergaard Madsen et al., *State of Economic Piracy 2011*, http://oceansbeyondpiracy.org/publications/economic-cost-somali-piracy-2011; *State of Economic Piracy 2013*, http://oceansbeyondpiracy.org/publications/state-maritime-piracy-2013, ii; Anna Bowden and Dr. Shikha Basnet, *The Economic Costs of Somali Piracy* 2011, 1, http://oceansbeyondpiracy.org/publications/economiccost-somali-piracy-2011.

23. Article 101, the United Nations Convention on the Law of the Sea 1982 (UNCLOS).

24. Sam Bateman, "Maritime Security Governance in the Indian Ocean Region," *Journal of the Indian Ocean Region* 12, no. 1 (2016): 16.

25. United Nations Convention on the Law of the Sea, Dec. 10, 1982, art. 101.

26. Erik Barrios, "Casting a Wider Net: Addressing the Maritime Piracy Problem in Southeast Asia," *Boston College International and Comparative Law Review* 28, no. 1 (2005): 153.

27. "Convention for the Suppression of Unlawful Acts against the Safety of Maritime Navigation, Protocol for the Suppression of Unlawful Acts Against the Safety of Fixed Platforms Located on the Continental Shelf," http://www.imo.org/en/About/Conventions/ListOf Conventions/Pages/SUA-Treaties.aspx.

28. Omer Elagab, "Somali Piracy and International Law," *Australian and New Zealand Maritime Law Journal* 59, http://www.austlii.edu.au/au/journals/ANZMarLawJl/2010/8.pdf, 63.

29. Ambassador Ahmedou Ould-Abdallah, comp., *Piracy Off the Somali Coast: Final Report, Assessment and Recommendations*, report of Workshop Commissioned by the Special Representative of the Secretary General of the UN to Somalia, Nairobi, Kenya, 10–21 November 2008.

30. Security Council resolutions (which form an international legal basis for CTF-151): UN Security Council resolution 1816, The Situation in Somalia, S/RES/1816 (2 June 2008), http://unscr.com/files/2008/01816.pdf; UN Security Council resolution 1838, The Situation in Somalia, S/RES/1838 (7 October 2008), http://unscr.com/files/2008/01838.pdf; UN Security Council resolution 1846, The Situation in Somalia, S/RES/1846 (2 December 2008), http://unscr.com/files/2008/01846.pdf; UN Security Council resolution 1851, The Situation in Somalia, S/RES/1851 (16 December 2008), http://unscr.com/files/2008/01851.pdf; UN Security Council resolution 1897, The Situation in Somalia, S/RES/1897 (30 November 3 2009), http://unscr.com/files/2009/01897.pdf.

31. Lauren Ploch, Christopher M. Blanchard, Ronald O'Rourke, R. Chuck Mason, and Rawle O. King, *Piracy Off the Horn of Africa*, no. R40528 (Washington, DC: Congressional Research Service April 27, 2011), 19–21.

32. US Department of State, "International Response," undated, http://www.state.gov/t/pm/ppa/piracy/contactgroup/.

33. "UN Piracy Brochure," http://www.un.org/undpa/sites/www.un.org.undpa/files/ckfiles/files/UN%20Piracy%20Brochure.pdf.

34. Naval cooperation entailed "ensuring effective naval operational co-ordination and supporting the building of the judicial, penal and maritime capacity of Regional States to ensure they are better equipped to tackle piracy and maritime security challenges." Safety4Sea,

"UN Contact Group on Piracy off the Coast of Somalia," 13 July 2012, http://www.safety4sea.com/un-contact-group-on-piracy-off-the-coast-of-somalia/.

35. US Department of State, "International Response: Contact Group on Piracy off the Coast of Somalia," undated, http://www.state.gov/t/pm/ppa/piracy/contactgroup/.

36. Ibid, 2. As the GAO observed during a subsequent evaluation, "This plan implements the *National Strategy for Maritime Security* (September 2005) and the *Policy for the Repression of Piracy and other Criminal Acts of Violence at Sea* (June 2007) as applied to piracy off the Horn of Africa." John H. Pendleton, *Maritime Security, Actions Needed to Assess and Update Plan and Enhance Collaboration Among Partners Involved in Countering Piracy Off the Horn of Africa* (Washington, DC: GAO, September 2011), 2.

37. James Kraska, "Fresh Thinking for an Old Problem: Report of the Naval War College Workshop on Countering Maritime Piracy," *Naval War College Review* 62, no. 4 (autumn 2009): 153.

38. The White House, *The National Strategy for Maritime Security*, 20 September 2005, https://georgewbush-whitehouse.archives.gov/homeland/maritime-security.html.

39. National Security Council, "Countering Piracy off the Horn of Africa: Partnership & Action Plan," December 2008, 8, https://www.hsdl.org/?view&did=232031.

40. Pendleton, *Maritime Security*, 31–34, http://www.gao.gov/new.items/d10856.pdf.

41. Ibid., 19.

42. US Government Accountability Office, *Maritime Security: Ongoing U.S. Counterpiracy Efforts Would Benefit from Agency Assessments*, June 2014, 14.

43. https://combinedmaritimeforces.com/ctf-150-maritime-security/.

44. International Chamber of Commerce—Commercial Crime Services, "Coalition Warships Set Up Maritime Security Patrol Area in the Gulf of Aden," 26 August 2008, http://www.icc-ccs.org/news/473-coalition-warships-set-upmaritime-security-patrol-area-in-the-gulf-of-aden.

45. Andrew Shapiro, assistant secretary, Bureau of the Political-Military Affairs in the Department of State testified that "U.S. Naval Forces Central Command (NAVCENT) has also worked with partners to set up a 463-mile-long corridor through the Gulf of Aden, called the Internationally Recommended Transit Corridor or IRTC for short." Andrew J. Shapiro, Assistant Secretary, Bureau of Political-Military Affairs, "Confronting Global Piracy," Statement before the Subcommittee on Terrorism, Nonproliferation and Trade of the House Foreign Affairs Committee, Washington, DC, 15 June 2011, http://www.state.gov/t/pm/rls/rm/166249.htm.

46. Thomas Tsilis, "Counter-Piracy Escort Operations in the Gulf of Aden," (MA thesis, Naval Postgraduate School, 2011).

47. Pendleton, *Maritime Security*.

48. Participating nations have included Australia, Canada, Denmark, France, Germany, Italy, Republic of Korea, Netherlands, New Zealand, Pakistan, Portugal, Singapore, Spain, and Turkey, and the United Kingdom. For more detail see CTF 150's website, https://combinedmaritimeforces.com/ctf-150-maritime-security/.

49. Quoted in Navy News Service, "New Counter-Piracy Task Force Established," 8 January 2009, http://www.navy.mil/submit/display.asp?story_id=41687.

50. The states participating in the CMF consisted of Australia, Bahrain, Belgium, Canada, Denmark, France, Germany, Greece, Iraq, Italy, Japan, Jordan, Republic of Korea, Kuwait, Malaysia, the Netherlands, New Zealand, Norway, Pakistan, The Philippines, Portugal, Saudi Arabia, Seychelles, Singapore, Spain, Thailand, Turkey, UAE, United Kingdom, United States, and Yemen.

51. Combined Maritime Forces, http://combinedmaritimeforces.com/about/.

52. Lauren Ploch et al., *Piracy off the Horn of Africa*, 25.

53. Ibid.

54. Eaglespeak, "Pirate Fighting: Roundtable with RADM McKnight, CTF-151," Maritime Global Net, 29 January 2009, http://www.eaglespeak.us/2009_01_01_archive.html.

55. "Operation Allied Provider," North Atlantic Treaty Organisation Factsheet, 2 December 2008, http://www.nato.int/issues/allied-provider/081202-allied-provider-factsheet-en.pdf.

56. "Counter-Piracy in the Gulf of Aden: Operation Allied Provider," *North Atlantic Treaty Organisation News*, 10 October 2008.

57. Operation Allied Protector, http://www.mc.nato.int/ops/Pages/Operation-Allied-Protector.aspx.

58. Raymond Knops, rapporteur, *The Challenge of Piracy: International Response and NATO's Role*, Report of the Sub-Committee on Future Security and Defence Capabilities, NATO Parliamentary Assembly, November 2012, 8, https://www.tbmm.gov.tr/ul_kom/natopa/docs/raporlar_2012/sa3.pdf.

59. For the breakdown of ships deployed by NATO see "Operation Shield," http://www.mc.nato.int/about/Pages/Operation%20Ocean%20Shield.aspx.

60. Marianne Riddervold, "New Threats—Different Response: EU and NATO and Somali Piracy, European Security," *European Security* 23, no. 4 (2014): 547.

61. Michael Evans, "EU Navies Join Forces to Fight Somali Pirates: Military Matters Land, Sea and Air, Cautious Common Sense, Is the Way to Counter Piracy," *The Times*, 12 September 2009, 105. Note that Northwood also serves as NATO's piracy headquarters.

62. Julian Hale, "EU Extends Anti-Piracy Effort to Seychelles," *Defense News*, 1 June 2009, 22.

63. Official Journal of the European Union, "Amending Joint Action 2008/851/CFSP on a European Union Military Operation to Contribute to the Deterrence, Prevention and Repression of Acts of Piracy and Armed Robbery Off the Somali Coast," Council Decision 2014/827/CFSP of November 21, 2014, http://eur-lex.europa.eu/legal-content/EN/TXT/?uri=CELEX%3A32014D0827

64. For further details, see "Deployed Units," European External Action Service at http://eunavfor.eu/deployed-units/mpras/#news-tabs.

65. Damien Helly, "EU NAVFOR Somalia: The EU Military Operation Atalanta," in *European Security and Defence Policy: The First 10 Years*, ed. Giovanni Grevi, Damien Helly, and Daniel Keohane (Paris: Institute for Security Studies, 2009), 396.

66. Alexandru Voicu and Ruxandra-Laura Bosilca, "Maritime Security Governance in the Fight against Piracy off the Coast of Somalia: A Focus on the EU Response," Centre for European Studies, EURINT Proceedings, 2015, 382, http://cse.uaic.ro/eurint/proceedings/index_htm_files/EURINT2015_VOI.pdf,

67. European Council, "EUNAVFOR Somalia Operation Atalanta: Operation's Mandate Extended until 31 December 2018," 28 November 2016, http://www.consilium.europa.eu/en/press/press-releases/2016/11/28-eu-navfor-somalia-operation-mandate-extended/.

68. Cf. "Operation Atalanta and Chinese Navy Work Together to Ensure World Food Programme Ship Remains Safe from Pirates," 16 May 2016, http://eunavfor.eu/operation-atalanta-and-chinese-navy-work-together-to-ensure-world-food-programme-ship-remains-safe-from-pirates/.

69. Christina Lin, "NATO-China Cooperation: Opportunities and Challenges," *ISPSW Strategy Series: Focus on Defense and International Security*, no. 189 (Berlin: Institute for Strategic, Political, Security and Economic Consultancy [ISPSW], April 2012), 5.

70. Jonathan Holslag, "The Reluctant Pretender: China's Evolving Presence in the Indian Ocean," *Journal of the Indian Ocean Region* 9, no. 1 (2013): 50.

71. Idrees Ali, "US Watches Piracy Increase off Somalia, See Ties to Famine," Reuters, 23 April 2017, http://www.reuters.com/article/us-usa-mattis-africa-idUSKBN17P0C7.

72. US Department of Homeland Security, "Uncommon Operational Picture," *S&T Snapshots* 2, no. 4 (July 2008), http://www.bal4.com/files/snapshots_v2n4.pdf.

73. Ibid.

74. As one draft report notes, "The US has the financial and technical resources to pursue this approach [CENTRIXS], but NATO does not." (7/19). Besides, in addition to different technical capabilities and investment patterns, American and NATO command and control arrangement are not seamless. DRAFT, ver. 0.9 NATO UNCLASSIFIED/Releasable to Internet 11:37 AM 14/03/2005 RL Parker "A NATO PERSPECTIVE ON CENTRIXS," http://www.dodccrp.org/events/10th_ICCRTS/CD/papers/007.pdf.

75. Kees Homan and Susanne Kamerling, "Operational Challenges to Counterpiracy Operations off the Coast of Somalia," in *The International Response to Somali Piracy Challenges and*

*Opportunities*, ed. Bibi van Ginkel and Frans-Pail van der Putten (Leiden: Brill Online, 2010): 88. CENTRIXS is a system "rooted in the efforts to interoperate during the Rim of the Pacific (RIM-PAC) exercise in 1998." Jose Carreno, Frank Bantell, George Galdorisi, and Russell Grall, "Enabling Multinational Communications with CENTRIXS," presented at the 15th ICCRTS, The Evolution of C2, *Proceedings of the 15th International Command and Control Research and Technology Symposium* (ICCRTS '10), http://www.dodccrp.org/events/15th_iccrts_2010/presentations/098.pdf.

76. Paul T Mitchell, "1000-Ship Navies, Maritime Domain Awareness and Networks: The Policy Nexus," in *Naval Networks: The Dominance of Communications in Maritime Operations: 2007 King-Hall Naval History Conference Proceedings*, ed. David Stevens (Sydney, Australia: Seapower Centre, 2012), 211–238, http://www.navy.gov.au/spc/sites/default/files/publication-documents/KH07-web-version.pdf.

77. Andrew S. Erickson and Austin M. Strange, "China's Blue Soft Power: Antipiracy, Engagement, and Image Enhancement," *Naval War College Review* 68, no. 1 (winter 2015), 78.

78. Helly, "EU NAVFOR Somalia," 399.

79. Quoted in "It's Good to Talk: Ad Hoc Networking across the Seas," *Jane's International Defense Review* 47, no. 2 (February 1, 2014): 47–51.

80. Gordon Van Hook, "How to Kill a Good Idea," *U.S. Naval Institute Proceedings* 133, no. 10 (October 2007), 34.

81. Shishir Upadhyaya, "Multilateral Maritime Security Cooperation in the Indian Ocean Region: Status and Prospects," *Journal of the Indian Ocean Region* 12, no.1 (2016): 42. Other accounts call SHADE "European Union–led." Both the United States and the EU may have contributed to developing SHADE, but CMF provided the deconfliction function before EUNAVFOR arrived. Joshy M. Paul, "Cooperative Security in the Indian Ocean Region: The IONS Way," no. 055, *RSIS Commentaries* (Singapore: Nanyang Technological University 2010), https://www.rsis.edu.sg/rsis-publication/idss/1345-cooperative-security-in-the-in/#.V1qiQFeUU3E.

82. Andrew Erickson and Austin Strange, "China and the International Antipiracy Effort," *The Diplomat* (1 November 2013), available at http://thediplomat.com/2013/11/china-and-the-international-antipiracy-effort/?allpages=yes.

83. For details on SHADE, see Christian Bueger, "Counter-piracy, Communities of Practice, and New Security Alignments," *Journal of Regional Security* 8, no. 1 (2013): 54.

84. Confidential interview with the authors, Brussels, 26 July 2016.

85. OBP roughly estimates the total cost of deterring piracy as $1.3 billion in 2015. Oceans beyond Piracy, *The State of Maritime Piracy: Assessing the Economic and Human Cost* (Bloomfield, CO: Oceans beyond Piracy 2016). See table "Costs of Deterring Piracy" in the section on "Somali Piracy in the Western Indian Ocean Region," http://oceansbeyondpiracy.org/reports/sop2015/east-africa.

86. Rosemary A. DiCarlo, Remarks by Ambassador Rosemary A. DiCarlo, US Alternate Representative for Special Political Affairs at the Signing of the "New York Declaration," at the United Nations, 9 September 2009, http://usun.state.gov/remarks/4465.

87. http://oceansbeyondpiracy.org/matrix/new-york-declaration.

88. Ploch et al., *Piracy off the Horn of Africa*, 23.

89. Confidential interview, 26 July 2016.

90. Cf. "Piracy Forces Kenya Cruise Tourism Down 95 Percent," *Voice of America*, 31 May 2010, http://www.voanews.com/content/piracy-forces-kenya-cruise-tourism-down-95-percent-95324914/154676.html.

91. Somalia's Attorney General Ahmed Ali Dahir, cited in Patsy Athanase and Betymie Bonnelame, "A Riddle: If Pirate Attacks Drop to Zero, Should Contact Group on Piracy Still Exist?" *Seychelles News Agency*, 31 May 2016, http://www.seychellesnewsagency.com/articles/5276/A+riddle+If+pirate+attacks+drop+to+zero,+should+Contact+Group+on+Piracy+still+exist.

92. Jeffery Gettleman, "Somali Pirates Attack, Raising Fears That a Menace Is Back," *New York Times*, 4 April 2017, https://www.nytimes.com/2017/04/04/world/africa/somalia-pirates.html?_r=0.

93. Christian Bueger, "Zones of Exception at Sea: Lessons from the Debate on the High Risk Area," Working Paper of the Lessons Learned Consortium of the Contact Group on Piracy off the Coast of Somalia, November 2015, http://www.lessonsfrompiracy.net/files/2015/10/Bueger-Lessons-from-the-HRA-debate.pdf: 8.

94. Ali, "US Watches Piracy Increase off Somalia, See Ties to Famine."

95. Currun Singh, "Al Shabab Fights the Pirates," *International New York Times*, 23 October 2013, 9. For an underlying analysis, see Currun Singh and Arjun Singh Bedi, "War on Piracy: The Conflation of Somali Piracy with Terrorism in Discourse, Tactic and Law," Institute of Social Studies Working Paper no. 543 (The Hague, The Netherlands: Institute of Social Studies, May 2012).

96. Confidential interview, Brussels, 26 July 2016.

97. See "Operation Ocean Shield," undated, http://www.mc.nato.int/about/Pages/Operation%20Ocean%20Shield.aspx.

98. Athanase and Bonnelame, "A Riddle?"

99. Confidential interview, Brussels, 26 July 2016.

100. Jonathan Stevenson, "Jihad and Piracy in Somalia," *Survival* 52, no. 1 (February–March 2010): 31.

101. Testimony of Ray Mabus, Secretary, Department of the Navy, "Proposed Fiscal 2012 Budget for the U.S. Navy," Hearing by the Senate Armed Services Committee, 8 March 2011, quoted in Lauren Ploch et al., *Piracy off the Horn of Africa*, 30.

102. David Gollust, "Clinton Announces US Anti-Piracy Measures," *Voice of America* (15 April 2009), http://www.voanews.com/content/a-13-2009-04-15-voa58-68799152/411974.html.

## 6. Navigating the Proliferation Security Initiative and Informal Sponsorship

1. Indeed, most are contested. There are very few global norms. See Simon Reich, *Global Norms, American Sponsorship and the Emerging Pattern of World Politics* (Basingstoke, UK: Palgrave Macmillan, 2010), 22–31.

2. Ibid.

3. For a discussion of this point, see Stephen D. Krasner, *Sovereignty: Organized Hypocrisy* (Princeton, NJ: Princeton University Press, 1999), especially 4.

4. Euan Graham, "Maritime Counter-Proliferation: The Case of MV *Light*," RSIS Commentaries no. 096 (Singapore: Nanyang Technological University, 2011), http://hdl.handle.net/10220/8049.

5. British Broadcasting Corporation, "US Navy 'Stopped North Korean Vessel Bound for Burma,'" BBC News, 13 June 2011, http://www.bbc.co.uk/news/world-asia-pacific-13747912.

6. Federation of American Scientists, "DDG-51 ARLEIGH BURKE-class," http://fas.org/man/dod-101/sys/ship/ddg-51.htm.

7. Ibid.

8. Cf. William J. Perry and Brent Scowcroft, *U.S. Nuclear Weapons Policy* (New York: Council on Foreign Relations, 2009). President Obama reinforced that view. See his remarks in Prague, "Remarks by President Barack Obama in Prague, Czech Republic," The White House, 5April2009,http://www.whitehouse.gov/the_press_office/Remarks-By-President-Barack-Obama-In-Prague-As-Delivered.

9. Barry R. Schneider, "Nuclear Proliferation and Counter-Proliferation: Policy Issues and Debates," *Mershon International Studies Review* 38, no. 2 (October 1994): 216.

10. Maria Rost Rublee, *Nonproliferation Norms: Why States Choose Nuclear Restraint* (Athens: University of Georgia Press, 2009).

11. Jacques E. C. Hymans, "Theories of Nuclear Proliferation," *Nonproliferation Review* 13, no. 3 (November 2006): 459.

12. Dan Reiter, "Preventive Attacks against Nuclear, Biological, and Chemical Weapons Programs: The Track Record," in *Hitting First: Preventive Force in U.S. Security Strategy*, ed.

William W. Keller and Gordon R. Mitchell (Pittsburgh, PA: University of Pittsburgh Press, 2006) 27–44; Schneider, "Nuclear Proliferation and Counter-Proliferation," 225–227.

13. As Eliot Cohen noted, "Publicly available evidence does not suggest that air attacks destroyed any Scud." Eliot A. Cohen, "The Mystique of U.S. Air Power," *Foreign Affairs* 73, no. 1 (January–February 1994): 109–124, quote is on 121.

14. Barry R. Schneider, *Radical Responses to Radical Regimes: Evaluating Preemptive Counter-Proliferation* (Honolulu: University Press of the Pacific, 2004).

15. Liviu Horovitz, "Beyond Pessimism: Why the Treaty on the Nonproliferation of Nuclear Weapons Will Not Collapse," *Journal of Strategic Studies* 38, no. 1–2 (2015): 126–158; quote from 22.

16. Ben Sanders, "What Nonproliferation Policy?" *Nonproliferation Review* 1, no. 1 (fall 1993): http://cns.miis.edu/npr/pdfs/sander11.pdf.

17. Amy Zegart, "Running in Place: An Institutional Analysis of U.S. Nonproliferation Organization since the Cold War," *Nonproliferation Review* 10 no. 2 (summer 2003): 15.

18. William Clinton, "Remarks to the 48th Session of the United Nations General Assembly," 23 September 1993, http://www.state.gov/p/io/potusunga/207375.htm.

19. To date, the text of PDD/NSC 18 has not been released, but Secretary of Defense Les Aspin discussed the initiative extensively in a speech on Pearl Harbor Day (December 7) in 1993, http://fas.org/irp/offdocs/pdd18.htm.

20. Ibid.

21. Andrew C. Winner, "The Proliferation Security Initiative: The New Face of Interdiction," *Washington Quarterly* 28, no. 2 (spring 2005): 130–131.

22. Michael Kimo Quaintance, "From Bad Weapons to Bad States: The Evolution of U.S. Counterproliferation Policy" (Ph.D. diss., University of St. Andrews, 2009), especially 160–193, https://research-repository.st-andrews.ac.uk/bitstream/10023/820/6/Michael%20K.%20 Quaintance%20PhD%20thesis.PDF.

23. For an account of the bureaucratic conflicts over this issue, see Chris Williams, "DOD's Counterproliferation Initiative: A Critical Assessment," in *Fighting Proliferation: New Concerns for the Nineties*, ed. Henry Sokolski (Washington: US Government Printing Office, 1996), 249–256.

24. Ibid., 251.

25. "Jane's Interview: Ashton Carter," *Jane's Defence Weekly*, 30 July 1994, 40.

26. For details of the *Yinhe* incident and its impact, see the 2008 Report to Congress of the US-China Economic and Security Review Commission, 110th Congress, Second Session, November 2008, 129–130, and 170nn17–18, http://origin.www.uscc.gov/sites/default/files/ annual_reports/2008-Report-to-Congress-_0.pdf.

27. For an official account, see Commission on the Intelligence Capabilities of the United States regarding Weapons of Mass Destruction. *Report to the President* (Washington, DC: WMD Commission 2005), especially chapter 3, http://www.wmd.gov/report/.

28. Rodger Payne and Peter Dombrowski, "Global Debate and the Limits of the Bush Doctrine," *International Studies Perspectives* 4, no. 4 (November 2003): 395–408; Peter Dombrowski and Rodger Payne, "The Emerging Consensus for Preventive War," *Survival* 48, no. 2 (summer 2006): 115–136.

29. "Text of Bush's Speech at West Point," *New York Times*, 1 June 2002, http://www. nytimes.com/2002/06/01/international/02PTEX-WEB.html?pagewanted=2.

30. Department of Defense, *National Strategy to Combat Weapons of Mass Destruction* (Washington, DC: Department of Defense, December 2002), http://www.state.gov/documents/ organization/16092.pdf.

31. Logically speaking, the intelligence collection and planning underpinning interdiction of the *BBC China* predated PSI, and the practical dimensions of PSI collaboration had barely started.

32. Eben Kaplan, "The Proliferation Security Initiative," Council on Foreign Relations Backgrounder, 19 October 2006, http://www.cfr.org/border-and-port-security/proliferation-security-initiative/p11057.

33. David Albright and Corey Hinderstein, "The A. Q. Khan Illicit Nuclear Trade Network and Implications for Nonproliferation Efforts," *Strategic Insights* 5, no. 6 (July 2006), http://calhoun.nps.edu/bitstream/handle/10945/11090/albrightJul06.pdf?sequence=1. For a timeline of events see New York Times Staff, "Chronology: A. Q. Khan," *New York Times*, 16 April 2006.

34. On A. Q. Khan and his network, see Gordon Corera, *Shopping for Bombs: Nuclear Proliferation, Global Insecurity, and the Rise and Fall of the A. Q. Khan Network* (New York: Oxford University Press 2009).

35. The original PSI Core group consisted of Australia, France, Germany, Italy, Japan, the Netherlands, Poland, Portugal, Spain, the United Kingdom, and the United States.

36. "Proliferation Security Initiative: Statement of Interdiction Principles," PSI.info, German Federal Foreign Office, http://www.psi-online.info/Vertretung/psi/en/07-statement/Interdiction-Principes.html.

37. "President Announces New Measure to Counter the Threat of Weapons of Mass Destruction (WMD)," Remarks by the President on Weapons of Mass Destruction Proliferation at Fort Lesley J. McNair—National Defense University, Washington, DC, 11 February 2004, http://2001-2009.state.gov/t/ac/rls/rm/2004/29291.htm.

38. Charles Wolf, Jr., Brian G. Chow, and Gregory S. Jones, *Enhancement by Enlargement: The Proliferation Security Initiative* (Santa Monica, CA: RAND, 2008).

39. See "Joint Statement by President Obama and Prime Minister Najib of Malaysia," 27 April 2014, https://www.whitehouse.gov/the-press-office/2014/04/27/joint-statement-president-obama-and-prime-minister-najib-malaysia-0.

40. "Remarks by President Barack Obama in Prague."

41. Winner, "The Proliferation Security Initiative," 136.

42. Aaron Dunne, "The Proliferation Security Initiative: Legal Considerations and Operational Realities," SIPRI, Policy Paper 36, May 2013, 43, http://books.sipri.org/files/PP/SIPRIPP36.pdf.

43. In Kenneth C. Brill and John H. Bernhard, "A Convention on Nuclear Security: A Needed Step against Nuclear Terrorism," *Arms Control Today*, June 2015, 17. See also the International Atomic Energy Agency (IAEA), "Incident and Trafficking Database," 9 December 2014, http://www-ns.iaea.org/security/itdb.asp.

44. The Pakistani A. Q. Khan network case is an exception, albeit because of its tacit approval by key government officials.

45. One major, if now aged, exception is Robert J. Einhorn and Michele A. Flournoy, *Protecting Against the Spread of Nuclear, Biological, and Chemical Weapons: An Action Agenda for the Global Partnership* (Washington DC: Center for Strategic and International Studies, 2003).

46. Michael C. Horowitz and Neil Narang, "Poor Man's Atomic Bomb? Exploring the Relationship between 'Weapons of Mass Destruction,'" *Journal of Conflict Resolution* 58, no. 3 (2013): 509–535.

47. These figures therefore underestimate the challenge. Richard R. Young, Matthew Peterson, Linda Novak, Meghan Flannery Hayes, and Frederick Tillotson, "Limiting the Worldwide Flow of Weapons and their Components through Established Maritime Transport," *Journal of Transportation Security* 7 (2014): 28.

48. Rohan Gunaratna, "The Post-Madrid Face of Al Qaeda," *Washington Quarterly* 27, no. 3 (2004): 91–100.

49. Anomalously, few Middle Eastern states have chosen to join the PSI. Three explanations have currency: (1) they might be implicated in PSI operations, (2) they fear entanglement in interdiction operations, and (3) at some point they might avail themselves of proliferation networks.

50. Robert S. Litwak has made the case that naming matters and traces the evolution of the term *rogue* and associated sobriquets in a series of articles and books. Robert S. Litwak, "What's in a Name? The Changing Foreign Policy Lexicon," *Journal of International Affairs* 54 no. 2 (spring 2001): 375–392; Robert S. Litwak, *Rogue States and U.S. Foreign Policy: Containment after the Cold War* (Washington/Baltimore: Woodrow Wilson Center Press with Johns Hopkins University Press, 2000); Robert S. Litwak, *Outlier States: American Strategies to Change, Contain, or*

*Engage Regimes* (Washington/Baltimore: Woodrow Wilson Center Press with Johns Hopkins University Press, 2012).

51. See John Bolton, "A Dictatorship at the Crossroads," Remarks in Seoul, South Korea, 31 July 2003, http://www.state.gov/t/us/rm/23028.htm, for a politically expedient interpretation of the proliferation threat. Scholarly accounts notably include Pakistan and China. Cf. Chaim Braun and Christopher F. Chyba, "Proliferation Rings: New Challenges to the Nuclear Nonproliferation Regime," *International Security* 29, no. 2 (fall 2004): 5–49.

52. Little political attention has been paid to "outliers" such as Pakistan's trafficking in technologies with China because Pakistan was an ally. On the Bush administration, see Wade Boese, "The Khan Network: Bush Outlines Proposal to Stem Proliferation," *Arms Control Today*, March 2004, especially 24. On the Clinton administration. See Karl Inderfurth interview, 18 February 2004; Strobe Talbott interview, February 8, 2004.

53. Bruce W. Jentleson and Christopher A. Whytock, "Who 'Won' Libya? The Force-Diplomacy Debate and Its Implications for Theory and Policy," *International Security* 30, no. 3 (winter 2005–6), 47–86; and J. W. de Villiers, Roger Jardine, and Mitchell Reiss, "Why South Africa Gave up the Bomb," *Foreign Affairs* 72, no. 5 (November–December 1993): 98–109.

54. Tom Bielefeld, "Mexico's Stolen Radiation Source: It Could Happen Here," *Bulletin of the Atomic Scientists*, 23 January 2014, http://thebulletin.org/mexico%E2%80%99s-stolen-radiation-source-it-could-happen-here.

55. See Matthew Bunn, Martin B. Malin, Nickolas Roth, and William H. Tobey, *Advancing Nuclear Security: Evaluating Progress and Setting New Goals* (Cambridge, MA.: Project on Managing the Atom, Belfer Center for Science and International Affairs, Harvard University, March 2014).

56. Alex P. Schmid and Charlotte Spencer-Smith, "Illicit Radiological and Nuclear Trafficking, Smuggling and Security Incidents in the Black Sea Region since the Fall of the Iron Curtain—An Open Source Inventory," *Perspectives on Terrorism* 6, no 2 (2012), http://www.terrorismanalysts.com/pt/index.php/pot/article/view/schmid-illicit-radiological/html.

57. Jason D. Ellis, "The Best Defense: Counterproliferation and U.S. National Security," *Washington Quarterly* 26, no. 2 (spring 2003): 125.

58. Harald Mueller, "Germany and WMD Proliferation," *Nonproliferation Review* 10, no. 2 (summer 2003): 1–20.

59. The *So San* carried disassembled Scud missiles. Thomas E. Ricks and Peter Slevin, "Spain and U.S. Seize N. Korean Missiles: Scuds Were on Ship Bound for Yemen," *Washington Post*, 11 December 2002, A01.

60. Lukasz Kulesa, "Poland and the Proliferation Security Initiative," *Korean Journal of Defense Analysis* 22, no. 1 (March 2010): 22.

61. John Bolton, US undersecretary of state for Arms Control and International Security, cited in Kaplan, "The Proliferation Security Initiative."

62. The term *nonparticipation* is ambiguous. Nonsignatories to the PSI Statement of Interdiction Principles nonetheless often join PSI conferences and tabletop games on a case-by-case basis. Some even observe and join operational field exercises.

63. Brill and Bernhard, "A Convention on Nuclear Security" 18.

64. Charles Allen, "Countering Proliferation: WMD on the Move," *Georgia Journal of International and Comparative Law* 40, no. 15 (2013): 16–36. Quote is on 34.

65. Natalie Klein, "The Right of Visit and the 2005 Protocol on the Suppression of Unlawful Acts against the Safety of Maritime Navigation," *Denver Journal of International Law and Policy* 35, no. 2 (2006): 287–332, see especially 311–312.

66. Caitlin A. Harrington, "Heightened Security: The Need to Incorporate Articles 3BIS(1)(A) and 8BIS(5)(E) of the 2005 Draft SUA Protocol into Part VII of the United Nations Convention on the Law of the Sea," *Pacific Rim Law and Policy Journal* 16, no. 1 (2007): 107–136; quote on 109.

67. Helmut Tuerk, "Combating Terrorism at Sea—The Suppression of Unlawful Acts against the Safety of Maritime Navigation," *University of Miami International and Comparative Law Review* 15 (2014): 337–367, especially 358–365.

68. Scott D. MacDonald, "The SUA 2005 Protocol: A Critical Reflection," *International Journal of Marine and Coastal Law* 28 (2013): 485–516.

69. John E. Noyes, "U.S. Policy and the United Nations Convention on the Law of the Sea," *George Washington International Law Review* 30 (2007): 621–638, quote on 636.

70. See as examples, Ticy V. Thomas, "The Proliferation Security Initiative: Towards Relegation of Navigational Freedoms in UNCLOS? An Indian Perspective," *Chinese Journal of International Law* 8, no. 3 (2009): 657–680; and Jinyuan Su, "The Proliferation Security Initiative (PSI) and Interdiction at Sea: A Chinese Perspective," *Ocean Development and International Law* 43, no. 1 (2012): 96–118.

71. Patrick J. Bonner, "Neo-Isolationists Scuttle UNCLOS," *SAIS Review of International Affairs* 33, no. 2 (summer–fall 2013): 135–146. Thomas Wright, "Outlaw of the Sea: The Senate Republicans' UNCLOS Blunder," *Foreign Affairs* (7 August 2012), https://www.foreignaffairs.com/articles/oceans/2012-08-07/outlaw-sea.

72. Author interviews, July 2015.

73. Kenneth C. Brill and John H. Bernhard, "A Convention on Nuclear Security: A Needed Step against Nuclear Terrorism," *Arms Control Today*, June 2015, 18.

74. Ian Williams, "The Proliferation Security Initiative (PSI) at a Glance," July 2013, http://www.armscontrol.org/factsheets/PSI.

75. Kaplan, "The Proliferation Security Initiative."

76. Shirley A. Kan, *China and Proliferation of Weapons of Mass Destruction and Missiles: Policy Issues*, CRS Report to Congress RL31555 (Washington DC: Congressional Research Service, 7 November 2012).

77. James Kraska and Brian Wilson, "China Wages Maritime Lawfare," *Foreign Policy*, 12 March 2009, http://experts.foreignpolicy.com/posts/2009/03/11/china_wages_maritime_lawfare.

78. Cf. Joseph S. Nye Jr., "Avoiding Conflict in the South China Sea," *Project Syndicate*, 3 June 2015, http://www.project-syndicate.org/commentary/south-china-sea-conflict-by-joseph-s--nye-2015-06#AXMthFjyJlIcZxo2.99.

79. Evan Medeiros, *Reluctant Restraint: The Evolution of China's Nonproliferation Policies and Practices, 1980–2004* (Palo Alto, CA: Stanford University Press, 2007); Rosemary Foot and Andrew Walter, *China, the United States, and the Global Order* (New York: Cambridge University Press, 2011).

80. See Neil Narang, Erik Gartzke, and Matthew Kroenig, eds., *Nonproliferation Policy and Nuclear Posture: Causes and Consequences for the Spread of Nuclear Weapons* (New York: Routledge Global Security Studies, October 2015).

81. See Thomas B. Smith and Marc Tranchemontagne, "Understanding the Enemy: The Enduring Value of Technical and Forensic Exploitation," *Joint Forces Quarterly* 75 (2014): 125.

82. Susan J. Koch, "Proliferation Security Initiative: Origins and Evolution," Occasional Paper no. 9 (Washington DC: National Defense University, Center for the Study of Weapons of Mass Destruction, June 2012), 23.

83. Quoted in ibid., 30.

84. On the role of scientists, engineers, and knowledge, see Jacques E. C. Hymans, *Achieving Nuclear Ambitions: Scientists, Politicians, and Proliferation* (London: Cambridge University Press, 2011).

85. See Rose Gottemoeller, "Cooperative Threat Reduction beyond Russia," *Washington Quarterly* 28, no. 2 (2005): 145–158.

86. Cited in Philip E. Coyle, III and Victoria Samson, "The Proliferation Security Initiative: Background, History, and Prospects for the Future," International Commission for Nuclear Non-Proliferation and Disarmament, January 2009, 7, http://icnnd.org/Documents/Proliferation_Security_Initiative.pdf.

87. Amy F. Woolf, Paul K. Kerr, and Mary Beth D. Nikitin, "Arms Control and Nonproliferation: A Catalog of Treaties and Agreements," *Current Politics and Economics of the United States* 16, no. 4 (2014): 517. Note that "this is an edited, reformatted and augmented version of a Congressional Research Service publication, No. RL33865, dated 28 April 2014."

88. U.S. Government Accountability Office, *Nonproliferation: U.S. Agencies Have Taken Some Steps, but More Effort Is Needed to Strengthen and Expand the Proliferation Security Initiative* (Washington, DC: GAO, November 2008).

89. US Government Accountability Office, *Proliferation Security Initiative: Agencies Have Adopted Policies and Procedures but Steps Needed to Meet Reporting Requirement and to Measure Results* (Washington, DC: GAO, March 2012), 20.

90. Simon Reich and Peter Dombrowski, "The Strategy of Sponsorship," *Survival: Global Politics and Strategy* 57, no. 5 (October–November 2015): 121–148.

91. This issue is discussed in Graham Allison, *Nuclear Terrorism: The Ultimate Preventable Catastrophe* (New York: Times Books, 2004).

92. Nick Miller, "U.S. Nonproliferation Policy Is an Invisible Success Story," *Washington Post,* 16 October 2014, http://www.washingtonpost.com/blogs/monkey-cage/wp/2014/10/16/u-s-nonproliferation-policy-is-an-invisible-success-story/. For Miller's detailed argument, see Nicholas L. Miller, "Nuclear Dominoes: A Self-Defeating Prophecy?" *Security Studies* 23, no. 1 (2014): 33–73.

93. Susan J. Koch, "Proliferation Security Initiative: Origins and Evolution," Center for the Study of Weapons of Mass Destruction, Occasional Paper No. 9 (Washington, DC: National Defense University Press, 2012), 24.

94. Thomas E. Ricks and Peter Slevin, "Spain and U.S. Seize N. Korean Missiles; Scuds Were on Ship Bound for Yemen," *Washington Post,* 11 December 2002; and David E. Sanger and Thom Shanker, "Threats and Responses: War Matériel; Reluctant U.S. Gives Assent for Missiles to Go to Yemen," *New York Times,* 12 December 2002.

95. Government Accountability Office, *Proliferation Security Initiative: Agencies Have Adopted Policies and Procedures but Steps Needed to Meet Reporting Requirement and to Measure Results Report,* GAO-12-441 (Washington, DC: GAO, March 2012), http://www.gao.gov/assets/590/589632.pdf.

96. Kenneth N. Waltz, "Why Iran Should Get the Bomb: Nuclear Balancing Would Mean Stability," *Foreign Affairs* 91, no 4 (July–August 2012), 2–5.

97. Michael Byers, "Policing the High Seas: The Proliferation Security Initiative," *American Journal of International Law* 98, no. 3 (July 2004): 526–545.

## 7. Racing for the Arctic with a Strategy of Restraint

1. Tom Parfitt, "Russia Plants Flag on North Pole Seabed," *The Guardian,* 2 August 2007, http://www.theguardian.com/world/2007/aug/02/russia.arctic.

2. Klaus Dodds, "Flag Planting and Finger Pointing: The Law of the Sea, the Arctic and the Political Geographies of the Outer Continental Shelf," *Political Geography* 29 (2010): 63–73.

3. C. J. Chivers, "Russians Plant Flag on the Arctic Seabed," *New York Times,* 3 August 2007, http://www.nytimes.com/2007/08/03/world/europe/03arctic.html.

4. N.B.: Only the Northern Sea Route is currently passible for limited periods, although it poses significant challenges for shipping. Atle Staalesen, "Russia's Northern Sea Route Saw Downturn in Cargo Transits in 2015," Updated 28 September 2016, adn.com, https://www.adn.com/arctic/article/new-low-northern-sea-route/2016/02/16/.

5. Alex Shoumatoff, "The Arctic Oil Rush," *Vanity Fair,* May 2008, http://www.vanityfair.com/news/2008/05/arctic_oil200805.

6. Doug Struck, "Russia's Deep-Sea Flag-Planting at North Pole Strikes a Chill in Canada," *Washington Post,* 7 August 2007, http://www.washingtonpost.com/wp-dyn/content/article/2007/08/06/AR2007080601369.html.

7. Nicholas Breyfogle, "Russia and the Race for the Arctic," *Origins: Current Events in Historical Perspective* 5, no. 11 (August 2012), http://origins.osu.edu/Article/russia-and-race-arctic.

8. Staalesen, "Russia's Northern Sea Route."

9. Chris Mooney and Jason Samenow, "The North Pole Is an Insane 36 Degrees Warmer than Normal as Winter Descends," *Washington Post,* 17 November 2016, https://www.washingtonpost.com/news/energy-environment/wp/2016/11/17/the-north-pole-is-an-insane-36-degrees-warmer-than-normal-as-winter-descends/?tid=ss_mail&utm_term=.9fee1cb6a80d.

10. Lawson Brigham, "Think Again: The Arctic," *Foreign Policy*, October/November 2010, http://foreignpolicy.com/2010/08/06/think-again-the-arctic/.

11. US Geologic Survey, *Circum-Arctic Resource Appraisal: Estimates of Undiscovered Oil and Gas North of the Arctic Circle*, USGS Fact Sheet 2008–3049 (2008), http://pubs.usgs.gov/fs/2008/3049/fs2008-3049.pdf.

12. "The Arctic: Special Report," *The Economist*, 16 June 2012, 10.

13. James Kraska and Betsy Baker, *Arctic Security Challenges: CNAS Policy Brief* (Washington, DC: Center for a New American Security, March 2014).

14. John McCain "The Real Arctic Threat: Obama Focuses on Global Warming while Putin's Neo-Imperialist Dreams Continue to Spread North," *Wall Street Journal*, 1 September 2015, http://www.wsj.com/Articles/the-real-arctic-threat-1441149448.

15. Some analysts interpret Russia's intentions and capabilities more benignly. Lincoln Edson Flake, "Russia's Security Intentions in a Melting Arctic," *Military and Strategic Affairs* 6, no. 1 (2014): 99–116.

16. Admiral Papp's testimony, 2, http://docs.house.gov/meetings/FA/FA14/20141210/102783/HHRG-113-FA14-Transcript-20141210.pdf.

17. Howard I. Kushner, "'Seward's Folly'? American Commerce in Russian America and the Alaska Purchase," *California Historical Quarterly* 54, no. 1 (spring 1975): 4–26.

18. See "U.S. Coast Guard History," https://www.uscg.mil/history/h_index.asp.

19. For a brief review of US naval operations, see David W. Titley and Courtney C. St. John, "Arctic Security Considerations and the U.S. Navy's Roadmap for the Arctic," *Naval War College Review* 63, no. 2 (spring 2010): 41–42.

20. Steven E. Miller, "The Arctic as a Maritime Theater," in *Arctic Alternatives or Militarism in the Circumpolar North*, ed. Franklyn Griffiths, Canadian Papers in Peace Studies no. 3 (Ontario, Canada: Science for Peace, 1992), 211–236.

21. Scott G. Borgerson, "Arctic Meltdown: The Economic and Security Implications of Global Warming," *Foreign Affairs* 87, no. 2 (March/April 2008): 63–77.

22. "National Security Presidential Directive 66," http://fas.org/irp/offdocs/nspd/nspd66.htm.

23. Barack Obama, *National Strategy for the Arctic Region* (Washington, DC: Executive Office of the President, May 2013), 6, http://www.whitehouse.gov/sites/default/files/docs/nat_arctic_strategy.pdf.

24. Karen Parrish, "Hagel Announces Arctic Defense Strategy," American Forces Press Service, 22 November 2013, http://archive.defense.gov/news/newsarticle.aspx?id=121220.

25. At present, US-Russian "relations are based on the Ilulissat Declaration signed by the 'Arctic Five' in May 2008, which states that the UNCLOS was recognized as the legal basis for drawing borders, and that the parties intended to resolve problems through negotiations." Alexander Serguninab and Valery Konyshev, "Russia in Search of Its Arctic Strategy: Between Hard and Soft Power?" *Polar Journal* 4, no. 1 (2014): 76.

26. Ibid.

27. Ibid., 8–9.

28. R. Douglas Brubaker, *The Russian Arctic Straits* (Leiden, Netherlands: Brill, 2005), chapter 1.

29. Matthew Carnaghan and Allison Goody, *Canadian Arctic Sovereignty*, Political and Social Affairs Division, Canadian Library of Parliament, 26 January 2006, http://www.parl.gc.ca/Content/LOP/ResearchPublications/prb0561-e.htm.

30. David R. Rothwell, "The United States and the Arctic Straits: The Northwest Passage and the Bering Straits," in *International Law and Politics of the Arctic Ocean: Essays in Honor of Donat Pharand*, ed. Suzanne Lalonde and Ted L. McDorman (Boston: Brill Nijhoff, 2014), 160–179, quote on 166.

31. Donat Pharand, "The Arctic Waters and the Northwest Passage: A Final Revisit," *Ocean Development and International Law* 38, no. 1–2 (2007): 3–69.

32. US Department of Defense, "Report to Congress on Arctic Operations and the Northwest Passage" (Washington, DC: Office of the Under Secretary of Defense for Policy, May 2011), http://www.defense.gov/pubs/pdfs/tab_a_arctic_report_public.pdf.

33. For a journalistic example, see Duncan Depledge, "How Russia Could Annex the Arctic," *Defense One*, 23 March 2015, http://www.defenseone.com/threats/2015/03/how-russia-could-annex-arctic/108229/; among politicians, see John McCain, "The Real Arctic Threat"; and note that President Putin apparently views potential American sea-based, antiballistic missile deployments as a reasonable justification for Russia's military activities in the Arctic. Alexei Anishchuka, "Russia Needs Arctic Presence to Guard against U.S. Threat: Putin," *Reuters Online*, 3 December 2013, http://www.reuters.com/Article/2013/12/03/us-alrussia-putin-arctic-idUSBRE9B20VT20131203.

34. For an assessment of Asian involvement, see Olav Schram Stokke, "The Promise of Involvement: Asia in the Arctic," *Strategic Analysis* 47, no. 4 (2013): 474–479.

35. James Kraska, "Arctic Strategy and Military Security," in *Changes in the Arctic Environment and The Law of The Sea*, ed. Myron H. Nordquist and Thomas H. Heidar (Netherlands: Martinus Nijihoff Publications, 2010), 261–263. Such speculation is neither official policy nor practical given the large number of Russian ICBMs. On Russian perceptions, see Vladmir Dvorkin, "Postcrisis Perceptions: The Prospect for Cooperation among the United States, NATO, and Russia on Ballistic Missile Defense," in *Missile Defense from a Global Perspective*, ed. Catherine Kelleher and Peter Dombrowski (Palo Alto, CA: Stanford University Press, 2015).

36. Norwegian Armed Forces, "Cold Response 2016," https://forsvaret.no/en/coldresponse.

37. Marcus Weisgerber, "Now NATO's Prepping for Hybrid War," *Defense One*, 27 August 2015, http://www.defenseone.com/management/2015/08/now-natos-prepping-hybrid-war/119687/.

38. NATO, "Exercise Cold Response 2016 Wraps Up in Norway," https://shape.nato.int/2016/exercise-cold-response-2016-wraps-up-in-norway.

39. Cf. "From Cold War to Hot War," *The Economist*, 14 February 2015, http://www.economist.com/news/briefing/21643220-russias-aggression-ukraine-part-broader-and-more-dangerous-confrontation.

40. Jane Perlez, "Hague Tribunal Rejects Beijing's Claims in South China Sea," *New York Times*, 12 July 2016, http://www.nytimes.com/2016/07/13/world/asia/south-china-sea-hague-ruling-philippines.html?emc=eta1.

41. Stephan Frühling and Guillaume Lasconjarias, "NATO, A2/AD, and the Kaliningrad Challenge," *Survival: Global Politics and Strategy* 58 no. 2 (March 2016): 95–116.

42. Some have argued that the Northwest and Northeast passages are less attractive than conventionally believed. Stephen M. Carmel, "The Cold, Hard Realities of Arctic Shipping," *Proceedings Magazine* 139, no. 7 (July 2013): 1–4, http://www.usni.org/magazines/proceedings/2013-07/cold-hard-realities-arctic-shipping.

43. Katarzyna Zysk, "Russia's Arctic Strategy Ambitions and Constraints," *Joint Force Quarterly* 57 (April 2010): 103–110.

44. Paal Sigurd Hilde, "The 'New' Arctic—The Military Dimension," *Journal of Military and Strategic Studies* 15, no. 2 (2013): 145.

45. Alexander Sergunin and Valery Konyshev, "Russia in Search of Its Arctic Strategy: Between Hard and Soft Power?" *Polar Journal* 4, no. 1 (2014): 86.

46. "Russia Establishes Arctic Strategic Military Command," *Radio Free Europe/Radio Liberty*, 1 December 2014.

47. Jonathan Masters, "The Russian Military," *CFR Backgrounder*, updated 20 March 2015, http://www.cfr.org/russian-federation/russian-military/p33758.

48. Associated Press, "'Cold' War Games: Russian Military Drills in Arctic," CBS News Online, 16 March 2015, http://www.cbsnews.com/news/russian-military-launches-massive-war-games-in-arctic/.

49. "'Norway Will Suffer': Russia Makes Nuclear Threat over US Marines,'" *The Local* (Norway), 31 October 2016, http://www.thelocal.no/20161031/norway-will-suffer-russia-makes-nuclear-threat-over-us-marines.

50. Andrew E. Krameraug, "Russia Stakes New Claim to Expanse in the Arctic," *New York Times*, 4 August 2015, http://www.nytimes.com/2015/08/05/world/europe/kremlin-stakes-claim-to-arctic-expanse-and-its-resources.html?_r=0.

51. For a review of the Soviet perspective, see Evgenia Issraelian, "Gorbachev's Murmansk Initiative," in *Arctic Alternatives: Civil or Militarism in the Circumpolar North*, ed. Franklyn Griffiths, Canadian Paper in Peace Studies no. 3 (Toronto: Science for Peace, 1992), 269–277.

52. Yuri Golotyuk, "Safeguarding the Arctic," *Russia in Global Affairs* 3 (9 August 2008), http://eng.globalaffairs.ru/number/n_11281. Russia's Arctic, for example, is rife with smuggling.

53. Kristian Åtlanda, "The Introduction, Adoption, and Implementation of Russia's 'Northern Strategic Bastion' Concept, 1992–1999," *Journal of Slavic Military Studies* 20, no. 4 (2007): 499–528; and Yuri Golotyuk, "Safeguarding the Arctic."

54. Atle Staalesen, "In Remotest Russian Arctic, a New Navy Base," *Barents Observer*, 17 September 2013, http://barentsobserver.com/en/security/2013/09/remotest-russian-arctic-new-navy-base-17-09.

55. Heather A. Conley, "Coast Guard Arctic Implementation Capabilities," Testimony to the House Coast Guard and Maritime Transportation Subcommittee, US Congress, 12 July 2016, 3, https://csis-prod.s3.amazonaws.com/s3fs-public/congressional_testimony/ts160712_Conley_testimony_coast_guard_arctic.pdf.

56. Kraska, "Arctic Strategy and Military Security."

57. For details, see Ronald O'Rourke, *Changes in the Arctic: Background and Issues for Congress* (Washington, DC: Congressional Research Service, April 25, 2013), especially 61–62.

58. Testimony of Mr. Andrew Holland, senior fellow for energy and climate, American Security Project, Hearing Before the Subcommittee on Europe, Eurasia, and Emerging Threats of the Committee on Foreign Affairs, House of Representatives, 113th Congress, Second Session, Serial No. 113-235 (10 December 2014), 35, http://docs.house.gov/meetings/FA/FA14/20141210/102783/HHRG-113-FA14-Transcript-20141210.pdf.

59. Douglas Ernst, "U.S. Cedes Arctic to Russia: 'We're Not Even in the Same League,' Says Coast Guard Chief," *Washington Times*, 8 July 2015, http://www.washingtontimes.com/news/2015/jul/8/us-cedes-arctic-russia-were-not-even-same-league-s/?utm_source=RSS_Feed&utm_medium=RSS.

60. US Chief of Naval Operations, "U.S. Navy: Energy, Environment, and Climate Change," http://greenfleet.dodlive.mil/climate-change/.

61. Jonathan Greenert, "A New Maritime Crossroad: The Arctic," 1 November 2013, http://cno.navylive.dodlive.mil/2013/11/01/a-new-maritime-crossroad-the-arctic/#sthash.q59gVAiz.dpuf.

62. Steven Beardsley, "Navy Spots an Arctic Future, But Struggles to Plot a Course," *Stars and Stripes*, 24 March 2014.

63. Scott G. Borgerson, "The Great Game Moves North: As the Arctic Melts, Countries Vie for Control," *Foreign Affairs Postscripts*, 25 March 2009, http://www.foreignaffairs.com/Arcticles/64905/scott-g-borgerson/thegreat-game-moves-north.

64. Lance M. Bacon, "Lawmaker Presses Navy to Buy an Icebreaker," *Navy Times*, 13 April 2015, A20.

65. Government Accountability Office, *Coast Guard: Efforts to Identify Arctic Requirements Are Ongoing, but More Communication about Agency Planning Efforts Would Be Beneficial*, GAO-10-870 (Washington, DC: GAO, September 2010), 18.

66. "Welcome to Thule, 'The Top of the World,'" http://www.peterson.af.mil/shared/media/document/AFD-100412-027.pdf.

67. Jordain Carney, "Alaska Senator Launches Arctic Caucus," *The Hill*, 4 March 2015, http://thehill.com/blogs/floor-action/senate/234659-alaska-senator-launches-arctic-caucus.

68. Juliet Eilperin, "Obama and Nordic Leaders: Economic Activity in the Arctic Must Pass Climate Test," *Washington Post*, 13 May 2016, https://www.washingtonpost.com/news/energy-environment/wp/2016/05/13/obama-and-nordic-leaders-economic-activity-in-the-arctic-must-pass-climate-test/.

69. John H. Herz, *Political Realism and Political Idealism* (New York: Cambridge University Press, 1951).

70. Kristian Åtlanda, "Interstate Relations in the Arctic: An Emerging Security Dilemma?" *Comparative Strategy* 33, no. 2 (2014): 145–166.

71. Atle Staalesen, "Hillary Warns against Russia in Arctic," *Barents Observer*, 3 April 2014, http://barentsobserver.com/en/arctic/2014/04/hillary-warns-against-russia-arctic-03-04.

72. Canadian Ministry of Foreign Affairs, Trade, and Development, "Canada Takes Principled Stand on Arctic Council Meetings," 15 April 2014, http://www.international.gc.ca/media/arctic-arctique/news-communiques/2014/04/15a.aspx?lang=eng.

73. "Appendix: Conference on Arctic Security: Summary and Perspectives," *Journal of Military and Strategic Studies* 15, no. 2 (2013): 163; "Summary of Conference at the University of Southern Denmark, 5 November 2012: Exploring the Foundations for Arctic Order: Collective Security, Collective Defense, or Something New."

74. Duncan Depledge, "Hard Security Developments," 59–68, and Alyson J. K. Bailes, "Wider Security Angles," 69–74, both in *Arctic Security Matters*, ed. Juha Jokela (Paris: EU Institute for Security Studies, 2015), http://www.iss.europa.eu/uploads/media/Report_24_Arctic_matters.pdf.

75. Marc A. Levy, "Is the Environment a National Security Issue?" *International Security* 20, no. 2 (fall 1995): 35–62, quote on 36–37.

76. BP, "Deepwater Horizon Accident and Response," http://www.bp.com/en/global/corporate/gulf-of-mexico-restoration/deepwater-horizon-accident-and-response.html.

77. Erica Martinson, "Trump Energy Plan Calls for More Drilling and Fewer Environmental Protections," ADN.com, updated 14 July 2016, https://www.adn.com/politics/2016/05/26/trump-pledges-to-back-more-oil-drilling-including-in-alaska/; Juliet Eilperin and Brady Dennis, "Trump, Reversing Obama, Will Push to Expand Drilling in the Arctic and Atlantic," *Washington Post*, 27 April 2017, https://www.washingtonpost.com/politics/trump-reversing-obama-will-push-to-expand-drilling-in-the-arctic-and-atlantic/2017/04/27/757fa06c-2aae-11e7-b605-33413c691853_story.html?utm_term=.08313ceb549a.

78. Michael Klare, *Resource Wars: The New Landscape of Global Conflict* (New York: Metropolitan Books, 2001); and Michael Klare, *Rising Powers, Shrinking Planet: The New Geopolitics of Energy* (New York: Holt Paperbacks, 2009).

79. Michael T. Klare, "From Scarcity to Abundance: The Changing Dynamics of Energy Conflict," *Penn State Journal of Law and International Affairs* 3, no. 2 (February 2015): 37. See earlier, Michael T. Klare, "Rushing for the Arctic's Riches" *New York Times*, 7 December 2013, http://www.nytimes.com/2013/12/08/opinion/sunday/rushing-for-the-arctics-riches.html?pagewanted=all.

80. Oran R. Young, "The Future of the Arctic: Cauldron of Conflict or Zone of Peace?" *International Affairs* 87, no. 1 (January 2011): 185–193.

81. Kirk Johnson, "Exuberance and Disappointment at Shell's About-Face in the Arctic," *New York Times*, 28 September 2015, http://www.nytimes.com/2015/09/29/us/exuberance-and-disappointment-at-shells-about-face-in-the-arctic.html?emc=eta1.

82. Jonathan Greenert, *U.S. Navy Arctic Roadmap, 2014–2030* (Washington, DC: US Navy, February 2014), http://www.navy.mil/docs/USN_arctic_roadmap.pdf.

83. Ibid., 18.

84. Ibid., 17.

85. William J. Aceves, "The Freedom of Navigation Program: A Study of the Relationship Between Law and Politics," *Hastings International and Comparative Law Review* 19, no. 2 (1996): 259–326.

86. Sam J. Tandgredi, "The Maritime Commons and Military Power," in *Conflict and Cooperation in the Global Common*, ed. Scott Jasper (Washington, DC: Georgetown University Press, 2012), 72.

87. Andreas Kuersten, "Assessing the U.S. Navy's Arctic Roadmap," *CIMSEC*, 21 June 2015, http://cimsec.org/assessing-the-u-s-navys-arctic-roadmap/17117.

88. Statement for the Record by the Honorable Mead Treadwell, Lieutenant Governor, State of Alaska, Before the United States House of Representatives Committee on Transportation and Infrastructure, Subcommittee on Coast Guard and Maritime Transportation, "America is Missing the Boat" (Washington, DC: 1 December 2011).

89. For a discussion of this point, see David Curtis Wright, *The Dragon Eyes the Top of the World: Arctic Policy Debate and Discussion in China*, China Maritime Study No. 8 (Newport, RI:

Naval War College Press, August 2011), https://www.usnwc.edu/Research-Gaming/China-Maritime-Studies-Institute/Publications/documents/China-Maritime-Study-8_The-Dragon-Eyes-the-Top-of-.pdf.

90. On China's energy dependence and its impact on policies, see, for one prominent example, Aaron L. Friedberg, A *Contest for Supremacy: China, America, and the Struggle for Mastery in Asia* (New York: W. W. Norton, 2012), 228–230.

91. Binyamin Applebaum, "On Trade, Donald Trump Breaks With 200 Years of Economic Orthodoxy," *New York Times*, 10 March 2016, http://www.nytimes.com/2016/03/11/us/politics/-trade-donald-trump-breaks-200-years-economic-orthodoxy-mercantilism.html?_r=0.

92. Ye Jiang, "China's Role in Arctic Affairs in the Context of Global Governance," *Strategic Analysis* 38, no. 5 (November/December 2014), 913–916.

93. "Chinese Investments Shore Up Russia's Arctic LNG Project—Total CEO," *RT*, 25 September 2015, https://www.rt.com/business/316477-china-russia-investments-arctic/.

94. Zhong Xiang Zhang, "China's Energy Security, the Malacca Dilemma and Responses," *Energy Policy* 39, no. 12 (December 2011): 7612–7615.

95. Cf. Dave Majumdar, "The U.S. Navy and Russia: Heading Towards a Crisis in the Mediterranean?" *National Interest*, 1 July 2016, http://nationalinterest.org/blog/the-buzz/the-us-navy-russia-heading-towards-crisis-the-mediterranean-16834.

96. Ronald O'Rourke, *Coast Guard Polar Icebreaker Modernization: Background and Issues for Congress* (Washington, DC: Congressional Research Service, 27 May 2016).

97. U.S. Navy Task Force Climate Change, "The United States Navy Arctic Roadmap for 2014–2030," (Washington, DC: US Navy, February 2014), 3, http://www.navy.mil/docs/USN_arctic_roadmap.pdf.

98. Scott G. Borgerson, "Arctic Meltdown: The Economic and Security Implications of Global Warming," *Foreign Affairs* 87, no. 2 (March/April 2008): 63–77.

99. Department of Defense, *Report to Congress on Arctic Operations and the Northwest Passage* (May 2011), 12.

100. Douglas C. Nord, "Responding to Change in the North: Comparing Recent Canadian and American Foreign Policies in the Arctic," in *The Arctic Contested*, ed. Keith Batterbee and John Erik Fossum (New York: P.I.E. Peter Lang, 2014), 59.

101. On McCain, see John McCain, "The Real Arctic Threat"; on Trump, see Richard Clifford, "Decision 2016; Trump's Arctic," *Polar Observer*, October 19, 2016, http://polarconnection.org/trump-arctic-policy/.

102. Nicholas Fandos, "Trump Weighs Cuts to Coast Guard, T.S.A. and FEMA to Bolster Border Plan," *New York Times*, 9 March 2017, https://www.nytimes.com/2017/03/09/us/politics/trump-budget-coast-guard.html.

103. Andrew Revkin, "Trump's Defense Chief Cites Climate Change as National Security Challenge," *Pro Publica*, 14 March 2017, https://www.propublica.org/article/trumps-defense-secretary-cites-climate-change-national-security-challenge?utm_campaign=bt_twitter&utm_source=twitter&utm_medium=social.

104. Author witness, US Coast Guard Headquarters, Washington, DC, 2012.

## 8. Controlling the Southern Maritime Approaches with an Isolationist Strategy

1. Examples are plentiful but cf. Eugene Scott, "Trump Vows to Build Border Wall to Address New Hampshire 'Drug Epidemic,'" CNN, 6 February 2016, http://www.cnn.com/2016/02/06/politics/donald-trump-new-hampshire-drug-epidemic/.

2. See David E. Sanger and Maggie Haberman, "In Donald Trump's Worldview, America Comes First, and Everybody Else Pays," *New York Times*, 26 March 2016, http://www.nytimes.com/2016/03/27/us/politics/donald-trump-foreign-policy.html?_r=0.

3. Department of State, "Chinese Immigration and the Chinese Exclusion Acts," Undated, https://history.state.gov/milestones/1866-1898/chinese-immigration. Mark Aspinwall and Simon Reich, "Who is Wile E. Coyote? Power, Influence and the War on Drugs," *International Politics* 53, no. 2, 2016: 155–175.

4. "Submarine with Cocaine Seized off Costa Rica," *NBC News*, 20 November 2006, http://www.nbcnews.com/id/15811689/ns/world_news-americas/t/submarine-cocaine-seized-costa-rica/.

5. David Kushner, "Drug-Sub Culture," *New York Times*, 23 April 2009, http://www.nytimes.com/2009/04/26/magazine/26drugs-t.html.

6. Lt. Kelley Chufo, "USS *McInerney*, Coast Guard Bust Submarine Loaded with Cocaine," US Navy, 18 September 2008, http://www.navy.mil/submit/display.asp?story_id=39839.

7. Ibid.

8. "Coast Guard, Navy Intercept Submersible Carrying $200M in Cocaine," *Fox News*, 27 March 2016, http://www.foxnews.com/us/2016/03/27/coast-guard-navy-intercept-submersible-carrying-200m-in-cocaine.html.

9. "USS *McInerney* (FFG 8)," http://navysite.de/ffg/FFG8.HTM.

10. Lisa M. Novak, "U.S. to Transfer Frigate to Pakistan Navy," *Stars and Stripes*, 7 August 2009, http://www.stripes.com/news/u-s-to-transfer-frigate-to-pakistan-navy-1.93820.

11. "Pakistan to Get Refurbished Warship from US," *Times of India*, 19 October 2008, http://timesofindia.indiatimes.com/World/Pakistan/Pakistan_to_get_refurbished_warship_from_US/rssarticleshow/3615200.cms.

12. Homepage of the Commander, US Naval Forces Southern Command/US 4th Fleet, http://www.public.navy.mil/comusnavso-c4f/Pages/default.aspx.

13. Commander, US Naval Forces Southern Command/US 4th Fleet, "Mission Statement," http://www.public.navy.mil/comusnavso-c4f/Pages/USNAVSO_4th%20Fleet.aspx.

14. Alex Smedegard, "Multinational UNITAS Pacific Naval Exercise Completed," US Southern Command, 4 November 2015, http://www.southcom.mil/newsroom/Pages/Multinational-UNITAS-Pacific-exercise-completed.aspx.

15. Christopher Lagan, "Drug Subs 2.0," *Coast Guard Compass: Official Blog of the U.S. Coast Guard*, 13 July 2010, http://coastguard.dodlive.mil/2010/07/drug-subs-2-0/.

16. Nicholas B. Dial, "At the Territorial Limit: Is the United States' Extraterritorial Response to Smuggling Submersibles on the High Seas Legitimate?" *Transnational Law and Contemporary Problems* 22 (fall 2013): 695.

17. In Byron Ramirez and Robert J. Bunker, eds., *Narco-Submarines: Specially Fabricated Vessels Used for Drug Smuggling Purposes* (US Army Foreign Military Studies Office, 2015), 4, http://fmso.leavenworth.army.mil/Collaboration/Interagency/NarcoSubmarines.pdf.

18. Testimony of Vice Admiral Charles D. Michel, Deputy Commandant for Operations, on "Drug Interdiction Operations" before the House Coast Guard and Maritime Transportation Subcommittee, 16 June 2015, http://transportation.house.gov/uploadedfiles/2015-06-16-michel.pdf.

19. James Traub, "Do Americans Really Want a Wall?" *Foreign Policy*, 4 March 2016, http://foreignpolicy.com/2016/03/04/do-americans-really-want-a-wall-trump-sanders-clinton-election-isolationism/.

20. John Grady, "SOUTHCOM CO Tidd: Not Enough Ships, Aircraft Available to Fight Drug War," USNI News, 10 March 2016, http://news.usni.org/2016/03/10/southcom-co-tidd-not-enough-ships-aircraft-available-to-fight-drug-war.

21. Pew Charitable Trusts, "Immigration Enforcement along U.S. Borders and at Ports of Entry: Federal, State, and Local Efforts," February 2015, 1 and Figure 1, 4, http://www.pewtrusts.org/~/media/assets/2015/02/borderenforcement_brief_web.pdf.

22. See CT Strategies, "FY16 Homeland Security Appropriations Act: U.S. Customs & Border Protection Funding," http://ct-strategies.com/wp-content/uploads/2016/02/CT_STRATEGIES_FY16_CBP_Appropriations.pdf.

23. Nicholas Fandos, "Trump Weighs Cuts to Coast Guard, T.S.A. and FEMA to Bolster Border Plan," *New York Times*, 9 March 2017, https://www.nytimes.com/2017/03/09/us/politics/trump-budget-coast-guard.html.

24. John Grady, "SOUTHCOM CO Tidd: Not Enough Ships, Aircraft Available to Fight Drug War," USNI News, 10 March 2016, http://news.usni.org/2016/03/10/southcom-co-tidd-not-enough-ships-aircraft-available-to-fight-drug-war.

25. Peter Andreas, *Smuggler Nation: How Illicit Trade Made America* (London: Oxford University Press, 2014).

26. Randall G. Holcombe, "The Growth of the Federal Government in the 1920s," *Cato Journal* 16, no. 2 (1996): 175–200.

27. Federal Bureau of Investigation, "The Lawless Years: 1921–1933," https://www.fbi.gov/about-us/history/brief-history/brief-history#Lawless.

28. Joseph A. Ricci, "Use All Force!" *Naval History* 27 no. 3 (June 2013): 50–55.

29. George W. Baer, *One Hundred Years of Sea Power* (Palo Alto, CA: Stanford University Press, 1994), chapter 6, "Treaty Navy: 1922–1939," especially 111.

30. Alfred Thayer Mahan's goal in increasing the size of the Navy was to enhance both territorial and hemispheric security, and project American power abroad. But, as George Baer has presciently observed, "The Caribbean Sea is the strategic key to the two great oceans, the Atlantic and the Pacific, our own chief maritime frontiers." Ibid., 25.

31. Emily Dufton, "The War on Drugs: How President Nixon Tied Addiction to Crime," *The Atlantic*, 26 March 2012, http://www.theatlantic.com/health/archive/2012/03/the-war-on-drugs-how-president-nixon-tied-addiction-to-crime/254319/.

32. Peter Andreas and Angelica Duran-Martinez, "The International Politics of Drugs and Illicit Trade in the Americas," Watson Institute for International Studies, Research Paper No. 2013–05, 16 September 2013. SSRN: http://ssrn.com/abstract=2326720 or http://dx.doi.org/10.2139/ssrn.2326720.

33. Office of the President, *Caribbean Border Counternarcotics Strategy* (Washington, DC: Office of the President, January 2015), 24, https://www.whitehouse.gov/sites/default/files/ondcp/policy-and-research/caribbeanstrategy5.pdf.

34. US Department of State, "Counternarcotics Strategy in Latin America," Testimony by Anne W. Patterson, Assistant Secretary of State, Bureau for International Narcotics and Law Enforcement Affairs, before the House International Relations Committee, Subcommittee on the Western Hemisphere, 30 March 2006.

35. *National Security Strategy* (Washington, DC: The White House, May 2010), 49, at https://www.whitehouse.gov/sites/default/files/rss_viewer/national_security_strategy.pdf.

36. *A Cooperative Strategy for 21st Century Seapower: Forward, Engaged, Ready* (March 2015), 6, https://www.uscg.mil/seniorleadership/DOCS/CS21R_Final.pdf.

37. Earlier strategic documents had made similar commitments. See, for example, J. T. Conway, G. Roughead, and T. W. Allen, *A Cooperative Strategy for 21st Century Seapower* (October 2007), https://www.ise.gov/sites/default/files/Maritime_Strategy.pdf.

38. Vesna Markovic, "The Contemporary Face of Transnational Criminal Organizations and the Threat They Pose to U.S. National Interest: A Global Perspective," in *The "New" Face of Transnational Crime Organizations (TCOs): A Geopolitical Perspective and Implications to U.S. National Security*, ed. Ben Riley and Kathleen Kiernan (Washington, DC: US Army, March 2013), chapter 6, 110.

39. John P. Sullivan and Robert J. Bunker, "Drug Cartels, Street Gangs, and Warlords," *Small Wars and Insurgencies* 13, no. 2 (2002): 40–53.

40. Max G. Manwaring, ed., *Gray Area Phenomena: Confronting the New World Disorder* (New York: Westview Press, 1993).

41. Jason M. Breslow, "The Staggering Death Toll of Mexico's Drug War," *Frontline*, 27 July 2015, http://www.pbs.org/wgbh/frontline/article/the-staggering-death-toll-of-mexicos-drug-war/.

42. Christopher Woody, "A Massive Cemetery': Mexico's Deadly Violence Shows no Signs of Relenting," *Business Insider*, 24 December 2016, http://www.businessinsider.com/homicides-drug-related-killings-in-mexico-in-2016-2016-12.

43. UNODC, *Global Study on Homicide, 2013: Trends, Context, Data*, UN Vienna, https://www.unodc.org/documents/gsh/pdfs/2014_GLOBAL_HOMICIDE_BOOK_web.pdf, Statistical Annex, Tables 8.1 and 8.2.

44. Max G. Manwaring, *A "New" Dynamic in the Western Hemispheric Security Environment: Zeta and Other Private Armies* (Carlisle, PA: Strategic Studies Institute, September 2009), 1, http://www.strategicstudiesinstitute.army.mil/.

45. John L. Hirsch and Robert B. Oakley, *Somalia and Operation Restore Hope: Reflections on Peacemaking and Peacekeeping* (Washington, DC: United States Institute of Peace, 1995).

46. For a description of significant examples of American intervention in Mexico, see Aspinwall and Reich, "Who is Wile E. Coyote?"

47. Rashi K. Shukla, Jordan L. Crumpe, and Emelia S. Chrisco, "An Evolving Problem: Methamphetamine Production and Trafficking in the United States," *International Journal of Drug Policy* 23, no. 6 (November 212): 426–435.

48. "U.S. Southern Command's Role in Combatting Illicit Trafficking," *National Security and Armed Conflict Law Review* 12 (2013–2014): 12–28, quote on 16.

49. Office of National Drug Control Policy, "Transit Zone Operations," undated, https://www.whitehouse.gov/ondcp/transit-zone-operations

50. Ronald O'Rourke, *Homeland Security: Navy Operations: Background and Issues for Congress* (Washington, DC: Congressional Research Service, 2004).

51. Wesley Hester, "Exploratory Study of Operational Approaches to Increase Narcotics Interdiction in the Maritime Domain," (Master's thesis, US Army Command and General Staff College, Leavenworth, Kansas, 2012), 24.

52. Department of Defense, *Naval Operations Concept 2010* (Washington, DC: US Government Printing Office, 2010), 43.

53. Joint Publication 3-28, Civil Support (September 2007), F-2.

54. See JIATF-South's webpage, http://www.jiatfs.southcom.mil/index.aspx.

55. Argentina, Brazil, Canada, Chile, Colombia, the Dominican Republic, Ecuador, El Salvador, Mexico, Peru, and the United States, and France, the Netherlands, Spain, and the United Kingdom from Europe.

56. "The Hidden Struggle at Sea: Counter-Narcotics in the Caribbean," *Jane's Navy International* 120, no. 1 (1 February 2015), unpaginated document.

57. Warren H. Bong, Paul Beery, and Eugene P. Paulo, "Applying Systems Engineering to Interagency Coordination in Support of Combatant Commands," *Journal of Defense Resources Management* 3, no. 2 (2012): 23–40.

58. Evan Munsing and Christopher J. Lamb, *Joint Interagency Task Force-South: The Best Known, Least Understood Interagency Success*, Strategic Perspectives 5 (Washington, DC: National Defense University Press, 2011), 26, http://ndupress.ndu.edu/Portals/68/Documents/stratperspective/inss/StrategicPerspectives-5.pdf.

59. "Le Joint Interagency Task Force-South (JIATF-S)," *Marine Nationale*, 1 February 2011, http://www.defense.gouv.fr/marine/operations/zoom-sur-la-marine-en-outremer/la-lutte-contre-le-narcotrafic-aux-antilles/le-joint-interagency-task-force-south-jiatfs.

60. Ibid.

61. Cf. Tomas Ayuso and Magnus Boding Hansen, "A Fragile Peace in Colombia," *Slate*, 25 March 2016, http://www.slate.com/articles/news_and_politics/roads/2016/03/colombia_and_farc_maintain_a_fragile_peace_while_working_toward_a_formal.html.

62. Clare Ribando Seelke et al., *Latin America and the Caribbean: Illicit Drug Trafficking and U.S. Counterdrug Programs*, CRS Report for Congress R41215 (Washington, DC: Congressional Research Service, 19 March 2012), 5–7.

63. US Department of State, *2014 International Narcotics Control Strategy Report (INCSR)*, vol. 1, *Drug and Chemical Control* (Washington, DC: Department of State, March 2014), 18, http://www.state.gov/documents/organization/222881.pdf.

64. US Department of State, *2014 International Narcotics Control Strategy Report (INCSR)*, vol. 2, *Money Laundering and Financial Crimes* (Washington, DC: Department of State, March 2014), http://www.state.gov/documents/organization/222880.pdf.

65. For a discussion of this point, see US Department of the Treasury, *Money Laundering Risk Assessment 2015*, https://www.treasury.gov/resource-center/terrorist-illicit-finance/Documents/National%20Money%20Laundering%20Risk%20Assessment%20%E2%80%93%2006-12-2015.pdf, 1–4 and 14–17; US Department of State, *2016 International Narcotics Control Strategy Report*, http://www.state.gov/j/inl/rls/nrcrpt/2016/index.htm.

66. Joint Chiefs of Staff, *Joint Counterdrug Operations* (Washington, DC: Joint Chiefs of Staff, 17 February 1998), III-37.

67. Among the Department of Defense assets used for air and surface early warning and surveillance are the Caribbean Basin Radar Network, ground-based radars, airborne radars,

and relocatable over-the-horizon backscatter radar, fixed radars, airborne radar platforms (including E-3 Airborne Warning and Control System [AWACS], E-2C, and P-3 aircraft), and antiair warfare-capable ships. Ibid., VI-8.

68. R. B. Watts, *Implementing Maritime Domain Awareness* (Master's thesis, Naval Postgraduate School, 2006), 48.

69. Munsing and Lamb, *Joint Interagency Task Force-South*, 77.

70. As South American–produced drugs also began to flow to Europe, several European countries dispatched vessels to support JIATF-South. They represent a modest (but symbolic) contribution, focusing on flows bound for Europe.

71. Jean Grace, "Ship Shortages Restricting Latin American Counter-Narcotics Operations, Say US Officials," *Jane's Navy International* 119, no. 9 (1 November 2014), unpaginated document.

72. Josh Phillips, "A Hunting We Will Go: Naval Air Tracks Drug Smugglers," *Naval Aviation News* 94, no. 4 (fall 2012), 26–29.

73. The resources from the Coast Guard are largely drawn from US Coast Guard Districts Seven and Eight, based in Miami, Florida, and New Orleans, Louisiana, respectively. Together the two districts control more than eighty cutters (i.e., any Coast Guard vessel sixty-five feet in length or greater, having crew accommodations).

74. Government Accountability Office, *Coast Guard: Resources Provided for Drug Interdiction Operations in the Transit Zone, Puerto Rico, and the U.S. Virgin Islands* (Washington, DC: GAO, June 2014), 10, http://www.gao.gov/products/GAO-14-527.

75. Ibid., 15.

76. "CBP provides a major share of maritime patrol aircraft support to JIATF-S, while the Navy provides both aircraft and vessel support. According to JIATF-S, in fiscal year 2013, CBP provided over 6,134 maritime patrol aircraft hours to JIATF-S. The U.S. Navy provided 2,100 maritime patrol aircraft hours." Ibid., 9.

77. Ibid., 24.

78. Munsing and Lamb, *Joint Interagency Task Force-South*, 3.

79. Statement of Rear Admiral Charles Michel in *Border Security Threats to the Homeland: DHS's Response to Innovative Tactics and Techniques*, Hearings Before the Subcommittee on Border and Maritime Security of the House Committee on Homeland Security (2012). http://homeland.house.gov/sites/homeland.house.gov/files/TestimonyMichel.pdf.

80. Seelke et al., *Latin America and the Caribbean*, 2–3.

81. While the figure quoted of "$20 billion to $25 billion a year on counternarcotics efforts over the last decade" accounts for more than interdiction efforts, the order of magnitude it represents is a proxy for the cost to the federal budget. Eduardo Porter, "Numbers Tell of Failure in Drug War," *New York Times*, 3 July 2012, http://www.nytimes.com/2012/07/04/business/in-rethinking-the-war-on-drugs-start-with-the-numbers.html?pagewanted=all&_r=0.

82. Written Statement of Rear Adm. Charles Michel, Director, JIATF-S, before the Subcommittee on Border and Maritime Security of the House Committee on Homeland Security (2012), 6, https://homeland.house.gov/files/Testimony-Michel.pdf.

83. "Budget Cuts Could Pull Navy Out of the War on Drugs," *Congressional Documents and Publications*, 5 March 2013.

84. Daniel Wasserbly, "SOUTHCOM Chief Sees Waning Interdictions," *Defence Weekly* 49, no. 13 (7 March 2012).

85. Government Accountability Office, *Drug Control: Cooperation with Many Major Drug Transit Countries Has Improved, but Better Performance Reporting and Sustainability Plans Are Needed*, GAO-08-784 (Washington, DC: GAO, July 2008), 26, http://www.gao.gov/assets/280/278210.pdf.

86. Ibid., 29–32.

87. Arnold H. Taylor, *American Diplomacy and the Narcotics Traffic, 1900–1939* (Durham, NC: Duke University Press, 1969).

88. United Nations, "The United Nations and Drug Control Abuse," publication no. E.87.I.8 (New York: United Nations, 1987), 63.

89. Taylor, *American Diplomacy and the Narcotics Traffic*, 22, 35–37, 197–209, and chapter 8.

90. For a list of countries who have acceded to these conventions, and when, as of December 31, 2013, see *U.S. Department of State, 2014 International Narcotics Control Strategy Report (INCSR)*, vol. I, *Drug and Chemical Control* (Washington, DC: Department of State, March 2014), 27–31. A full list of international agreements is on vi, http://www.state.gov/documents/organization/222881.pdf.

91. Baytoram Ramharack, "Cooperation in Narco-Trafficking: The United States and the English-Speaking Caribbean," *Social and Economic Studies* 46, no. 4 (December 1997): 102.

92. Holger W. Henke, "Drugs in the Caribbean: The 'Shiprider' Controversy and the Question of Sovereignty," *European Review of Latin American and Caribbean Studies / Revista Europea de Estudios Latinoamericanos y del Caribe* 64 (June 1998): especially, 37–41.

93. Joseph E. Kramek, "Bilateral Maritime Counter-Drug and Immigrant Interdiction Agreements: Is This the World of the Future?" *University of Miami Inter-American Law Review* 31, no. 1 (spring, 2000): 123.

94. Brian Wilson, "Submersibles and Transnational Criminal Organizations," *Ocean and Coastal Law Journal* 17, no. 35 (2011): 3.

95. Ann Marie Brodarick, "High Seas, High Stakes: Jurisdiction over Stateless Vessels and an Excess of Congressional Power under the Drug Trafficking Vessel Interdiction Act," *University of Miami Law Review* 67 (October 2012): 256.

96. Ramharack, "Cooperation in Narco-Trafficking," 102.

97. Richard A. Best, Jr., *Intelligence and Law Enforcement: Countering Transnational Threats to the U.S.*, CRS Report for Congress 30252, Updated December 2001, 7.

98. Ernesto Zedillo, "Overview," in *Rethinking the "War on Drugs" Through the U.S.-Mexico Prism*, ed. Ernesto Zedillo and Haynie Wheeler (New Haven, CT: A Yale Center for the Study of Globalization eBook, 2012), 9.

99. Peter Reuter, Gordon Crawford, and Jonathan Cave, *Sealing the Borders: The Effects of Increased Military Participation in Drug Interdiction* (Santa Monica, CA: RAND Corporation, January 1988), 37.

100. Ibid., 2.

101. Doug Bandow, "Keeping the Troops and the Money at Home," *Current History* 93, no. 579 (January 1994): 8–13; and Patrick J. Buchanan, "America First—and Second, and Third," *National Interest* 19 (spring 1990): 77–82.

102. Paul D. Miller, "Five Pillars of American Grand Strategy," *Survival: Global Politics and Strategy* 54 (October–November 2012): 7–44, especially the section describing the homeland defense pillar.

## Conclusion: Moving beyond the Current Debate

1. Simon Reich and Richard Ned Lebow, *Good-Bye Hegemony! Power and Influence in the Global System* (Princeton, NJ: Princeton University Press, 2014), 133–139.

2. Cf. Zbigniew Brzezinski, *The Grand Chessboard: American Primacy and Its Geostrategic Imperatives* (New York: Basic Books, 1997).

3. See G. John Ikenberry, "Grand Strategy as Liberal Order Building," Unpublished paper, 29 May 2007, 2. Relatedly, see Stephen G. Brooks, H. John Ikenberry, and William C. Wohlforth, "Don't Come Home, America: The Case against Retrenchment," *International Security* 37, no. 3 (Winter 2012/13): 36. This is a central theme of G. John Ikenberry, *Liberal Leviathan: The Origins, Crisis, and Transformation of the American World Order* (Princeton: Princeton University Press, 2011), notably chapter 1.

4. See, for example, Simon Dalby, "Geopolitics, Grand Strategy and the Bush Doctrine," Institute of Defense and Strategic Studies, October 2005, http://www.isn.ethz.ch/Digital-Library/Publications/Detail/?id=27169&lng=en; Hussein Ibish, "Obama's Flawed Doctrine Laid Bare," *The National*, 12 March 2016, http://www.thenational.ae/opinion/comment/obamas-flawed-foreign-policy-doctrine-laid-bare.

5. Micah Zenko and Rebecca Friedman Lissner, 'Trump Is Going to Regret not Having a Grand Strategy,' *Foreign Policy*, 13 January 2017, http://foreignpolicy.com/2017/01/13/

trump-is-going-to-regret-not-having-a-grand-strategy/. They define 'tactical transactionalism' as "united by three core attributes: first, a focus on short-term tactical wins rather than longer-term foresight; second, a "zero-sum" worldview where all gains are relative and reciprocity is absent; third, a transactional view of American foreign policy that is devoid of moral or ethical considerations."

6. Henry Kissinger interviewed by Jeffrey Goldberg, "The Lessons of Henry Kissinger," *The Atlantic*, December 2016, http://www.theatlantic.com/magazine/archive/2016/12/the-lessons-of-henry-kissinger/505868/.

7. For a recent example, see John J. Mearsheimer and Stephen M. Walt, "The Case for Offshore Balancing: A Superior Grand Strategy," *Foreign Affairs* 94, no. 4 (July–August 2016): 70–83, https://www.foreignaffairs.com/articles/united-states/2016-06-13/case-offshore-balancing.

8. For a discussion of this point, see Hal Brands, *What Good Is Grand Strategy? Power and Purpose in American Statecraft from Harry S. Truman to George W. Bush* (Ithaca, NY: Cornell University Press, 2014).

9. Whether these historical comparisons between the current and earlier periods are appropriate is, of course, debatable. Cf. John Rapley, "The New Middle Ages," *Foreign Affairs* 96, no. 3 (May/June 2006): 95–103.

10. Cf. "President Bush Links War in Iraq to War on Terrorism," *PBS Newshour*, 24 May 2007, http://www.pbs.org/newshour/bb/white_house-jan-june07-terrorism_05-24/.

11. Richard Higgott and Simon Reich, "Globalisation and Sites of Conflict: Towards Definition and Taxonomy," Working Paper No. 1, Centre for the Study of Globalisation and Regionalisation, Warwick University, June 1998, http://www2.warwick.ac.uk/fac/soc/csgr/research/workingpapers/1998.

12. Scott Shane, "The Lessons of Anwar al-Awlaki," *New York Times Magazine*, 27 August 2015, http://www.nytimes.com/2015/08/30/magazine/the-lessons-of-anwar-al-awlaki.html?_r=0. For an illustration, see Shereena Qazi, "Afghan Taliban: Haibatullah Akhunzada Named New Leader," *Al Jazeera*, 26 May 2016, http://www.aljazeera.com/news/2016/05/afghan-taliban-haibatullah-akhunzada-leader-160525045301080.html.

13. The Review on Antimicrobial Resistance, "Tackling Drug Resistant Infections Globally: Final Report and Recommendations," 19 May 2016, http://amr-review.org/sites/default/files/160518_Final%20paper_with%20cover.pdf.

14. For interstate and intrastate war figures, see Erik Melander, *Organized Violence in the World 2015: An Assessment by the Uppsala Conflict Data Program*, especially Figure 7, 7, http://www.pcr.uu.se/digitalAssets/61/61335_1brochure2.pdf.

15. For a popularized form of this argument, see Ted Koppel, *Lights Out: A Cyber Attack, a Nation Unprepared, Surviving the Aftermath* (New York: Penguin Random House, 2015).

16. Andrew S. Erickson, Lyle J. Goldstein, and William S. Murray, *Chinese Mine Warfare: A PLA Navy "Assassin's Mace" Capability* (Newport, RI: China Maritime Studies Institute, Naval War College, 2009).

17. Cf. Andrew Krepinevich, *7 Deadly Scenarios: A Military Futurist Explores the Changing Face of War in the 21st Century* (New York: Bantam, 2010), chapter 5.

18. See James Dobbins, John G. McGinn, Keith Crane, Seth G. Jones, Rollie Lal, Andrew Rathmell, Rachel M. Swanger, and Anga R. Timilsina, *America's Role in Nation-Building: From Germany to Iraq* (Santa Monica, CA: RAND Corporation, 2003), http://www.rand.org/pubs/monograph_reports/MR1753.html.

19. Eric Schmitt, "Pentagon Contradicts General on Iraq Occupation Force's Size," *New York Times*, 28 February 2003, http://www.nytimes.com/2003/02/28/us/threats-responses-military-spending-pentagon-contradicts-general-iraq-occupation.html; Thomas E. Ricks, *Fiasco: The American Military Adventure in Iraq, 2003 to 2005* (New York: Penguin Press, 2006), especially 155–156.

20. Basil Henry Liddell Hart, *Strategy*, 2nd rev. ed. (London: Faber & Faber, 1967), 322.

21. Cf. G. John Ikenberry, "American Grand Strategy in the Age of Terror," *Survival: Global Politics and Strategy* 43, no. 4 (winter 2001–2): 25–26.

22. Another alternative to resolving this tension is to rely on the strategist as heroic. By this reasoning, a master strategist—a Napoleon, Bismarck, or even a Kissinger—manages to

maintain strategic coherency by faithfully embodying a grand strategy while recognizing the opportunities represented by contingencies, and the adjustments required to adapt to circumstances.

23. Barry R. Posen, *Restraint: A New Foundation for Grand Strategy* (Ithaca, NY: Cornell University Press, 2014), 5.

24. Ibid., 1.

25. Micah Zenko and Rebecca Friedman Lissner, "Trump Is Going to Regret Not Having a Grand Strategy," *Foreign Policy,* 13 January 2017, http://foreignpolicy.com/2017/01/13/trump-is-going-to-regret-not-having-a-grand-strategy; Stephen M. Walt, "America's New President Is Not a Rational Actor," *Foreign Policy,* 25 January 2017, http://foreignpolicy.com/2017/01/25/americas-new-president-is-not-a-rational-actor/; David Rothkopf, "Trump's Pox Americana," *Foreign Policy,* 26 January, 2017, http://foreignpolicy.com/2017/01/26/trumps-pox-americana-the-retreat-of-the-indispensable-nation; Colin Kahl and Hal Brands, "Trump's Grand Strategy Train Wreck," *Foreign Policy,* 31 January 2017, https://foreignpolicy.com/2017/01/31/trumps-grand-strategic-train-wreck/.

26. Gary Shapiro, "The Trump Administration Might Put the 'Extreme' in 'Extreme Vetting,' *Washington Post,* 17 April 2017, https://www.washingtonpost.com/opinions/the-trump-administration-might-put-the-extreme-in-extreme-vetting/2017/04/17/8e81f7ca-1ecb-11e7-be2a-3a1fb24d4671_story.html?utm_term=.02cce3e257f6; Maria Sacchetti, "ICE Immigration Arrests of Noncriminals Double under Trump," *Washington Post,* 16 April 2017, https://www.washingtonpost.com/local/immigration-arrests-of-noncriminals-double-under-trump/2017/04/16/98a2f1e2-2096-11e7-be2a-3a1fb24d4671_story.html?utm_term=.701b8eba2861; Anu Joshi, "Donald Trump's Border Wall – An Annotated Timeline," *Huffington Post,* 1 March 2017, http://www.huffingtonpost.com/entry/donald-trumps-border-wall-an-annotated-timeline_us_58b5f363e4b02f3f81e44d7b.

27. Jenna Johnson, "Trump on NATO: 'I Said It Was Obsolete. It's No Longer Obsolete,'" *Boston Globe,* 13 April 2017, https://www.bostonglobe.com/news/world/2017/04/12/trump-nato-said-was-obsolete-longer-obsolete/j6LUBSclegPmkVA22wEP2J/story.html; "Final two F-35As Arrive for Europe Training Deployment," *InsideDefense.com,* 25 April 2017, https://insidedefense.com/daily-news/final-two-f-35as-arrive-europe-training-deployment.

28. "Trump: 'Armada' Heading toward North Korea," CNN, 4 April 2017, http://www.cnn.com/videos/world/2017/04/12/trump-armada-north-korea-fox-news-sje-orig.cnn.

29. Ibid., 147–149.

30. Robert R. Tomes, "Relearning Counterinsurgency Warfare," *Parameters* 3, no. 1 (spring 2004): 16–28.

31. See for example, Fred Kaplan, *The Insurgents: David Petraeus and the Plot to Change the American Way of War* (New York: Simon & Schuster, 2013); and Stanley McChrystal, Tantum Collins, David Silverman, and Chris Fussell, *Team of Teams: New Rules of Engagement for a Complex World* (New York: Portfolio/Penguin, 2015).

32. Robert R. Tomes, *U.S. Defense Strategy from Vietnam to Operation Iraqi Freedom: Military Innovation and the New American Way of War* (London: Routledge, 2007), especially chapter 4.

33. On the 1980s, see William M. LeoGrande, *Our Own Backyard: The United States in Central America, 1977–1992* (Chapel Hill: University of North Carolina Press, 2000); and Thomas Carothers, *In the Name of Democracy: U.S. Policy toward Latin America in the Reagan Years* (Berkeley: University of California Press, 1991). On the 1990s see, for example, David Halberstam, *War in a Time of Peace: Bush, Clinton, and the Generals* (New York: Scribner and Sons, 2001); and Wesley K. Clark, *Waging Modern War: Bosnia, Kosovo, and the Future of Combat* (New York: Public Affairs, 2001).

34. Cf. Andrew J. Bacevich, *The Limits of Power: The End of American Exceptionalism* (New York: Holt Paperbacks, 2009).

35. Andrew J. Bacevich, *America's War for the Greater Middle East: A Military History* (New York: Random House, 2016).

36. Christopher A. Preble, *The Power Problem: How American Military Dominance Makes Us Less Safe, Less Prosperous, and Less Free* (Ithaca, NY: Cornell University Press, 2009).

37. Peter Dombrowski and Simon Reich, "The Strategy of Sponsorship," *Survival: Global Politics and Strategy* (October/November 2015) 57, no. 5: 121–148.

38. Roger Barnett identifies "adaptability" as one of the core components of the Navy's organizational culture. Roger W. Barnett, "Strategic Culture and its Relationship to Naval Strategy," *Naval War College Review* 60, no. 1 (winter 2007): 24–34.

39. For example, the "MQ-4C TRITON: Like a big, fast, powerful eye in the sky, the soon-to-be-operational Triton drone is an unmanned aircraft system (UAS) designed to provide broad area maritime surveillance (BAMS). With a 130-ft. wingspan comparable to a 737, it can fly 24 hours a day and seven days a week with an operational range of over 8,000 nautical miles and with 360-degree sensory capabilities—at an altitude close to 60,000 feet and speeds approaching 350 MPH. And its crew includes an air vehicle operator, a mission commander and two sensor operators manning the controls from a station on the ground." https://www.navy.com/about/equipment/drones.html#aerial-drones.

40. Michèle Flournoy and Shawn Brimley, "The Contested Commons," *Proceedings* 135/7/1,277, July 2009, 1, http://indianstrategicknowledgeonline.com/web/The%20Contested%20Commons,%20Flournoy,%20Brimley.pdf. See also Robert Gates, "A Balanced Strategy," *Foreign Affairs* 88, no. 1 (January/February 2009): 28–40.

41. Mark D. Faram, "Navy Dumps Unpopular Recruiting Slogan during Army Game," *Navy Times*, 15 December 2014, http://www.navytimes.com/story/military/pentagon/2014/12/15/navy-recruiting-slogan-changes/20443467/.

42. Benjamin S. Lambeth, *American Air Power at the Dawn of a New Century* (Santa Monica, CA: RAND National Defense Research Unit, 2005), 10.

43. Ibid., 37, n35.

44. Ibid., 17.

45. *Final Report to Congress: Conduct of the Persian Gulf War*, April 1992, 79.

46. Ibid., 446.

47. Meagan Eckstein, "Stackley: Would Increase SSN, DDG, Amphib Production Rate to Reach 350-Ship Navy," *USNI News*, 1 December 2016; David B. Larter, "Donald Trump Wants to Start the Biggest Navy Build-up in Decades," *Navy Times*, 15 November 2016.

48. Wayne P. Hughes, Jr., "A Bimodal Force for the National Maritime Strategy," *Naval War College Review* 60, no. 2 (spring 2007): 40.

49. Laurence E. Lynn, Jr. and Richard I. Smith, "Can the Secretary of Defense Make a Difference?" *International Security* 7, no. 1 (summer 1982): 45–69. The quote is from 55.

50. "Department of Defense Dictionary of Military and Associated Terms," 8 November 2010 (as amended through 15 February 2016).

51. For a short, accurate, and accessible history of the Joint Staff by someone who helped craft the Goldwater-Nichols legislation see, James R. Locher III, "Has It Worked? The Goldwater-Nichols Reorganization Act," *Naval War College Review* 54, no. 4 (autumn 2001): 95–115, https://www.usnwc.edu/getattachment/744b0f7d-4a3f-4473-8a27-c5b444c2ea27/Has-It-Worked-The-Goldwater-Nichols-Reorganization.

52. Aaron L. Friedberg, *Beyond Air–Sea Battle: The Debate over US Military Strategy in Asia* (London: The International Institute for Strategic Studies 2014), especially chapter 3. On A2/AD approaches, see Sam J. Tangredi, *Anti-Access Warfare: Countering A2/AD Strategies* (Annapolis, MD: US Naval Institute Press, 2013).

53. Jon Tetsuro Sumida, *Inventing Grand Strategy and Teaching Command: The Classic Works of Alfred Thayer Mahan Reconsidered* (Washington, DC: Woodrow Wilson Center Press, 1999).

54. Edward Rhodes, "Do Bureaucratic Politics Matter? Some Disconfirming Findings from the Case of the U.S. Navy," *World Politics* 47, no. 1 (October 1994): 34.

55. Geoffrey Till, *Seapower: A Guide for the Twenty-First Century* (New York: Routledge, 2013), 57.

56. Philip A. Crowl, "Alfred Thayer Mahan: The Naval Historian," in *Makers of Modern Strategy from Machiavelli to the Nuclear Age*, ed. Peter Paret, Gordon A. Craig, and Felix Gilbert (Princeton, NJ: Princeton University Press, 1986), 477.

57. The conventional wisdom in the 1970s and early 1980s was that the Navy's role was peripheral. Yet, by the end of the Carter administration, the Navy was busily developing the so-called Maritime Strategy that posited "an aggressive global role for U.S. Navy in the event of a conventional war with the Soviet Union, including early attacks on Soviet ballistic missile submarines (SSBNs) in arctic waters, offensive strikes against Soviet bases on the Soviet

mainland, and attacks against Third World countries allied to the Soviet Union." Steven van Evera, "Preface," in *Naval Strategy and National Security: An International Security Reader*, ed. Steven E. Miller and Stephen Van Evera (Princeton, NJ: Princeton University Press, 1988).

58. John M. Richardson, *A Design for Maintaining Maritime Superiority*, version 1.0, January 2016, http://www.navy.mil/cno/docs/CNO_STG1.pdf, 2.

59. Ibid., 6.

60. Admiral Jonathan Greenert, "CNO's Sailing Directions," http://www.navy.mil/cno/cno_sailing_direction_final-lowres.pdf.

# Index

CPSIA information can be obtained
at www.ICGtesting.com
Printed in the USA
LVHW091143090821
694884LV00009B/291/J